Queens of Romance

*A collection of bestselling novels by
the world's leading romance writers*

**Two intense, passionate novels
from international bestselling author**

MICHELLE REID

"…a sizzler with two volatile characters and
explosive chemistry blended into an
emotionally gripping story."
—*Romantic Times* on *Ethan's Temptress Bride*

"Michelle Reid's latest is dynamite. Shannon
and Luca share a vibrant chemistry along with
some powerful emotional scenes that make
this book a definite must-read."
—*Romantic Times* on *The Salvatore Marriage*

100 Reasons to Celebrate

We invite you to join us in celebrating
Mills & Boon's centenary. Gerald Mills and
Charles Boon founded Mills & Boon Limited
in 1908 and opened offices in London's Covent
Garden. Since then, Mills & Boon has become
a hallmark for romantic fiction, recognised
around the world.

We're proud of our 100 years of publishing
excellence, which wouldn't have been achieved
without the loyalty and enthusiasm of our
authors and readers.

Thank you!

Each month throughout the year there will
be something new and exciting to mark the
centenary, so watch for your favourite authors,
captivating new stories, special limited
edition collections…and more!

MICHELLE REID

A Passionate Bargain

Containing

**Ethan's Temptress Bride
& The Salvatore Marriage**

*M&B™ and M&B™ with the Rose Device
are trademarks of the publisher.
Harlequin Mills & Boon Limited, Eton House,
18-24 Paradise Road,
Richmond, Surrey TW9 1SR*

A Passionate Bargain © by Harlequin Books S.A. 2008

Ethan's Temptress Bride and *The Salvatore Marriage* were
first published in Great Britain by Harlequin Mills & Boon
Limited in separate, single volumes.

Ethan's Temptress Bride © Michelle Reid 2002
The Salvatore Marriage © Michelle Reid 2003

ISBN: 978 0 263 86594 3

025-0408

*Printed and bound in Spain
by Litografía Rosés S.A., Barcelona*

Ethan's Temptress Bride

MICHELLE REID

The
Queens of Romance
Collection

Dear Reader,

Mills & Boon is celebrating its centenary this year, and what an extraordinary achievement that is. I would hazard a guess that there were many people back in 1908 who said, "A publishing house dedicated to romance? It will never succeed." Well, not only did Mills & Boon succeed, but it quickly became one of the most instantly recognisable publishing names throughout the entire world! And, as one among the millions of us who love to read romance, I'm so very pleased that it did!

I'm immensely proud, too, to play a small part in their success story. In 1987, when I dared (yes, it took plenty of courage) to send in a manuscript to Mills & Boon I never expected them to like it. Then in true romantic style *the call* came – on Christmas Eve! My daughter answered the telephone and turned to say to me, in a stunned little whisper, 'It's for you, Mum. It's Mills & Boon…' The joy of that call will live with me for ever, and it just grows with each of my books that are published.

So I want to say my own special thank you, Mills & Boon, for taking a chance on me as a writer, and for allowing me the most fabulous career I could have wished for.

The very warmest of congratulations for your glorious first century, and as you stride proudly into your second century know that both readers and writers are so very glad that you're here.

Michelle Reid

Michelle Reid grew up on the southern edges of Manchester, the youngest in a family of five lively children. But now she lives in the beautiful county of Cheshire, with her busy executive husband, and she has two grown-up daughters. She loves reading, the ballet and playing tennis when she gets the chance. She hates cooking, cleaning and despises ironing! Sleep she can do without, and produces some of her best written work during the early hours of the morning.

Look for the latest novel from Michelle Reid, *The Markonos Bride*, next month, May 2008, in Mills & Boon® Modern™.

CHAPTER ONE

PARADISE was a sleepy island floating in the Caribbean. It had a bar on the beach, rum on tap and the unique sound of island music, which did seductive things to the hot and humid late afternoon air, while beyond the bar's open rough-wood construction the silky blue ocean lapped lazily against a white-sand shore.

Sitting on a bar stool with a glass of local rum slotted between his fingers, Ethan Hayes decided that it didn't get any better than this. Admittedly it had taken him more than a week to wind down to the point where he no longer itched to reach for a telephone or felt naked in bare feet and shorts instead of sharp suits and highly polished leather shoes. Now he would even go as far as to say that he liked his new laid-back self. 'No worries,' as the locals liked to say, had taken on a whole new meaning for him.

'You want a refill for that, Mr Hayes?' The soft melodic tones of an island accent brought his gaze up to meet that of the beautiful brown girl who was serving behind the bar. Her smile held a different kind of invitation.

'Sure, why not?' He returned a smile and released his glass to her—without acknowledging the hidden offer.

Sex in this hot climate was the serpent in Paradise. As one's body temperature rose, so did that particular appetite, Ethan mused, aware that certain parts of him were suggesting he should consider the offer in the bar-girl's velvet-brown eyes. But he hadn't come to the island to indulge that specific pleasure, and all it took was the tentative touch of a finger to the corner of his mouth to remind him why he was wary of female entanglement. The bruising to his lip and jaw had faded days ago, but the injury to his dignity hadn't. It still throbbed in his breast like an angry tiger in dire need of succour for its nagging wound. If a man had any sense, he wouldn't unleash that tiger on some poor, unsuspecting female; he would keep it severely locked up and avoid temptation at all cost.

Though there was certainly a lot of that about, he acknowledged, as he turned to observe the young woman who was hogging the small bare-board dance floor.

The serpent's mistress, he named her dryly as he watched her sensual undulations to the music. She was a tall and slender toffee-blonde with a perfect Caribbean tan, wearing a short and sassy hot-pink slip-dress that was an almost perfect match for the pink hibiscus flower she wore tucked into her hair.

Eye-catching, in other words. Too irresistible to leave to dance alone, so it wasn't surprising that the young men in the bar were lining up to take their turn with her. She had class, she had style, she had beauty, she had grace, and she danced like a siren, shifting from partner to partner with the ease of one who was used to taking centre stage. Her eager young cohorts were enjoying themselves, loving the excuse to get up close and personal, lay their hands on her sensational body and gaze into big green beautiful eyes or watch her lovely mouth break into a smile that promised them everything.

And her name was Eve. Eve as in temptress, the ruin of man.

Or in this case the ruin of these brave young hunters who were aspiring to be her Adam. For she was the It girl on this small Caribbean island, the girl with everything, one of the fortunate few. A daddy's girl—though in this case it was Grandpa's girl, and the sole heir to his fabulous fortune.

Money was one hell of an aphrodisiac, Ethan decided cynically. Make her as ugly as sin and he could guarantee that those same guys would still be worshipping at her dainty dancing feet. But as so often was the way for the fabulously wealthy, stunning beauty came along with this package.

She began to laugh; the sound was soft and light and appealingly pleasant. She pouted at her present young hunter and almost brought the poor fool to his knees. Then she caught Ethan's eyes on her and the cynical look he was wearing on his face. Her smile withered to nothing. Big green come-and-get-me-if-you-dare eyes widened to challenge his cynicism outright. She knew him, he knew her. They had met several times over the last year at her grandfather's home in Athens, Ethan in his professional role as a design-and-build architect renowned for his creative genius for making new holiday complexes blend into their native surroundings, Eve in her only role as her grandfather's much loved, much spoiled, gift from the gods.

They did not like each other. In fact mutual antipathy ran in a constant stream between them. Ethan did not like her conceited belief that she had been put on this earth to be worshipped by all, and Eve did not like his outright refusal to fall at her feet. So it was putting it mildly to say that it was unfortunate they should both find themselves holidaying in the same place. The island was small enough for them to be thrown into each other's company too often for the comfort of either. Sparks tended to fly, forcing hostility to raise its ugly head. Other people picked up on it and didn't know what to do or say to lighten the atmosphere. Ethan usually solved the problem by withdrawing from the conflict with excuses that he had to be somewhere else.

This time he withdrew by turning away from her, back to the bar and the drink that had just been placed in front of him. But Eve's image remained standing right there, dancing on the bar top. Proud, defiant, unashamedly provocative—doing things to other parts of him he did not want her to reach.

His serpent in paradise, he grimly named this hot and nagging desire he suffered for Theron Herakleides' tantalising witch of a granddaughter.

Eve was keeping a happy smile fixed on her face even if it killed her to do it. She despised Ethan Hayes with an absolute vengeance. He made her feel spoiled and selfish and vain. She wished he had done his usual thing of getting up and walking out, so that she wouldn't have to watch him flirt with the barmaid.

Didn't Ethan know he was treading on dangerous ground there, and that the barmaid's strapping great sailor of a lover would chew him up and spit him out if he caught him chatting up his woman? Or was it the girl who was doing the chatting up? Then Eve had to settle for that as the more probable alternative, because Ethan Hayes was certainly worth the effort.

Great body, great looks, great sense of presence, she listed reluctantly. In a sharp suit and tie he was dynamic and sleek; now simple beach shorts and a white tee shirt should have turned him into something else entirely, but didn't—dynamic and sleek still did it for her, Eve decided as she ran her eyes over him. She began at his brown bare feet with their long toes that were curling lovingly round one of the bar stool crossbars, then moved onwards, up powerfully built legs peppered with dark hair that had been bleached golden by the sun.

How did she know the sun had bleached those hairs? Eve asked herself. Because she'd seen his legs before— had seen *all* of Ethan Hayes before!—on that terrible night at her grandfather's house in Athens, when she'd dared to walk uninvited into his bedroom and had caught him in a state of undress.

Prickly heat began to chase along to her nerve ends at the memory—the heat of mortification, not attraction though the attraction had always been there as well. She had gone to Ethan's room to confront him over something he had seen her doing in the garden with Aidan Galloway. Bristling with self-righteous indignation she had marched in through his door, only to stop dead with her head wiped clean of all coherent thought when she'd found him standing there still dripping water from a recent shower, and as stark staring naked as a man could be—not counting the small hand towel he had been using to dry his hair. The towel had quickly covered other parts of him, but not before she'd had a darn good owl-eyed look!

Oh, the shame, the embarrassment! She could feel her cheeks blushing even now. 'I presume Mr Galloway ran back to his fiancée, so you thought you would come and try your luck here.' Eve winced as Ethan's cutting words came back to slay her all over again.

'Your foot, sorry,' her present dance partner apologised.

He had misinterpreted the wince. 'That's okay,' she said, smiling sweetly at Raoul Delacroix without bothering to correct his mistake—and wished she'd had the wits to smile sweetly at Ethan Hayes that night, instead of running like a fool and leaving him with *his* mistake!

But she had run without saying a single word to him in her own defence, and by the next morning embarrassment had turned to stiff-necked pride; hell could freeze over before she would explain anything to him! As a result he had become the conscience she knew she did not deserve, because all it took was a glance from those horribly critical grey eyes to make her feel crushingly guilty!

It wasn't fair, she hated him for it. Hated his dark good looks too because they did things to her she would rather they didn't. But most of all she hated his cold, grim, English reserve that kept him forever at a distance, thereby stopping her from beginning the confrontation that she knew would completely alter his perception of her.

Did she need to do that? Eve asked herself suddenly. And was horrified to realise how badly she did.

'Have dinner with me tonight...' Her present dance partner was suddenly crowding her with his too eager hands and the fervent darkening of his liquid brown eyes. 'Just the two of us,' Raoul huskily extended. 'Somewhere quiet and romantic where no one can interrupt.'

'You know that's a no-no, Raoul.' Smiling to soften the refusal, she also deftly dislodged one of his hands from her rear. 'We're here as a group to have fun, not romance.'

'Romance can be fun.' His rejected hand lifted up to brush a finger across her bottom lip with a message only a very naïve woman would misinterpret.

Eve reached up and firmly removed the finger and watched his beautifully shaped mouth turn down in a sulk. Raoul Delacroix was a very handsome French-American, with eyes dark enough to drown in and a body to die for—yet he did nothing for her. In a way she wished that he did because he was her age and her kind of person, unlike the disapproving Ethan Hayes who added a whole new meaning to the phrase, the generation gap.

And what was that gap—her twenty-three years to his thirty-seven? Big gap—yawning gap, she mocked it dryly. 'Don't sulk,' she scolded Raoul. 'Today is my birthday and we're supposed to be having lots of fun.'

'Tomorrow is your birthday,' he corrected.

'As we all know, my grandfather is arriving here tomorrow to help me celebrate, which means I will have to behave with proper decorum all day. So tonight we agreed that we would celebrate my birthday a day early. Don't spoil that for me, Raoul.'

It was both a gentle plea and a serious warning because he had been getting just a little bit too intense recently. Raoul Delacroix was the half-brother of André Visconte who owned the only hotel on the island. So like the rest of the crowd whose families owned property here, they'd all been meeting up for holidays since childhood. They were all good close friends now who'd agreed early on that romance would spoil what they enjoyed most about each others' company. Raoul knew the rules, so attempting to change them now was just a tiny bit irritating—and a shame because he was usually very good company—when he wasn't thinking of other things, that was.

'The beach is strewn with good prospects for a handsome Frenchman to play the romantic,' she teased him. 'Take your pick. I can guarantee they will swoon at your feet.'

'I know, I've tried one or two,' Raoul returned lazily. 'But this was only in practice, you understand,' he then added, 'to prepare myself for the woman I love.'

Implying that Eve was that woman? She laughed, it was so funny. After a moment, Raoul joined in the laughter, and the mood between them relaxed back into being playful. The music changed not long after, calypso taking the place of reggae, and Eve found Raoul's place taken by another admirer while he moved on to pastures new.

Viewing this little by-play via the mirror on the wall behind the drinks optics, Ethan wasn't sure he liked the expression on Raoul Delacroix's face as he'd turned away from Eve. Raoul's look did nasty things to Ethan's insides and made him curious as to what Raoul and Eve had been talking about. They'd parting laughing, but Raoul's turning expression had been far from amused.

None of your business, he then told himself firmly. Eve knew what kind of dangerous game she was playing with all of these testosterone-packed young men. My God, did she know, he then added with a contempt that went so deep it reflected clearly on his face when, as if on cue, Aidan Galloway walked into the bar. The darkly attractive young Irish-American paused, found his target and made directly for Eve.

The last time Ethan had seen Aidan Galloway had been a month ago in Athens when he had been a guest of Eve's grandfather, along with several members of the Galloway family. On the face of it, the younger man had only had eyes for the beautiful fiancée he'd had hanging from his arm. But since coming to this island, Ethan had seen no sign of the fiancée and Aidan Galloway now only had eyes for Eve.

Someone slid onto the stool next to him, offering him a very welcome alternative to observing the life and loves of Eve Herakleides. It was Jack Banning who managed the only hotel on the island for owner, André Visconte. Jack was a big all-American guy, built to break rocks against but as laid-back as they came.

'Marlin have been spotted five miles out,' Jack informed him. 'I'm taking a boat out tomorrow. If you're interested in some big-game fishing, you're welcome to come.'

'Early start?' Ethan quizzed.

'Think sunrise,' Jack suggested. 'Think deep yawns and black coffee and no heavy partying the night before if you don't want to spend your time at sea throwing up.'

The barmaid interrupted by appearing with a glass of

rum for Jack. The two of them chatted boss to employee for a few minutes, but the girl's eyes kept on drifting towards Ethan, and when she had moved away again Jack sent Ethan a very male glance.

'Considering a different kind of game?' Jack posed lazily.

'Not today, thanks.' Ethan's smile was deliberately benign as he took a sip at his drink.

'Or any day that you've been here, from what my sources say.'

'Was that an idle question or a veiled criticism of my use of the island's rich and varied hospitality?'

'Neither.' A set of even white teeth appeared to acknowledge Ethan's sarcastic hit. 'It was just an observation. I mean—look at you, man,' Jack mocked him. 'You've got the looks, you've got the body parts, and I know for a fact that you've had more than one lovely woman's heart fluttering with anticipation since you arrived, but I've yet to see you take a second look at any of them.'

He was curious. Ethan didn't entirely blame him. The island was not sold on its monastic qualities. The women here were, in the main, beautiful people and a lot of them had made it clear that they were available for a little holiday romance.

But Ethan was off romance, off women, and most definitely off sex—or at least he was in training to be off it, he amended, all too aware that his body was trying to tempt him with every inviting smile that came his way.

Then there was that other sexual temptation, the one that hit him hard in his nether regions every time he looked at Eve Herakleides and recalled an incident when she'd walked into his room to find him standing there naked. She'd looked—no *stared*—and things had happened to him that he hadn't experienced since he'd been a hormone-racked teenager. What was worse than the reaction was knowing she'd witnessed it.

So why his eyes had to pick that precise moment to glance in the mirror was something he preferred not to analyse. She was dancing with Aidan Galloway, and the body language was nothing like what it had been when she'd danced with the other men. No, this was tense, it was serious. It reminded him of that kiss he had witnessed in her grandfather's garden in Athens. The two of them had been so engrossed in each other that they hadn't heard his arrival—nor had they known they'd also been watched by Aidan's fiancée, who'd almost fainted into the arms of another young Galloway.

Eve was a flirt and a troublemaker, a woman with no scruples when it came to other women's men. Her only mission in life was to slay all with those big green you-can-have-me eyes.

Ethan loved those eyes…

The unexpected thought jolted him, snapped his gaze down from the mirror to his glass. What the hell is the matter with you? he asked himself furiously. Too much sun? Too much time on your hands? Maybe it was time he got back into a suit and unearthed a mobile telephone.

'And you?' He diverted his attention back to Jack Banning. 'Do you sip the honey on a regular basis here?'

Jack gave a rueful shake of his head. 'The boss would have my balls for trophies if I imbibed,' he murmured candidly. 'No…' picking up his glass he tasted the rum '…I have this lovely widow living on the next island who keeps me sane in that department.'

With no ties, and no commitment expected or desired, Ethan concluded from that, knowing the kind of woman

Jack was talking about because he'd enjoyed a few of them himself in his time.

'She's a good woman,' Jack added as if he needed to make that point.

'I don't doubt it,' Ethan replied, and he didn't. In the time he had been here, he had got to know and like Jack Banning. Being in the leisure business himself—though in a different area—he wasn't surprised that André Visconte had a man like Jack in place. In fact he was considering doing a bit of head-hunting because they could do with Jack running the new resort his company was in the process of constructing in Spain.

Though that idea was shot to pieces when Jack spoke again. 'Her husband was caught out at sea in a hurricane four years ago,' he said quietly. 'He left her well shod but heavily pregnant. Left her with a badly broken heart too.'

Which told Ethan that Jack was in love with the widow. Which in turn meant there was no hope of getting him to leave for pastures new.

'So what's your excuse for the self-imposed celibacy?' Jack asked curiously.

Same as you, Ethan thought grimly. I fell for a married woman—only her husband is very much alive and kicking. 'Too much of a good thing is reputed to be bad for you,' was what he offered as a dry reply.

Glancing at him, he saw Jack's gaze touch that part of Ethan's jaw where the bruising had been obvious a few days ago. He had been forced to wear the mark like a banner when he'd first arrived on the island. Speculation as to how he'd received the bruise had been rife. His refusal to discuss it had only helped to fire people's imagination.

But the expression in Jack's eyes told him that Jack had drawn a pretty accurate conclusion. He sighed, so did Jack.

Both men lifted their glass to their mouths and said no more. It had been that kind of conversation: some things had been said, others not, but all had been taken on board nonetheless. Turning on his stool, Jack offered the busy bar room a once-over with his lazy-yet-shrewd manager's eye, while Ethan studied the contents of his glass with a slightly bitter gaze. He was thinking of a woman with dark red hair, silk-white skin and a broken heart that was in the process of being mended by the wrong man, as far as he was concerned.

But the right man for her, he had to add honestly, felt the tiger stir within and wished he knew of a good cure for unrequited love.

'Try the sex,' Jack said suddenly as if he could read his mind. 'It has to be a better option than lusting after the unattainable.'

Unable to restrain it, Ethan released a hard laugh. 'Is that advice for me or for yourself?'

'You,' Jack answered. Then he grimaced as he added, 'Mine is a hopeless case. You see, the widow's son calls me Daddy.' With that he got up and gave Ethan's shoulder a man-to-man, sympathetic pat. 'Let me know about the Marlin trip,' he said and strolled away.

Turning to watch him go, Ethan saw Jack stop once or twice to chat to people on his way out of the bar. One woman in particular came to meet him. It was Eve the temptress. A quick look around and he found Aidan Galloway standing at the other end of the bar. He was ordering a drink and he didn't look happy. Join the club, Ethan thought, as his eyes then picked out Raoul Delacroix who was watching Eve with an expression on his face that matched Aidan Galloway's.

As for Eve, her long slender arms were around Jack's neck and she was pouting up at him in a demand for a kiss. Amiably Jack gave it and smiled at whatever it was she was saying to him. Without much tempting she managed to urge the manager into motion to the music, his big hands spanning her tiny waist, his dark head dipped to maintain eye contact. Like that, they teased each other as they swayed.

Suddenly Ethan knew it was time to leave. Downing the rest of his drink, he came to his feet, placed some money on the bar and wished the girl behind it a light farewell. As he walked towards the dancers he thought he saw Eve move that extra inch closer to Jack's impressive body.

Done for his benefit? he asked himself, then shot that idea in the foot with a silent huff of scorn to remind himself that Eve Herakleides disliked him as much as he disliked her.

Outside the air was like warm damp silk against his skin. The humidity was high, and looking out to sea Ethan could see clouds gathering on the horizon aiming to spoil the imminent sunset. There could be a storm tonight, he predicted as he turned in the direction of his beach house. Behind him the sound of a woman's laughter came drifting towards him from inside the bar. Without thinking he suddenly changed direction and his feet were kicking hot sand as he ran toward the water and made a clean racing dive into its cool clear depths.

'Don't even think about it,' Jack cautioned. 'He's too old and too dangerous for a sweet little flirt like you.'

Dragging her eyes away from the sight of Ethan Hayes in full sprint as he headed for the ocean, Eve looked into Jack Banning's knowing gaze—and mentally ran for cover. 'I don't know what you're talking about,' she said.

Jack didn't believe her. 'Ethan Hayes could eat you for a snack without touching his appetite,' he informed her without a hint of mockery to make the bitter pill of truth an easier one to swallow.

'Like you, you mean,' she said with a kissable pout, which was really another duck-and-run. 'Big bad Jack,' she murmured as she moved in closer then began swaying so provocatively that he had to physically restrain her.

He did it with a white-toothed, highly amused, grin. 'Minx,' he scolded. 'If your grandfather could see you he would have you locked up—these messages you put out are dangerous.'

'My grandpa adores me too much to do anything so primitive.'

'Your grandfather, my little siren, arrives on this island tomorrow,' Jack reminded her. 'Let him see this look you're wearing on your face and we will soon learn how primitive he can be...'

CHAPTER TWO

ETHAN took his time swimming down the length of the bay to come out of the water opposite the beach house he was using while he was here. It belonged to Leandros Petronades, a business associate, who had understood his need to get away from it all for a week or two if he wasn't going to do something stupid like walk out on his ten-year-strong working partnership with Victor Frayne.

Victor... Ethan's feet stilled at the edge of the surf as the same anger that had caused the rift between the two of them rose up to burn at his insides again.

Victor had used him, or had allowed him to be used, as a decoy in the crossfire between Victor's daughter, Leona, and her estranged husband, Sheikh Hassan Al-Qadim. In the Sheikh's quest to recover his wife, Leona and Ethan had been ambushed then dragged off into the night. When Ethan had eventually come round from a knockout blow to his jaw, it had been to find he'd been made virtual prisoner on Sheikh Hassan's luxury yacht. But if he'd thought his pride had taken a battering when he'd been wrestled to the ground and rendered helpless with that knockout blow, then his interview with the Sheikh the next morning had turned what was left of his pride to pulp.

The man was an arrogant bastard, Ethan thought grimly. What Leona loved about him he would never understand. If *he* had been her father, he would have been putting up a wall of defence around her rather than aiding and abetting her abduction by a man whom everyone knew had been about to take a second wife!

19

Leona had been out of that marriage—*best* out of that marriage! Now she was back in it with bells ringing and—

Bending down he picked up a conch shell then turned and hurled it into the sea. He wished to goodness he hadn't had that conversation with Jack Banning. He wished he could stuff all of these violent feelings back into storage where he had managed to hide them for the last week. Now he was angry with himself again, angry with Victor, and angry with Sheikh Hassan Al-Qadim and the whole damn world, probably.

On that heavily honest assessment, he turned back to face land again. Leandros Petronades had been his saviour when he'd offered him the use of this place. Not that the Greek's motives had been in the least bit altruistic, Ethan reminded himself. As one of the main investors in their Spanish project, Leandros had been protecting his own back, plus several other business ventures his company had running with Hayes-Frayne. A bust up between Ethan and Victor would have left him with problems he did not need or want. So when he'd happened to walk in on the furious row the two partners had been locked in, had seen the huge purple bruise on Ethan's face and had heard enough to draw his own conclusions as how the bruise got there, Leandros had immediately suggested that Ethan needed a break while he cooled off.

So here he was, standing on the beach of one of the most exclusive islands in the Caribbean, and about the lush green hillside in front of him nestled the kind of properties most people only dreamed about. The Visconte hotel complex occupied a central position, forming the hub around which all activities on the island revolved. Either side of the hotel stood the private villas belonging to those wealthy enough to afford a plot of land here. André Visconte himself owned a private estate. The powerful

Galloway family owned many properties, forming a small hamlet of their own in the next bay. But if the size of a plot was indicative of wealth, then the villa belonging to Theron Herakleides had to be the king.

Painted sugar-pink, it sat inside a framework of ancient date- and fabulous flame-trees about halfway up the hill. From the main house the garden swept down to sea level via a series of carefully tended terraces: sun terraces, pool terraces, garden terraces that wouldn't be believed to be real outside a film set. There were tennis courts and even a velvet smooth croquet lawn, though Ethan could not bring himself to imagine that Theron Herakleides had ever bothered to use it. Then there were the guest houses scattered about the grounds, all painted that sugar-pink colour which came into its own with every burning sunset. Almost on the sand sat the Herakleides beach house, the part of her grandfather's estate that Eve was using while she was here.

It had to be the worst kind of luck that the Petronades and the Herakleides estates were beside each other, because it placed her beach house right next door to his, Ethan mused heavily, as he trod the soft sand on his way up the beach. Other than for Eve's close proximity he was happy with his modest accommodation. The beach houses might be small but they possessed a certain charm that appealed to the artist in him. Nothing grand: just an open-plan living room and kitchen, a bathroom and a bedroom.

All he needed, in other words, he acknowledged as he came to a stop at the low white-washed wall that was there to help keep the sand back rather than mark the boundary to the property. Set into the wall was a white picket gate that gave access to a simple garden and the short path that led to a shady veranda. Next to the gate was a concrete tub overhung by a freshwater shower head. Pulling his wet tee shirt off over his head he tossed it onto the wall, then stepped into the tub and switched on the tap that brought cool water cascading over his head.

His skin shone dark gold in the deepening sunset, muscles rippled across his shoulders and back, as he sluiced the sand and salt from his body. Standing a few short yards away on the hot concrete path that ran right around the bay, Eve watched him with the same fascination she had surrendered to the last time she had chanced upon Ethan Hayes like this.

Only it wasn't the same, she reminded herself quickly. He was dressed, or that part of him which caused her the most problems was modestly covered at least. But as for the rest of him—

Water ran off his dark hair down his face to his shoulders. The hair on his chest lay matted in thick coils that arrowed down to below his waist. She hadn't noticed the chest hair the last time—hadn't noticed the six-pack firmness of his abdomen. He was lean and he was tight and he was honed to perfection, and she wished she—

'You can go past. I won't bite,' the man himself murmured flatly, letting her know that he had seen her standing here.

Fingers curling into two fists at her sides, Eve released a soft curse beneath her breath. I hate him, she told herself. I *really* hate him for catching me doing this, not once but *twice*!

'Actually I quite like the view,' she returned, determined not to let him embarrass her a second time. 'You strip down quite nicely for an Englishman.'

More muscles flexed; Eve's lungs stopped working. She wished she understood this fascination she had for his body, but she didn't. She could not even say that he possessed the best body she had ever seen—mainly because it was the *only* one she had seen in its full and flagrant entirety. That, she decided, had to be the cause of this wicked fascination she had for Ethan Hayes. It fizzed through her veins like a champagne cocktail, stripped her mouth of moisture like crisp dry wine. Tantalising, in other words. The man was a stiff-necked, supercritical, over-bearing boor, yet inside she fluttered like a love-struck teenager every time she saw him.

The shower was turned off. He threw one of those cold-eyed looks at her then slid it away without saying a word. He was going to do his usual thing and walk away as if she didn't exist, Eve realised, and suddenly she was determined to break that arrogant habit for good!

'You've missed a bit,' she informed him.

He turned a second look on her. Looks like that could kill, Eve thought as, with a scrupulously bland expression, she pointed to the back of his legs where beautifully pronounced calf muscles were still peppered with fine granules of sand.

Still without saying a word he turned on the shower again. A sudden urge to laugh brought Eve's ready sense of humour into play and she decided to have a bit of fun at the stuffy Ethan Hayes' expense.

'Jack just warned me off falling for you,' she announced, watching him wash the sand off his legs. 'He thinks you're dangerous. The eat-them-for-a-snack-as-you-walk-out-of-the-door kind of man.'

'Wise man, Jack.' She thought she heard him mutter over the splash of water, but she couldn't be sure.

'I laughed because I thought it was so funny,' she went on. 'I mean—we both know you're too much the English gentleman to do anything so crass as to love them and leave them without a backward glance.'

It was not a compliment and Ethan didn't take it as one.

'You keep taking a dig at my Englishness, but you're half English yourself,' he pointed out.

'I know.' Eve sighed with mocking tragedy. 'It worries the Greek in me sometimes that I could end up falling for a die-hard English stuffed-shirt.'

'Fate worse than death.'

'Yes.'

He switched the shower off again and Eve rediscovered her fascination with his body as he turned to recover his wet tee shirt; muscles wrapped in rich brown flesh rippled in the red glow of the sunlight, droplets of water clung to the hairs on his chest.

Ethan turned to catch her staring. The prickling sensation between his thighs warned him that he had better get away from here before he embarrassed himself again. Yet he didn't move, couldn't seem to manage the simple act. His senses were too busy drinking in what his eyes were showing him. He liked the way she was wearing her hair twisted cheekily up on her head with a hibiscus flower helping to hold it in place. He liked what the pink dress did for her figure and the slender length and shape of her legs. And he liked her mouth; it was heart-shaped—small with a natural provocative yen to pout. He liked her smooth golden skin, her cute little nose, and those eyes that had a way of looking at him as if she...

Go away, Eve, he wanted to say to her. Instead he dragged his eyes away, and looked for something thoroughly innocuous to say. 'I thought you were all off to a party this evening.' Flat-voiced, level-toned, he'd thought he'd hit innocuous perfectly.

But Eve clearly didn't. She stiffened up as if he had just insulted her. 'Oh, do let's be honest and call it an orgy,' she returned. 'Since you believe that orgies are more my style.'

Time to go, he decided, and opened the picket gate.

'While you do what you're probably very good at, of course,' she added, 'and play whist with the cheese and wine set at the hotel.'

He went still.

Eve's heart stopped beating on the suspicion that she had finally managed to rouse the sleeping tiger she'd always fancied lurked within his big chest. Sometimes—usually when she was least expecting it—Ethan Hayes could take on a certain quality that made her think of dangerous animals. This was one of those times, and her biggest problem was that she liked it—it excited her.

'How old are you?' he asked.

He knew exactly how old she was. 'Twenty-three until midnight,' she told him anyway.

He nodded his wet head. 'That accounts for it.'

This was blatant baiting, Eve recognised, and foolishly took it. 'Accounts for what?'

'The annoyingly adolescent desire to insult and shock.'

He was so right, but oh, it hurt. Why had she willingly let herself fall into that? Eve had no defence, none at all and she had to turn to stare out to sea so that he wouldn't see the sudden flood of weak tears that were trying to fill her eyes.

And who was the adolescent who made that cutting comment? Ethan was grimly asking himself, as he looked at her standing there looking like an exotic flower that had been cut down in its prime. Oh, damn it, he thought, and walked through the gate, meaning to get the hell away from this before he—

He couldn't do it. Muscles were tightening all over his body on wave after wave of angry guilt. What had she ever done to him after all? If you didn't count a couple of teasing come-ons and letting him catch her in a heated clinch with someone else's man.

She'd also caught him naked and had had a full view of his embarrassing response, but he didn't want to think about that. Instead he took in a deep breath and spun back to say something trite and stupid and hopefully less—

But he found he was too late because she had already walked off, a tall slender figure with a graceful stride and a proud yet oddly vulnerable tilt to her head. Still cursing himself for the whole stupid conversation, Ethan made himself walk up the path. Though, as he reached the shade of the veranda, he couldn't resist a quick glance sideways and saw Eve was about to enter her house. One part of him wanted to go after her and apologise, but the major part told him wisely to leave well alone.

Eve Herakleides could mean trouble if he allowed himself to be sucked in by her frankly magnetic appeal. He didn't need that kind of stimulation. He didn't want to end up in the same fated boat he had been in before with a woman just like her.

What was it that Jack had called it? 'Lusting after the unattainable.' Eve was destined to higher things than a mere architect had to offer—as her grandfather would be happy to tell him. But it was the word lust that made Ethan go inside and firmly close his door.

CHAPTER THREE

EVE tried to enjoy the party. In fact she threw herself into the role of life and soul with an enthusiasm that kept everyone else entertained.

But the scene with Ethan Hayes had taken the edge off her desire to enjoy anything tonight. And she was worried about Aidan. He had been drinking steadily since he'd arrived at the bar on the beach late this afternoon and his mood suited the grim compulsion with which he was pouring the rum down his throat.

Not that anyone else seemed to have noticed, she realised, as she watched him do his party trick with a cocktail shaker and bottle of something very green to the laughing encouragement of the rest of the crowd, whereas she felt more like weeping.

For Aidan—for herself? In truth, she wasn't quite sure. On that low note she surrendered to the deep doldrums that had been dogging her every movement tonight and slid open one of the glass doors that led onto the terrace. Then she stepped out into the warm dark night, intending to walk across the decking to the terrace rail that overlooked the sea—only it came as a surprise to discover that she was ever so slightly tipsy, so tipsy in fact that she was forced to sink onto the first sunbed she reached just in case she happened to fall down.

Well, why not? she thought with a little shrug, and slipping off her shoes she lifted her feet up onto the cool, cushioned mattress, then relaxed against the raised chair back with a low long sigh. The air was soft and seductively

27

quiet, the earlier threatened storm having passed them by. Reclining there, she listened to the low slap of lazy waves touching the shore, and wondered dully how much longer she needed to leave it before she could escape to brood on her own terrace without inviting comment here?

At least Aidan was already in the right place for when he eventually sank into a drunken stupor, she mused heavily. This was his home, or the one he liked to call home of several the family had dotted around this tiny bay. With a bit of luck he was going to slide under a convenient table soon and she could get some of the guys to put him to bed, then forget about him and his problems for a while and concentrate on her own.

She certainly had a few, Eve acknowledged through the mud of her half-tipsy state. Ethan Hayes and his horrible attitude towards her was one of them. Her grandfather in his whole, sweet, bullying entirety was another. The older he got, the more testy he became, and more determined to run her life for her. She smiled as she thought that about him though, and allowed her mind to drift back to the last conversation she'd had with him over the phone before she'd flown out here from her London flat.

'Grandpa, will you stop trying to marry me off to every eligible man you happen to meet?' she scolded, 'I am only twenty-three years' old, for goodness' sake!'

'At twenty-three you should be suckling my first grandson at your breast while the next grows big in your belly,' he complained.

'Barefoot I presume, while making baklava for my very fat husband.'

Eve hadn't been able to resist it, she chuckled into the night at the outrageous scenario.

'Spiridon is not fat.'

'But he is twice my age.'

'He is thirty-nine,' the old man corrected. 'Very hand-some. Very fit. The ladies worship him.'

'And you ought to be ashamed of yourself for trying to foist me off with the most notorious rake in Greece,' she rebuked. 'I thought you loved me better than this.'

'You are the unblemished golden apple of my eye!' Theron Herakleides announced with formidable passion. 'I merely want you to remain that way until I see you safely married before I die.'

'Die?' she repeated. He was bringing out the big guns with that remark. 'Now listen to me, you scheming old devil,' she scolded, 'I love you to bits. *You* are the love of my life! But if you stick one—*just one*—eligible man in front of me I will never speak to you again—under-stand?'

'*Ne*,' the old man answered, gruff-voiced and tetchy. 'Yes, I understand that you bully a sick and lonely old man.'

Sick, she did not believe, but lonely she did. 'See you soon, Grandpa,' she softly ended the conversation.

And she would do—sooner than she'd thought too—because her grandfather was making a flying visit here tomorrow just to spend her birthday with her. The prospect softened her whole face. She loved that stubborn, bad tempered old man almost to distraction. He had been both her mother and father for so many years now that she could barely recall the time when she hadn't looked to him for every little thing she might need.

But not a husband, she quickly reminded herself. That was one decision in her life out of which he was going to have to learn to keep his busy nose!

Why a sudden image of Ethan Hayes had to flash across her eyes at that moment, Eve refused to analyse, but it put a dark frown upon her face.

'Here, try this…' Glancing up she found Raoul Delacroix standing beside her holding out a tall glass full of a pinkish liquid decorated with just about everything, from a selection of tropical fruit pieces to several fancy cocktail sticks and straws.

'What's in it?' she asked warily.

'Aidan called it tiger juice with a bite,' Raoul replied.

Tiger juice, how appropriate, Eve mused dryly, thinking of Ethan Hayes again.

'I'm game, if you are,' Raoul said, bringing her attention to the other glass of the same he was holding. 'It might help take the scowl from your face that you seem to have been struggling with all evening.'

Had her bad mood been that apparent? Eve accepted the glass without further comment, but as Raoul lowered himself onto the sunbed next to hers, she felt a fizz of anger begin to bubble inside because she knew whose fault it was that she was feeling like this!

If she didn't watch out, Ethan Hayes could be in danger of becoming an obsession.

'*Salute.*' Raoul's glass touching the edge of hers brought her mind swinging back to where it should be.

'Cheers,' she replied, unearthed a curly straw from the rest of the pretty junk decorating the glass, put it to her lips and sucked defiantly.

The drink tasted a little strange but not horribly so. She looked at Raoul, he looked at her. 'What do you think?' she asked him curiously.

'Sexy,' he murmured with a teasingly lecherous grin. 'I can feel my toes tingling. I will now encourage the sensation to reach other parts.' With that he took another pull on his straw.

Laughing at his outrageousness, Eve did the same, and it became a challenge as to which of them could empty the glass of Aidan's wicked brew first. After that she remembered little. Not the glass being rescued from her clumsy fingers nor the light-hearted banter that went on around her as the rest of the crowd discussed where the birthday girl should be placed to sleep it off. Aidan offered a bed, someone else suggested she was perfectly fine where she was. Raoul reminded them that her grandfather was due in on the dawn flight, so maybe the wisest place for him to find her tomorrow was in her own bed. This drew unilateral agreement because no one wanted to explain to Theron Herakleides why his precious granddaughter had been so rolling drunk she hadn't even made it home. Raoul offered to deliver her there since it was on the way to his villa, and he'd only had one glass of alcohol. Everyone agreed because no one else felt sober enough to make the drive.

It was all very relaxed, very light-hearted. No one thought of questioning Raoul's motives as they watched him carry Eve to his car. They were all such long-standing friends after all. All for one, one for all.

CHAPTER FOUR

ETHAN came shooting out of a deep sleep to the sound of a woman's shrill cry. Lying there in his bed with his heart pounding in his chest he listened for a few moments, uncertain that it hadn't been someone screaming in his dream.

Then the second cry came, and he was rolling out of bed and landing on his feet before the sound had come to a chillingly abrupt halt. Grabbing up a pair of beach shorts he pulled them on, then began moving fast out of his bedroom, across the sitting room and through the front door, where he paused to look around for some clue as to where the cries had come from.

It was pitch black outside and whisper-quiet; nothing stirred—even the ocean was struggling to make a sound as it lapped the shore. Peering out towards the sea, he was half expecting to see someone in difficulties out there, but no flailing silhouette broke the moon-dusted surface. The cries had been close—much closer to house than the water.

Then it came again, and even as he swung round to face Eve's beach house he saw the shadowy figure of a man slink down the veranda steps.

Eve was the screamer. His heart began to thump. 'Hey—!' he called out, startling the figure to a standstill halfway down the veranda steps. It was too dark to get a clear look at him but Ethan had his suspicions. He sure did have those, he thought grimly, as he began striding towards the boundary wall that separated the two properties. The name Aidan Galloway was burning like a light

32

bulb inside his head. 'What the hell is going on?' he demanded, only to prompt the other man to turn and make a sudden run for it.

His skin began to crawl with a sense that something was really wrong here. People didn't run unless they had a reason to. Thinking no further than that, he gave chase, sprinting across the dry spongy grass and vaulting the wall without even noticing. Within seconds the figure had disappeared around the corner of Eve's beach house. By the time Ethan rounded that corner all he saw were the red tail-lights of a car taking off up the narrow lane which gave access to the beach from the road above.

On a soft curse he then turned his thoughts to Eve. Spinning about, he stepped onto her veranda and began striding along its cool tiled surface until he came to the door. It was swinging wide on its hinges and he stepped warily through it into complete darkness.

'Eve—?' he called out. 'Are you all right?'

He received no answer.

'Eve—!' he called again, more sharply this time.

Still no reply came back at him. He had never been in here before so he had to strain his eyes to pick out the shapes of walls and pieces of furniture as he began moving forwards. He bumped into something hard, found himself automatically reaching out to steady a table lamp by its shade and had the foresight to switch it on. Light suddenly illuminated a floor plan that was much the same as his own. He was standing in the sitting room surrounded by soft-cushioned cane furniture; there was an open-plan kitchen in one corner and two doors which had to lead to a bathroom and the only bedroom.

'Eve?' he called out again as he wove through the cane furniture to get to the other two doors. One was slightly ajar; warily he lifted a hand and widened the opening enough to allow light to seep into the darkened room.

What he saw brought him to a dead standstill. The room looked like a disaster area, with Eve sitting in the middle of it like a discarded piece of the debris. Lamp light shone onto her down-bent head and her hair was all over the place, forming a tumbling screen of silk that completely hid her face. She was hugging herself, slender arms crossed over her body, long fingers curled like talons around the back of her neck. The tattered remains of the hot-pink dress lay in a crumpled huddle beside her on the floor.

'God in heaven,' he breathed, feeling his heart drop to his stomach when he realised what had clearly been going on here.

'Go away,' she told him, the whimpered little command almost choked through a throat full with tears.

Grimly ignoring the command, Ethan walked forward, face honed into the kind of mask that would have scared the life out of Eve if she'd glanced up and seen it. He came to squat down in front of her. He might not be able to see her face but he could feel her distress pulsing out towards him.

'Are you hurt?' he asked gruffly, reaching out with a hand to lightly touch her hair.

Her response was stunning. In a single violent movement she rose to her feet, spun her back to him, then began trembling as her battle with tears began to be lost.

Ethan took his time in rising to his full height and trying to decide what his next move should be. It was as clear as day that some sort of assault had taken place here, that Eve was shocked and distressed and maybe—

'I hate you, do you know that?' she choked out suddenly. 'I really—really hate you for coming in here like this!'

'I heard a scream, came out to investigate and saw someone leaving here,' he felt compelled to explain. 'There was something in the way he moved that made me—Eve—' he changed tack anxiously '—you're shaking so badly you look like you're going to collapse. Let me—'

'Don't touch me,' she breathed, then quite suddenly her legs gave away on her and she sank, folding like a piece of limp rubber down onto the edge of the rumpled bed.

Standing there, Ethan was uncertain as to what to do next. She didn't want him near her, she wanted him to go, but there was no way he could do that without making sure she was fit to be left on her own. His eyes fell on the hot-pink dress, then the scrappy pink bra lying beside it. His skin began to crawl again in response to the horror that was painting itself into his head. The evidence suggested rape, or at the very least a bungled attempt.

A thrust of bloody anger had him bending down to scoop up a white cotton sheet from the tangle of bedding on the floor, then carefully draping the sheet around her trembling frame. It wasn't that she was naked, because he'd noticed the pair of pink panties when she'd risen to her feet. But, as for the rest... His teeth clenched together as he lowered himself into a squatting position in front of her again.

She was clutching the sheet now, face still hidden, hunched shoulders trembling like mad. 'What happened here, Eve?' he questioned grimly.

'What do you think?' she shot back on a bitter choke. 'I suppose you think I deserved it!'

'No,' he denied that.

'Liar.' She sobbed and lifted the sheet up to use it to cover her face.

'Eve—nobody of sane mind would believe a woman deserves what appears to have happened here,' he insisted soberly.

'I'm drunk,' she admitted.

He could smell the alcohol.

'It was all my fault.'

'No,' he said again, his hands hanging limp between his spread thighs, though they desperately wanted to reach out and touch her.

'I can't feel my legs. I don't even know how I got here. I think he spiked my last drink.'

'Possibly,' Ethan quietly agreed, willing to feed her answering remarks if it helped him to understand just what had happened here.

She moved at last, rubbing the sheet over her face then slowly lowering it so he could get his first look at it. Her lips were swollen and he could see chafe marks from a man's rough beard. His jaw became a solid piece of rock as he noticed other things and tried to keep that knowledge off his face.

Maybe she saw something—he wasn't sure, but she released the sheet and rubbed trembling fingers over the side of her neck, then lifted the fingers higher to push back her hair and clutched at her head as she began to rock to and fro again.

Ethan's fingers twitched; she saw it happen. 'I'm all right,' she said jerkily. 'I just need to—'

Get a hold on what has happened to me, he finished for her mentally. 'How bad was it?' He had to ask the question even though he knew she did not want to answer it. But this could well be the kind of scene that required a doctor and the police to investigate.

But Eve shook her head, refusing to answer. Then, from seemingly out of nowhere, a huge sob shook her from shoulders to feet and she was suddenly gulping out the tears with a total loss of composure.

A silent sigh ripped at the lining of his chest. 'Look, Eve, will you let me hold you? You need to be held but I don't want to—'

'You hate me.' She sobbed.

'No, I don't.' This time the sigh was full-bodied and heavy. 'I'll go and call the police.' He went to get up.

'No!' she cried, and without any warning she slid to the ground between his spread knees and landed heavily against his chest, almost knocking him over in the process.

As he flexed muscles to maintain his balance, she began sobbing brokenly into his shoulder. It was a dreadful sound—the sound nightmares were made of. Her arms went around his neck and began clinging tightly. The sheet began to slip, and with his jaw locked like a vice against the gamut of primitive emotion building inside him, Ethan caught the sheet, replaced it over her shoulders, then took a chance and wrapped his arms round her to just hold her while she cried herself out.

Her tears began to wet his shoulder and neck, mingling with her breath as she sobbed and quivered. She smelt of alcohol and something much more sweetly subtle, and he hoped she hadn't noticed that her naked breasts were pressing against his equally naked chest. She felt warm and soft and so infinitely fragile it was like holding a priceless piece of art. As his eyes took in the debacle of their surroundings, he couldn't think of a less likely setting or situation to discover that he was holding the perfect woman in his arms.

The unexpected thought stopped his train of thought. Maybe he tensed; he was certainly shocked enough to have turned into a pillar of rock. Whatever, the sobbing grew less wretched, the grip on his neck began to ease. Old tensions erupted, defensive barriers began to climb back into place. He could actually feel Eve taking stock of the situation. The sobs quietened, silence came and within it her distress changed to a self-conscious embarrassment.

She had noticed the intimacy of their embrace.

Untangling her fingers from round his neck, Eve lifted her head out of his shoulder, then drew away from him just enough to gather the sheeting around her front. She couldn't believe she had done that—couldn't believe she had just sobbed her heart out on Ethan Hayes of all people, nor that she had done it with her bare breasts flattened against his naked chest.

So now what did she do? she asked herself helplessly, and put a hand up to cover the aching throb taking place behind her heavy eyes. He didn't speak, though she wished he would because she just didn't know what to say to him.

'I'm sorry,' were the weak words that eventually left her.

'Please don't be,' he returned, sounding so stiff and formal that she wanted to shrivel up and die.

But at least he moved at last by sitting back on his ankles to place some much needed distance between them, and Eve dared herself a glance at that hair-covered chest she could still feel warm and prickly against her breasts. She liked the sensation, just as she liked the way she could taste the moist warmth of his skin on her lips.

Oh—what is happening to me? In trembling confusion brought the sheet up to cover her face again. Beyond her hiding place the silence in the room throbbed. What was he thinking? What did he really want to do? Get up and leave? Wishing he hadn't come in here at all? Why not? She knew what Ethan Hayes thought of her. She knew he was seeing only what he would have expected to see.

In his eyes she was a flirt, a man-teaser with no scruples

to stop her from going that step too far. Well, Mr Hayes, she thought behind the now damp sheet. Here I am where you probably always predicted I would end up, hoisted by my own petard.

'Say something!' she snapped out. She couldn't bear the silence.

'Tell me what happened here.'

'I don't remember!' The words and their accompanying sob drove her to her feet. Only, her legs wouldn't support her; they felt like two rubber bands stretched so taut they quivered. And how he knew that, she didn't understand! But he was on his feet and using a hand on her arm to support her as he guided her down onto the edge of the bed.

She was in shock. In one part of her wretched head, Eve was aware of that. She was even able to appreciate that Ethan did not quite know what to do in the situation he found himself in.

'I'm sorry,' she said again. 'I can't seem to th-think straight.' Taking a deep breath she made a concerted effort to be rational. 'W-we were all at Aidan's beach house. It was my birthday party and I suppose we were all a little bit tipsy. Aidan was mixing cocktails…'

Her voice trailed off, her mind drifting back over the following few minutes when Raoul had sat down beside her and they'd talked and had drunk…

After that she could remember nothing until she'd found herself back here and Raoul had been undressing her. 'It's okay, Eve.' She echoed Raoul's soothing words back to herself, unaware that what had come before had only been replayed inside her head. 'You are back home. I am putting you to bed…'

Bed. Her stomach revolted, forcing her back to her feet and off that dreadful piece of furniture! On her rubber-band legs she stumbled, her hand went out to grab at something to steady herself with and it had to be a rock-solid bicep belonging to Ethan Hayes. The worst of it was, she didn't want to let go again. She *never* wanted to let go! Why was that? she asked herself dizzily. Why was it that this man with this cold hard expression that so disapproved of her, could fill her with such a warm feeling of strength of trust?

She didn't know. In fact she didn't think she knew anything for certain any more. 'I believed him.' Staring up at Ethan's mask-like face, her own revealed a shocked lack of comprehension at her own gullibility. 'How could I have *done* that?' she cried. 'How could I *not* have known there was more to his motives than…?'

'He spiked your drink,' Ethan gently reminded her. 'Don't knock yourself over something I don't believe you had any control over.'

Swallowing she nodded and clutched more tightly at his arm. 'I m-must have passed out again,' she went on shakily. 'Next thing I remember, I was being kissed. I thought it was a dream…' She stopped to swallow thickly, put trembling fingers up to her swollen lips and her expression crumpled on a wave of pained and frightened dismay because it had been no dream. 'I th-think I screamed. I th-think I hit him. I think I m-managed to scramble off the bed. I *know* I screamed again because I can still hear it shrilling inside my h-head—'

The stumbling words were halted by the way Ethan wrapped her close to him again. It was the sweetest, most comforting gift he could have given her right then.

But Ethan wasn't thinking of gifts, he was thinking of murder. He was seeing Aidan Galloway's handsome face and how it was going to look when he had restructured it. He was thinking about how this proud, feisty woman had been reduced to this, because one spoiled lout didn't know how to control his libido. He was also thinking about the way she came into his arms without hesitation, how she was nestling here.

'I thought he was my friend.'

Ethan recognised the pained feeling that went into that wretched comment. 'We all make poor judgements of people now and then.'

She nodded against his breastbone—he wished she wouldn't do that he thought, as other parts of him began to respond. He wished he understood it, wished he knew why this woman had the power to move him in ways he'd never previously known. It wasn't just the sex thing, he made that clear to himself. But he liked the way she clung to him, and how, despite the ordeal she had just been through here, she could trust him enough to cling.

'You're being too nice to me.'

'You would prefer it if I tore into you about the dangers of flirting with one too many young and sexually healthy men?'

'Like you just did, you mean?' Lifting her head she looked at him through eyes turned almost black by fright and whatever drug was swimming in her blood.

Vulnerable, he thought. Too—too vulnerable. It made him want to kiss away her fears— What he didn't expect was for Eve to suddenly fall on his neck and start kissing him!

Shock leapt upon him like a scalded cat with its claws unsheathed. Those claws raked a pleasurable passage across his senses before he found the wits to prize his mouth free from hers. He had to use tough hands on her waist to prize the rest of her away from him. 'What the *hell*?' he ground out forcefully as she stood staring up at him through those wide black unseeing eyes. By now he was feeling so damn shaken he was almost on the point of running himself! 'Dear God, Eve, what do you think you're playing at?'

The rough-cut rake of his voice brought her blinking back from wherever she had gone off to. She stared at him in horror then in dawning dismay. 'Oh,' she gasped out in a shaken whimper, and then it was she who tried to make a mortified bolt for it. But the moment she tried her legs gave away once more.

On a muttered curse Ethan caught her up, then dumped her unceremoniously back onto the bed. The whole thing was taking on a surreal quality. Standing there he stared down at her as if she was some kind of alien while she rocked and groaned with a hand flattened across her horrified mouth. It was then as he watched her that it really began to dawn on him that the swine must have spiked her drink with something pretty potent and it was still very much at work in her blood. 'I'm sorry,' she was saying over and over. 'I don't know what came over me. I don't—'

'You need a doctor,' Ethan decided grimly.

'No!'

'We need to call in the police and get them to track that bastard down so that we can find out what it is he's slipped you.'

'No,' she groaned out a second time.

But Ethan wasn't listening. He was too busy looking around for the telephone. As Eve saw him take a stride towards one sitting on a low table across the room, she erupted with a panic that flung her anxiously to her feet.

'No, Ethan—please—!' she begged him. 'No police. No doctor—I'm all right!'

Virtually staggering in her quest to put herself between him and the phone, she stood there trembling and looking pleadingly up at him while he looked down at her with an expression that grimly mocked her assurance.

'I *will* be all right in a minute or two!' she temporised, saw him take another determined step and felt the tears begin to burn in her eyes as fresh anxiety swelled like a monster inside. 'Please—' she begged again. 'You don't understand. The scandal, my grandfather—he will blame himself and I couldn't *bear* to let him do that!' I can't bear to know that he will never look on me in the same way again, Eve added in silent anguish. 'Look…' at least Ethan was no longer moving, and the panic had placed the strength back in her legs '…I was drunk. It was my own f-fault—'

'There is no excuse out there to justify date rape, Eve,' Ethan toughly contested.

'B-but it didn't get that far. I m-managed to stop him before he could—' The words dried up. She just couldn't bring herself to say them and had to swallow on a lump of nausea instead. 'I'll get over this—I will!' she insisted. 'But *only* if we can keep it a secret between you and me; please, Ethan—please—!' she repeated painfully.

She was pleading with him as if she was pleading for her life here, but Ethan could see the lingering horror in her eyes, see the shock and hurt and bewildered sense of betrayal, see the swollen mouth and the chafed skin, and the effects of some nasty substance that had turned her beautiful eyes black and had left her barely able to control her actions.

Did she really expect him to simply ignore all of that? In an act of frustrating indecision he sent his eyes lashing around the room. It looked like exactly what it was: the scene of some vile crime. The man was dangerous; he needed to be stopped and made to pay for his actions.

Flicking his gaze back to Eve, Ethan opened his mouth to tell her just that—then stopped, the breath stilling in his lungs when he saw the tears in her eyes, the trembling mouth, the anxiety in her pale face that was now overshadowing the incident itself. His mouth snapped shut. A sigh rattled from him. Surrender to her pleas arrived when he acknowledged that she was in no fit state to take any more tonight.

'Okay,' he agreed with grim reluctance. 'We will leave the rest until tomorrow. But for now you can't stay here on your own…'

He deliberately didn't add, '…in case he comes back'. But he saw by her shuddering response that Eve had added the words for herself. 'Thank you,' she whispered.

He didn't want thanks. He wanted a solution as to what he was going to do next. Glancing at Eve in search of inspiration, he found himself looking at a wilting flower again, only she was a slender white lily this time, covered as she was in the cotton sheet.

A sad and helpless slender white lily, he elaborated, and the image locked up a blistering kind of anger inside his chest. 'How are you feeling?' he asked gruffly. 'Do you think you can manage to get yourself dressed?'

'Yes,' she whispered.

'Good.' He nodded. At least she was managing to stand unsupported at last. 'Do that, then I'll walk you up to the main house,' he decided, aware that there was a small army of live-in staff up there to watch over her.

'No, not the house.' Once again she vetoed his suggestion. 'The staff will report to my grandfather and…' Her voice trailed away, and those big eyes were suddenly pleading with him again. 'Could I come and stay with you?' she asked. 'Just for the rest of tonight. I promise I won't be any more trouble, only…'

Again that voice trailed away to nothing, and that dark, sad, vulnerable look cut into him with a deeply painful thrust. Hell, how was it he seemed to attract these kind of situations? he wondered, racking his brain for an alternative solution only to find there wasn't one. Beginning to feel a bit as if he'd been run over by a bus, he lifted up a hand in a hopeless gesture. 'Sure,' he said.

Why not? he asked himself fatalistically. He had conceded to just about everything else.

He was just about to leave her to it when he saw her mouth open to offer yet another pathetic thanks. 'Don't say it,' he advised grimly.

'No,' she mumbled understandingly. 'Sorry,' she offered instead.

His shoulder muscles rippled as they flexed in irritation. 'Don't say that either,' he clipped out tightly. 'I don't want your thanks or your apologies.' What he really wanted, he thought as he turned for the bedroom door, was to close his hands around Aidan Galloway's throat.

He was angry, Eve realised. She didn't blame him. She had probably managed to thoroughly ruin his holiday with all of this. Feeling sick to her stomach, as weak as a kitten, and still too shocked and dizzy to really comprehend even half of what had happened to her tonight, she turned away from him with the weary intention of doing as she'd been told and finding some clothes to put on—only to go still on a strangled gasp when she found herself confronted with her own reflection in the mirror on the opposite wall.

The sound brought Ethan's departure to a halt. Glancing back, he followed her gaze, found himself looking at her reflection in the mirror and instantly understood.

She'd seen her swollen mouth, her chafed skin—had

caught sight of the telling discolouration on the side of her neck that Ethan had been trying very hard to ignore from the moment he'd seen it himself. And perhaps most telling of all was the pink hibiscus still trying its best to cling to her hair.

The tears bulged in her eyes. 'I look like a harlot,' she whispered tremulously, lifting shaking fingers to remove the poor flower.

A sensationally beautiful, very special harlot, he silently extended, and on that provoking thought he threw in the metaphorical towel. 'Blow the clothes,' he decided harshly and walked back to her side. His arm came to rest across her sheet swathed shoulders. 'Let's just get you out of here.'

With that he grimly urged her into movement. Still shocked at the sight of herself, Eve tripped over the trailing sheet. On a muttered curse, Ethan went the whole hog and scooped her up high against his chest.

'I can walk!' she protested.

'Enjoy the ride,' was his curt response, as he began carrying her out of the bedroom and out of the house with his cast-iron expression brooking no argument.

Neither saw the dark figure standing in the shadows, whose eyes followed their journey from one beach house to the other by the conventional route of paths and gates. Eve's attention was just too occupied with that old fascination, which was this man called Ethan Hayes and the structure of his—she was thinking, handsome, but the word was really too soft to describe such a forcefully masculine face. His chin was square and slightly chiselled, his eyelashes long and thick. His eyebrows were two sternly straight black bars that dipped a little towards the bridge of his nose and added a disturbing severity she rather liked. She liked his eyes too, even with that a dark steely glint they were reflecting right now, and she loved his mouth, its size, its shape, its smooth firm texture— Her lips began to pulse with the sudden dark urge to taste him in that same wild, uncontrolled way she had done a few minutes ago.

Had she really done that? Shock ricocheted through her. *Why* had she done it? What kind of substance could Raoul have stirred into her drink that had had the power to make her do such an outrageous thing? She shifted uncomfortably, disturbed by the knowledge that such an out-of-control person could actually be lurking inside her, seemingly waiting the chance to leap out and jump all over a man. What must he be thinking about it, and her, and—?

'About that kiss earlier...' she said, approaching the subject tentatively.

Long eyelashes flickered, steely grey irises glinting as he glanced down at her upturned face. 'Forget it,' he advised, and looked away again because Ethan was trying not to think at all.

It was hard enough trying not to be aware that what he was carrying was feather-light and as slender as a reed, and that the warm body beneath the sheet was shapely and sleek. He didn't need the added provocation of looking into her beautiful face, nor to be reminded of that unexpected kiss.

So he concentrated his mind on the different ways he could make Aidan Galloway sorry for what he had done to Eve tonight. Date rape—for want of something to call it—and the use of sexually enhancing drugs to get what he desired, made Galloway the lowest form of human life.

That was where Eve's kiss had come from, he reminded himself. Nothing more, nothing less, therefore not worth a second thought.

So why can you still feel the imprint of her mouth against your own? he asked himself grimly.

Because she was beautiful, because she was dangerous, and—heaven help him—he liked the danger Eve Herakleides represented. It was called sexual attraction, and he would have to be a fool not to be aware that Eve felt the same pull. That little wriggle she'd just performed had been full of sexual tension—though he had to concede that the drink probably had had a lot to do with it too.

Either way, it was a danger he could not afford to be tempted by. His life was complicated enough without the tempting form of Eve Herakleides.

So what do you think you are doing now? he then scoffed to himself as he carried Eve in through his own front door. And discovered it was not a question he wanted to answer right now, as he lowered her feet to the floor then turned to close the door.

CHAPTER FIVE

THE beach houses were all very picturesque outside, but very basic inside; just one bedroom, a bathroom, small kitchen and a sitting room. Really they were meant for nothing more than a place to cool off during a day spent on the beach. Or as in Ethan case, the perfect place for the single person to use for a holiday. Problems only arose when the single person doubled to two.

It was a problem that only began to dawn on Eve as she watched Ethan close the door. The fact that it had dawned on him too at about the same moment became apparent when, instead of turning to face her, he went perfectly still.

A thick and uncomfortable silence settled between them. Clutching the sheet to her throat, Eve tried to think of something to say to break through the awkward atmosphere. Ethan tried to break it by taking off round the room to switch on the table lamps.

The light hurt her eyes, forcing her to squeeze them shut. He noticed. 'Sorry,' he murmured. 'I didn't think—'

'It's okay.' She made herself open them again. She didn't look at him though—she couldn't. Instead she made a play of checking out her surroundings—surroundings she already knew as well as she knew her own, because she had been in and out of the Petronades beach house since early childhood.

'Bedroom through that door, bathroom the other...'

She looked and nodded. Her mouth felt paper dry.

'Would you like a drink? Something hot like tea or coffee?'

Yes—no, Eve thought in tense confusion. Her head was beginning to pound, a sense of disorientation washing over her in ever increasing waves. She felt strange, out of place and—

'This was a mistake,' she pushed out thickly. 'I think I had better—'

One small step in the direction of the front door was all that it took for the whole wretched nightmare to come crashing back down upon her head. She swayed dizzily, felt her legs turn back to rubber; she knew she was going to do something stupid like drop to the floor in a tent of white sheeting.

Only it never happened, because he was already at her side and catching hold of her arms to steady her. She was trembling so badly her teeth actually chattered.

'Are you frightened of being alone here with me, or is this a delayed shock reaction?' he questioned soberly.

Both, Eve thought. 'Sh-shock, I think,' was the answer she gave out loud. Then she confessed to him shakily, 'Ethan, I really need to sit down.'

'What you need is a doctor,' he clipped back tautly.

'No,' she refused.

Sighing at her stubbornness. 'Bed, then,' he insisted. 'You can at least sleep off the effects there.'

He was about to lift her back into his arms when Eve stopped him. 'W-what I would really love to do is take a shower,' she told him. 'W-wash his touch from my skin...'

There was another one of those tense pauses. 'Eve, he didn't—?'

'No,' she put in quickly. 'He didn't.' But the tremors became shudders, and neither of them bothered to question why she was suddenly shuddering so badly.

'The bathroom it is, then,' he said briskly, and the next thing she knew Eve was being lifted into his arms again and carried into the bathroom. He set her down on the lowered toilet seat, then turned to switch on the shower. 'Stay right there,' he instructed then as he was disappearing through the door.

His departure gave Eve the opportunity to sag weakly. He was back in seconds, though, forcing her to straighten her backbone before he caught her looking so darn pathetic.

'Fresh towels,' he announced, settling them on the washbasin. 'And a tee shirt of mine.' He placed it on her lap. 'I thought it might be more comfortable to wear than the sheet.'

It was an attempt to lighten the thick atmosphere with humour, Eve recognised, and did her best to rise to it. 'White was never my colour,' she murmured, referring to the sheet.

The tee shirt was white. They both stared down at it. It was such a stupid, mild, incidental little error that certainly did not warrant the flood of hot tears it produced. Ethan saw them—of course he did—when had he missed a single thing since he'd barged into her bedroom?

He came to squat down in front of her. 'Hey,' he murmured gently. 'It's okay. I am not offended that you don't like my tee shirt.'

But she did like it. She liked every single thing about this man, every single thing he had done for her. And the worst of it was that he had done it all even though he actively disliked her! 'I'm so very sorry for dumping on you like this.' The sheet was covering her face again.

'I thought we'd agreed that you were not going to apologise,' he reminded her.

'But I feel so wretched, and I know you have to be hating this.'

'I hate what happened to you to put us both in this

situation,' he tempered. 'And the rest I think is best left until tomorrow when you should be feeling more able to cope.'

He was right. Eve nodded. 'I'll take that shower now,' she said bracingly.

'You will be okay on your own? You won't fall over or—?'

'I'll be okay.' She nodded.

He didn't look too sure about that. His eyebrows were touching across the bridge of his nose as he studied her, and his eyes were no longer steely but dark and deep with genuine worry and concern. Could she *ever* look more pathetic than this? Eve wondered tragically. And did it *have* to be Ethan Hayes who witnessed it?

The sheet was used as a handkerchief again, and they weren't her fingers that lifted it to wipe the tears from her cheeks, they were his gentle fingers. The caring act was almost her complete undoing.

'I'll be fine!' she promised in near desperation. Any second now she was going to throw herself at him again if she didn't get him out of here! 'Please go, Ethan— please,' she repeated plaintively.

Maybe he knew because he rose up to his full height. 'Don't lock the door,' was his final comment. 'And if you need me, shout.'

But Eve didn't shout, and while he waited for her to reappear, Ethan prowled the place. He was like a pacing tiger guarding his territory—he likened his own tense and restless state. In the end he put his restless energy to use and tidied the bedroom, remade the bed and, as a belated thought, pulled another clean tee shirt out of the drawer and slid it over his head, then went to make a pot of tea. He had just been placing a tray down on the coffee table when the bathroom door opened.

He glanced up. Eve paused in the doorway. She had a towel wrapped around her hair and she was wearing the tee shirt. It covered her to halfway down her thighs and the short sleeves almost brushed her slender wrists.

She was wrong about the colour, he thought, quickly dropping his eyes away. 'Tea?' he offered.

'I… Yes, please,' she answered and, after a small hesitation that told him Eve was as uncomfortable with this situation as he was, she walked forward and took the chair next to the sofa. Having been told how she liked her tea, Ethan poured and offered her the mug then folded himself into the other chair. Neither spoke as they sipped, and the atmosphere was strained, to put it mildly. Eve was the first to attempt to ease it. Putting the cup down on the tray, she removed the towel from her hair and shook out its wet and tangled length. 'Would you have a comb or something I could use?'

'Sure.' Glad of the excuse to move, he got up and found a comb. 'Hair-dryer's in the bathroom,' he said as he handed over the comb.

She nodded in acknowledgement of something he suspected she already knew. He sat down again and she began combing the tangles out of her hair. It was all very domestic, very we-do-this-kind-of-thing-all-the-time. But nothing could have been further from the truth.

'I'll take the couch,' she said.

'No, you won't,' he countered. 'I have my honour to protect. *I* take the couch.'

'But—'

'Not up for discussion,' he cut in on her protest. One brief glance at his face and she was conceding the battle to him. Suddenly she looked utterly exhausted yet so uptight that the grip she had on his comb revealed shiny white knuckles.

'Come on, you've had enough.' Standing up again, he swung himself into action which felt better than sitting there feeling useless. Taking hold of her wrist, he tugged her to her feet, gently prized the comb from her fingers, and began trailing her towards the bedroom.

'My hair…' she prompted.

'It won't fall out if you leave it to dry by itself,' was his sardonic answer. But really he knew he was rushing her like this because it was himself that had suddenly had enough. He needed some space that didn't have Eve Herakleides in it. He needed to get a hold on what was churning up his insides.

And what was that? he asked himself. He refused to let himself look for the answer because he knew it was likely to make him as bad as that swine Aidan Galloway.

The bedroom was ready and waiting, its shadows softened by the gentle glow from the bedside lamp. He saw Eve glance at the bed, then at the room as a whole, and her nervous uncertainty almost screamed in this latest silence to develop between them.

'You're safe here, Eve,' he grimly assured her, making that assurance on the back of his own sinful thoughts.

She nodded, slipped her wrist out of his grasp and took a couple of steps away. She looked so darn lost and anxious that he had to wonder if she was picking up on what his own tension was about.

Yet what did she do next? She floored him by suddenly spinning to face him. White-faced, big-eyed, small mouth trembling. 'Will you stay?' she burst out. 'Just for a few minutes. I don't want to be alone yet. I…'

The moment she'd said it, Eve was wishing the stupid words back. Just the expression on his face was enough to tell her she could not have appalled him more if she'd tried. Oh, damn, she thought and put a trembling hand up to cover her face. He didn't even like her; hadn't she always known that? Yet here she was almost begging him to sleep with her—or as good as.

'Pretend I never said that,' she retracted, turned away and even managed a couple more steps towards the wretched bed! She felt dizzy and confused and terribly disorientated—and she wished Raoul Delacroix had never been born!

The arm that reached round her to flip back the bed covers almost startled her out of her wits. 'In,' Ethan commanded.

In, like a child being put to bed by a stern father, she likened. *In* she got, curling onto her side like a child and let him settle the covers over her. When I leave here tomorrow I am *never* going to let myself set eyes on Ethan Hayes again! she vowed. 'Goodnight,' she made herself say.

'Shut up,' he returned and the next thing she knew he was stretching out beside her on top of the covers. 'I'll stay until you go to sleep,' he announced.

'You don't have to,' Eve responded with a hint of bite. 'I changed my mind. I don't—' The way he turned on his side to face her was enough to push the rest of her words back down her throat.

'Now listen to me, you aggravating little witch,' he said huskily. 'Any more provocation from you and I am likely to lose my temper. If you need me here, I'll stay, if you want me to go, I'll go. Your decision.'

Her decision. 'Stay,' she whispered.

Without another word he flopped onto his back and stared rigidly at the ceiling. Curled up at his side, Eve imagined his silent curses that were probably all very colourful ways of describing what he was feeling about this mess.

I'm sorry, she wanted to say, but she knew he didn't want to hear that, so she did the next best thing she could think of and shut her eyes then willed herself to fall asleep.

Five minutes, Ethan was thinking grimly. I'll give her five minutes to fall asleep then I'm out of here. With that, he took a look at his watch. Two o'clock.

A sigh whispered from her. Turning his head it wrenched at his heart to see the trace of tears still staining her cheeks. She had just endured a close encounter with what had to be a woman's worst nightmare and here he was putting a time limit on how long he was going to support her through the rest of this.

A sigh whispered from him. Eve liked the sigh. She liked the comfort she gained from hearing his closeness and the sure knowledge that if she was safe anywhere then it had to be right here with him.

Tomorrow was destined to be another thing entirely. By tomorrow, she predicted, it would be back to hostilities, with him backing off whenever she threatened to come close. But, for now, she was content to think of him as her guardian angel, and on that comforting thought she let herself relax into sleep.

Another five minutes, Ethan decided. She'd relaxed at last and her breathing was steady. He would give her another five minutes to slip into a deep slumber, then he would swap the comfort of the bed for the discomfort of the living-room couch.

His eyelids began to droop; he dragged them back up again and captured a yawn on the back of his hand. Eve moved and mumbled something, it sounded like, 'Don't.' He tagged on another five minutes because the last thing he wanted was for her to wake up in a strange bed alone and frightened. Another five minutes wouldn't kill him, would it?

Eve came thrashing up from a deep dark sleep to that halfway place where haunted dream mixed with confusing reality. A sound had disturbed her, though she wasn't sure what it had represented, only that it had made her pulse accelerate and had pushed up her eyelids so she found herself staring directly into the sleeping face of Ethan Hayes. He was lying kiss-close to her on the same pillow with his arms and legs wrapped warmly around her—or were her limbs wrapped around him? She didn't have time to consider the puzzle because the sound came again and even as she lifted her head off the pillow she was aware that Ethan was now awake also. They turned together to look towards the open bedroom doorway, then froze on a heart-stopping clutch of stunning dismay.

Theron Herakleides stood filling the doorway, looking like his favourite god, Zeus, with his thickly curling grey locks framing a rough, tough, lived-in face that was clearly preparing to cast thunderbolts down on their heads.

'Grandpa,' Eve only managed on a strangled whisper. Ethan hissed out a couple of quick curses beneath his breath. The old man flicked devil-to-pay black eyes from one to the other and conjured up an image of themselves, which showed them what he was seeing. It was so utterly damning neither found the ability to speak in their own defence.

Theron did it for them when hard as rock, he threw his first thunderbolt. 'One hour, in my study at the main house,' he instructed. 'I will expect you both there.'

Then he was gone, leaving them lying there in a tangle of limbs and white bedding, feeling as culpable as a pair of guilty lovers who'd been caught red-handed in the act of sex.

'Oh, dear God.' Eve found her voice first, groaning out the words as she fell back heavily against the bed.

Ethan went one stage further and snaked his legs free of the tangle then landed on his feet beside the bed. He did not want to believe that any of this was really happening.

'How did you get here?' Eve had the absolute stupidity to ask him.

'How did *I* get here?' Ethan swung round to lance at her. 'This is *my* bed!'

They'd both reacted on pure instinct. Now reality hit, clearing away the last muddy remnants of sleep. Eve began to remember. Ethan watched it happen in a slide-frame flicker, as she passed through last night's ordeal to this morning's shocked horror. She went as pale as alabaster, clamped a hand across her trembling mouth, and just stared at him through huge dark nightmare-ridden eyes that turned his insides into a raging inferno of anger and gave him a desire to break someone's neck.

His own at the moment, he acknowledged grimly, and released the air from his lungs on a pressured hiss. 'My fault,' he conceded. 'I fell asleep. I'll go and talk to him.'

Decision set in his mind, he was already turning towards the door when Eve's half hysterical, 'No!' hit his ears. 'He won't believe you. I have to do it!' She began scrambling shakily to the edge of the bed. All long limbs, flying hair and utterly shattered composure, she landed on her feet beside him and began searching the floor.

'Shoes,' she mumbled anxiously.

'You didn't come in shoes. I carried you, remember?'

The hand was at her mouth again as a second barrage of memories came flooding in. No shoes, no clothes; Ethan was seeing it all with her. He was also seeing another bed that had looked not unlike this one, with its covers lying in the same damning tangle, half on the floor half on the bed.

Had Theron Herakleides seen that other bed too? His skin began to prickle as he began to fully appreciate what the older man had to believe from the evidence. A passionate interlude spent in his granddaughter's bed before they'd transferred to this one to repeat the whole orgy all over again.

The air left his lungs on yet another hard hiss. This whole mad scenario was going to take some serious explaining. 'I'll do the explaining,' he grimly insisted. 'You can stay here while I—'

'Will you listen to me, Ethan—? He will not believe you!' Eve stated fiercely. 'Trust me. I know him. He has seen what he's seen.'

'The truth is out there, Eve,' he reminded her. 'It has a name and a face—and when I get my hands on him he will be happy to spill out the truth to your grandfather.'

While his eyes began to darken at the delightful prospect of bringing Aidan Galloway face to face with his sins, Eve's eyes did the opposite and turned bright green, glinting like the eyes of a witch who was busy concocting her next wicked spell. She started walking towards the door.

'Where are you going?' he demanded.

'To see Grandpa before you do,' she stated firmly.

'Eve—'

'No!' She turned on him. 'I said I will deal with it!' The eyes were now glinting with tears, not wicked spells. 'Y-you don't understand. You will *never* understand!' And on that she was gone, running out of the room and leaving him standing there wondering what the heck that last outburst had been all about?

He'd understood! Of course he'd understood, he claimed arrogantly. From the moment he'd stepped into her bedroom last night, he'd understood without question what it was he'd been seeing!

Now it hurt that *she* didn't see that understanding. What did she think he was going to do? Paint her character all the lurid colours he could think of just to make his own part in this fiasco seem prettier?

Well, he was damned if he was going to slink away and hide in some dark corner while Eve fought his battles for him. Theron Herakleides was expecting the two of them to present themselves in his study and that was what would happen.

CHAPTER SIX

UNDERSTANDING anything about Eve Herakleides flew out of the window the moment Ethan found himself confronting her grandfather. Because Eve, he all too quickly discovered, had got in first with her version of events leading up to what Theron had witnessed. Now Ethan was angrily trying to make some sense of what it was he was supposed to have done.

Standing tall and proud behind his desk, Theron Herakleides looked on Ethan as if he was seeing a snake in the grass. 'You have to appreciate, Mr Hayes,' he was saying, 'that in Greece we expect a man to stand by his actions.'

'Are you implying that I wouldn't?' Ethan demanded stiffly.

The older man's brief smile set his temper simmering. 'You stand here claiming no intimacy between yourself and my granddaughter,' he pointed out. 'Are those not the words of a man who is trying to wriggle off the hook he finds himself caught upon?'

'We were not intimate,' Ethan insisted angrily.

A pair of grey-cloud eyebrows rose enquiringly. 'Now you expect this old man to question what his own eyes have already told him?'

Not only his own eyes, Ethan noted, as he sent a murderous glance at Eve who was standing quietly beside her grandfather. Gone was the seductress in sexy hot-pink. Nor was there any sign of the broken little creature he'd taken under his wing. No, from the neatly braided hair to the clothes that had been chosen with modesty in mind, here stood a picture of sweet innocence wearing a butter-wouldn't-melt-in-her-mouth smile that told clearly that he was going to be made the scapegoat here!

'Of course,' Theron Herakleides broke into speech again, 'you could be attempting to protect Eve's reputation, in which case I most sincerely apologise for implying the opposite. But your protection comes too late, I'm afraid,' he informed him gravely. 'For what I saw with my own eyes had already been substantiated by one of the men that guard my property. He saw you carry my granddaughter from our beach house to your beach house covered only by a sheet, you see...'

Damned by his own actions, Ethan realised. Then he said frowningly, 'Just a minute. If your guard was watching the beach house, then where was he when Eve—?'

Eve moved, drawing his glance and lodging the rest of his challenge in his throat when he found those eyes of hers pleading with him to say no more. Anger erupted as he glared at her and felt frustration mount like a boiling lump of matter deep within his chest.

I should stop this right here, he told himself forcefully. I should tell Eve's grandfather the unvarnished truth and finish this craziness once and for all. But those pleading eyes were pricking anxiously at him, reminding him of the conversation he and Eve had had the night before.

Ethan looked back at her grandfather, and Eve held her breath. If he talked, it was over. If he talked, her life was never going to be the same again.

'I think it's time you explained to me where you are going with this, Theron,' Ethan invited very grimly.

A deep sense of relief relaxed the tension out of Eve's shoulders. Thank you, she wanted to say to him. Thank you from the bottom of my heart for this.

'I am going to give you the benefit of the doubt,' her grandfather smoothly announced, 'and presume that your intentions towards my granddaughter are entirely honourable…'

It wasn't a question but a rock-solid statement. Eve watched nervously as Ethan's full attention became riveted on the older man's face. Her heart stopped beating in the throbbing silence, her mouth running dry, as she tried to decide whether to jump in and take over before Ethan said something ruinous or to remain quiet and keep praying that he didn't let her down.

Ethan didn't know what he was doing. The word 'honourable' was playing over and over inside his head while he stared at Theron's perfectly blank expression. Then he switched his gaze to Eve who was standing there looking like a diehard romantic who'd just had her dearest wish voiced out loud.

I've been well and truly set up, he finally registered, and the knowledge was threatening to cut him off at the knees.

Eve came to his rescue—if it could be called a rescue. Leaving her grandfather's side she rounded the desk and came to thread her fingers in with his then had the gall to lean lovingly against him like an ecstatic bride. 'You guessed our secret.' She pouted at her darling grandpa. 'I'm so happy! This is turning out to be the most wonderful birthday of my entire life.'

Slowly turning his dark head Ethan looked down at her through narrowed, steely I'm-going-kill-you eyes. 'Oh, don't be cross.' She pouted at him also. 'I know you wanted to wait a while before we told anyone about us. But Grandpa can keep a secret—can't you, Grandpa?' It was Grandpa's turn to receive the full spell-casting blast of her wide green witch's eyes.

The old man smiled. It was an action that smoothed

every hard angle out of him. 'But why be secretive, my
little angel?' he quizzed fondly. 'You are in love with each
other. Don't hide it, celebrate! We will announce your betrothal in front of the family when we return to Athens
next week…'

He's remembered he hates me, Eve realised nervously.
Ethan had washed and changed before coming up to the
main house, but even wearing a smart blue shirt and grey
trousers she could still see the man sitting in the beach bar
feeding her his utter contempt.

'Please, Ethan,' she said, panting as she hurried after
him down the path that led the way back to the beach. 'Let
me explain—'

'You set me up,' he rasped. 'That doesn't need explaining.'

'It was the only way I could think of to—'

'Get a marriage proposal?' he cut in contemptuously.

'You're not that good a catch!' she retaliated.

He stopped striding and swung round to face her. Sensational, Eve thought with an inner flutter. Ethan Hayes in
the throws of a blistering fury was exciting and dangerous
and—

'Then, *why* me?' he bit out.

'He dotes on me…'

Ethan responded to that with a hard laugh. 'Now tell
me something I haven't worked out.'

'He's built this shining glass case around me that he
likes to believe protects me from the realities of life.'

'Take my advice, and smash the case,' Ethan responded.
'Before someone else comes along and smashes it for you.'
On that he turned and started walking again.

So did Eve. 'That's the whole point,' she said urgently.
'I know I need to smash the case, but gently, Ethan!' she

pleaded with him. 'Not with a cold hard blow of just about the ugliest truth I could possibly think of to hurt him with.'

'He deserves the truth,' he insisted. 'You are insulting him by protecting him from it!'

'No.' Her hand gripping his arm pulled him to a stop again, like a miniature tyrant she stepped right in front of him to block his path. Her eyes pleaded, her mouth pleaded, the fierce grasp of her fingers pleaded. 'You don't understand. He's—'

Eve watched him go from sizzling fury to another place entirely. His shoulders flexed, his teeth gritted together, his wide breastbone shifted on an excess of suppressed air. 'Don't tell me again that I don't understand,' he bit out roughly, 'when all I need to understand is that you are using me, Miss Herakleides. And that sticks right here.' He stabbed two long fingers at his throat.

'Yes, I can see that...' she nodded '...and I'm sorry...'

'Good. Now let me pass so I can go and do what I need to do.'

'Which is what?' she asked warily.

The morning sun dappling through the tree tops suddenly turned his face into a map of hard angles that made her insides start to shake. 'Find the cause of this mess and make him wish he'd never been born before I deliver him into the hands of your grandfather,' Ethan answered grittily and went to step around her.

'You can't!' Once again Eve stopped him. 'H-he isn't here!' she exclaimed. 'H-he left the island by launch at first light. I know because I checked before I went to see Grandpa. H-he must have known I—'

'You checked,' Ethan repeated, his eyes narrowing on her pale features and her worriedly stammering lips. 'Now, why should you want to go and do that?' he questioned silkily.

'I w-wanted to talk to him, f-find out why he did it,' she explained. 'I really needed to know if I had brought it all upon myself! H-he was a friend—a long-standing friend. Friends don't do that to each other, do they? So I had to at least try to find out why!'

Ethan really couldn't believe he was hearing this. 'After everything he put you through last night.' Grimly he stuck to the main issue here. 'You went to confront him—on your own?'

Anxiety was darkening those big green eyes again. 'If I'd asked you to come with me, I knew you would want to kill him!'

Time to stop looking in those eyes, he decided. 'And you don't want him dead,' he persisted.

'No,' she breathed. 'I'm trying to avoid trouble not stir it up! A war will erupt between the two families if what happened last night ever got out.'

But that wasn't the real reason, Ethan thought grimly. She was hiding something, he was sure of it.

Then that something was suddenly clawing its way up his spine and attacking the hairs at the back of his neck. It was written all over her, in those big green apprehensive eyes, in the unsteady tremor of her lovely mouth—in the very words she had said!

'You're in love with the bastard.' He made the outright accusation. No wonder she'd felt compelled to find out why he had done what he had done! Why she didn't want Ethan to go anywhere near him—why she was trying to protect the swine now!

Her chin shot up. 'I'm what?' she questioned in shrill surprise.

But Ethan was no longer listening. 'I can't believe what a fool I've been,' he muttered. For him it was like lightning striking twice! First, he had got embroiled in Leona's love problems. Now he found himself embroiled in Eve's!

'How dare you?' she gasped out, dropping the surprise for indignant fury.

'No.' Ethan hit back by turning on her furiously. 'How dare *you* get me mixed up in your crazy love life?'

He was angry; she was angry; the old hostile sparks began to fly. The air crackled with them, 'That's rich,' Eve mocked, 'coming from a man who is only here on this island because he's in hiding after being caught red-handed with another man's wife!'

The sparks changed into a high-voltage current. It was unstable—very unstable. 'Who told you that?' Ethan demanded.

Eve shrugged. 'Leandros Petronades is a relative of Grandpa's. He told Grandpa, and Grandpa thought I should know before I committed myself to you.'

'It's a lie,' he declared.

Eve didn't believe him. 'Don't insult my intelligence,' she denounced. 'Do you think I didn't notice the bruise on your face when you arrived on the island? Everyone noticed it. In fact it was the source of much speculation.'

'And the bruise on your neck?' Ethan went in with the metaphorical knife and took some satisfaction from seeing her snap her hand up to cover the mark.

'I forgot!' she gasped out in impressive horror.

Ethan didn't believe her. The brazen hussy hadn't even bothered to cover the damn thing up! 'How many more people have seen it and been equally imaginative about how it was put there?'

She blushed and looked uncomfortable. Ethan released a harsh laugh. 'My God,' he breathed, 'you are unbelievable! Take my advice, Eve,' he offered as his grim farewell. 'Go back up to the house and tell your grandfather the truth before I do it for you.'

'You wouldn't...'

He was turning away when she said that. It brought him swinging back again. 'I would,' he promised. 'And you know why I would do it? Because you are a danger to yourself,' he told her. 'You flirt with every man you come into contact with, uncaring what your flirting is doing to them. Then you have the rank stupidity to fall in love with a piece of low life like Aidan Galloway— And even after what he tried to do to you last night, you are *still* standing here protecting him! That makes you dangerous,' he concluded, and tried to ignore her greyish pallor, the hint of tears, the small shocked jerk she made that somehow cut him so deeply he almost groaned out loud.

Instead he walked away, striding down the path towards the beach with so much anger burning inside him he had to reign in on just about every emotion he possessed, or he'd be doing something really stupid like—

Like going back up the path and taking back every rotten, slaying word he'd spoken, because he knew what it was like to be in love with the wrong person, didn't he?

At least Leona was warm and kind and unfailingly loyal to her husband, he grimly justified his reason for not turning back. Aidan Galloway was a different kind of meat entirely. He was poison; he needed exposing before he tried the same thing with some other woman.

From a window in the main house, Theron Herakleides observed the altercation on the path down to the beach through mildly satisfied eyes. He wasn't quite sure what the altercation was actually about, but he had a shrewd idea. Ethan Hayes had just been well and truly scuppered by his enterprising granddaughter and he was now in the middle of a black fury.

Served him right for seducing her, Theron thought coldly. If he hadn't been so sure that Eve truly believed she was in love with the rake, the hell being wrought down there on his path would have been happening right here at his own orchestration.

But if his beautiful Eve thought he was going to let her throw herself away on a man like Ethan Hayes, she was so wrong it actually hurt him to know that he was going to have to show her just how wrong she was. So what if the man was an outstandingly gifted architect? So what if he, Theron Herakleides, had actually held him in deep respect until today? By tomorrow Ethan Hayes would be out of the picture, Theron vowed very grimly, and Eve was going to learn to recover from her little holiday romance.

With those thoughts in mind, Theron turned away from the window to pick up the telephone. 'Ah—*yassis*, Leandros,' he greeted pleasantly, and fell into light conversation with his nephew while glancing back out of the window to see the way Eve had been left standing on the path, looking like a thoroughly whipped peasant instead of the proud and brave goddess he believed her to be.

Ethan Hayes would pay for that, he vowed coldly. He was going to pay in spades for playing with the heart of a sweet angel when everyone knew he was in love with Leona Al-Qadim!

'I am about to call in that favour you owe to me,' he warned Leandros Petronades, then went on to explain what he required of him. 'The sooner the better would be good for me, Leandros…'

Standing there on the sunny path, feeling as if she had just been reduced to dust by a man angry enough to tear down a mountain, Eve was carefully going over everything Ethan had tossed at her so she could be certain she had heard him correctly.

Aidan— 'Oh, good heavens,' she gasped as the whole thing began to get even more confused and complicated. Ethan believed it was Aidan, not Raoul, who'd been with her in her bedroom last night!

The telephone was ringing as Ethan let himself into the beach house. He stood glaring at the contraption, in two minds whether to ignore it. He didn't want to speak to anyone. He did not want to do anything but stew in the juices of his anger.

But, in the end, he gave in and picked up the receiver, if only to silence its persistent ring. It was Victor Frayne, his business partner, which did not improve his mood any. 'What do you want, Victor?' he questioned abruptly.

'Still as mad as hell at me, I see,' Victor Frayne drawled sardonically.

Mad as hell at the world, Ethan grimly extended. 'What do you want?' he repeated with a little less angst.

Victor went on to tell him that they had an emergency developing in San Estéban and that Leandros Petronades wanted Ethan back there to sort it out.

'Can't you see to it?' Ethan snapped out impatiently. He had no will to feel accommodating towards Victor nor Leandros Petronades for that matter, the latter being the spreader of gossip about his rich and varied love life!

'It's a planning dispute with the Spanish authorities,' Victor explained. 'Apparently we've breached some obscure by-law and they are now insisting we pull down the new yacht club and rebuild it somewhere else.'

'Over my dead body,' Ethan pronounced in fatherly protection of what happened to be one of his proudest achievements in design. 'We have not breached any by-law. I know because I checked them all out personally.'

'Which makes you the man with the answers, Ethan,' Victor relayed smoothly. 'Therefore, it makes this your fight. I have to warn you that they are threatening to bull-doze the place themselves if we refuse to do it.'

'I'll be on the next plane,' Ethan announced, and was surprised to discover how relieved he felt to reach that decision. Now he could get the hell out of paradise and leave the serpent to look for a fresh victim to mesmerise before she bit!

'Have you heard from Leona?' he then heard himself ask, and could have bitten himself for being so damned obvious.

'She's fine,' Leona's father assured him. 'She is cruising the Med as we speak and thoroughly enjoying herself, by the sound of it.'

Which puts me right in my place, Ethan thought as he replaced the receiver. Out of sight, out of mind and where I belong.

'Damn,' he muttered. 'Damn all women to hell.' And, on that profound curse, he picked up the telephone again with the intention of reserving a seat for himself on the three o'clock plane to Nassau, where he could catch a connecting flight to London, and then on to Spain. Only he didn't get quite that far because a movement at the door caught his eye.

CHAPTER SEVEN

SHE looked pale and fragile, as if someone had come along with an eraser and had wiped out all that wonderful animation which made Eve Herakleides the fascinating creature she was. His heart dipped. Had he done that? Or was the white-faced frailty Aidan Galloway's handiwork, and it was just that he had been too angry with her earlier to remember that she had been put through one hell of an ordeal only the night before.

No, he then told himself as a softening in his mood began to weaken his firm stance against her machinations. Eve is trouble. You've done enough. Send her packing and get out of here.

'What now?' he demanded in a hard, grim tone that told Eve he only had to look at her now to see trouble standing at his door.

But Eve wasn't Ethan Hayes' real trouble, she'd just come to realise. No, his trouble had been evident in the deep dark husky quality of his voice when he had spoken that other woman's name.

Suddenly she wanted to run, she wanted to hide, she wanted to pretend she had not overheard his conversation, because she knew for sure now that Ethan had lied before, and he was tragically, painfully in love with Leona Al-Qadim.

At that precise moment she felt like trouble because she had this blistering urge to knock some sense into him! Would someone like to tell her, please, how a man like Ethan Hayes could allow himself to fall in love with a very married woman? Was she a witch? Had she cast a spell over him? Had they been such passionate lovers that he'd been blinded by the sex and he couldn't see it took a certain type of woman to cheat on her husband?

No wonder the Sheikh had bruised his jaw for him! He deserved it, the fool! And she only hoped to goodness that the lovely Leona had received her just desserts too!

'Speak, Eve,' Ethan prompted, when she still hadn't managed to say anything. 'I'm in a rush. I have a plane to catch.'

A plane to catch, she silently repeated. Well, didn't that just about say everything else about him! Her eyes turned to crystal, backed by an ocean of burning green anger. 'So.' She stepped forward into his house and into his life with the grim intention to sort it out for him. 'You're going to leave the island and drop me in it because of one stupid phone call.'

The burning accusation flicked him like a whip. Ethan fielded it with the kind of small mocking smile that further infuriated Eve. 'That one stupid phone call was from my business partner informing me of an emergency that has developed on one of our projects in Spain,' he explained. 'And you dropped yourself in it,' he then coolly reminded her, 'by telling a pack of lies to your grandfather.'

'You had the chance to refute those lies. You didn't,' Eve pointed out. 'So now I'm afraid you are stuck with me.'

'As my future wife? Not in this life, Miss Herakleides,' he informed her. 'You know already what I think you should do, but if you still can't bring yourself to *drop* Aidan Galloway *in it* with your grandfather, then, with my speedy exit from here, at least you won't have to worry about me destroying your grandfather's trust in your honesty.'

With that cutting bit of arrogance he turned to walk away from this conversation—as if Eve was going to let him!

'Oh, you're so pompous sometimes.' She sighed as she trailed him across the sitting room. 'Do you ever stop to listen to yourself? I have no wish to be the wife of anyone,' she announced as she arrived in the bedroom doorway in time to see him settle a suitcase out on the bed. 'But, while we are on the subject of marriage, I'll point out that at least I am at liberty to be your wife if I wanted to be!'

The remark made him turn. Eve felt her skin start to prickle as she was reminded of wild animals again. 'Meaning—what?' he demanded.

She offered a shrug, that warning prickle forcing her to backtrack slightly. 'Meaning I don't have the wish, so why are we arguing about it?'

He knew she had backed out of what she had been going to say. It was there, written in the way she lowered her eyes from his—which in turn had his own narrowing threateningly. 'I don't know,' he incised. 'You tell me.'

His was an outright challenge for her to get off her chest whatever was fizzing inside it. He knew she knew about Leona. He knew she'd overheard his discussion with Victor just now.

But Eve was discovering that she just did not want to discuss his very married lover with him. She wanted to discuss *them*. 'Aidan Galloway,' she prompted, watching his face toughen up like a rock. 'I came here, because something you said on the path just now made me realise we seem to have been talking at cross purposes about what actually happened last night.'

Some of the challenge leaked out of him. 'He attempted to rape you.' Ethan named it.

'No.' Eve frowned. 'It wasn't—'

Ethan spun his back to her and walked over to the wardrobe to begin removing clothes from their hangers. 'Still protecting him, I see,' he drawled.

The comment stung. 'No,' she denied the charge. 'I don't need to protect Aidan. Not in this context anyway,' she felt pressed to add. 'And will you stop *doing* that and listen to me!' she snapped out, when he continued to pack his suitcase as if she wasn't even there.

Ignoring her demand, he made to walk back to the wardrobe. On a fit of irritation she went to stand directly in his path. She felt like a mouse challenging a giant and, the worst of it was, it excited her. Her insides came alive as if sparkling diamonds were showering her with the urge to reach out and touch.

'I am trying to tell you that Aidan Galloway was *not* the one who spiked my drink last night!' she told him furiously. 'You've been blaming the wrong man!'

Looking down into those rich green earnest eyes, Ethan had to wonder how such beautiful eyes could lie as well as they did? For some unaccountable reason the way she was still insisting on defending the bastard made him want to kiss that lying little mouth senseless.

Instead he released a very soft, very deriding laugh, took hold of her stubborn chin between finger and thumb and gave it a condescending shake. 'But you would say that, being so in love with him,' he taunted softly, then he side-stepped her and continued with what he was doing.

I knew I hated him, now I remember why, Eve thought, and took in a deep breath of air to give her the will to continue when really she wanted to beat out an angry tattoo on his back!

'We were at Aidan's beach house. It was my birthday party and we were all enjoying ourselves...' Except for me, because I was brooding over you! she added silently.

'Aidan was the one who was mixing the drinks. But it was *not* Aidan who slipped something potent into my drink. It was *not* Aidan who brought me home and—did what he did!'

'Who then?' he shot at her.

Ah, Eve thought, and snapped her lips shut. Having seen his burning desire to rip Aidan from limb to limb, she decided it might be wise to keep the name of the real culprit to herself for now. 'Who it was doesn't matter any more.' She therefore evaded the question. 'I just needed to tell you that it wasn't Aidan.'

'You're lying,' he pronounced with a withering glance at her.

'I'm not!' she denied. 'Aidan is one of the nicest people I know!' she insisted in defence of that look. 'And he's going through his own bit of hell right now—so he doesn't need you accusing him of something he would not think of doing in a million years!'

'Are we talking about the same man who could lose himself in the embrace of another woman while his fiancée, his cousin and myself, looked on from the sidelines?' he mocked. Then on a sudden burst of impatience, he tossed the clothes he had been holding onto the bed and took a hard grip her shoulders. 'Stop protecting him, Eve,' he shook her gently. 'The man just isn't worthy of it!'

'I am telling you the truth,' she insisted. 'If you will just shut up and listen, I will explain about the kiss—'

'You're in love with him,' he repeated the outright accusation. 'That doesn't need explaining.'

'You're in love with another man's wife,' Eve retaliated in kind. 'What does that say about your right to moralise over me?'

His eyes began to darken ominously. Eve's senses began to play havoc with her ability to breathe or think. His mouth was hard and tight and angry, hers was soft and quivery and hurt. He was too close—she liked it. Her hands even went up to press against his shirt front. She felt his heat, the pound of his heart, the elixir of sheer masculine strength.

She wanted him to kiss her so very badly that it hurt.

Damn it all, but he wanted to kiss some sense into her, so badly it actually hurt, Ethan was thinking helplessly. 'He bruised your mouth, here,' he murmured, making do with running a finger over the soft smooth padding where the slight discolouration was still evident.

'She let her husband bruise yours,' Eve responded with a mimicking touch of a finger to the corner of his mouth.

He wasn't listening. 'And here,' he continued, moving that same gentle finger to the mark at her throat. 'I want to kill him for doing this to you.'

'It wasn't Aidan.' Somehow, some way she managed to hang onto a thread of sanity long enough to say that, even though she was becoming more engrossed in the pleasure of touching him.

'It wasn't Leona's husband who put the bruise on my face.'

'I still want to kill her just for breathing,' she confessed with enough green-eyed jealousy to make him laugh.

It was a strained, low, husky sound though, thick with other things, that made her insides begin to melt. Then he wasn't laughing. Instead he was taking her trailing finger in his and feeding it slowly into his mouth. Moist heat enveloped each sensitised nerve end, then spread right down to her toes. She released a soft breath of air and watched his steel-grey eyes turn to smoke. He was going to kiss her.

Yes, please, she begged him silently, and let him lower

her hand back to his chest, let him lower his dark head, and parted her lips in readiness for when his met them.

Then he was kissing her, kissing her hotly, kissing her deeply, kissing her urgently like a man stealing something he knew he shouldn't take. But Eve wanted him to take. In fact she wholly encouraged him by sliding her hands up his shirt front until they joined at the back of his neck, then she parted her lips that bit more to invite him to take as much as he liked.

Heat poured from one to the other. One of them released a pent-up sigh—maybe both of them did. His hands left her shoulders and spread themselves across her slender spine, firm yet gentle in the way they urged her into closer contact with him. She liked it—loved it. This man had been threatening to ignite her like this from the first moment she had ever set eyes on him.

She was warm, she was sweet, she was seduction itself. She was everything he had been fantasising she would be for so long now he couldn't remember when it had begun. His hands felt enlivened merely by touching her. His body was slowly drowning in sensual heat. If she moved any closer, he'd had it, he was sure of it; that dragging sensation between his thighs was telling him he was ready to leap.

And the kiss? It just went on and on as a fascinating swim through a million pleasure zones. He didn't want it to end. Yet it had to end.

'What is this?' he murmured, against her mouth. 'Mutual consolation?'

He was trying to cool things, though Eve could tell he didn't really want to cool anything. So what if it was consolation to him? she asked herself. If the power of his hunger was anything to go by, Ethan Hayes was more than ready to be consoled. 'I'm game, if you are,' she therefore confided with enough breathy seduction to slay any man.

'Eve the flirt, Eve the temptress.' Ethan fought a hard battle between his desire to be tempted and a need to break free from her magic spell. But, in doing so, he hadn't realised he had said the words out loud.

Eve broke all connection. It was so abrupt he didn't even have time to respond. She turned away—walked away—then wrapped her arms around her body in a way he recognised all too well.

Eve trying to hug her pain away. He named it with a sense of bitter self-contempt for being the one to make it happen this time.

'I'm sorry,' he murmured. 'I didn't mean—'

'Yes, you did,' she cut in on him in a thin little voice.

A sigh eased itself from his body. 'All right,' he admitted it. 'So I think you like to tease men's senses.' She had been teasing his senses since the day they'd first met—was still teasing them! Even with whole chasms between them right now, he could still feel her lips and the impression of her body where it had pressed against his.

Damn it to hell! 'Aidan Galloway isn't the only man I've watched you turn inside out with a smile,' he added, angry with himself now for allowing that kiss to happen at all! 'Jack Banning isn't immune and neither is Raoul Delacroix.'

She stiffened sharply. 'Meaning what?' She spun on him. 'That I *did* get what I deserved last night?'

'I didn't say that.' Ethan sighed wearily. 'I will never say that!'

'But it's interesting that you're clocking up a whole list of men who could have been mad enough for me to want to spike my drink! We could even add your name, since you've just given in against your better judgement and kissed Eve the flirt!'

Ethan had no defence. 'I'm sorry,' was all he could say helplessly. 'But I was not making a judgement on you! If anything I was making a judgement on them! On me— it—oh, I don't know.' He sighed, heavily aware that he'd dug his own grave as deep as it needed to go.

'In other words the name doesn't really matter, just the one they revolve around,' Eve misunderstood him—deliberately he suspected.

'One name matters.' He grunted.

'As in, who tried the big seduction of Eve the flirt?' Ethan winced. Eve nodded, feeling that she'd more than deserved that telling wince. 'Well, let's go through all the candidates shall we?' She was beginning to warm to her sarcastic theme. 'We both know it wasn't you, so we can cross your name from the list. Jack Banning has a job to protect, so, even if it was him, he isn't going to come out and admit he so much as looked at me the wrong way. If it was Aidan, I'm in trouble because the Galloways are rich and powerful, and very clannish, they protect their own in ways you would not believe. As for André Visconte, he will defend his half-brother to his very last breath—as he has done on countless occasions before! Then there is my grandfather to consider—another rich man with too much power at his fingertips. If he finds out someone has dared to overstep the line, he will yell very loudly for the head of the man who tried to seduce his innocent granddaughter while she was under the influence of drink. War will be declared between the two involved families. But who do you think will come out of it with the damaged reputation? Me,' she threw at him. 'Eve the flirt. Eve the temptress. Eve the spoiled little rich girl who likes to lead men on for the fun of it and has finally received her just desserts!'

She was near to tears and didn't want him to know it, so she spun away again taking with her the image of him just standing there staring at her as if she'd just grown two heads. Well, maybe she had! She certainly felt as if she had two heads rocking on her neck. She was tired through lack of sleep, exhausted with lingering shock and whatever else was still permeating her bloodstream. And she was hurting inside because she still couldn't bring herself to understand why Raoul had believed he could do to her what he had tried to do! Nor could she quite manage to justify that she hadn't deserved what had happened.

That was the toughest pill to swallow. Self-contempt. She named it bleakly as she stared out of the window, while a deathly silence crowded in from behind. What was he thinking? she wondered painfully. What was now going on inside his cynical head?

Ethan was struggling to think anything much. She was amazing, was his one main impression, and that came from the gut not the brain. But, standing there with the light coming in from behind her, she seemed to shimmer like a proud goddess sent down from the heavens to mess up his life. No wonder her grandfather worshipped her. He was beginning to understand what that felt like.

He was also stunned by what she'd thrown at him. Worse, he wanted to refute what she'd predicted was bound to happen but knew that he couldn't. It was the way of the world. Since the beginning of time, woman had been cast in the role of temptress and man merely as a slave to her seductive wiles. He was as guilty as anyone of assuming the same thing about Eve. He'd even likened her to the serpent in paradise, when in truth the serpent had been his own desire to tap into that special magic that was Eve.

Man being man at the expense of woman, in other words, blaming her for his weakness.

It was not a nice thing to admit about oneself.

'So…' He sighed in what he knew was his surrender to the whole darn package that was Eve. 'Tell me what it is you want to do,' he invited.

Eve turned to look at him. All he saw was a pair of tear-washed wounded eyes. 'Do you mean it?' she asked him in an unsteady voice that finally finished him.

Ask me to bite the apple, Eve, and I will do it, he mused ruefully, well aware that man's oldest weakness was still very much alive inside him; after all he had just admitted to himself. 'Yes, I mean it,' he confirmed and even felt like smiling at his own downfall.

Her fingers released their comforting clutch on her arms. He watched them lower to her sides then turn themselves into two tight, hopeful little fists. He wanted to claim those fists. He wanted to prize those fingers open and feed them inside his shirt so they could roam at their leisure.

'Continue to play the charade—just for a few weeks,' she begged him. 'Give me time to let Grandpa down about this marriage thing—without my having to admit the truth to him.'

Well, he'd asked, now he knew. He was to play the love-struck lover of Eve until she decided it was no longer necessary. Why not? he asked himself. Why the hell not? At this precise moment he was even prepared to lie down on the floor and let her walk all over him.

Time to move, time to react. She was waiting for an answer. Dragging his eyes away from the inner vision of himself lying at her beautiful feet, he looked at his watch and tried to concentrate well enough to read it.

Twelve o'clock, he saw. 'You've got approximately two hours to pack a bag and say your farewells,' he announced with a smoothness that in no way reflected what was really happening inside him.

'Why, where am I going?'

Well, there's an interesting question, he mused. And wished he knew the answer. 'You can't come to despise me enough to jilt me while you're here in the Caribbean and I'm in Spain,' he pointed out. 'So you are going to have to come to Spain with me.'

CHAPTER EIGHT

EVE was late.

Standing by the car he aimed to return to the hire company at the tiny airport on the other side of the island, Ethan was beginning to wonder if she'd had a change of heart about coming away with him, when he caught sight of her coming along the path that led to the lane behind the beach houses.

She was pulling her suitcase behind her through the dappled sunlight cast by the shady overhang of the trees. Tall and slender, as always faultlessly sleek, gone was the sweet Miss Modesty look she'd created for her grandfather's benefit. Now the smooth and slinky siren was back in a misty-lavender skimpy camisole top edged with lace, and matching narrow skirt that did wonderful things to her figure as she moved. She had also let her hair down so it swung like spun toffee around her shoulders, and a pair of silver-framed sunglasses pushed up on her head held it away from her face.

A face that wasn't happy, Ethan noticed as she came closer. A face that was not just pale any more but sad and very grim.

'You're late,' he said as she reached him. 'I was beginning to think you weren't going to bother.'

'Well, I'm here, as you see.' And there was nothing loverlike, pretend or otherwise, in the way she flipped the sunglasses down over her eyes before she handed over her case then climbed into the car without offering another word.

Grimacing to himself, Ethan stashed the case then joined her. As they drove off up the lane he noticed that she didn't spare a glance for the sugar-pink gate posts that guarded her grandfather's property.

'He was okay about you leaving with me?' he dared to probe a little.

'Yes,' she answered, but he saw the tension line around her mouth and knew she was lying... Again, he tagged on, and wondered why it was that even the lies weren't bothering him any more.

'You surprise me,' he remarked mildly. 'Having flown in from Greece this morning specifically to spend your birthday with you, I expected him to be very annoyed that you were now walking out on him.'

'He didn't fly in from Greece, he flew from Nassau,' she corrected, 'where he always intended to return tomorrow, because his mistress is waiting there for him.'

Mistress. Ethan's opinion of the seventy-year-old Theron Herakleides altered slightly with that piece of information. 'I didn't know he had a mistress.'

'He has several,' his granddaughter supplied.

Ethan almost allowed himself a very masculine grin. 'Then, why not bring her here with him and save himself several island-hopping journeys?'

'A Greek male does not introduce his mistress to his family.'

'Ah.' Ethan began to see the light. 'And neither should a Greek woman introduce her lover to her family?'

'You are not my lover.'

'He thinks I am.'

'He also thinks you are only marrying me for my money,' she responded tartly. 'Says a lot about my personal pulling power, don't you think?'

It said a lot about his character too, Ethan noted grimly,

and stopped the car. Turning towards her he viewed her profile through a new set of eyes, and released a heavy sigh. 'You fed him a very carefully constructed catalogue of lies to save his feelings and he disappointed you by not appreciating the gesture,' he deduced.

She didn't answer, but those hands were locked into fists again.

It made him wonder if she was having second thoughts about this and was being just too stubborn to admit as much. 'If you would rather stay,' he offered. 'I can understand if you—'

'No, you don't understand,' she suddenly flashed at him. 'And, like it or not, I am coming with you!'

'Then why are you so angry?'

'I am not angry,' she denied.

Reaching over, Ethan whipped the sunglasses from her eyes.

'Okay,' she conceded, 'So, I'm angry. Grandpa is angry,' she tagged on with telling bite. 'He was lying before when he appeared to be sanctioning our relationship. He now claims that there is no way he is going to let you marry me.'

'Good for him,' Ethan commended. 'It means he has your best interests at heart. I admire him for that.'

Her chin came up. 'Do you also admire him for setting up this so-called emergency in Spain, just to get you off the island and away from me?'

No, Ethan did not admire Theron for stooping that low. 'Are you sure about that?'

'He told me himself,' Eve confirmed.

'Oh, what a tangled web we weave…' Ethan murmured, then sat back in his seat with a sigh. 'Go back and tell him the truth, Eve,' he advised heavily. 'This has gone too far.'

'I will have my tongue removed before I will tell him

the truth now!' she exclaimed. 'This is my life, Ethan! I have the right to make my own choices without interference from anyone!'

'So do I,' he announced with a sudden resolve that had him starting the car engine again.

'W-what are you doing?'

'Going back,' he said.

'Why?' she challenged. 'Because you've suddenly realised that he might decide to take the Greek project away from you if you let me step on that plane with you?'

Ethan stilled again. 'He threatened to do that?'

Her mutinous expression gave him his answer. Without another word he turned the car round and drove back down the lane and in through the sugar-pink gate posts, then along the driveway to pull up outside the palatial frontage of the Herakleides holiday home.

He was angry now, burning with it. Getting out of the car he walked round to open the passenger door. 'Out,' he said, reaching down to take hold of Eve's hand so he could aid her arrival at his side.

'What are you going to do?' she asked.

'Call his bluff,' he declared. This was no longer a case of helping Eve out of a situation. It had become a case of his honour and integrity being placed into question, and he didn't like that.

In fact he didn't like it one little bit.

Eve wasn't sure that she was looking forward to what was coming. It was one thing *her* being angry with her grandfather, but it was quite a different thing entirely to discover that she'd managed to make Ethan angry with him too. She loved that cantankerous old man. She understood where he was coming from; Ethan did not.

'Don't upset him,' she burst out suddenly.

Pausing in the process of closing the car door, 'Are you going to tell him the truth?'

He looked down at her, and she looked up at him, her heart flipped over. He was so much her kind of man that Grandpa couldn't be more wrong about anything! 'No,' she answered mutinously.

His dark head nodded. Her hand was grasped. He began trailing her behind him up white marble steps set between tall pink pillars. The front door was standing open; Ethan took them inside. The house was quiet, so their footsteps echoed on the cool white tiling as they trod the way across the huge hallway to Theron's inner sanctum. The man himself was lounging behind his desk talking on the telephone. But the moment he saw them appear through the door, the phone call was severed and he was rising to his feet.

'So he brought you back. I expected as much.' The eyes of a cynic lanced Ethan with a dismissive look before they returned to his granddaughter. 'Which part did it, hmm? The part about me threatening to leave you nothing if he married you, or the part about the Greek project hanging in the balance?'

'Neither.' Striding forward with Eve still in tow, Ethan lifted up their linked hands and brought them down, still linked, upon Theron's desk. It was a declaration of intent, and Theron took it as such, his smug expression turning slightly wary as he looked at the other man.

'My submission for the Greek project is now formally withdrawn,' Ethan announced. 'Written confirmation will arrive on your desk as soon as I can have it typed up. As for your money—tell him Eve…'

Tell him Eve… Tell him what? A current of communication was running between them via those firmly linked hands, but for the life of her she didn't know what it was Ethan was expecting her say. Her grandfather was looking at her, Ethan was keeping his eyes fixed on her grandfather, and her mouth had gone dry as the idea sank in that Ethan was waiting for her to come clean with the whole nasty truth, so her grandfather would know then that this was all nothing but a terrible sham.

'Ethan doesn't want your m-money,' she began, having to moisten her lips with the tip of her tongue before she could find the will to speak. 'M-money isn't what this is about. He only w-wanted to—'

'Love a woman whom I think is worthy of being loved for herself,' Ethan took over. 'But you don't seem to agree,' he informed the older man. 'So while I provide written confirmation of my withdrawal from the Greek project, I suggest you protect Eve from my evil intentions and provide formal notice that none of your money can be accessed or offered in any way shape or form, to me.'

He meant it—he really meant it! 'Ethan—no!' Eve cried out. 'I can't let you throw away your livelihood because I—'

He kissed her to shut her up—did he kiss her! In front of her grandfather and without compunction, he kissed her until her knees went weak.

Theron watched that kiss, saw its passion, and felt its intensity like the pulsing beat of a drum. Eve emerged in a state of blushing confusion. Ethan Hayes was black-eyed, tight-jawed—and hot. If it wasn't for that troubling rumour about a certain married lady, Theron would be convinced that Ethan Hayes was as much in love with Eve as she clearly was with him!

But there was that niggling rumour, the old man reminded himself. Which then made him wonder if Ethan Hayes was executing one very convincing bluff here? Was he now expecting Theron to withdraw all threats, then sit back and think that all was right in his granddaughter's world?

'I will have all the relevant documentation drawn up and ready for you to sign when you reach Spain,' Theron announced, smoothly calling a double bluff.

It took the two lovers a long moment to respond. Their eyes were still locked, as were those dramatically clasped hands. Ethan Hayes stood one very handsome dark head taller that his sweet Eve, and Theron was willing to admit that they made a strikingly fetching pair.

'Why should I go to deal with an emergency that never was?' Ethan prompted.

Theron merely gave an indolent shrug. 'The emergency is real,' he confessed. 'The difference being that your business partner was attempting to deal with it himself without breaking into your holiday. Apparently my request for help to get you off this island merely tied in with what your people were already intending to do.' He even grimaced at the irony. 'So go and catch your plane,' he invited as a form of dismissal, 'for we have nothing left to discuss on this subject, other than to confirm that I will expect to see you both in Athens in two weeks for the formal announcement of your betrothal.'

Unless Mr Hayes had found a way to wriggle out of it by then, was the silent addition Theron kept to himself. Ethan Hayes was frowning down at him, unconvinced by his all-too easy climb-down. On the other hand, his beautiful Eve was breaking his heart with angry daggers for eyes.

'I don't want your money,' she announced.

Theron just smiled a silky smile. 'But you are getting it, my sweet angel,' he returned. 'Every single hard-earned drachma. And not one coin will be spent on him.' Theron looked at Ethan, bluff and counter-bluff stirring spice into his old blood. 'Perhaps you can recommend one of your competitors to take over the Greek project?' he intoned.

'You already had the best, and you know it,' Ethan countered. 'So be sure to inform Leandros that you've chucked me off the job. I can promise you that he is going to be absolutely ecstatic.'

With that neat and final arrogantly confident cut, Ethan turned to Eve. 'Say your goodbyes properly,' he commanded. 'I don't want you with me if you're going to be angry with him.'

Then he kissed her fully on the mouth again and strode away, leaving grandfather and granddaughter staring after him as if they could not quite believe he was real.

Ethan himself didn't know if he was real. He certainly felt different—alive, pumped up, energised, as if someone had slipped him the elixir of life.

That kiss with Eve perhaps?

Oh, shut up, he told himself frowningly. This is all just a sham, remember?

Just a great sham. Think of Aidan Galloway, he reminded himself. Whatever Eve liked to pretend, she had something going on with the Irishman. Love, sex—call it whatever—it was there, a throbbing pulse that said it was of a lot more than mere friendship.

'Watch him,' Theron advised, forcibly dragging Eve's attention away from the long, straight-shouldered stride of Ethan's retreat. 'He has your measure, my girl, and I don't think you are going to like that.'

Like it? She loved it. In fact it was tumbling around inside like a barrow load of sins desperately trying to get out. She wanted to run after him, take his hand again, laugh up into his arrogant face. She wanted to wind her arms around his neck and kiss him to heaven and back.

'You mean, *you* don't like it.' She turned a wry, knowing smile on this other man. She knew *he* had her measure, and wondered if he had guessed that all of this was just a sham?

A sham. Yes, a sham, she reminded herself, and felt the smile fade away like day turning to night. 'Grandpa—don't spoil this for me,' she heard herself say tremulously.

'He's dangerous,' Theron stated.

'I know.' Her eyelashes flickered. 'I like it.' It was a terrible confession to make.

'He is in love with another woman.' The reminder was supposed to be deadly to fragile emotions.

'I know that too.' Eve nodded. 'But he's what I want. I can make him love me instead of her, given a bit of time and space.'

'So this isn't just a ploy to bring poor Aidan Galloway to his senses about you?'

Aidan? Eve blinked. Her grandfather as well—? 'Aidan is still in love with Corin!' she protested, as if he had just suggested something terrible.

Theron took his time absorbing that declaration. It worried him, because if it wasn't Aidan, then this was exactly what it seemed to be. Yet his instincts were picking up all kinds of messages that conflicted with what he was being shown here. He couldn't work it out. He needed to work it out.

Getting up from his chair, he reached into a drawer then came round the desk to stand in front of Eve. In his hand he held a gaily wrapped package. 'Happy birthday, my angel,' he murmured softly as he fed the package into her hands then placed tender kisses on both of her cheeks.

He received his reward with the kind of unfettered shower of affection he'd come to expect from Eve. 'I love you, Grandpa.'

'I know you do, child.' And he did know it. It was the

substance his whole life had been built upon since she'd been a shocked and grief-stricken child of ten years' old. 'Now, go catch your plane,' he told her. He had been going to say go catch your man, but something held him back.

Eve left with a promise to call him as soon as she arrived in Spain. As the door closed behind her, Theron was already reaching for the telephone.

'Ah—*yassis*, Giorgio,' he greeted. 'I have a job for you to do for me, my friend. Write this name down: Ethan Alexander Hayes. *Ne*.' He nodded. 'Anything you can find. Dig hard and dig deep and do it quickly.'

CHAPTER NINE

Eve felt so stupidly shy when she settled into the passenger seat next to Ethan. 'Thank you for that,' she said a trifle self-consciously. 'I would have hated to leave him angry with me.'

Ethan made no response. Eve shot him a wary glance. His profile looked relaxed enough, but there was something about the shape of his mouth that suggested he was angry about something.

With her, with her grandfather, or with himself for allowing himself to become so embroiled in her problems?

The car engine came to life, the air-conditioning kicked in and began circulating cool air filled with the scent of him. His knuckle brushed her thigh as he shifted the gear stick. Suffocation seemed imminent, and Eve didn't know whether it was due to that so seductive scent, or to the sensation of his accidental touch which had left her body thickened.

Or maybe it had more to do with knowing that her grandfather was right. I'm letting myself in for a lot of heartache here, she mused. He doesn't love me, he loves someone else. Eve put a hand up to her trembling lips and felt Ethan's lips there instead. Her hand was pulled down again; it was trembling too.

'Say something, for goodness' sake.' The words left her lips on a shaken whisper.

Say what? Ethan thought frustratedly. I don't know what I'm doing here? I don't know what you are doing, coming away with me like this? You should be back there, home safe with your grandfather, because you certainly aren't safe here with me!

'What's in the packet?' Did he really just offer something as benign as that?

His fingers flexed on the steering wheel. The afternoon sunlight was shining on her bent head, threading red highlights through spun toffee like fire on silk. He'd never noticed the threads of fire before. Why was he noticing them now? Her skirt had rucked up, showing more thigh than he wanted to see. He could still feel the touch of her smooth skin against his knuckle and he wanted to feel more of it. All of it. Hell, damn it—everything.

'Grandpa's birthday present,' she answered huskily.

Husky was seductive. It was vibrating along almost every skin cell like a siren's melody. 'You haven't opened it.'

His voice had a rasp to it that was scraping over the surface of her skin like sand in a hot seductive breeze. 'He doesn't like me to open presents in f-front of him, just in case I don't like what he's chosen and he sees the disappointment on my f-face.' She was stammering. Stop stammering! Eve told herself fiercely.

She was stammering. Was she crying? Ethan couldn't tell because she had her head bent and her hair was hiding her face. 'Does it happen often?' Now he sounded husky, he noticed heavily.

'Never.' She shook her head. 'I always love anything he gives to me. You would think he had worked that out by now.' Another soft laugh and her fingers were gently stroking the present.

'Open it,' he suggested.

'Later,' she replied. She had enough to contend with right now without weeping all over Grandpa's gift as well.

They reached the top of the lane and turned onto the

only proper road on the island. It went two ways—to the lane they'd just left, or to the small town with its even smaller airport, passing the entrance that led into the Galloways' bay on its way.

Two ways, Eve repeated. Forward, or back the way they had come. Did she want to go back? Did he want her to go back?

'Eve—if you've changed your mind about this, I can soon turn around and—'

'I'm coming with you!' The words shot out like bullets from a gun, ricocheting around the closed confines of the car.

Ethan snapped his mouth shut. His fingers flexed again. Eve sat simmering in her own hectic fallout, and silence reigned for the rest of the way.

It took ten minutes to get there. Ten long minutes of throat-locking hell. Eve gripped her birthday gift. Ethan gripped the wheel. They slid into a parking spot by the car-hire shop and both of them almost tumbled out of the car in their eagerness to breath hot humid air.

The nine-seat Cessna was waiting on the narrow runway. A porter ran up to collect their luggage to take it to the plane. Ethan appeared out of the car-hire shop, still feeding his credit card back into his wallet as he came. His dark head was bent, his hair gleaming blue-black against his deeply tanned face. He was wearing another blue shirt with grey trousers, and over his arm lay a jacket to match. Eve clutched at the strap to her shoulder bag, over which hung the cardigan that matched her top—and wished she didn't find the man so fascinating to watch.

He looked up. She looked quickly away. She looked beautiful, and his heart pulled a lousy trick on him by squeezing so tightly it took his breath away.

Nassau was a relief. They had a two-hour stopover,

which meant they could both make excuses to go their separate ways for a while. Eve went window-shopping; Ethan went to hunt out somewhere he could access his website and download some documents so he could read them on the flight.

On his way back to find Eve, he spied a furry tiger with its tail stuck arrogantly in the air. He began to grin. Eve would never get the joke, but he couldn't resist going into the shop and buying if for her. While the toy was being gift-wrapped, he went browsing further down the line of shop windows and came back to collect the tiger with a strangely stunned expression on his face.

Eve was sitting with a fizzy drink can and a whole range of gifts packed into carrier bags. 'Souvenirs for my friends in London,' she explained. 'They expect it.'

Ethan just smiled and sat down beside her, then offered her his gift. 'Happy birthday,' he said solemnly.

She stared at him in big-eyed surprise. It was amazing, he mused, how much he adored those eyes. 'Open it,' he invited, tongue-in-cheek. 'I'm not at all sensitive to disappointment.'

He was smiling, really smiling, with his mouth, with the warm soft grey of his wonderful eyes. Eve smiled back, really smiled back, then handed him her can so she could give her full attention to ripping off the gold paper from her present. Meanwhile Ethan drank from her can and watched with interest as the tiger emerged.

There was a moment's stunned silence, an unexpected blush, then she laughed. It was that wonderfully light, delighted laugh he'd heard her use so often for other people but never for him before. 'Good old Tigger—you idiot.' She turned to him. 'How did you know I have a whole roomful of Tiggers back home?'

He hadn't known, but he did now, which rather sent his

private joke flat, because Tigger was not quite the animal he had been thinking about when he'd bought the furry toy. Still, did it matter? She liked it, that was enough.

'ESP,' he confided, tapping his temple.

With her old exuberance, Eve leaned over to kiss him, realised what she was about to do and hesitated halfway there. Wary eyes locked on his, and a black eyebrow arched quizzically over one of them. Her heart gave a thud. Irresistible, she thought. I'm falling head over heels and don't even care any more. She closed the gap, knowing by the dizzying curling sensation inside that a kiss was about the most dangerous thing she could offer right now, even here in the transit lounge of a busy airport with hundreds of people playing chaperone… Because he might think he was fatally in love with Leona Al-Qadim, but he fancies the pants off me!

And I'm available, very available, she added determinedly. Their lips met—briefly—and clung in reluctance to part.

Yes, Eve thought triumphantly, he does want me. 'Thank you,' she murmured softly.

'You're welcome,' he replied, but he was frowning slightly. Eve wished she knew what thoughts had brought on his frown.

Thoughts of Leona Al-Qadim? Was he sitting here with one woman's kiss still warm on his lips and daring to think of another? Like a coin flipping over, she went from smiling certainty of her own power to win this man, to dragging suspicion that the other woman would always win.

Tigger was receiving a mangling, Ethan noticed, and wondered what the poor tiger had done to deserve such abuse? Then he had to smother a sigh, because he knew it was him she was thinking about as she twisted the poor animal's tail round in spirals. They kept kissing when they shouldn't. They kept responding to each other when they shouldn't. He was not the right man for her, and she was most definitely *not* the right woman for him.

'Here, do you want this?' He offered the drink can back to her.

Eve shook her head. 'You can finish it if you want.'

He didn't want it, but he knew what he did want. On that grim thought he got to his feet, too tense and restless to sit still any longer in this—crazy situation that should never have begun in the first place!

Walking over to the nearest waste-disposal bin he dropped the can in it, took a deep, steadying breath, then turned to go back the way he had come. Eve was no longer sitting where he had left her. Alarm shot through his veins like an injection of adrenalin, that quickly changed to a kind of thick gluey stuff that weighed him down so heavily he couldn't move an inch.

Why? Because her hair lay like silk against her shoulders, her bags of shopping hung at her sides. Tall and tanned and young and lovely, she was drawing interested gazes from every man that passed her by because she had class, she had style. She was an It girl, one of the fortunate few—and right at the present moment in time she was looking in the same jeweller's window he'd stood looking in only minutes before. Same place, same tray of sparkling jewels, he was absolutely certain of it. His feet took him over there, moving like lead in time with the heavy pump of his heart.

'Which one do you like?' he asked lightly over her shoulder.

She jumped, startled, glanced up at him, then looked quickly away again, blushing as if he'd caught her doing something truly sinful. 'The diamond cluster with the emerald centre,' she answered huskily.

Husky was back, he noticed, and husky he liked. Reaching down, he took her bags from her then placed a free hand to the small of her back. 'Let's go and try it,' he murmured softly.

'What—? But we can't do that!'

She was shocked, she was poleaxed—he even liked that. The lead weights dropped away from his body; he sent her a wry grin that made her eyes dilate. 'Of course we can,' he disagreed. 'It's tradition.'

Tradition, Eve repeated and felt her mind start turning somersaults, as the hand on her back firmly guided her into the shop. Ethan placed her bags on the floor at his feet, kept her close and calmly asked for the tray of rings. It arrived in front of them, sparkling beneath the lights. Long, lean, tanned male fingers plucked the diamond and emerald cluster off its velvet bed. While the assistant smiled the smile used for lovers, Ethan lifted up her left hand and gently slid the ring onto her finger.

'What do you think?' he prompted softly.

Eve wasn't thinking anything, she discovered. 'It fits,' was all she could manage to come up with to say.

'But do you like it?' he persisted.

'Yes,' she answered, so gruffly she didn't know her own voice.

'Good. So do I,' Ethan said. 'We'll take it,' he told the smiling sales assistant.

'But—look at the price!' she gasped as the assistant went away with Ethan's credit card.

'A lady doesn't check the price,' he told her dryly.

'But I can't let you buy something that expensive! Can you afford it? We shouldn't even be doing it.' Eve was beginning to panic in earnest now, Ethan noted, feeling his few minutes of pure romanticism turned to ashes as she spoke. 'W-we told Grandpa we were going to keep all of this a secret.'

'There will be nothing secret about us living together in Spain, Eve,' he dryly pointed out, and earned a startled look from those eyes for saying that. Yes, he thought grimly, take a moment to consider that part about us living together, Eve. 'But if you really don't want the ring—'

'No— Yes, I want it!'

'Good.' He nodded. 'A sham is not a good sham without all the right props to go with it.'

Eve's heart sank to her shoes as reality came rushing in. Here she was thinking—while he was only thinking— a sham. She swallowed on the thickness of her own stupidity. 'Then we'll go halves on the cost,' she decided.

If she said it to hit back at him then she certainly succeeded, Eve noted, as he stiffened. 'You really do think that because I can't match your grandfather's billions I must be as poor as a church mouse, don't you.'

Eve gave a noncommittal shrug for an answer. 'I just don't want you to be out of pocket just because I dumped myself on you like this.'

'Well, think of how much relief you will feel on the day you throw it back at me.'

The assistant arrived back to finish the sale then. Maybe it had been a timely interruption, Eve thought, as she watched him sign the sale slip and receive back his passport and credit card, because the sardonic tilt to his tone when he'd made that last remark had been aimed to cut her down to size. When, in actual fact, she suspected they both knew it was Ethan Hayes who'd taken the blow to his ego.

But the ring had suddenly lost value, its sparkle no longer seemed so fine. Their flight was called, and in the time it took them to gather up their belongings the whole incident was pushed away out of sight, even as the ring winked on her finger every time she moved her hand.

The plane was full, but first-class was quiet, with new state-of-the-art seating that offered just about every comfort that might be required. As they settled themselves in for the long journey, Eve unearthed Tigger from her hand luggage and sat him on the arm between their two seats.

You were my favourite birthday present, she told the stuffed tiger—not counting Grandpa's present, of course, she then added loyally, which she intended to open when she wasn't feeling so miffed at Ethan Hayes. *As for you*, she looked down at the ring sparkling like a demon on her finger, *you're just a prop, which means you are as worthless as paste.*

Within an hour of taking off, Ethan was deep into a stack of printed literature he'd managed to get someone in Nassau to pull off his website. Eve wasn't talking. Now he was glad he hadn't confided in her that the ring was the very one he'd picked out himself only minutes before she'd picked it out. Silly stuff like that provoked curious questions. Questions provoked answers he didn't want to give. It had been a stupid gesture anyway. He wished he hadn't done it. Now the damn ring kept on sparkling at him every time she turned a page of the magazine she'd brought with her onto the plane.

'Would you like a refill for that, Mr Hayes?' the flight attendant asked him. Glancing up at the woman he saw the look in her eyes was offering a whole lot more than a second cup of coffee.

Spice of life, he mocked grimly and refused the offer. As she went to move away he saw the flight attendant glance at Eve, then at her finger. *That's right*, he thought acidly, *I've already been hooked.*

By a toffee-haired witch with a sulk to beat all female sulks.

'And you, Miss Herakleides?'

'No, thank you,' Eve refused. And keep your greedy eyes off my man, she thought.

A man who had a way with a black ballpoint pen that held her attention with the same rapt fascination she would have given to Picasso if she'd had the opportunity to watch him at work. It wasn't as if he was actually doing anything special—just drawing circles round sentences then scrawling comments over the printed words. He was sitting back against the seat with an ankle resting across his other knee. He stopped writing, frowned, used the pen to relieve an itch on the side of his chin; he used it to tap out an abstract drum beat; he drew another circle, then scrawled comments again.

He sighed at something. His chest moved, and as she glanced sideways at it she realised she could see glimpses of deeply tanned flesh in the gaps between shirt buttons. Nice skin, warm skin, tight let-me-touch skin, she thought.

Close your eyes, Eve, and stop this! she railed at herself.

It wasn't long after she closed her eyes that the magazine began to slip from her slackened grip. Ethan rescued it and folded it away, then rescued Tigger as he too began to slip off his perch.

Tigger: fun, bouncy, always in trouble—he wasn't so old that he couldn't remember the animal's appeal. He had to smile at the irony because *his* tiger was neither fun nor bouncy, but it certainly meant to cause him a lot of trouble where Eve Herakleides was concerned.

Reaching over he gently placed Tigger on Eve's lap, then sent him a wry man-to-man look. 'Lucky guy,' he told the toy, and pressed a button that would recline her into a more comfortable position for sleep. A sigh whispered from her as she resettled her body. A glance at her eyes to check if he had disturbed her showed him the fine bruising around the sockets, which told him she was still suffering the effects of last night.

He'd forgotten about that. How had he forgotten about that? Because his mind had become fixed on more lusty things, of which he really ought to be ashamed.

He returned to his papers for a little while, but not very much later succumbed to the need to sleep himself. Halfway across the Atlantic he woke up to find that Eve had curled up on her side facing him, and her hand was splaying across his chest. But that wasn't all—not by a long shot because a couple of her fingers had somehow found their way into the gap between his shirt buttons and were now resting against his warm skin.

He liked them there, had no wish to move them, even though a call of nature was nagging at him. So he closed his eyes again and saw his own fingers slipping down the front of her gaping top in a quest to caress the warm golden globe he'd caught sight of as he'd glanced at her.

Then he thought. No way. He forced his eyes back open—just in case he might do in sleep what he had been fantasising about while awake. Been there, done that once already today, he ruefully reminded himself. Instead he gave in to the other desire and gently removed her hand from his chest so that he could get up.

She was awake when he came back, and her seat had been returned to its upright position. 'Drink?' he suggested.

'Mmm.' She half yawned. 'Tea, I think, and can you see if they can rustle up a sandwich?'

'Sure.' He went off to find a flight attendant. When he came back Eve was not there and he presumed she'd gone where he'd just been. She slipped back into her seat as the flight attendant arrived with a china tea service and a plate of assorted sandwiches.

She'd freshened up, he'd freshened up, both looked a bit better for it. Ethan poured the tea while Eve checked the fillings between neat triangles of bread. 'Any preference?' she asked him.

You, he thought soberly. 'I don't mind,' he answered. 'I'm starving. We slept through dinner apparently.'

'You too?' she quizzed.

'Mmm,' he answered.

'Did you manage to finish your work before you slept?'

'Mmm,' he said again.

'Is that all you can say?' she mocked. 'Mmm?' It was like talking to a bumble-bee, Eve thought impatiently.

No, it wasn't all he could say, she discovered the moment he turned his head to look at her. Dark grey eyes locked with green, and the air was suddenly stifled by the kind of feelings that didn't belong in the cabin of an aeroplane. He wanted her. She wanted him. If they touched they would go up in a plume of fire and brimstone, it was so sinful what was happening to both of them.

They didn't touch. Eve looked away, picked up her cup and grimly drank the hot tea in the hope that it would outburn everything else. That damn ring flashed again and Ethan wished he hadn't put it there. It had been a mad impulsive gesture to make. This arrangement was a sham. The ring was a sham. But when he looked at that thing, Eve belonged to him.

CHAPTER TEN

THE rest of the flight was a lesson in how to avoid giving off the wrong kind of signals. They dropped down into Heathrow airport in the early morning local time, then had to hurry through transit to catch their connection to Malaga. That flight was full and noisy with excited children off on holiday to Spain. It was early afternoon by the time they cleared the formalities there.

Ahead of them lay a two-hour drive south to San Estéban, but one glance at Eve put the cap on that plan. Travel fatigue was casting a greyish pallor over her beautiful skin and she looked fit only to drop down and sleep where they stood.

Ethan had used a hand to guide her into a convenient seat in the airport arrival lounge. 'Sit,' he quietly commanded.

Subsiding without a single murmur, she watched him park their luggage trolley next to her through listless eyes and didn't even seem to notice that he then walked off without telling her where he was going.

He came back five minutes later to find her sitting more or less how he had left her. As he came to stand in front of her she looked up and, stifling a yawn, she pointed at their assorted luggage. 'Just think,' she said, 'how convenient it would be if we ever got married.'

Following the direction of her pointing finger, Ethan found himself looking at two sets of suitcases, both of which wore the same initials embossed on their leather like a sign from the devil of what the future held for them. He didn't like it. His mouth turned down in a show of dismay because those near-matching suitcases spoke of one giant step over that fragile line between, I can deal with this, and, The hell I can.

Eve saw he didn't like it. 'It was a joke, Ethan,' she sighed out wearily.

'Time to go,' was all he said—heavily.

Taking hold of her arm he pulled her to her feet when all Eve wanted to do was curl up in a dark corner somewhere, go to sleep and not wake up again while he was still in her life!

Then what did he do to throw that last thought right out of her head? He placed an arm around her shoulders, gently urged her to lean against him then kept her that close while pushing the trolley in front of them as they walked outside.

I like him this close, she confessed to herself. I love it when he makes these unexpected gestures of concern. 'You've no sense of humour,' she muttered in grim rejection of her own weakness.

'Or your sense of timing is lousy,' he suggested sardonically.

Maybe he was right. Maybe it hadn't been the most diplomatic observation to make when they were in effect walking alongside a whole pack of lies. She released a sigh; he acknowledged it by giving her arm a gentle squeeze that could have been sympathising with that weary little sigh. And, because it felt right to do it, she slipped her hand around his lean waist—and leaned just that bit more intimately into him.

As the automatic exit doors slid open for them, a small commotion just behind them made them pause and glance back to see a group of dark-eyed, dark-suited Spaniards heading towards the doors with a pack of photographers on their trail. It was only as the group drew level with them that Eve realised the men were clustered around an exquisite looking creature with black hair, dark eyes and full-blooded passion-red mouth.

'Miss Cordero, look this way,' the chasing pack were pleading. Camera bulbs flashed. Miss Cordero kept her eyes fixed directly ahead as her entourage herded her towards the exit doors Eve and Ethan had conveniently opened for them. As they swept by, someone called out to Miss Cordero. 'Is it true that you spent the night in Port Said with your lover, Sheikh Rafiq?'

Eve felt Ethan stiffen. Glancing up at his face she saw a frown was pulling the edges of his brows across the bridge of his nose. 'What?' she demanded. 'Who is she?'

'Serena Cordero, the dancer,' he replied.

Eve recognised the name now. Serena Cordero was the unchallenged queen of classical flamenco. Her recent world tour had brought on a rash of Spanish dance fever, causing schools dedicated to the art to open up all over the place. It wasn't just classical dance she performed with sizzling mastery. Her gypsy fire dance could put an auditorium full of men into a mass passion meltdown.

None of which explained why Ethan was standing block-still with a frown on his face, she mused curiously. Unless... 'Do you know her?' she asked him, already feeling the sting of jealousy hit her bloodstream at the idea that Ethan might know what it was like to have the exotic Serena dance all over him!

But he gave a shake of his dark head. 'I only know *of* her,' he said, making the chilly distinction.

'Then why the frown?'

'What frown?'

He looked down at her. Eve looked up at him. The now familiar sting of awareness leapt up between the two of them. 'That frown,' she murmured, touching a slender long finger to the bridge of his nose where his eyebrows dipped and met. It was too irresistible not to trail that fingertip down the length of his thin nose. Her hand was caught, gently crushed into his larger hand and removed.

The question itself was no longer relevant: Serena Cordero had suddenly ceased to exist. Mutual desire was back, hot and tight and stifling the life out of everything else.

'Let's go,' Ethan murmured, striving to contain it.

He wanted her, she wanted him. It was going to happen some time, Eve was sure of it. 'Okay,' she said.

Attention returned to the exit doors, they stepped outside into the afternoon heat. Coming here from the Caribbean should have meant they were acclimatised to it by now. But the Spanish heat was so dry it scorched the skin, whereas the Caribbean heat was softened by high humidity and cooled slightly by trade winds coming off the sea.

The Cordero entourage had disappeared already. There was a chauffeur-driven car standing by the kerb waiting for them. Eve was glad to escape into the air-conditioned coolness of its rear seat. Having helped to stash their luggage in the car boot, Ethan joined her. The heat emanating from his body made her shiver, though she didn't know why it did.

Two hours of this, she was thinking breathlessly, as they took off with the smoothness of luxury. The prospect brought back the aching tiredness, the tiredness thankfully dulled the aching pulse of desire. Settling back into soft leather, Eve had just reconciled herself to this final leg of their journey when, to her surprise, they hadn't even left the airport perimeter before they were turning in through a pair of gates and drawing to a halt next to a gleaming white helicopter bearing the Petronades logo on its side.

'What now?' she asked curiously.

'Our transport to San Estéban, courtesy of your cousin, Leandros,' Ethan sardonically supplied. 'Having been so instrumental in getting us both here, I thought it was time he helped make this final part a bit easier.'

Easier, truly said it. Their two-hour drive south was cut by two-thirds. As they skipped over the top of a lush green headland, Ethan said, 'San Estéban.'

Glancing out of the window, Eve felt her heart stop beating in surprise. 'Oh,' she said, gasping in astonishment, unsure what it was that she had been expecting, but knew that it certainly wasn't this.

Her gaze took in the modern example of a Moorish castle guarding the hill top, then it flicked down the hill to a beautiful deep-water harbour with its mosaic-paved promenade that linked it to the pretty white-washed town. In the quest to create something magical, that same Moorish style repeated itself in a clever blend of modern with ancient. Nothing clashed—nothing dared. It was no wonder that her grandfather had been so eager to have Hayes-Frayne apply their magic touch to his project, she realised. From up here she could see the same sense of vision that must have inspired her grandfather when Leandros had suggested he come out here and take a look for himself.

Turning her face she looked into Ethan's grey eyes and saw a different man looking steadily back at her. The artist—the man with the vision that inspired others; the sensitive romantic who perhaps could fall in love with the unattainable, and maybe even go so far as to love *because* that person was out of his reach. It was a well-known fact that artists liked to suffer; it was a natural part of their persona to keep the creative juices flowing by desiring what could never be.

Was that part of her attraction? Eve then found herself

wondering curiously. With her grandfather openly stating that Ethan was not what he wanted for his only grandchild, had Theron unwittingly lifted her to the same desirable heights as the very married Leona Al-Qadim?

His eyes were certainly desiring her, she noted, but, for the first time, she didn't like what she could see. Don't raise me up onto a pedestal, she wanted to warn him, because she had no intention of remaining there, safely out of reach.

The helicopter dropped them onto a helipad custom-built to service the Moorish castle which, she realised, was really a hotel set in exquisite grounds. A car was waiting to transport them along the hill top that surrounded the bay where exclusive villas lay hidden behind screens of mature shrubs and trees. Eventually they pulled in through wide arched gates into a mosaic courtyard belonging to one of those villas.

Ethan unlocked the front door while the driver of their car collected their luggage and stacked it neatly by the door. Ethan knew the man; they'd chatted in Spanish throughout the short journey and continued chatting until the driver got back into his car and drove way.

Almost instantly silence tumbled down around them as it had done once before when they'd found themselves suddenly on their own like this.

'Shall we go in?' Ethan cut through it with his light invitation.

'Yes.' Eve made an effort to smile and didn't quite manage it as she walked into the villa while he brought the luggage inside then closed the door behind him.

Fresh tension erupted. Eve didn't quite know what to do next and Ethan didn't seem too sure himself, so they both started speaking at the same time.

'Is this one of your own designs?' she asked him.

'Would you like to freshen up first or—? No.' He answered her question.

'Yes, please.' She answered his.

He sighed, ran a hand round the back of his neck and looked suddenly bone-weary. Eve chewed nervously on her bottom lip and wished herself back in the Caribbean lying on a beach.

'Guest bedroom's this way...' Picking up her luggage he began leading the way over pale blue marble beneath arched ceilings painted the colour of pale sand. As they walked, they passed by several wide archways that appeared to lead to the main living space. But Eve was way beyond being curious enough to show any interest in what those rooms held. All she wanted was to be on her own for a while, to take stock, maybe even crash out on the large bed she'd caught sight of in the room Ethan was leading her into.

'Bathroom through that door,' he said as he placed her luggage on the top of a cedarwood ottoman. 'You can reach the terrace through there...' He pointed to the silk-draped full-length windows. 'Make yourself at home...' He turned toward the door, had seconds thoughts, and turned back again. 'I'll be working out on the terrace if you want me. Other than that...take your time...'

Lightly said, aimed to make her feel comfortable with whatever she wanted to do, he did not take into account that he hadn't once allowed his eyes to make contact with her eyes since they'd entered the villa.

Which meant that he was feeling as uncomfortable with this new situation as she was. 'Right. Fine,' she said.

He left her then; like a bat out of hell he got out of that room and made sure he shut the door behind him as he went. Eve wilted, had a horrible feeling that he was standing on the other side of that door doing exactly the same thing, and really, really wished she hadn't come.

Ethan was beginning to wonder if she'd made a run for it when, over an hour later, Eve still hadn't put in an appearance. At first he'd been glad of the respite, had taken a shower, had enjoyed a home-made pot of tea out here on the terrace with only the view and a dozen telephone calls to keep him company.

But as time had drifted on without him hearing a peep from Eve, he'd begun to get edgy. Now he felt like pacing the terrace because the tiger inside him was making its presence felt again.

What time was it? Six p.m., his watch told him. Two minutes later than it had been the last time he'd looked. He grimaced, then sighed to himself and walked over to the terrace rail to look down the hillside where San Estéban lay basking in the early evening sun. This time yesterday he had been sitting in the bar on the beach in the Caribbean drinking local rum and chatting with Jack Banning.

No, you were not, you were watching Eve dance with her eager young men and wishing you weren't there to witness it, a grim kind of honesty forced him to admit.

A sound further along the terrace caught his attention. His stomach muscles instantly tightened when he recognised the sound as one of the terrace doors opening. Eve appeared at last, wearing a plain straight dress with no sleeves, a scooped neck and a hemline that rested a quiet four inches above her slender knees.

Quiet—why quiet? he asked himself as he watched her walk over to the rail then stand looking out over the bay. There was nothing quiet about Eve Herakleides, not where he was concerned anyway. Her hair, her face, her wonderful figure— Even that sudden and unexpectedly shy expression on her face rang bells inside him as she turned and saw him standing there.

CHAPTER ELEVEN

'SORRY,' she murmured in apology. 'I fell asleep.'

'That's okay,' he replied, feeling all of that restlessness ease out of him to be replaced with—damn it—sex. The thought of it anyway. 'I've been working. Didn't notice the time.'

'This is a lovely view,' she remarked, turning her attention back to the bay. 'Nothing looks new or out of place; everything simply blends as if it's been like this for centuries.'

'That was the plan.' After a moment's hesitation he went to stand beside her and began to point out the different features the resort had to offer. She smelt of shampoo and something subtly expensive. Her voice, when she inserted a comment, played feather-like across his skin. 'We haven't even begun developing that area yet,' he said, indicating toward one of the farthest edges of the bay, and went on to describe what would be seen there within the next year or two.

His arm caught her shoulder, his voice vibrated along her flesh, raising goose-bumps on her skin as she listened to him—no—that she *absorbed* with a breathless kind of concentration every detail he relayed to her and wished she could remember a single one of them.

But she couldn't. It was the man who held her wrapped in fascination, the rest was just wallpaper pasted on for appearances' sake. 'Quite utopian,' she murmured eventually. 'And all your own?'

'No.' He denied that with a wry shake of his head. 'I

would love to say it was, but a very austere Spaniard called Don Felipe de Vazquez owns all the land. Victor and I are just the men who transformed his ideas into reality.'

'All of this doesn't reflect an austere temperament.' Eve frowned. 'I see the heart of a romantic at work here.'

'Maybe he has hidden depths.' But, by his tone, it seemed he didn't think so. 'It's more likely he has a good instinct for what will return a healthy dividend on his land.'

'You don't like him,' Eve said, presuming from that.

'It's not my place to like or dislike him.' Ethan took the diplomatic line.

Turning against the rail, Eve folded her arms beneath her breasts then looked up at him sagely. 'But you don't like him,' she repeated stubbornly.

Ethan laughed, it was a soft dryly rueful sound that brought his eyes down to meet with hers. It was a mistake; the wrong move. Things began to happen to him that he had been determined he would not let happen. Don Felipe was tossed into oblivion; San Estéban with all its beauty may as well have not been there at all. Eve the witch, the beautiful siren, was all that he was seeing. She had relaxed with him at last, was actually smiling with her eyes, with her lovely mouth. Don't spoil it, he told himself. Don't so much as breathe in case you ruin the mood.

This wasn't easy, Eve was thinking. Maintaining this level of relaxed friendliness was tough when what she really wanted to do was kiss him so badly that it was like a fire in her brain. She'd fallen asleep thinking of this man, had woken up thinking of this man and didn't dare look into what had gone on in between.

Dreams were ruthless truth-tellers, she mused. 'Don Felipe,' she prompted, though she wasn't interested in the slightest in the Spaniard; it was important that she kept the conversation going, or she might give in and make an absolute fool out of herself.

His eyelashes flickered—long dark silky things that made her lips tingle as if they'd flickered against them. He took in a measured breath that expanded his ribcage and made her breasts sting into peaks. His mouth parted to speak but it wasn't what he was going to say that held her captive.

'You have to know a man to draw a considered opinion as to whether you like him or not...' Ethan dragged his eyes away from her before he did something he shouldn't. 'He's a strange man: very private, cold and remote. Rumour has it that he was disinherited by his father in favour of his half-brother, and didn't take the decision very well. Went a bit mad for a while, got into a couple of fights, had an accident, which left him scarred in more ways than one. Since then he has been out to prove something—with this resort and all the other investments he has made during the last few years that have earned him a fortune big enough to throw in his family's face. But does all of that make him a romantic?' His tone was sceptical to say the least.

'Then you must be the romantic at work here,' Eve announced decidedly.

Me—a romantic? Sending a fleeting glance over San Estéban, Ethan shook his dark head. 'I'm just an architect who likes to leave a place looking as untouched as it was before I arrived...'

Another silence fell. It had probably had to, because neither of them were really thinking about the discussion in hand. Words were appearing from within the mists of other things.

'Drink,' Ethan said, filling the gap again.

'Yes,' she agreed. Relieved to have an excuse to move,

she straightened away from the rail at the same moment that Ethan shifted his stance and made the fatal mistake of looking down at her. That was all that it took to flip the mood right into that one place they'd both been trying to keep away from. Eve saw his eyes dilate, saw the breath grow still in his chest. Her smile began to die along with her relaxed manner, because she knew for certain now what was really going on inside his head.

His tension began to fight with hers. 'And food,' he added. 'We need to eat. The kitchen is stocked with all the usual provisions, but we can eat out if you prefer.'

Eat in or out? Eve tried to make a decision, found she couldn't because sexual desire lay too thickly in the atmosphere to think of anything else. It would take only one more move, one tiny gesture from either of them, to lick desire into a flame.

'In,' she said, choosing. 'I've had enough of crowded places for one day.' She even managed to send him a semblance of a smile to accompany the reply.

But the smile was the gesture. It made him look at her mouth. Eve released a soft gasp as if she'd just been surprised with a kiss. The flame was licked, her arms unfolded and he was taking their place. They went into each other's arms without another sane thought, and all it took was the first light brush of their lips to plunge them right back to where they'd cut off on the plane over the Atlantic.

Hungry and hot, it was the kind of kiss that worked on every sense until she was trembling so badly she needed to hang onto something. That something was his neck where the tips of her fingers had curled and had dug in. And he was no better, taking what she offered with an urgency that fed the need. His hands explored her body, his touch sure with knowledge, sensually driven by man at his most practiced: He was not the fumbling boy Raoul had been the night before, a slave to his own urgent needs.

Eve knew the difference. And so Ethan should have understood that—being the sophisticated lover he was reputed to be. But he shot back so abruptly it was like being severed at the neck. 'What am I doing?' He began cursing himself. 'Great move, Ethan,' he told himself harshly. 'Great damn move!'

'You started it!' Eve threw at him as if he'd implied otherwise.

It swung him round. 'Do you think I don't know that?' he tossed back harshly. 'You suffered a bad experience only yesterday. If I took advantage of you now, it would make me no better than the bastard who did that to you! I apologise,' he clipped out. 'If I ever attempt anything like that again you have my permission to cry—'

Rape, Eve finished when he so obviously couldn't. And there it was, she realised. In one ill-thought-out sentence Ethan had brought this whole ugly situation back to where it really belonged.

So it is me who makes this happen, she realised. You don't get two men in one day thinking you're open to that kind of thing without you giving off something that tells them that!

'You're wrong, so stop thinking it,' he said.

'Why wrong?' He had to explain that or it meant nothing!

Ethan made himself look her in the eyes, made himself take the slap of those pained tears that glittered there. 'You wanted me,' he explained. 'You did not want him.'

It was true. Was it true? Too shaken to think straight, she looked away from his grim hard face, and down at her body where she could still feel the lingering pleasure of his touch. With Raoul she'd felt revulsion, only revulsion.

But that didn't mean she hadn't *asked* for what he'd tried to do! Did it make a difference that she hadn't known she'd been doing it? No, it did not. A flirt was a flirt. A tease was a tease. She looked back at Ethan through pain-bright eyes filled with a terrible self-disillusionment.

'No,' he denied, knowing what was raking around inside her head. 'No!' he repeated and walked back to take her by the shoulders and issue a gentle shake. 'With him, you screamed, Eve,' he pointed out gruffly. 'Even under the influence of whatever he gave you, you screamed loud enough to waken me.'

But that doesn't mean I didn't bring it on myself! she thought painfully.

'You're beautiful, stunning—irresistible in many ways,' he went on as if he could read the thoughts tumbling through her head. 'But ninety-nine per cent of the male population will resist you—unless you don't want them to.'

And I did not want you to resist me. 'But you stopped it anyway,' she whispered shakily.

'Because it was wrong. Because it is not what we're here for.'

'You pompous swine,' she said and turned to walk back to her room.

She didn't get very far. He exploded so spectacularly it came as a shock. 'What is it you actually want from me, Miss Herakleides?' he roared at her furiously as he strode towards her. 'I thought you wanted my help, so I gave it.' His hands found her shoulders. 'I thought you wanted my support with your lies, so I gave you that!' Those hands spun her round to face the fury he was giving out. 'You're here. *I'm* here, living a lie that should never have been allowed to start in the first place!' Cold steely eyes raked her face like cutthroat razors. 'Now I can't even honour that deal without you making me out to be some kind of rat!'

'I didn't mean—'

'Yes, you did,' he cut in thinly.

'I thought—'

'You don't think, Eve, that's your trouble!'

'Will you stop shouting at me,' she yelled back. 'I wanted what I thought you wanted! My mistake. I apologise. Now let go of me!'

He did. She staggered. His hands came back to steady her. She released a pathetic little sob. He muttered something. She looked up at him. Like lightning striking a volcano, a whole ocean of molten emotion came boiling out.

'He was there; he hurt me. You were the last person on earth I expected to understand! I liked it—your kindness, your caring, the strength that you let me lean on.' Stop trembling! she told herself. 'I liked the way you could be so stern with me, but make love to me with your eyes at the same time. You're doing it now!' she choked out shrilly. 'You're angry but you want me. I am *not* misreading the messages! How dare you imply that I am?'

It was a damning indictment. She was right, every word of it. Standing there, watching this beautiful woman shimmer with anger, hurt and a million other emotions beside, Ethan took it all full in the face and wondered what he was supposed to say or do now.

Then, he thought, oh to hell with it. He even released a short laugh because he knew what he was going to do with it. He was going to throw off his high moral stance and surrender to Eve—as he had been doing since this whole crazy thing had begun.

'Don't laugh at me,' she protested unsteadily, hurt tears sparkling across dark green irises.

'I'm not laughing at you,' he denied. 'I'm laughing at myself.'

'Why?'

Ethan kissed those tear-washed eyes, ran his lips down her cute little nose and settled at the corner of her trembling mouth. 'Because of this,' he murmured huskily, and made his surrender, falling into it without allowing himself another sane thought.

'If you're playing games with me, I'll—'

'No game,' he promised and, because they'd done enough talking, he moved his lips until they'd covered her own then gently parted them to receive the moist caress of his tongue.

It was different. Eve could feel it was different. Not just the kiss but the way he was holding her—not with anger nor that driving compulsion that had pulled their mouths together before. He was going to take what she had placed on such open offer, and for a fleeting, fleeting, moment Eve wondered if she had made a terrible mistake by making herself so easy for him. Then he lifted his head, and she saw the slightly awry smile he offered that told her he wasn't thinking this was easy at all.

'Beautiful Eve,' he murmured and covered her mouth again, picked her up and carried her down the terrace, into her bedroom and over to the bed before he let her feet slide down to the floor.

Shy, she felt agonisingly shy suddenly, which was stupid after everything that had gone before. He cupped her face, felt the burn in her cheeks, brushed his thumbs across them gently and felt her small tremor as he tilted her head back enough to receive his next kiss.

Only, not just a kiss but a deep and desirous prelude to what was about to come. It was a warm and unhurried awakening of the senses that held her captivated and compliant, wanting to go only where he led her.

He noticed, of course he did. 'A passive Eve?' he mocked her gently.

'Yes,' she whispered. 'Do you mind?'

'No.' But that awry smile was on his lips again. 'Just so long as it doesn't mean you're having second thoughts and don't know how to tell me.'

'No second thoughts.' And to prove it, she wound her arms around his neck and brought his mouth back to hers again, then mimicked his long seductive kiss.

He led her through an erotic undressing by drawing the zip of her dress down her spine with caressing expertise that took her breath away. His fingers trailed feather-light over exposed skin, sun-kissed shoulders, slender backbone, the shockingly sensitised concaved arch at the nape of back. She moved against him and could tell that he liked that. It emboldened her into pressing the bowl of her hips even closer to what was happening to him.

He released a sigh; it shook with feeling. Eve matched that too, and he caught the sound on his tongue then fed it back to her, while his hands drifted up her arms until they reached her hands still locked around his neck. Drawing them downwards he encouraged her dress to slither down her body, then laid her hands against his shirt front. 'Undress me,' he urged.

It was the calling song of a mating bird. Shy though she still felt, Eve complied, while the caress of his hands and his mouth urged her on. Did he know? she wondered mistily. Could he tell she'd never done this before, and was that why he was taking it all so slow and easy?

Shirt buttons slid from their buttonholes to reveal more and more of that wonderful chest she loved to look at so much. Now she allowed herself the pleasure of touching, placing her fingers on his chest where dark hair coiled into the hollow between tight pectoral muscles. Then, because she couldn't resist, the moist tip of her tongue followed suit.

The air left his lungs on a heavy rush that brought her head up sharply. She looked up at him, he looked down at her, and the pace suddenly altered dramatically. They fell on each other's mouths with a series of deep hot hisses while his urgent hands stripped her flimsy scrap of a bra away and hers pushed the shirt off his back.

Then it was flesh on flesh, pleasure tangling up with pleasure as the whole thing shot off on its own natural journey. His arms were crushing her, his kiss was deep, their laboured breathing hissed into the warm golden light of the slow-dying day as he manoeuvred her down onto the bed. He came down with her, his skin was moist, she yearned to taste it but the kiss was just too good to break away from. His hands began caressing her with so much sensual expertise that she arched and flexed as sensation washed over her in waves and scraped restless fingernails over his shoulder blades with enough urgency to make him shudder in response.

'Sorry,' she whispered helplessly.

He released a thick laugh and said, 'Do it again.'

The exchange of words broke the kiss. Without the kiss she was free to indulge herself by tasting him. He liked her nails so she ran them down his back, loving the feel of his muscles flexing pleasurably, loving the groan he uttered just before he claimed one of her breasts with his mouth.

Desire stirred and writhed like an unleashed serpent deep within her abdomen. He must have known, because his hand was suddenly playing her stomach, moving downward, fingertips slipping beneath the scrappy fabric of her briefs. She knew he was going to touch her, knew that this was it, the moment she had been waiting for for what seemed the whole of her life. A tight and tingling breath-taking anticipation sent her still, which made him lift his head and send her a sharp questioning look.

'What?' he said.

'You,' she said in a sexually tense little voice.

He understood. His eyes went black, his features tightening into a very male, passionate cast. The hand slipped lower, fingertips drifting through dusky curls to seek out warm moist tissue that was the centre of her world right now. She groaned then gasped as pleasure licked with stunning intensity through to her toes and fingertips. He murmured something she didn't hear—it could have been her name or it could have been a curse because she knew she was rocketing right out of control here.

He encouraged her though. With the mastery of the sea-soned lover, he orchestrated her pleasure trip through the senses. Did he know? He had to know. Surely no man took this much care to please the woman he was making love to without expecting some similar stimulation back by return, unless he knew that this was her first experience?

The last of her clothing was trailed away; she was vaguely aware of him ridding himself of his own. When his hands were busy elsewhere his mouth took up the burning seduction of her breasts, her navel, brushing hot moist kisses along the inner surface of her golden thighs.

Flesh burned against flesh; long restless limbs tangled in a love-knot caress. They rolled. He came above her, her hands locked around his neck. It was then that she felt the probing force of his masculinity and as her insides curled in anticipation she uttered his name on a sensual breath.

He liked it; she felt his response in the small shudder

that ripped through his body. She liked that, and responded with a lithe flexing of her hips that made her exquisitely aware of the power he was still keeping in check.

'Eve, give me your mouth.'

She gave him her mouth, willingly, hungrily. She gave him every little bit of herself that she could possibly give. He took it all. Like a man leaping into a fiery furnace knowing he was about to get severely burned, he made a single strangled sound in his throat then, swift and sure, he claimed the passage he had prepared for himself.

It was wild, it was shocking, it was shamelessly exhilarating. Barriers broke; she winced on a soft little gasp. He paused, touched her cheek with unsteady fingers, gently combed her hair away from her face.

'Eve,' he breathed.

She opened her eyes and made contact with the burning black density of his. He looked different, darker, masculine, more her man than ever.

'Yes,' she breathed, closed her eyes again, then made a single stretching movement that fastened her to him as a whole new hot probing journey held her in its spectacular thrall. He took her to places she hadn't known existed; he taught her things about her that held her trapped on the pin-piercing pinnacle of discovery for long agonising seconds before he tipped her over the edge with the sudden increased rush of masculine thrust. She learned what it was like to lose touch with everything but a swelling pulsing pleasure of the senses.

When it was over it was all she could do to hang onto him while he lay heavily on top of her with their pounding heartbeats throbbing all around.

He went to move. She stopped him. 'Wait,' she whispered. She didn't want to miss a single sense-soaring moment in this act of momentous importance to her. She had waited so very long for this to happen, had never been slightly tempted to experiment because she had been so determined to wait for the right man to come along—the one she would know instinctively was the one man for her. Marriage, wedding gowns, playing the shy virgin bride had never come into her perfect dream. It had just had to be the right man. She'd found that man, and nothing—no moment in time—was ever going to feel as special as this.

CHAPTER TWELVE

EVE'S sigh was soft against his shoulder; it whispered the pleasure still permeating her blood. Ethan knew the feeling; it was with him also. But that didn't mean he was feeling good about this.

What had he done—?

What the hell had he done? He didn't deserve this, he did not deserve one half second of what she had just given to him. Now he was desperate to move, to separate from this incredible creature so that he could take stock—come to terms with what this was going to mean to the both of them.

He felt her begin to stir beneath him. It became the most sensually evocative stretch of the female body that began at her shoulders and arched her slender spine and flexed the cradle of her hips where he received the full kick of the movement because they were still joined.

At least with that stirring she also gave him permission to move by slackening the grip her arms had around him. Using his forearms as braces to take his weight, he levered himself away from her, and shuddered at her soft quivering gasp as he withdrew other parts. The gasp didn't surprise him. He might be wishing himself a million miles away at this precise moment, but his body certainly wasn't agreeing.

It wanted more—already. It wanted him to begin the whole wildly exciting process all over again.

'Say something,' she murmured.

The soft sound of her voice brought his head round to

look at her. She was lying there beside him with her cheek resting on her forearm and gazing at him through shy, dark, vulnerable eyes. His heart pitched and rolled. She looked gloriously, stunningly, *achingly* lovely with her hair spreading out across the pillow and her face wearing that satiated bloom.

'I was your first lover.' It was the only thing rattling around his head that was fit to be said.

The bloom deepened, her eyelashes flickered down in a bid to hide away from that soul-blazing truth. But not for long; not this woman who had so much spirit; she wasn't going to let a bit of shy self-consciousness beat her. So the lashes rose up again, gave him a view of deep green, slightly mocking, eyes packed full of the new knowledge he had given to her. 'Thank you for making it such a memorable experience,' she said softly, and smiled.

That smile… He felt it reach right down inside and grasp hold of certain parts. The urge to roll towards her and recreate the whole magic again was so tantalising he could actually taste it.

Or taste Eve, he amended grimly, and sat up. 'You should have told me,' he censured.

There was a moment's silence, a moment's total stillness, a moment in which he felt muscles clench all over him because his gruff, curt attitude had just wiped the pleasure right out. He felt it leave like an actual entity, unfolding itself from their flesh and slipping silently through the open terrace window.

Not Eve though. She still lay beside him; he could see her slender bare feet, the sensual curl of her toes and the gold silk length of her slender legs.

'Why?' she challenged. 'Is there some unwritten rule somewhere that says all first-timers must announce that fact before proceeding?'

Put like that, he wanted to laugh. But the bottom line still read like ten vicious swear words. 'I had a right to know.'

'You believe you had a right of say over my virginity? Rubbish,' she denounced. 'For what purpose?' she demanded. 'So that you could make the decision as to whether you wanted to take it or not?'

'No.' This, Ethan realised, was not going to be easy.

'Then, what?'

The silky gold legs disappeared from his vision, the slender feet, the sensually curling toes. His eyes followed them as they slid across smooth white sheeting to snake out of his sight as she pulled herself up—not to sit but to kneel somewhere behind him. He felt her rise upwards, smelt the sweetly seductive scent of her skin, felt her sigh brush his nape, just before her arms appeared over his shoulders and long delicate fingers with nails painted hot-pink came to rest in the hair matting his chest. Her lips caught his ear lobe, her teeth gently bit, and sensation sprinkled through him like a thousand pinpricks, the tips of her breasts pressing like two hard buttons against his back.

'It wasn't your special moment, it was mine,' she told him. 'Go all Neanderthal on me and I might not let you teach me how good it can be the second time…the third…' She bit his lobe again. 'To infinity and beyond,' she whispered sensually.

His short huff of amused laughter found voice this time. Eve the flirt, Eve the temptress, Eve the serpent in paradise, whom he seemed to have transported with him across half the world. Now it was Eve the dangerous seductress. Though she might have just enjoyed her first experience in making love, even now he knew he could teach her nothing. She was a natural, born to it. Special and rare.

What had that small burst of laughter been for? Eve wondered anxiously. Was he thinking she was incorrigible? Was he thinking she must be a real little hussy to make so light of what they'd just done?

But Eve didn't feel light about anything. She was worried. She was scared in case he took the honourable path and decided her virginity came with a price tag he might be forced to pay, when all he'd really been doing had been giving in to the temptation she'd so blatantly thrown his way.

She loved him, she wanted him, but not without him loving and wanting her above anything else.

Anything? she then questioned. One woman, she amended. One unavailable woman, who had no right to keep the heart she could never cherish. Well, move over, Leona, she thought possessively. Because you've just lost out and this beautiful man's heart is going to belong to me!

'I need a shower,' she murmured huskily against that tasty ear lobe. 'And so do you.'

Invitation—demand. Ethan stared down at the place against his chest where his ring winked defiantly up at him. She's all yours, mate, it seemed to be telling him. For now at any rate.

Well, to hell with it—why not? he decided. He was a big boy, he could take it when it was over and it was time to get out! So he turned to look at her, dislodging her arms in the process so she sat back on her haunches looking at him through wide green wary eyes. She wasn't sure what was coming but he knew.

He looked her over, his eyes stripping off a layer of skin with their silver-bright possessive blast. Then he swung himself off the bed, turned, and pressed Eve up against his chest so that her eyes were level with his and her thighs were clinging to his narrow waist. 'Your grandfather,' he said, 'should have locked you away years ago.'

She grinned; her eyes began to shine; she had the audacity to put out her tongue and lick the shape of his mock-stern mouth. 'Jack Banning said the very same thing,' she informed him. Then before he could respond, she kissed him—hell, did she kiss him! She kissed him all the way into the adjoining bathroom, then the shower and, as promised, beyond.

Eve was in the kitchen and was humming to herself as she waited for the toast to pop up from the toaster. Sunlight was pouring in through the open door which led onto the terrace and behind her lay the remnants of the meal they'd eaten in here the night before—though for the life of her she couldn't remember what that meal had consisted of.

It didn't matter. Nothing mattered, other than for the huggable knowledge that she had spent the night in Ethan's home, in Ethan's bed, in Ethan's arms, making wonderful love. She was now wearing Ethan's shirt as she prepared his breakfast, while his voice filtered into her from out on the terrace where he was sounding very smooth, very slick, very informed as he spoke in fluent Spanish to some authoritative body. She loved his voice; she loved its rich deep texture and what it did to her tummy muscles as she listened to him. She loved this feeling of complete contentment as she prepared breakfast for him.

He stopped talking as the toast popped up, his footsteps sounding on pale blue tiling as they brought him into the kitchen to look for her. She smiled as his hands came to cup her hips, crushing fine cotton against her cool flesh. 'Mmm, that smells good,' he said, then buried his mouth in the side of her throat.

It really was quite sinful the way she responded, turning

round in his grasp to demand that mouth for her own. His hands shaped her body and hers stroked the smooth clean surface of his freshly shaved face. Things would have moved onto something else if the telephone hadn't started ringing.

He was reluctant to let her go, Eve equally so. But she liked the evidence of frustration in his eyes as he dug his mobile out of his pocket and placed it to his ear.

'Ethan Hayes,' he announced in that deep smooth drawl that made her toes curl into the floor. He was wearing a light grey suit, white shirt and grey tie and was looking dynamic, again, she noticed with a wry little smile as she turned back to the toast while he discussed local by-laws.

The call ended just as she finished slotting triangles of toast into a toast rack. There was a short sharp silence that alerted her before she even turned round and saw his face.

He was gazing ruefully at the breakfast tray she had prepared ready to take out onto the terrace. 'You're going to be angry with me for this,' he warned her. 'But I'm afraid I'll have to miss breakfast. I have a meeting in ten minutes down at the yacht club.'

Disappointment curled inside her tummy but she kept it from showing on her face by hiding it behind an understanding smile. It was what he had rushed back here to Spain for, after all. 'So much for my display of domesticity,' she mocked.

'I shouldn't be long,' he assured her. 'You'll be all right here on your own until I get back?'

'I'll try my best not to go into too deep a decline while you're gone,' she promised.

'What about my decline?' he countered quizzically.

It was nice of him to say it, but he was in no danger of wasting away from not having her within touching distance. He was already pumped up and eager to go and take on the whole Spanish government.

Folding her arms beneath her breasts, Eve leaned against the worktop and sent him a dry look. 'Go,' she said.

'Right,' he said, but still didn't move. Instead he looked at her, really looked at her, with a slight tilt to his head and a slight frown to his brow, as if he was trying to work something out about her but couldn't quite grasp what that something was. Then he seemed to give up on it and, with a brief smile, he brushed a kiss across her cheek. 'I'll be as quick as I can,' he said.

Then he was gone, striding out of the kitchen and away from her with his car keys jangling in his hand as he made for the rear courtyard, where she'd noticed the set of four garages when they'd arrived the afternoon before.

Left on her own, breakfast lost some of its appeal, though the aroma of fresh coffee was too inviting to ignore. So she carried the tray out onto the terrace and sat at one of the tables there to drink it and watch San Estéban glitter with the early morning crystal-clarity that came with the promise of a perfect summer's day. After that she spent some time tidying the kitchen, then decided to take a long shower and dress before exploring the rest of the villa, since she hadn't bothered to notice anything much the day before.

She took the terrace route to her bedroom, noticed she hadn't even got around to unpacking her suitcase, and wondered if Ethan had unpacked his? A quick shower and she was just slipping into a short blue skirt and a white sun top, her next intention to explore the villa, when a telephone began ringing somewhere, it was the land-line kind that announced itself as such by its distinctive tone.

Ethan? she wondered, and felt her heart leap. He had only been gone a couple of hours yet he was missing her so much he had to give her a call? Hurrying out of the bedroom, she began to follow the sound down the wide arched hallway. The villa suddenly felt big and empty, and she wasn't sure she liked Ethan's taste in décor. It surprised her to think that because she liked just about every other thing about Ethan, she mused with a smile as she walked between pale sand walls on the same pale blue tiling that seemed to cover the floors throughout. It was all very cool, very Lawrence-of-Arabia, nothing shouted, nothing scarred the eyes. Yet...

She found the telephone in one of the reception rooms. As she moved towards it, it suddenly stopped ringing and the answering machine kicked in. As she waited to hear if it was indeed Ethan trying to contact her before she decided to pick up the receiver, she began to look around the room.

A stranger's voice suddenly filled the air space. Deep and smooth, it possessed the same rich English tones as Ethan's voice, only it lacked his toe-curling attraction.

'Ethan,' the voice said. 'It's Victor. When you get a spare minute, give me a call. I'm at the London office and that cantankerous devil, Theron Herakleides, has decided to go silent about the Greek project.'

Grandpa. Eve smiled at the cantankerous description, frowned at the part about the Greek project because she'd forgotten about her grandfather's threats. She remained standing there waiting for Victor Frayne to finish his message so that she could call up her grandfather and try and convince him he would be cutting off his nose to spite his own face if he pulled Hayes-Frayne's submission.

Maybe she shouldn't have come here. For the first time she began to have doubts about her own motives. Selfish, she was being selfish, and maybe she should let Ethan off the hook and tell her grandfather the truth about what had happened. It wasn't right; it wasn't fair that Ethan should be forced to make sacrifices just because she'd managed to wriggle her way beneath his tough façade and basically run rings around him.

Is that what she'd done? Yes, it was exactly what she'd done, she admitted. She'd wept, she'd fought, she'd begged and had seduced and had turned him upside down and inside out—and all in twenty-four wild and dizzying hours, too!

'Oh, by the way…' Victor Frayne's voice cut through her train of thinking at about the same moment Eve's eyes settled on a row of framed photographs sitting on a long low cedarwood sideboard. '…the door to Leona's bedroom is sticking. Can you get someone up there to take a look at it?'

The call to her grandfather was forgotten. A cold chill of dismay was settling on her skin. Ethan couldn't—surely—have brought her to stay at the home of Victor Frayne and Leona Al-Qadim?

CHAPTER THIRTEEN

THE meeting had taken longer than Ethan had expected but by the end of it Ethan was satisfied that the new yacht club building was no longer under threat. As he shook hands with the local planning officials, he was aware that his site managers were standing to one side waiting to do the usual post-mortem on the meeting, but he was eager to get away.

He kept thinking of Eve and how she'd looked when he'd left her, wearing nothing but his cast-off shirt and a becoming flush to her lovely face.

As soon as the officials departed, one of his managers stepped up. 'Victor has been trying to contact you,' the man informed him. 'Something to do with Theron Herakleides and the Greek project?'

Theron, Ethan began to frown. He had forgotten all about Eve's grandfather and his threats. 'I'll deal with it.' He nodded. He glanced at his watch, realised he'd been away from Eve for over two hours, and wished he knew at what point it had been that he had become so obsessed with her that she was virtually wrapped around his every thought. 'If everything is back on track here, can we rain check the post-mortem? I need to be somewhere else.'

He was talking to all three of his site managers, and they instantly developed distinct masculine gleams in their eyes. 'We heard all about the souvenir you brought back with you from the Caribbean,' one of them teased him lazily, telling him also that the company grapevine was still working efficiently.

This kind of man-to-man camaraderie was to be expected on building sites. One either sank or swam with it. Ethan usually swam.

'The *souvenir* goes by the name of Eve Herakleides,' he informed them dryly. 'And if you value your jobs here I would suggest you curb the joky comments, because she also happens to be my future wife.'

A stunned silence fell. Ethan looked at the three men and saw their slack-jawed trance. But their shock came nowhere near the shock that he found himself experiencing. He felt as if he had just stepped off a very high cliff.

Had he really said that? Yes, he had said that, he was forced to grimly face the fact.

They were looking at him as if they expected him to laugh now and withdraw what he'd said. After all, this had to be a classic example of building-site camaraderie where the jokes flew back and forth with quick-flitting wit that did not always need to tell the truth if the punch-line served got the right results?

So—okay, this was supposed to be part of an elaborate deception, he tried to reason. But it didn't feel like a lie. Was that why he was suddenly feeling as if he'd jumped into a free fall from a fatal height?

'Nothing to say?' he mocked, working like mad to keep the jaunty flow going now that he had opened his big mouth.

'Congratulations,' one man muttered uncomfortably. The others mimicked their colleague like puppets that had just had their strings well and truly jerked.

'Thank you,' he murmured, while thinking Eve would have loved to be here to witness this. It placed the act she'd put on for her grandfather the day before yesterday right into the shade. 'Be sure to make it a good whip-round for my wedding gift when the time comes.'

They should have laughed then—told him what a fool he was for getting caught after managing to stay single for all these years. But their expressions had now shifted to something else entirely.

What else? he puzzled. What exactly was now going on inside their heads while they stood there looking at him like that?

Then it hit him. Leona. His free fall through space stopped abruptly as cold anger erupted in his breast. Did everyone in San Estéban suspect his relationship with Leona had been something other than what it was?

Now he was glad that Eve wasn't here to witness this scene, or every single suspicion she had about him and Leona would be buzzing around her possessive head.

Oh, but he liked Eve possessive; he liked her weepy and vulnerable and high-tempered and snappy; he liked her wearing hot-pink, like the dress she'd had on in the bar on the beach, and she'd had painted onto the nails she'd drawn down his chest last night.

Where the hell did he think he was going with this kind of crazy thinking? Crazy really said it. The last twenty-four hours in their entirety had been one long walk through insanity! But in those twenty-four hours, he realised he'd come to care a great deal what Eve thought about him.

'So watch the snide remarks in her presence,' he cautioned more seriously. 'She's special. I expect her to be treated as special. Make sure you pass the warning on.'

And if this performance didn't convince them that he and Leona were not an item, then what would?

'Right, Boss,' they said in solemn unison.

As he left, Ethan wondered how long it would take for this juicy snippet of information to make it right round San Estéban?

Eve was standing in the sunny lounge holding a picture

frame between trembling fingers when she heard Ethan return. She was trying to decide whether to be hurt, insulted or just plain angry. She'd certainly been hurt when she'd picked up this frame, and had found herself staring at the tableau it presented of a beautiful woman standing with—not one—but *four* incredibly spectacular looking men!

One of the men was Ethan. *All* of them looked ready and willing to worship at the woman's feet. And why not? she acknowledged. The lady was really quite something special with her flowing red hair, exquisite face and the kind of smile that dropped men to their knees.

'It was taken at Leona's civil wedding in England,' Ethan's voice quietly informed her.

Looking up she saw him standing in the archway. The jacket to his suit had gone but the tie still rested neatly against his shirt front. As always, he looked heart-stoppingly attractive, even with that guarded look he was wearing on his face.

She looked away from him and back at the photograph. 'She's beautiful,' she murmured huskily.

His answering smile was more like a grimace as he walked forward to glance down at the photograph. 'Victor Frayne,' he indicated with a long finger. 'Leona, of course, and Sheikh Hassan Al-Qadim. The giant is Sheikh Hassan's brother, Sheikh Rafiq Al-Qadim—though he refuses to acknowledge the title,' he added grimacing.

'Why?'

'Long story. Remind me to tell it to you sometime— preferably before you meet him.' Said with humour, there was nothing funny in the way he took the frame from her then stood frowning down at it before putting it back in its place.

'Is there a chance that I'll meet him?' Eve was already

stiffening her insides ready for the blow she thought was coming her way. If the Al-Qadim family were here in San Estéban... If they were staying in this same house then she was...

'Not really,' he murmured. 'He goes nowhere without his brother, and his brother is cruising the Mediterranean as we speak.'

'This is their villa, isn't it?' she stated.

Did he hear the accusation in her tone? If he did, his face didn't show it as he turned with what Eve read as reluctance from the photo to look at her. 'It's the company villa,' he corrected. 'Victor designed it, Leona furnished it. We all use it as a convenient place to live when we are here in Spain.'

Convenient, just about said it for Eve, and her mind was suddenly tripping over itself as it painted lurid pictures in her head of Ethan and Leona in their convenient love-nest with dear Papa along as one lousy chaperone!

'And where's Leona now?' she demanded.

'With her husband on their yacht. Victor flew back to London yesterday, once he knew I was coming here to take over for him.'

'So you thought, Why not bring Eve here and *conveniently* slot her in where Leona should be?'

Ethan's eyes narrowed at her waspish tone. 'What is that supposed to mean?'

'It means,' she lashed at him, 'that I do not appreciate playing substitute to anyone!'

'Substitute to who, exactly?'

He wanted her to spell it out for him. Well, she could do that! 'Leona's clothes hang in the wardrobe,' she told him. 'The next bedroom to yours as a matter of fact!'

'It bothers you?' he murmured.

'It bothers me.' She nodded. 'It more than bothers me

that you dared to bring me here to your sordid little love-nest and make love to me in the same bed in which you probably made love to her!'

His grey eyes narrowed some more and Eve was suddenly thinking about dangerous animals again, and felt the fizz of excitement leap inside.

She was trembling like mad, Ethan noticed, and he was angry! 'A small piece of advice,' he offered thinly. 'Loose talk is dangerous when the Al-Qadim family is involved. So hold your foolish tongue and listen. Leona and I are not, and never have been, lovers,' he stated it with ice-cold precision. 'Take that on board and heed it, Eve, because I won't repeat it again.'

But he would say that, wouldn't he, to protect his true love? Eve had never felt so used in her entire life. 'I'm leaving,' she decided.

He didn't say anything, but just stood there looking at her through cold hard gun-metal-grey eyes.

Her heart was bursting, because she didn't really want to go. But she turned anyway and began walking towards the archway the led to the hall.

'Back to Aidan Galloway?' he fed silkily after her. 'Back to the young bloods you can handle better than you can handle me?'

She stopped. 'At least Aidan cares about my feelings.'

'By spiking your drink so he can enjoy you without needing to put much effort into it?'

She swung round. 'I told you it wasn't Aidan that did that to me!'

'Ah, yes, the other nameless young blood,' he drawled, and Eve noticed that the cynicism was back. 'Funny how you remembered him only after I threatened to tear Galloway limb from limb.'

He still didn't believe her about Aidan! she realised. 'It

was Raoul Delacroix who spiked my drink!' she insisted furiously.

Raoul Delacroix. Any other name, Ethan was thinking, and he would have laughed in her lying face! But he was recalling the look on Raoul's face as he'd turned away from her in the bar at the beach. He was recalling the stinging sensation he'd experienced at the back of his neck, that reminded him he didn't like what he'd seen on the young Frenchman's face.

'And I don't know what right you think you have to throw my love life back at me when nothing could be more sordid than the set-up you have going here!'

'Leave Leona out of this,' he bit at her.

'Leave Aidan out of it!'

Stalemate. They both recognised it for what it was. She was standing there shimmering with offence and fury and he was standing there simmering in the midst of a jealous rage! He couldn't believe it. Couldn't bring himself to accept that in forty-eight short hours she could have actually brought him down to this.

'Go if you are going,' he said as the damning remark to come straight out of that last angry thought.

She turned—but not before he had seen that heart-shaped pink mouth that had a propensity to pout, quiver, and her eyes sparkle with the promise of tears. Hell, he cursed, when he knew what was going to happen: he was going to give in. He could feel it bubbling up inside him, hot and out of control.

'But—I'm coming with you.' The decision itself set his feet in motion. As he strode towards her he saw his ring sparkling on her finger when she lifted her hand up to brush a tear from her cheek.

My tears, my ring—my woman, he claimed possessively. He took all three, grabbing his woman around the waist, crushing the ring in the clasp of one of his hands, and spinning her about so that he could lick the tears from her cheek. 'Anywhere,' he murmured, while he did it. 'Hotel, an apartment in San Estéban. We can even take one of the other villas if that's what you prefer.'

Preference didn't really come into it, Eve thought helplessly. She preferred not to love him this badly. But she did. Bottom line. 'I would prefer it if Leona Al-Qadim didn't exist,' she told him honestly.

'Forget Leona,' he muttered impatiently.

'If you forget Aidan,' she returned, determined to maintain some level of balance around here.

She looked into his eyes; he looked into hers; both sets were angry because they were giving in. Their bodies liked it though, Eve noticed. They were greeting each other like hungry lovers.

'So, where are we going to go to continue this?' His voice rasped with impatience, his body pulsed with desire.

The fact that hers was doing the same thing made the decision for her. So she reached up, touched her mouth to his, and remained that close while she murmured, 'Here seems very convenient, don't you think...?'

CHAPTER FOURTEEN

THE little minx. An absolute witch, sent to torment the life out of him, Ethan was thinking irritably. There was nothing convenient about having Eve Herakleides running riot through his life.

The telephone rang. He picked it up. 'What?' he barked.

It was his secretary in London. Sitting there behind his desk, Ethan dealt with a list of queries while his angry gaze remained fixed on the little scene taking place outside his site-office window, where Eve stood laughing, surrounded by a whole rugby scrum of big, tough, very much hands-on builders wearing yellow helmets, dust-covered steel-capped boots, tight tee shirts and jeans.

And what was Eve wearing?

Hot-pink. It was her favourite colour, he had come to realise during the last ten days. Today it was hot-pink trousers that skimmed her hips and thighs and stopped just above her slender calf muscles, and a baby-pink top that left a lot of golden midriff on show.

Too much midriff. 'I don't know about that, Sonia,' he murmured. 'I can't be sure I'll be back in London to attend that meeting. You'd better ask Victor if he can do it.'

Eve's hair was up in a natty little twist that did amazing things to the length of her neck, and in profile she looked like the sweetest thing ever to be put onto this earth. Every time she moved he saw his ring flash in the sunlight. Every time she laughed he saw his men almost fall to their knees.

'I know they wanted me,' he rasped out testily. 'But they can't have me.'

I'm already engaged, he thought, to a woman with no sense of what's right or proper to wear on a building site! In the last ten days he'd also come to realise the full meaning of the term *engaged*.

'Heard anything from Theron Herakleides?' he thought to enquire.

There was another person who was irritating the hell out of him. Since their tough talk in the Caribbean, he hadn't had a single peep out of Eve's grandfather. His own letter formally withdrawing his submission for the Greek project had not been acknowledged. The promised contract making sure Ethan didn't get his greedy hands on the old man's money had never appeared. No one at Hayes-Frayne could get to speak to Herakleides, and even Leandros was complaining that the Greek had dropped off the face of the earth. As far as Ethan could make out, Theron was only answering calls from his precious granddaughter. She'd been talking to him every day, but even she couldn't get him to come clean as to what he was going to do about the Greek project. He'd just said, 'I'll see you in two weeks.' Then it had been one week. Now it was down to just a few days.

Their official betrothal. His ring on Eve's finger winked at him. 'Nothing,' he heard his secretary say.

The ring sparkled again as Eve lifted up her hand to brush some dry plaster from one man's bulging bicep. The guy grinned a very macho, very sexy, Spanish grin. Ethan felt his gut tighten up in protest. Abruptly finishing the telephone conversation, he stood up and knocked on the window-pane.

Eve turned. So did the men. She sent him a wide white brilliant smile. The men's smiles were more—manly, as in, You lucky devil, Mr Hayes.

'He wants his souvenir back,' he heard one man say to the others.

Eve laughed, as she had done from the first time she'd heard herself referred to as that. She liked it. Damn it, *he* liked it! He liked what it did to him when she sent him that teasing little smile that said, Some souvenir, hmm?

He was in love with her. He'd known it for days, weeks, maybe even months. She filled his every thought, his every sense, his every desire. He looked at her and felt a multitude of conflicting emotions, none of which on their own could adequately describe what he was having to deal with inside.

Bidding a light farewell to her macho fan club, she began walking towards his office door. He watched her come, watched her soft mouth take on a different look that was exclusively for him. It was a kiss, a sensual kiss, offered to him from a distance. She was a flirt; she was a tease; he found himself wearing an irresistible grin.

'What are you doing here?' he demanded though, the moment she came into the cool confines of his air-conditioned office. 'I thought we'd agreed you would keep away from the site so you don't cause accidents.'

She laughed; she thought he was joking, but Ethan wasn't sure that he was. Heads turned when Eve walked by. The fact that those heads were on bodies with feet balancing on ladders or on scaffolding made it dangerous.

'I needed to ask your advice about something.'

'Try the phone.'

'Oh, don't be a grouch.' She pouted up at him as she walked around his desk. Then she boldly pulled the cord that closed the sunblinds across the window and reached up to transform the pout into a kiss that wound its tentacles around him and left him wanting more.

I love this man, Eve thought, as she drew away again.

I love him so much that I daren't let myself think about Athens and the fact that we have only three days to go before we are expected there.

It was frightening. She held his cheek, looked deep into his eyes and wished she knew how much of what they relayed to her was just sexual desire and how much was still rooted in pretence. What she did know was that they had been so happy here. No spats, since the first day. No mention of anything likely to start a war.

Except for Grandfather, of course. He was discussed on a daily basis. But never in a way that could remind either of them of how this whole thing had started out.

'Was that it?' he prompted. 'You wanted my advice on how well you kiss?'

Eve refocused her attention and saw one of his eyebrows had arched and his mouth was wearing a lazily amused smile. It would be the easiest thing in the world to say yes, and leave it at that, keep the rest until later when he came home.

But keeping Ethan on his toes was her aim in life. So, she said airily, 'Oh, no. I already know what a great kisser I am.'

Stepping away from him, she applied her surprise tactics by unzipping her trousers and peeling them back from her hips. 'What do you think?' she asked innocently.

Innocent was not the word Ethan was thinking as he stared down at her silk-smooth abdomen. He was thinking, Minx, again. Outrageous and unpredictable minx. For there, nestling in the hollow of her groin, just above the tantalisingly brief panty line, and right on the spot of an erogenous zone he knew so well he could actually feel its response against the flat of his tongue, lay a heart. A small red painted heart.

'It's a tattoo,' he announced.

'What do you think?' she repeated.

'I think you're not safe to be let out on your own,' he replied. 'What were you thinking of, marking your lovely skin with something like that?'

'I thought you might like it.' The pout was back, Ethan noticed, the one that begged to be soothed into something else.

Well, not this time. 'You idiot,' he snapped. 'That's going to hurt like blazes by tonight.'

'No, it won't,' she denied. 'Because it isn't real. I found this amazing little shop down one of the back streets in San Estéban where they apply these temporary tattoos. It will disappear in about a month. I think its great.' Eve looked down to view her latest impulse. 'I might have it replaced with a permanent one next time.'

'Over my dead body,' he vowed, but he had to reach out to run his thumb pad over the painted heart. As he did so he heard her breath quiver in her throat and felt the sound replay itself in other parts of himself.

He knew that sound. He looked at her face and saw her innocent green eyes had darkened into those of an outright sinner. His body quickened; she saw it happen; her mouth stretched into a knowing smile. 'It will be interesting to see if you change your mind about that,' she taunted silkily.

It was no use, Ethan gave up—as he always seemed to do. Swinging his chair around, he sat himself down then drew her in between his spread thighs. 'No,' he refused, knowing exactly what she believed was going to come. Instead he tugged the zip shut on her trousers, then took a firm grip on both of her hips and brought her tumbling down on his lap. Kisses on the mouth were much less evocative than kisses elsewhere. This way at least he would manage to hang onto some of his dignity if anyone should happen to walk in here.

By the time the kissing stopped, her eyes were glazed—but then so were his. 'I'm going to send you packing now,' he told her huskily.

'But you would rather come with me.'

It was no lie. 'If that tattoo hurts later, we are going to have a row,' he warned.

'It won't,' she stated confidently.

The telephone on his desk began to ring. Maybe it was good timing on its part because it put a stop to what was still promising to develop into something else.

'Up,' he commanded, and used his hands to set her back on her feet, then urged her towards the door. 'Now go and don't come back.' On that brisk dismissal he reached out for the phone. 'And leave my labourers alone!' he added as she was about to walk out of the door.

She turned, sent him a look that stirred his blood. Then she caught him off guard, yet again. 'I did it for you, you know,' she softly confided. 'You're going to love it, I promise you.'

'Ethan Hayes,' he announced into the telephone, as he stood up to open the blinds so he could watch Eve walk towards the car he had hired for her to use.

The whole site had come to a stop. He watched it happen, watched her take no notice of any of the remarks that flew her way. He also saw her pause, look back and wave to let him know that she knew he was watching her. By the time she'd turned away again he knew that his own departure wasn't going to be that far away.

He was right, but for the wrong reasons. 'Ethan—' it was Victor '—you are not going to like this, but I need to ask you to do me a very big favour...'

Eve had been back at the villa for less than half an hour

when she heard Ethan come in through the door. Not expecting him for hours yet—even with the invitation she had left behind her earlier—she had just curled up in a shady spot on the terrace with the book her grandfather had given her for her birthday. It was a rare first edition of classical Greek love poems to add to the collection he had been building for her since her first birthday.

But the moment she heard Ethan's step, the book was forgotten, a look of surprised delight already lighting her face at this major triumph in managing to get him to come back early because he couldn't resist the invitation she'd so blatantly left him with.

'I'm on the terrace!' she called out and uncurled her feet from beneath her then stood up to go and meet him halfway. She reached the door through to the sitting room as he appeared in the arch leading into it from the hall. He stopped, she stopped. It took less than a second to make her welcoming smile fade from her face when she saw the expression on his. It was like being tossed back eleven days to that bar on the Caribbean beach, he looked so different.

CHAPTER FIFTEEN

'WHAT'S wrong?' she asked sharply, absolutely sure that something had to be, because no man changed so very much in such a short space of time without having a reason for doing so.

He didn't reply, not immediately anyway. Instead he built the tension by grimly yanking the tie loose from his collar and tossing it aside then releasing his top shirt-button before issuing a heavy sigh.

'We need to talk,' he said on the back of that sigh. That was all, no warm greeting, no teasing comment about the little red heart she was wearing for him.

Fear began to walk all over her self-confidence, 'W-what about?'

'You and me,' he replied, ran a hand round the back of his neck as if to attempt to ease the tension she could see he was suffering from. 'We've been living a lie for the last ten days, Eve. Have you ever stopped to think about that?'

Think about it? She lived with it! Ate, slept and made love to it!

'For me it stopped being a lie from the first time we made love, Ethan,' she answered. 'So maybe you had better tell me whether you've thought about it much recently.'

Her sarcasm hit a nerve, but instead of an answer he made a grimace that she just did not like. Something had happened; it had to have done to change the man she had left only an hour ago into this person who was so uptight she could actually feel his tension cutting through the air like a sharp knife. And worse: he had stopped looking at her.

'I have to go away for a few days,' he suddenly announced.

That was the root of all of this tension? 'Well, that's all right,' she murmured, unable to believe that was the answer to what was bothering him. Forcing herself to walk forwards on legs that weren't all that steady, she tried to look calm as she placed her book down on a nearby table then turned to look expectantly at him. 'Business?' she asked.

'Yes—no.' He changed his mind and began to frown. 'It's more an errand of mercy…' Then he muttered, 'Damn this, Eve—I'm trying to find out if you intend to still be here when I get back.'

Was that all? Staring at him, Eve couldn't believe the sense of relief that went flooding through her. 'Of course!' she exclaimed. 'Why ever not?'

For some bewildering reason, her reply only filled him with exasperation and he strode forward to grasp her left hand then lifted it up to her face. 'Because this ring,' he uttered tightly, 'will become a formal engagement ring on Saturday in Athens. So if you want out, you have to say so now.'

'Do you want out?'

'No.' He sighed. 'I do not want out. I just needed to know where I stand with you before I—'

'Well, I don't want out,' she cut in softly, and her smile came back to her eyes, to her slightly quivering mouth. 'I want you.'

He loved that mouth, Ethan reaffirmed something he already knew. He loved this woman. But was her 'I want you' enough to make him declare himself?

Was it enough to get him through the rest of what he

had to tell her. 'Enough to trust me?' he therefore had to ask.

'Trust you about what?'

Well, here it comes, he thought, the bottom line to all of this. He took a deep breath, let it out again, desperately wanted to kiss her first, but held back on the need and looked deep into her beautiful green eyes. 'Victor Frayne called me as you were leaving the office. He needs a very big favour from me. Due to unfounded rumours involving me and his daughter Leona, her marriage is under threat. So I am flying out to Rahman to help scotch those rumours—at her husband Sheikh Hassan's request.'

He added Hassan's name to give it all sanction. He hoped it would hold a lot of sway. But silence came back at him, though it wasn't really silence because Eve's eyes told him a lot; their warm green slowly froze over until they'd turned to arctic frost. Her kissable mouth became a hard cold untouchable line, and loudest of all, she snatched her hand out of his and curled it into a tight fist at her side.

'You're still in love with her, you bastard,' she whispered.

'No.' He denied it. 'Leona needs—'

'To know she still has you dangling on a string.'

Coming from the very woman who had him dangling, Ethan couldn't help but laugh at that.

Eve's response was to step around him and walk coldly away.

She had never felt so betrayed. He'd manoeuvred that discussion, worked it and her like a master conductor until he'd got her to say what he'd wanted to hear, before he'd told her what he'd known she had not wanted to hear.

And for what purpose? Had he received a telephone call from her grandfather also? Did he now know, as she did, that the Greek project was about to be awarded to Hayes-Frayne?

'Don't do this, Eve,' he threaded heavily after her.

She didn't want to listen—refused to listen, and just kept on walking out of the sitting room and down the hall into the bedroom. *Their* bedroom. The one they'd been sharing since the first night he'd brought her here. She hated him for that. She now hated him so very badly that she could barely draw breath over that burgeoning hate.

He arrived in the doorway just as she was flipping her case open on the bed. A sense of *déjà vu* washed over her; only, last time this scene had been played their roles had been reversed.

'Eve—this is important.' He tried an appeal.

She almost laughed at his choice of words, coming hard on the back of what she had just been likening this moment to.

'We are talking about an Arab state here—a Muslim state where women are held sacrosanct. The smallest hint of a scandal and she can be cast out into the wilderness without a single qualm. I have to go.'

'I'm not stopping you,' she pointed out.

'This is stopping me!' he rasped back angrily.

'Okay.' She turned on him in the midst of her own sudden fury. 'You don't go and I don't go!'

It was the gauntlet tossed down on the tiles between them. Ethan even looked down as if he could see it lying there—while Eve held her breath, though it didn't stop her heart from thundering madly in her ears, or fine tremors from attacking her flesh.

Because this was do or die. He chose her over Leona or it was finished for them. He knew that, she knew that.

His eyes lifted slowly, dark lashes uncurling to reveal stone-cold reservoirs of determined grey. 'The rumours are lies,' he stated. 'Just a cruel and ruthless pack of lies put about by Sheikh Hassan's enemies with the deliberate intention of forcing him to reject his wife and take another one. His father is dying. A power struggle is on. Leona is caught right in the middle because she cannot bear his child. Those who don't want to unseat Hassan from power are pressurising him to take a second wife who can give him that child. If you have one small portion of understanding what that must be like for her, then you will accept that I cannot turn my back on her need for my support now.'

'How does your going to Rahman scotch those rumours?' Eve questioned with an icy scepticism that made him release a short tight laugh.

'If you knew the ways of Arab politics you would know that no Arab would invite his wife's lover into his house,' he explained. 'I am to be placed on show.' The laughter died. 'Held up in front of Rahman's best and most powerful as a man Hassan trusts and admires. And if you think I'm looking forward to that, then you're wrong,' he grimly declared.

'So you love her enough to put her needs before your own pride,' Eve concluded. And that was what this was really all about. Not whether he went or whether he stayed. It was about whether he still loved Leona enough to do it. The rest was just icing to cover an ugly cake.

'I'm going home, to Athens,' she told him flatly. 'This is it. We are finished.'

Ethan released another very bitter laugh. 'Well,' he said, 'at least you managed to do what you set out to do. You gave yourself two weeks to get around to jilting me. You're even slightly ahead of time. Well done, Eve.'

With that, it was Ethan who walked away.

Why? Because he had his answer. If she'd loved him,

she would have trusted him. If she'd cared about anyone but herself, she would have understood why he had to go.

Funny really, he thought, when only five minutes later he walked out of the villa and climbed into his car. A bit of encouragement on Eve's part and he would probably have invited her to go to Rahman with him. She would have enjoyed the novelty of watching him be foisted up as a pillar of good old-fashioned gentlemanly honour, when she knew the real man could take a sweet virgin and turn her into a sex goddess.

Too late now. He didn't want a woman that couldn't trust his word, and she didn't want a man who didn't jump to her bidding every time she told him to. On that most final of thoughts on the subject of Eve Herakleides, he started the car and drove out of the courtyard then turned to skirt San Estéban so he could meet the main road to Malaga.

While Eve still stood where he had left her, staring at nothing, feeling nothing—was too scared to feel.

The sound of the front door closing only five minutes later came as a big shock though. She hadn't expected him to leave so soon. She hadn't realised the end was going to be so quick and so cold.

She even shivered, found herself staring at Tigger who was sitting where he always sat, on the table beside the bed. He was looking at her as if to ask what kind of fool she was.

Well, she knew she was a fool. She'd worked so very hard to bring Ethan to the point where he'd want her to keep his ring on her finger. Now she'd thrown it all away.

Was that good or bad? Staring down at the ring, she watched its sparkle grow dim behind a bank of tears, and knew her failure was not in making Ethan want her, but in failing to make him love her.

Malaga airport was packed as always. Ethan arrived just in time to catch his flight to London, where he would have time only to go to his apartment, catch a couple of hours' sleep then pack a bag before he was due to link up with Victor for their trip to Rahman.

Eve took the easier option, and rang her cousin Leandros to beg the use of his helicopter to take her to Malaga. Therefore she arrived long before Ethan got there, and had taken off for Athens by the time he pulled his car into a long-stay slot.

London was cold. He didn't mind; the heavy grey skies suited his mood. It wasn't until he thought to check his emails before shooting off to meet Victor, that he found a note from his secretary telling him that Theron Herakleides had come out of hiding and was now making hopeful murmurings about Hayes-Frayne being awarded the Greek project.

'Well, shoot that in the foot,' he told the computer screen, and switched it off. As of now, Hayes-Frayne could kiss goodbye anything to do with Greece.

He wished he'd kissed Eve goodbye before he'd left…

Athens was hot, stifling beneath one of its famous heatwaves. Eve was glad to let the taxi cab drive her up into the hills where the air was more fit to breathe. Her grandfather's mansion house stood in a row of gracious old houses occupying one of the most prestigious plots the rambling city had to offer.

He was just sitting down to dinner when she walked in, unannounced. 'My angel!' he greeted in surprise, and got to his feet to come down the table for his expected embrace.

He was not expecting her to burst into a flood of tears though. 'Oh, Grandpa!' She sobbed as she walked into his arms. 'I hate him. I hate him so much!'

CHAPTER SIXTEEN

THE palace of Al-Qadim made an impressive sight standing against a backcloth of a star-studded night sky. Its rich sandstone walls had been flood-lit from below and, as they drove through the arched gateway into its huge inner courtyard, Ethan was reluctantly impressed with the sheer scale and beauty that met his eyes.

But he didn't want to be here. He was angry and fed up with role-playing for other people's benefit. He was sick to his stomach with the Mr Honourable tab people seemed to like to stick on him. The Mr you-can-depend-on-me-to-bale-you-out label.

He grimaced. Somewhere back there across a large tract of land and an ocean, he was being summarily sacked from his latest role with the none too tasty word *jilted* to wear as an epitaph to that little affair. While here, he was about to become the focus of critical Arab eyes, when he received his second sacking in twenty-four hours from the role as wicked lover to the Sheikha Leona Al-Qadim.

'Ethan—if you don't want to go ahead with this, then say so,' Victor murmured beside him.

'I'm here, aren't I?' he answered tersely, but then his whole manner had been terse since he'd climbed into his car in Spain and had driven away from Eve.

Eve the flirt, Eve the temptress, Eve the serpent, who'd made the last two weeks a perfect paradise—before she'd reverted to her original form. And what was that? he asked himself. Eve, the spoiled little rich girl, who wanted everything to go her way.

159

He was best out of it. He should have known that before it began. He should have seen the idiot he was making of himself every time he let her weave her magic spells around him.

The trouble was, he'd liked it. He'd liked playing slave to Eve Herakleides and her whims. She turned him on, hard and fast. She made him feel alive.

She'd had a heart temporarily tattooed onto one of her most erogenous spots just to tease him out of his mind.

'Only, in this mood, you aren't what I would call sociable,' Victor inserted carefully.

'Watch me turn on when the curtain goes up,' he promised. 'I'll be so sociable with your son-in-law that they will start to wonder if it's Hassan I've been having the affair with.'

'Don't be facetious.'

Victor was getting angry. Ethan didn't particularly blame him.

'You should have brought her with you if you can't last a day out of her arms without turning into a grouch.'

'Who are we talking about?' Ethan's eyes flashed a warning glance at the other man.

Victor just smiled one of those smiles that people smiled around him these days. 'I might not have been to San Estéban recently, but even the London-office cleaner knows about the *souvenir* you brought back from the Caribbean.'

Souvenir from hell, he amended bitterly.

Then he saw her expression just before he'd turned his back on her for the last time, and his insides knotted into a tight ball. He'd hurt her with all of this. He'd known that he would. That's why he'd tried to find out where she'd wanted their relationship to go, before he'd told her about this trip.

He'd wanted her to understand. He'd wanted her to trust him. See, for goodness' sake, that he couldn't be in love with another woman when she possessed every single inch of him!

So—what now? What was he doing here? A sudden and uncontrollable aching tension attached itself to his bones. He should be back there, arguing with Eve, not snapping at Victor! She was right in a lot of ways: he should have put her feelings first!

Oh, hell, damn it, he cursed.

The car came to stop in front of a beautiful lapis-lazuli-lined dome suspended between pillars made of white marble. Beyond the dome he could see a vast entrance foyer glittering beneath Venetian crystal. Victor got out of the car. Ethan did the same. As they stepped towards the dome, he shrugged his wide shoulders and grimly swapped Eve-tension for play-your-part-tension—so he could get the hell out of here.

Dressed in black western dinner suites, white shirts and bow ties, he and Victor stood out in a room filled with flowing Arabian colour. He saw Leona straight away. She was wearing gold-threaded blood-red silk and she looked absolutely radiant. Beside her stood the man she had adored from the first moment she'd set eyes on him just over five years ago, Sheikh Hassan Al-Qadim—who looked unusually pale for a man of his rich colouring.

Had the strain of the last few weeks begun to get to him? Victor had relayed some of what had been going on. Hassan had been fighting the battle of his life to keep the wife of his choice by his side *and* retain his place as his father's successor as ruler of Rahman. He had achieved success on both fronts—by the skin of his teeth.

Other than for this one last thing…

The hairs on the back of Ethan's neck began to prickle.

A brief, smooth scan of the room showed him what he had expected to see. People were staring at him—in shock, in dismay, in avid curiosity.

Were they expecting a scene? Were they looking like that because they expected Hassan to call for his sword and have his head taken off?

The prickle at the back of his neck increased, when what had been meant as a bit of sardonic whimsy suddenly didn't seem that whimsical at all. Then common sense returned, because what use would it be to have his head severed from his shoulders when all that would do would be to prove that Hassan believed the rumours about his beautiful wife?

What he was doing was far more subtle. The man had style, Ethan was prepared to acknowledge when, on catching sight of him standing here next to Victor, Hassan did not reveal a hint of the old dislike that usually flashed between the two of them. Instead Ethan saw him smile, then gently touch Leona's arm to draw her attention their way.

Leona turned to towards them. By now the room was held enthralled. Her lovely face began to lighten. A pair of stunning green eyes, that somehow were not quite as stunning to him as another pair of green eyes, flicked from her father's face to his face then quickly back again. Then, on a small shriek of delight, she launched herself towards them.

It seemed as if the whole assembly took a step backwards in shocked readiness for her to reveal her true feelings for this western man. Tall, lean and in very good shape for his fifty-five years, Victor Frayne received his daughter into his arms and accepted her ecstatic kisses to his face while Ethan felt the room almost sag in relief, or disappointment, depending on whether they were friend or foe to Sheikh Hassan Al-Qadim.

'What are you doing here? Why didn't you tell me?' Leona was scolding her father through a bank of delighted tears.

'Ethan—' She turned those starry eyes on him next and reached out to capture his hand. 'I can't believe this! I thought you were in San Estéban!'

'I only spoke to you this morning in London.' She was talking to her father again.

'No, a hotel, here.' Her father grinned at her. 'Thank your husband for the surprise.'

Hassan appeared at Leona's side to lay a hand on her slender waist. Leona turned those shining eyes onto him. 'I love you,' she murmured impulsively.

'She desires to make me blush,' Hassan said dryly, then offered his hand first to his father-in-law then to Ethan. 'Glad you could make it,' he said congenially. 'We are honoured to receive you into our home.'

'The honour is all mine,' Ethan replied with a smile that held only a touch of irony to imply that there was more to this invitation than met the eye.

Hassan sent him a slight grimace, then looked down at Leona who was too excited to notice any of the undercurrents flowing around her.

She didn't know, Ethan realised. She had no idea that he was here to help save her reputation. His estimation of Sheikh Hassan rose a couple of notches in recognition of the lengths he was prepared to go to for his love of Leona.

Could he have ever loved her like that? Looking at her laughing, beautiful face, he found himself superimposing another laughing, beautiful face over the top of it, and had to ask himself if he'd ever loved Leona at all? For this other face didn't just laugh at him, it teased and flirted and sent him secret little come-and-get-me smiles that made his insides sing. This other face looked at him and loved him.

Loved him? He stopped to question that.

Loved him, he repeated. His legs almost went from under him as his heart sank like a stone.

It was there, he could see it. It was there. He'd been blind!

'Ethan, are you feeling okay?'

He blinked and found himself looking down at Leona's anxious face. 'Fine.' He smiled. 'I'm glad to see you looking so happy.'

Stupidly, utterly, totally blind!

'I am!' She smiled. 'Deliriously happy.'

I need to get out of here...

'Good,' he said. 'This time make sure you hang onto it.'

In solemn response, she linked her arm with Hassan's arm. 'Hanging on,' she softly promised him.

He was supposed to laugh so he did laugh. Half the room turned to stare at the two of them and because Hassan must have seen all his hard work going down the tubes, he suddenly laughed as well and so did Victor.

As if cued by this brief moment of danger, another diversion was suddenly grabbing everyone's attention. People stopped talking. Silence rained down on the whole assembly as Hassan's half-brother, Rafiq, appeared pushing a wheelchair bearing Sheikh Khalifa ben Jusef Al-Qadim.

Ethan had only met the elderly sheikh once before, five years ago at his son's wedding. But he still couldn't believe the changes wrought since then. The old man looked so thin and frail against the height and breadth of his youngest son—a wasted shadow of his former self. But his eyes were bright, his mouth smiling and, in the frozen stasis brought on by everyone's shock at how ill he actually looked, he was prepared, and ready to respond. 'Welcome—welcome everyone,' he greeted. 'Please, do not continue to look at me as if you are attending my wake, for I assure you I am here to enjoy myself.'

After that everyone made themselves relax again. Some who knew him well even grinned. As Rafiq wheeled him towards the other end of the room, the old Sheikh missed no one in reach of his acknowledgement. 'Victor,' he greeted. 'I have stolen your daughter. She is now my most precious daughter, I apologise to you, but am not sorry, you understand.'

'I think we can share her,' Victor Frayne replied smilingly.

'And...ah.' The old sheikh then turned to Ethan. 'Mr Hayes, it is my great pleasure to meet Leona's very good friend.'

He had the floor, as it should be, so no one could miss the message being broadcast. 'Victor...Mr Hayes...come and see me tomorrow. I have a project I believe will be of great interest to you... Ah, Rafiq, take me forward for I can see Sheikh Raschid...'

And there it was, Ethan saw. In a simple exchange of pleasantries, the rumours had been scotched, dismissed and forgotten, because there wasn't a person here who would continue to question Leona's fidelity after Sheikh Khalifa himself had made his own opinions so very clear.

The old sheikh moved on, the spotlight shifted. For the next couple of hours, Hassan consolidated on what his father had put into place by taking Ethan and Victor with him around the room and introducing them to some very influential people.

I'm going crazy, Ethan decided. Because here I am smiling and talking to a lot of people I don't even care about, when I could be somewhere else with someone I do care about.

And where was Eve? Was she still at the villa in San Estéban, or had she made good her word and gone back to Athens? He wanted to know. He needed to know. His mobile phone began to burn a hole in his pocket.

In the end he couldn't stand it. He left the throng and went outside to see if he could get a signal. It wasn't a problem, so he stabbed the quick-dial button that would connect him to the villa, then stood breathing in the jasmine-scented night air while he waited to discover what his fate was going to be. What he got was the answering machine, which told him exactly nothing.

Frustration began to war with tension in his breast. Someone came to stand beside him. It was Hassan, looking less the arrogant bastard that he'd always seen him to be.

'Thank you,' Hassan said. 'I owe you a great debt of gratitude for coming here like this.'

Where it came from, Ethan had no idea, but he was suddenly so desperate to be somewhere else entirely that he knew he couldn't stay here a single moment longer. 'Do you think that debt of gratitude could stretch to a quick exit from here?' he asked curtly.

Hassan stiffened. 'You dislike our hospitality?'

'No.' He laughed. Only, it wasn't a real laugh because it erred too close to the threshold of panic. 'I just need to be somewhere else.'

She was calling him. Like the witch she was, she was casting a spell somewhere, he was sure of it. He could feel her tugging him back to her like a dog on a lead. And he wanted to go back. He didn't even mind the lead he could feel tightening around his neck. He wanted his woman. He *needed* his woman.

Maybe he knew. Maybe Sheikh Hassan Al-Qadim

wasn't all self-centred arrogance. Because he simply glanced at him, just glanced, once, read something in his face—heartache, heartbreak, heart-something anyway—and with a click of his fingers he brought a servant running.

'Have my plane made ready for an immediate departure,' he instructed smoothly. 'Mr Hayes, your transport to…somewhere…awaits,' he then drawled sardonically.

CHAPTER SEVENTEEN

EVE was casting spells in the garden. They wound around a tall, dark, idiot Englishman with no heart worth mentioning.

She wasn't happy. Everyone in her grandfather's house knew that she wasn't happy. She'd rowed with Grandpa. No one had ever heard Eve row with her grandpa.

But, like the Englishman, she had come to realise that Theron Herakleides had no heart either. He'd let her down. When she'd needed his comfort and support more than she'd ever needed it, he had withdrawn both with an abruptness that shocked.

'No, Eve,' he said. 'I will not let you do this.'

'But you don't have a say in the matter!' she cried.

'On this point I do,' he insisted. 'I gave you two weeks to come to your senses about that man. When you did nothing but claim how much you adored him, I gave in to your wishes, soft-hearted fool that I am, and went ahead with planning tonight's party. You are not, therefore, going to make the Herakleides name look foolish, by cancelling at this late juncture!'

'But I no longer have a man to become betrothed to!'

'Then find one,' he advised. 'Or you will dance alone tonight, my precious,' Theron coolly informed her, 'with your honour lying on the floor by your pretty feet and the Herakleides pride lying beside it.'

'You don't mean it,' she denounced.

But he did mean it. Which was why she was sitting in the garden wondering what she was supposed to do about a party she didn't want, meant to celebrate a betrothal she didn't want, to a man who wasn't here to share either even if she did want him!

Where was he?

Her heart gave a little whimper. Was he with Leona right now, worshipping the unattainable, while her long-suffering husband played the grim chaperone—just to save face?

I hope they've had him thrown into a dungeon, she decided savagely. I hope they've cast him out into the desert with no food and water and definitely no tent!

But *where* was he? her stupid heart cried.

Today was Saturday. Yesterday she'd left a message on the answering machine in San Estéban asking him to call her. Couldn't he have done that at least? He owed her that one small consideration for all the love she'd poured into him.

I want him back. I *don't* want him back. She stood up, sat down again, let her hands wring together, looked down to find the thumb from the right hand rubbing anxiously at a finger on the left where Ethan's ring used to be.

I miss it. I miss him. Come and get me, Ethan! Oh, good grief, she never knew anything could feel this wretched.

'Eve...'

'Go away, Grandpa.' She didn't want to speak to anyone.

'There was a telephone call for you—'

'From Ethan—?' She shot eagerly back to her feet. Seeing the pity in her grandfather's eyes made her wish the ground would open up and swallow her whole.

What have I let that man do to me?

'It was Aidan Galloway,' her grandpa told her. 'He is on his way from the airport. I said you would be glad to see him.'

'Why?' Her green eyes began to spark with aggression. 'Are you thinking that Aidan could stand in as substitute?'

It made her even angrier when he dared to laugh. 'That is not a bad idea, sweetness,' he mused lazily. 'He will be here in a few minutes. I will leave you to put the suggestion to him.' With that he strolled off, still grinning from ear to ear.

He was enjoying this, Eve realised. It amazed her that she hadn't realised before what a twisted sense of humour her grandfather possessed. Her life was on the line here— her one hope at happiness—and he thought it was funny to watch her tear herself apart?

Theron did pause for a moment to wonder whether he should put her out of her misery and tell her what he already knew. He had been in touch with Victor Frayne about the Greek project. Victor Frayne had, in turn, told him about Ethan's quick departure from Rahman.

If the man wasn't coming to claim his granddaughter, then his name wasn't Theron Herakleides. Keeping Eve unaware of this prediction was good for her character. Good things came too easily for Eve, he'd come to realise. She had sailed through her life without feeling the pangs that hunger breeds. She had wit, she had grace, she had charm and intelligence, and she knew how to use them all to reach her goals with ease. But love stood on its own as something that must be worked at if it was to develop into its fullest potential. Feeling the sharp-edged fear of losing love should make her appreciate and heed the fear of losing it again.

Why did he feel she needed to do that? Because Ethan Hayes was a man of hidden fibre, he'd discovered. To keep up with the sneaky devil she was going to have to learn dexterity and speed.

Ethan landed in Athens and had to utilise some dexterity

and speed to get through an airport that the rest of the world had seemed to decide to use at the same time.

He managed to grab a taxi by jumping the queue with the help of a British fifty-pound note. The drive through the city set his teeth on edge. The heat, the crowded streets, the knowledge that he had taken a chance and come here directly from Rahman, instead of checking out San Estéban, all helping to play on his stress levels. So, by the time he passed through the gates of the Herakleides mansion, he was beginning to regret this madly impulsive decision to chase after Eve.

The taxi pulled to a halt in front of a stone-fronted residence built to emulate Greek classicism at its most grand. A maid opened the door to him, smiled in recognition of the times he had been here before. When he asked to see Eve, she offered to take his suit bag from him then directed him towards the garden at the rear of the house.

His heart began to pump with the adrenaline rush of relief because he now knew his instincts had not let him down and he had been right to miss out San Estéban to come straight here.

It was mid-afternoon and as he stepped out onto the wide stone-flagged terrace the air was just taking on the warm golden glow that reminded him of the Caribbean. Striding forward he paused at the head of a set of wide shallow steps which led down into the garden. Standing on a hill as the house did, the garden itself sloped away from him in a riot of summer colour, so from up here he should easily be able to pick out Eve.

He did so immediately. It would have been impossible not to do when she was wearing a hot-pink stretchy top with a short lavender skirt. She stood out in this garden of colour like the most exotic flower ever created. As his heart began to pound in response to wrapping all of that vivid colour to him and never letting go of it again, he saw her move, realised that she wasn't alone, realised that she was also standing in the exact same spot he had seen her standing the last time he'd seen her here—and locked in the arms of the same man.

Aidan Galloway—she was locked in the arms of Aidan Galloway! Lightning was striking twice again, using a burning blast of cynical reality to hit him full in the face.

Aidan Galloway. It was a joke. He almost laughed. Only he didn't feel like laughing. Turn, he told himself. Leave, he told himself. Get away from here before she sees you and knows what a bloody fool you've made of yourself.

'Oh, Aidan,' Eve sobbed into his shoulder. 'I've made such a fool of myself!'

'Join the club,' Aidan said.

'He isn't going to come, and I've left this stupid message on his machine…'

'Now it's playing over and over in your head. I know.' Aidan sighed. 'Been there, done that, felt the agony.'

'I hate Ethan Hayes.' She sobbed into his shoulder.

'I wish I could learn to hate Corin,' Aidan murmured wistfully.

'Oh.' Eve touched his cheek. 'Is she still—?'

'Yes.'

Eve playing Eve, Ethan observed bitterly, as he watched her lift up her head and gaze into Galloway's eyes.

He felt his muscles go into violent spasm, as a need to go down there and commit murder swelled in his chest. He was about to take his first step towards assuaging that desire when a hand touched him on the shoulder, making him spin round and almost explode all that violence on Theron Herakleides instead.

'Come back inside, Mr Hayes,' Eve's grandfather said quietly.

'That's Aidan Galloway she's with,' he heard himself murmur hoarsely.

'Yes, I know it is.' Theron's steely head nodded. 'But angry men do not confront weaker men. So come inside,' he repeated the invitation. 'I have a matter I would like to discuss with you.'

Business, Ethan surmised, and shrugged the older man's hand from his shoulder. 'Keep your business proposals for someone else,' he said. He had taken enough from other people trying to direct his life. 'I'm leaving.' And he turned to stride back into the house.

Theron followed. 'Take care, Mr Hayes, what you say right now,' he quietly advised. 'For a man can still be chased through the courts here in Greece, for jilting his betrothed...'

There were several words used in that comment that stirred Ethan's blood. Jilting, was one of them, he chose to challenge another one. 'There was no betrothal,' he coldly denied. It was all just an elaborate sham thought up by the manipulating witch wearing hot-pink.

'How many witnesses do you think will I find in San Estéban who would be willing to swear the opposite to that?'

Ethan stopped walking, turned and looked at Eve's grandfather, aware that there was still more to come.

'Ah,' Theron said. 'I see you understand me. Then we will go in here and continue to discuss the small matter of a settlement...'

With that, Theron opened the door to his study and walked inside. After a small hesitation, Ethan followed him with the word settlement ringing warning bells in his head.

Theron's study was furnished to suit the man's big persona. Heavy furniture filled the floor space, heavy-framed portraits adorned the walls.

'So,' the big man began as he slotted himself behind his heavy oak desk. 'Did you really think that you could send my granddaughter back to me like used and broken goods without paying a heavy price?'

Broken. That word made Ethan release a hard mocking laugh. There had been nothing broken about the woman he'd seen wrapped in the arms of another man. 'Ask Aidan Galloway to pay the price,' he suggested. 'He has the money. You'll struggle to get a penny out of me.'

'Eve loves you.'

'Hell, damn it!' Ethan suddenly exploded spectacularly. 'Open your eyes, Theron! Eve only loves the thrill of the chase!'

Through the fine silk drapes covering the opened French window of her grandfather's study, Eve heard the deep rasping tones of Ethan's voice, froze for a split second, then spun around to stare at the house.

'Be assured that Aidan Galloway is more than willing to take your place tonight,' Theron smoothly replied. 'Oh, yes,' he confirmed at Ethan's sudden stillness. 'Eve's betrothal celebration will take place tonight whether or not it is you standing at her side. Eve is resigned to this. You've broken her heart, now she cares not about the man who will next share her bed.'

The words were used as well-aimed bullets that sank themselves deep into Ethan's head. Was that what Eve was doing out there—seducing Aidan Galloway to take his place? More bells began ringing, a red tide of anger came flooding in. He was very intimate with Eve's powers of persuasion. He knew only too well what it was like to fall into her sticky web.

'What do you want from me, Theron?' he demanded grimly.

'I want you to honour those promises you made to me in the Caribbean,' the big man said.

'I'll talk to her.' It was Ethan's only concession, though he was planning to do a lot more than just talk to Eve when he could get his hands on her. She played with men's feelings. She walked all over their self-respect. She made love like a natural-born seducer and he was damned if any other man was going to know how good that felt.

'Not without the right,' Theron smoothly said.

Ethan glared at him. 'Explain,' he insisted.

Theron went one better and slid several documents across the top of his desk. 'You know the score. Sign, and you can talk to my granddaughter. Don't sign, and you can leave her to Aidan Galloway's adequate care.'

Ah, Ethan thought. The contract to protect Theron's precious money. He almost laughed in the old man's face as he stepped up to the desk, picked up Theron's handy pen, and scrawled his signature in the allotted space.

'Now, if you will excuse me,' he concluded coldly.

'Don't you think you should have read what it is you've just put your signature to? It is an unwise man who signs a document without first ensuring himself that he has not just signed his entire wealth away.'

Wealth, Ethan thought. 'What wealth?' he mocked. His wealth stood outside in the arms of another man.

His wealth, his woman—hell, he was right back on track again; he felt so much better for realising that.

'You're a liar, Hayes,' Theron inserted, then suddenly let rip with a hearty laugh. 'Do you think I would let you seduce my granddaughter into marriage without having you thoroughly checked out? You are a Caledonian Hayes of the merchant shipping line. Your grandfather sold up in the sixties and died in the eighties, leaving you so much money you could even afford to buy me out!'

'Ah—my credentials,' Ethan acknowledged and the depth of his cynicism played havoc with his face. 'How long have you been planning this?' he demanded.

'Marrying you to my granddaughter? Two weeks ago you became worthy of consideration when my nephew, Leandros, let slip how much money you had invested in San Estéban,' Theron replied. 'A mere architect, no matter how gifted he is, could not earn that kind of money in a hundred years. I have an instinct for these things.' With a smugness that said he was enjoying himself, Theron touched a finger to the end of his nose. 'The nose twitched. So I decided to have you checked out for curiosity sake, you understand. And for Eve's sake, of course.'

Glancing down at the document he had just put his signature to, Ethan began to wonder what he had signed away. 'It won't do you any good,' he announced. 'I live off my earned income. Any money my grandfather left me is tied up in trusts for any children I might have.'

'Or my grandchildren.' Theron nodded. 'Exactly.'

So that was what this was all about. 'Eve is up for sale to the man with the biggest return.'

From sitting there wallowing in his own self-satisfied smugness, Theron was suddenly launching to his feet in a towering rage. 'Don't speak about Eve in that tone!' he bellowed. 'It is okay for you with your hidden millions to stand here mocking me whose wealth is well documented. But place yourself in Eve's shoes and tell me how *she* distinguishes between the man who will love her for herself and the one with love only for the money she will inherit one day!'

'So you think that by finding her a husband who is wealthier than herself, you are safeguarding her against disillusionment and a broken heart?' Ethan's tone poured contempt all over that concept as his own fury rose to match the older man's. 'Money in the bank is no guarantee for love, Theron!' he bit out furiously. 'It's just—money in the bank! I am as capable as the next man is of breaking her foolish, reckless heart!'

'If you were the kind of man to do that, you would not be standing here arguing with me about this!'

'She already thinks I'm in love with another woman!' he threw at Theron. 'Are you telling me that your investigation of me did not tell you that?'

'If it didn't, he knows now,' another quieter, heart-piercingly level voice inserted.

CHAPTER EIGHTEEN

BOTH men stiffened sharply, both turned to stare at the silk-draped window where Eve now stood. Both men went as pale as death.

'Eve, that wasn't said to—'

The flick of a hand silenced him; the expression on her face tore him apart. She was hurting, he was hurting. Ethan didn't even want to know what Theron was feeling like. Big, green how-could-you-both-hurt-me-like-this eyes flicked from one man to the other. She took in a breath of air. It seemed to pull all of the oxygen out of the room and left none for them to breathe.

Pale but composed, feeling as fragile as a lily about to snap in the soft warm breeze, Eve took a small step to bring herself into the very male-orientated surroundings of her grandfather's study, and announced. 'If you've both finished playing Russian roulette with my future. I would like to point out that women gained the right to choose for themselves some time during the last century.'

'You break my heart, child,' her grandpa told her painfully. 'I would be failing in my duty to you if I did not make this man formally declare his intentions.'

'He doesn't have any intentions!' Eve slashed at him.

'Yes, I do,' Ethan argued.

She turned on him, eyes burning like phosphorescence as they fixed themselves onto his. His chest swelled, his heart began to pump, other parts of him began to send taunting little signals out across his skin. She was waiting to hear more. More was coming, if he could only get past the sight of her in Galloway's arms.

'Will you marry me, Eve?' There, he'd said it.

'Oh.' She choked, and her eyes filled with tears. 'How could you let him browbeat you into saying that?'

'I didn't.' He was shocked.

'I'll never forgive you for this—never.' She sobbed, turned and ran outside leaving Ethan staring after her in thundering dismay!

'I would go after her if I were you,' Theron smoothly advised while calmly reading the contract Ethan had just signed.

On an act of sheer frustration Ethan snatched the document out of Theron's hands. 'I am sick and tired of other people meddling in my life!' he announced, then turned and walked out of the study—by the conventional route of the door through to the hallway.

Outside he was a mass of offended dignity. Inside he was bubbling with angry offence at the way Eve had rejected him. He'd had enough. Eve was impossible. He was happy to let Aidan Galloway have her. He strode down the hallway with every intention of leaving this house and never stepping foot in it again.

As he crossed the foot of the stairs, he heard a door on the upper landing shut. His feet came to a stop. Bubbling offence had changed to something else entirely, and he knew he wasn't going anywhere but up those stairs to open her shut door.

On a lethal curse, he changed direction. As he took the stairs, two at a time, he had even reached the point of asking how he thought he could walk away, when he could feel that lead still attached to his neck.

She tugged, he went where it pulled him.

Eve stood in the middle of her bedroom and shook from

fingers to toes. She couldn't believe he'd said that. She couldn't believe she'd actually looked her dearest in the face then had turned and had walked away from it!

How could he—how *could* he stand there in her grandfather's study wheeling and dealing her life away? He was just like Grandpa: money orientated, power orientated! If she had any sense left she would get out of here. She would disappear somewhere so remote that she would never be found! She hated men—all men. Young, old, they were all the same: arrogant self-obsessed bullies who liked to think they were in control of everything.

The bedroom door suddenly flew open. She spun round to find Ethan standing there. 'If you've come to offer another proposal of marriage then don't bother!' she snapped.

'You will have to get down on your knees to get another one of those out of me,' Ethan grimly returned.

Her knees tried to buckle. Eve felt like screaming. He looked lean and hard, and tough and angry; the bitter expression on his face was spoiling its handsome lines. She liked it. It meant he was hurting. If he was hurting then it had to be because of her—didn't it?

'Then what do you want?' she demanded coldly.

'You,' he said, 'to explain to me what the hell were you doing wrapped in Galloway's arms the moment my back was turned!'

The door slammed shut. Eve's eyes began to fire. 'What were *you* doing leaving me to go to *her*, just because she crooked her little finger at you?' she countered furiously.

Eve folded her arms across her front. Ethan leaned back against the door and did the same. Stalemate. They'd been here before. Excitement began to fizz in the air. Green eyes flashed with it; grey glinted with it. She wanted to go over there and kiss him stupid.

'It was hell,' he pronounced. 'I didn't have any idea how

rife the rumours were until I saw the way my arrival was received. I half expected to die the death of a thousand cuts!' He released a short laugh.

'You are still in love with her,' she tossed at him in pained accusation.

'No, I am not,' he tossed right back. 'I am in love with you—God help me!'

'Oh,' she said.

'Yes,' he agreed in grim, tight mockery.

'Then you shouldn't have gone!'

'You should have come. You would have enjoyed the spectacle.'

'You should have invited me.'

'If you hadn't been so pig-stubborn, I probably would have done.'

'Oh,' she said again, and silence settled.

Eve wanted to fill it by throwing herself into his arms and kissing her way back into his good graces. Ethan wanted to fill it by throwing her on that bed he could see across the room and loving her absolutely senseless.

Instead they both looked at the papers he held in his hand. Eve recognised them for what they were; resentment began to flare again.

'Rip it up,' she told him.

'Why?' he asked. 'He's only got me to sign my life away.'

'I don't want your money.'

'I didn't say money, I said life!' He flashed her a hard look. 'Are you telling me you don't want that, either?'

Her chin went up. Two steps and she was snatching the contract from him just as he had snatched it from Theron.

Eve ripped it up. She tossed it to the ground. She placed hands on hips and waited for his eyes to move up from the torn contract to her provocative pose, to her mouth which was wearing its angry pout, and finally to her eyes shot through with challenge. 'Okay,' she announced. 'I'll take your life.'

Ethan reached out, pulled her hard up against him then kissed her... Why not? It was what they both needed. Eve didn't so much as attempt to pull away.

'Now, tell me why were you kissing Aidan Galloway,' he murmured some very satisfying seconds later.

'I wasn't kissing him,' Eve denied. 'I was sobbing on his shoulder because you weren't here and I wanted you to be.'

Ethan brought up a finger to gently touch the corner of her kiss-trembling mouth. 'And the last time I saw you with him like that?' he probed. 'You weren't sobbing then.'

'You misread what you saw that night,' she explained, slid out her tongue and licked his finger and watched as his eyes grew darker in response. 'Aidan had just seen Corin wrapped in a heated clinch with his cousin. They were childhood sweethearts; he's adored her all of his life. He was devastated, I was comforting him when I heard them coming towards us, and I just reacted by kissing Aidan to give Corin a taste of her own nasty medicine.'

'Impulsive as usual.' He sighed.

'Well, you should know.' She flashed. 'When I realised you'd seen us, I knew what you would be thinking. So as soon as I could safely leave Aidan, I *impulsively* went to your room to explain. Only...'

'You found me standing there stark-naked, and decided it was more fun to stare me into embarrassing myself?'

'If that's what you like to think.' She wasn't taking the bait. Instead she caught hold of his finger then fed it across the surface of his own mouth. Already moistened by the tip of her tongue the finger left a film of moisture on his lips.

He licked it off. Sex was suddenly alive in the air. 'You can't control yourself around me,' she informed him smugly, 'which is why you made sure you kept your distance from then on.'

His own hand came to remove her teasing finger. 'You tease and flirt without conscience,' he condemned.

'Your fault,' she blamed. 'The more you disapproved of me the more outrageous I became.'

'Dangerous is the word that comes to my mind.'

He was referring to Raoul Delacroix, Eve realised. It altered the mood so abruptly that Ethan gave a sigh of regret when she withdrew right away from him then walked over to stare out of the bedroom window with her arms crossed over her body in a gesture he recognised as Eve needing to protect Eve.

He followed, unwrapped her arms and replaced them with his own. 'I'm sorry,' he said. 'I didn't mean to resurrect bad memories.'

'I've known Raoul almost all of my life,' she murmured. 'We—all the crowd on the island have been meeting up for holidays there since we were small children. Flirting and teasing was part of the group culture but no one ever took it further than that.'

'But he decided to.'

'We hadn't seen him for a couple of years,' she explained. 'When he came back to the island this summer, he'd changed. We all noticed it, wondered why, but Raoul refused to talk about it. So we drew our own conclusions and decided it had to be a failed love affair or a fall-out with his brother, André, for whom he'd always nurtured a resentment. But never in my wild imaginings did I think he had changed so much that he was capable of pulling something like that.'

'Forget it, it's over.'

'But maybe it was my fault. Maybe I did lead him on.'

'You know that isn't true, so we aren't getting into that,' Ethan said firmly.

Eve pressed back against him and said no more. Beyond the window she watched her grandfather's car taking off down the driveway. The roof was folded away so she could see Aidan sitting next to him. They would be going to a local café where they would drink coffee while Aidan told her grandfather all his woes, and her grandfather would relay wise advice, previously discussed and decided upon with Aidan's older brother, Patrick. It was how it had always worked since Eve had lost her parents and Aidan had lost his in the same car accident, leaving Grandpa to play the role of wise counsellor to both families. Strange really, she mused. But, thinking about it, Raoul had shown signs of resentment to that closeness too.

'Where's your ring?'

Glancing down, she realised that her hands were lost in the clasp of his and his thumb was stroking her naked ring finger in much the same way as her own had been doing every since she'd taken the ring off.

'Tigger has it,' she said.

'And where is Tigger?'

'In my dressing room with his friends.' She went to move. 'Do you want me to go and—?'

'No.' He stopped her. 'We haven't finished here yet.'

'Finished what?' Foolishly she turned in his arms to face him—foolishly, because she should have guessed what was coming, but didn't; so his kiss when it arrived took her breath away.

It was fierce and it was greedy. It brought her hands

around his neck and placed his hands on her hip-bones so he could pull her close. She came alive for the first time in too many days to dare think about.

He whispered something into her mouth. 'Marry me,' he said.

'I'm not on my knees.'

'You can go there later. Just say yes.'

'Yes,' she said.

Ethan released a soft laugh. 'Now tell me you love me.' He was going for broke here.

'I love you,' she softly complied.

After that, things moved on a pace. They found the bed, they lost their clothes, Ethan found his little red-painted heart. 'We shouldn't be doing this here,' he thought to remark when it was already way too late. 'This is your grandfather's house. It shows a lack of respect.'

'I don't recall you being so sensitive when you seduced me in Victor Frayne's house,' Eve pointed out.

It more or less put the lid on his conscience so that he could sink himself into what he had started.

Later, much later, they lay in a tangle of satiated limbs. 'You do know I love you to distraction, don't you?' he told her solemnly. 'Leona was—' He stopped, then started the same sentence from a different place. 'I think I only ever loved the idea of loving someone like Leona.' He thought that said it best. 'But in Rahman, when I looked at her, I couldn't even see her face because your beautiful face insisted on imprinting itself over the top of hers. No, don't cry.'

'I'm not crying.' But there were tears in her beautiful eyes, nonetheless. 'I just needed you to say that.'

It cut him to the quick—which he knew he deserved. 'I'm sorry I didn't say it a long time ago.'

She wound her arms around him; he drew her close.

They sighed together as their mouths joined. No complicating sex this time, just love and caring and—'

'Get dressed,' he decided suddenly.

'Why?' she protested. Eve was perfectly happy where she was.

'We are going to play the rest of this relationship by the book. So we get dressed, then we will go out and find you something amazing to wear in hot-pink for our official betrothal tonight. Then we get married—next week,' he added as a frowning afterthought. 'Because I don't think we can behave ourselves for longer than that.'

'You won't last a week,' Eve informed him a short ten minutes later as they left her room and his hand was already checking out the smooth line of her bottom.

'I suppose you are going to make it your mission to prove yourself right.'

'Oh, yes,' she said airily. 'I love a good challenge.'

She won, but then she usually did. Eve the flirt, Eve the temptress, went to her marriage bed every night that week.

The Salvatore
Marriage

MICHELLE REID

CHAPTER ONE

THE storm raging outside was killing the signal. Shannon uttered a soft, tense little curse as trembling fingers reset her cell-phone then hit 'redial' before pushing the phone back to her ear.

Fear was crawling over her skin like a swarm of invading spiders. She couldn't stop shivering—or was she trembling? She didn't know, didn't care, she just needed—*needed* to make this connection.

'Come on…' she prayed with teeth-gritting tension when still nothing happened.

Five minutes ago she had been dashing from a taxi to her apartment block with no other concern than to get out of the driving rain. She'd had a hell of a day from the moment she'd overslept that morning. In her haste to catch her flight to Paris, she'd rushed out of her flat forgetting to pick up her cell-phone as she left and had felt lost without it all day.

On top of that, her meeting had not been worth the time she had wasted on it. Temperamental supermodels and gifted graphic designers just did not mix, she'd discovered, especially when the supermodel in question took one look at the graphic designer's slender, long-legged figure and re-garded her as an instant threat. Why the heck the idiot had conjured up the idea that a five-foot-eight redhead could compete with a six-foot-tall sylph-slim blonde with cheek-bones to die for was anyone's guess. But all hope that the model was going to let Shannon design her self-promoting website went out of the window then and there.

Since then Shannon had flown back to London through the worst weather imaginable, struggled to get a taxi, then had got soaked getting from it to here. The first thing she saw on stepping through her front door was her cell-phone lying on the hall table, innocently telling her that she'd received a dozen missed calls—most of which were from her business partner Joshua demanding to know why the hell she wasn't answering her phone.

But it was another message awaiting her that had sent her mind into a complete meltdown. 'Shannon,' it said. 'Call me back on this number as soon as you can. There has been an—accident.'

An accident— Her throat closed on her effort to swallow. The relater of the message had not left his name but through the static his deep, smooth, accented voice had been familiar enough to put her into this state of raw panic. She guessed that the call was from her sister's husband Angelo—and if Angelo had left such a message then it could only be because the accident involved Keira.

'Damn,' she muttered when still nothing happened, and was hitting redial again when the doorbell gave a short, sharp ring.

Distracted, she turned to walk down the hallway, barely noticing that she had to step over the bag she'd left dumped in the middle of the floor as she made her way to the front door. A set of harried fingers made a wild scrape through the silk straight weight of her rain-dampened hair before continuing on to grasp the door latch. The phone still wasn't connecting. She tugged the door open, too preoccupied to wonder who might be standing on the other side of it so it came as a shock—a cold, hard, breath catching shock to find the last person on earth she ever expected to see standing there.

He stood over six feet two inches tall and was wearing a long black overcoat. The width of his shoulders almost spanned the doorway. For a few awful moments Shannon actually felt dizzy enough to clutch at the door while he stood there filling the opening like some dark, chilling force.

'Luca.' Dear God, she thought as her lips framed his name on a stunned whisper.

He didn't utter a single word but just reached out with a hand to ease the phone from her numbed fingers, then began ushering her backwards by the economical means of taking a step forwards.

Her breath feathered against her ribcage, the fact that she wasn't yelling at him to get the hell away from her said a lot about her state of near complete shutdown—though she did manage to register that both of them moved without touching anywhere. Like a dance between two opposing magnets, they made the manoeuvre into her hall without breaching each other's defensive space until she was standing with her back pressed against a wall, eyes wide and fixed unblinkingly on him as he turned his back on her and in grim, grim silence closed the door.

The size of her hall suddenly shrank to nothing, she felt strange suddenly, as if she too were shrinking into herself in an effort to get away from what she was being faced with here.

This man, this larger-than-life figurehead of the vast Salvatore empire. Luca Salvatore, of Florence, a man of power and of unrivalled passion. Ex-lover to Shannon Gilbraith, woman of sin and sister to his brother's wife.

He was also the man she had been going to marry. The man she had lived with like a wife for six wonderful months before it had all come crashing in. She'd loved him passionately; now she could barely have him look at her without feeling her heart wither in his presence.

He turned slowly to face her, shedding raindrops from his wide shoulders as he did so and filling the confined space with the smell of cold air and rain on wool. His long lashed gaze flicked her a glance then slid away to take in the bag dumped on the floor.

'You've been away,' he murmured levelly. His English was perfect, smooth and deep with the kind of accent that played across her senses like the brush of a lover's—

Don't go there, she told herself. 'P-Paris,' she said.

He nodded his dark head as if she'd just confirmed something for him, though for the life of her she couldn't work out what. She was shaking all over, racked by too many confusing conflicts, aware that she should be thinking about her sister but able to think only about him.

Keira… Her throat convulsed on a wave of anguish, the flat of her palms pressed into the wall. Lifting anxious blue eyes to the hard, tight lines of his profile, she parted her lips to demand he tell her what had happened to Keira, but Luca spoke first.

'Are we alone here?' he questioned, and when she just gaped at him, unable to believe he had dared to ask that question, he decided to find out for himself. Stepping over her bag, he began opening doors.

Shock was replaced by burning dismay when she realised what he was doing. Two years ago Luca had arrived at his apartment in Florence to find her making a hurried attempt to cover up the evidence of what she had been doing while he'd been out of the way. What followed had been a gruesome demonstration of what came to pass when you played a Salvatore for a fool.

That time he had dragged her from room to room with him as he'd checked all the places in which she could have hidden a lover. This time he was prepared to make the search on his own—not that he had any right to do so.

'You bastard,' she breathed, and found the strength to push herself away from the wall and walk on trembling legs into her sitting room.

She hadn't had a chance to come in here, she realised,

staring blankly into the room's chilly darkness that was soft-ened only by the halogen glow from an outside street lamp filtering in through the window. It was automatic to reach for the nearest switch and flood the room with proper light—automatic to cross to the window to tug the cream curtains over the rain-soaked glass.

When she turned she found him standing in the doorway staring at her through narrowed dark brown, gold-flecked eyes set in a face that wore the proud stamp of his Florentine lineage. He was handsome but hard; handsome but cold; forge a statue in his image and you would have yourself a reflection of a modern-day god.

But this man was no god, she reminded herself quickly. He might have the face and the body of one, might possess the kind of power and arrogance the old gods liked to wield, but inside he was as mortal as anyone. Flawed and fickle, she concluded as she waited for the shock to ease so that the old bitter emotions could come flooding in.

Emotions like pain and anger, and the miserable ache of a love cruelly ripped away from her—a passionately pro-fessed, returned love that she'd learned the hard way had never gone more than skin-deep for him.

It didn't happen. Standing here white-faced and tensed in readiness for it all to surge up and grab her, Shannon dis-covered that she continued to feel absolutely nothing, not even a slight twinge of that old sense of desperation with which mere thoughts of him used to fill her. Those eyes that used to turn her heart inside out were leaving her cold now, as did the slender mouth that used to act like a magnet to her own hungry lips. The slashing high cheek-bones, the dark golden skin, the magnificent body hidden beneath the heavy coat; she used to worship all of them with every touch, every breath or sensual homage she could find. The man in his whole god-like entirety was doing nothing for her any more.

It came as such a relief, because it had to mean that she was over him.

Over him at last and for ever.

'Satisfied with your search?' she asked with acid-tipped sarcasm. 'Or would you like to check behind the curtains too?'

There was a hint of a frown before he acknowledged the comment with a small grimace.

'No,' was all he said and he shifted his gaze to take in the décor with its soft pastel shades and neat modern furniture that was such a contrast to the antique luxury he'd furnished his own home with. Her small twin sofas were covered with cream linen, her floor was of pale polished wood. His floors displayed priceless rugs thrown over intricate inlaid wood parquetry and his sofas were made of rich brown leather that were big and deep enough to stretch out upon two at a time to canoodle and kiss in exquisite—

Once again she was forced to bring her wandering thoughts up short. Why recall all of that when it no longer meant anything? she asked herself crossly, and moved across the room to flick another switch, which sent flames leaping up over designer logs resting on a bed of pale pebbles in her open hearth.

This time when she turned she found that his attention had switched back to her again, his hooded gaze moving over her pencil-slim skirt with its natty little kick pleat at the back, which gave her long legs a rather sexy shape. Did he like her legs? Of course he liked her legs; he used to worship them with his hands and his mouth and the teasing lick from his tongue as it trailed upwards on its way to—

Oh, stop it! she told herself. He looked up suddenly, as if she'd said the words out loud. Their eyes connected. Tension erupted to rush screaming round the room on the back of a mutual, intimate knowledge that would never go away no matter how much they both might want it to.

They'd been lovers, gorgeous, greedy, sensually indulgent lovers. They knew every inch of each other, what made the other sigh with pleasure and what would send them toppling over the edge. But those thoughts did not belong here—*he* didn't belong here!

Say something, damn you! she wanted to scream at him. But he'd always been good at using silence to whittle down people's nerves, and he continued to stand there looking at her as if he was waiting for *her* to say something. Say what? she wondered. Was he expecting her to invite him to sit down?

The phrase about burning in hell first whipped through her head.

Maybe he heard it. Maybe he was still able to tune himself in to what was going on inside her head because the black silk lashes flickered slightly as he shifted his gaze yet again and fixed it on something over her right shoulder.

Shannon didn't need to look to know what it was that had now caught his attention. It had to be the framed wedding photograph standing alone on a shelf that showed the sweet face of her sister Keira smiling adoringly up at his handsome brother Angelo.

Behind the blissful couple and fortunately out of focus stood Luca, playing the dauntingly sophisticated best man to the groom and herself as the young and self-conscious chief bridesmaid. Luca had been all of twenty-eight years old to her own meagre eighteen at the time, but they'd enjoyed each other's company that day.

Odd, she thought, that she should remember that now when there were so many bad things about Luca she could be remembering instead.

'I think it might be best if you sit down.'

Muscles all over her body jerked suddenly, bringing her chin up sharply as her senses leapt in alarm. When someone told you to sit down it could only mean they were about to tell you something that was guaranteed to take the legs from under you, and the only way this man could do that to her was by bringing her bad news about—

'What's wrong with Keira?' she shot at him sharply.

A hand came out; long-fingered and lean, it indicated to one of the sofas. 'When you sit down,' he countered, then watched calmly as if he was expecting it as she sparked like a firework.

'Oh, stop being so bloody sensitive to my feelings, Luca, and tell me what's happened to my sister!' she cried. 'All I got was some static-splashed message telling me that there had been an accident and would I ring a stupid mobile phone number that did not exist!'

'It exists,' he murmured.

And like a lightning strike Shannon suddenly realised what a terrible—terrible—mistake she had made. 'It was your mobile number, wasn't it?' she bit out accusingly, struggling to believe that she could *ever* have mistaken the deep, terse tones of his voice for the warmer tones of his brother Angelo. 'Poor Luca,' she mocked with sudden bitterness, 'being forced to give the wicked witch his new number and risk a second flood of unwanted calls.'

His half-grimace acknowledged her right to toss that remark at him. Two years ago she'd tried every which way she could use to get him to talk to her. She'd called him on his cell-phone night and day until suddenly the number had been no longer obtainable. He'd cut off his main source of contact—just as she'd been ruthlessly cut off from everything else that had been important to her.

'Just speak, damn you,' she prompted huskily.

With a grim pressing-together of his lips, Luca looked ready to continue holding out until she sat down. Then she saw his eyes make a flickering inventory of the way she was standing there, fine-boned and slender enough that the tremors now shaking her body almost forced her down. Stubbornness held her upright; stubbornness and a defiance that had always been one of her most besetting sins in his eyes— though not her worst sin.

Then—no, she slammed a door shut on that kind of thinking. Stop going there! she told herself angrily. Don't think about anything. Don't even bother to notice the way he's looking at you again with a contempt he believes you deserve. So he hates and despises you. Let him, she invited. I don't care—I don't.

He moved then, and on a thick, inner quiver of fear she saw his expression alter from hard to grave. His eyes flicked away. He heaved in a deep breath. The fine hairs on her body started to tingle as he parted his mouth to speak.

Then the words came. 'There has been an accident—a car crash this morning,' he told her. 'People are hurt—badly hurt,' he then extended grimly.

'Keira—?' Her sister's name arrived as a fragile whisper.

'Yes.' He nodded. 'And I need you to be strong here, Shannon,' he warned then, 'because the prognosis is not good and we need to— Oh, hell—you mad, stubborn *idiota*!'

Shannon didn't know she'd swayed until his hands arrived hard on her shoulders and forcibly manoeuvred her into the nearest sofa. She landed with a bump, eyes wide and staring.

'Why can you *never* take good advice when it is offered to you?' he ground out as he came down on his haunches and took a strong grasp on her ice-cold hands. 'It was a simple request—a *wise* request. You almost collapsed as I knew you would. You are your own worst enemy, do you know that? I cannot believe you are still such a—'

She tugged her hands free. The action silenced his angry tongue, snapped his lips together and tightened the muscles in his face. In the new silence that developed Shannon struggled to get a hold of what was trampling through her. Her heart was palpitating wildly, her breathing reduced to tight and shallow catches of air. Keira was the only person left in this world that she truly cared about.

Keira, her beautiful Keira, whom everyone loved and wanted a piece of.

'Tell me what happened,' she whispered unevenly.

His mouth had developed a white ring of tension around it. She had to look away because she couldn't bear to see him while he said what he had to say. 'They were in the fast lane on the main *autostradale* into Florence when they ran into a heavy downpour of rain,' he explained. 'An articulated lorry skidded on the wet surface. It cricco-accoltellato—jackknifed directly in front of them, swerving right across the road. They did not stand a chance,' he uttered in a voice like thick gravel. 'With no room or time to take avoiding action they hit head-on and—'

The words stopped when he was forced to swallow. Silence returned, crawling all over the two of them while Shannon sat staring over the top of Luca's dark head as the whole wretched thing played itself like a macabre action movie in front of her eyes.

'Is she—?'

'No,' he cut in quickly—roughly.

Relief feathered through her, then she tensed again as the next dreaded thought flipped into her head.

'They. You said *they*,' she prompted shakily, and looked at him then, really looked at him and saw for the first time the strain etched into the fabric of his lean, hard features—and the pain burning in the deep, dark depths of his eyes. Realisation dawned, the muscles in her own face began to collapse, tears of a desperate, desperate understanding flooding into her eyes.

'Oh, no, Luca—no,' she choked out unevenly. 'Please,' she begged, 'not Angelo…'

But the answer she wanted to hear didn't come, and as a

set of her cold fingers jerked up to cover her trembling mouth Luca muttered something thick in Italian, then lowered his head to bury his face in his hands.

Dark mists of shock and grief wrapped around them. For what could have been an age Shannon couldn't move or think or even feel. Angelo and Keira—Keira and Angelo—the two precious names spun in her head on an ever dizzying spiral while the rain lashed wildly at the window and Luca remained squatting in front of her with his face covered and his wide shoulders taut as he fought his own battle with shock and grief.

Luca and his brother were close. They worked together, played together, laughed and talked together all the time. To think of one without thinking about the other was—

'Oh Luca…' Lifting her hand with its trembling fingers, Shannon gently touched them to his rain-dampened hair. 'I'm so s—'

It came without warning. At the first light brush of her fingers he was thrusting away from her with a violence that left her stunned and shaken as he climbed to his feet, turned his back on her and strode away several paces to then stand still and rigid while he fought a battle with his moment of complete collapse.

When he turned to face her he was back in control again, or as controlled as a man could be who'd just lost the brother he loved. Shannon hadn't moved, and as his gaze lashed over her she saw the ice, the cold hatred, and knew what he was thinking. He was thinking he did not deserve to lose his brother and she did not deserve to have her sister still.

Yes, she thought, he hated her enough to think like that.

Bitterness returned, and with it came a welcome sense of foggy calmness. Shannon climbed to her feet, wished with all her aching heart that she could just walk away from him, but there were still things she needed to know.

'Y-you said the prognosis for Keira isn't good,' she prompted, feeling the shake in her voice as well as in the fingers she used to smooth down the rucked fabric of her slender skirt. 'Why isn't it good?'

The tense shape of his mouth slackened slightly as he parted his lips to speak. 'Her injuries were extensive. She had to be cut out of the car—'

Shannon flinched and lowered her eyes from him, painfully aware that the *they* had now changed to *she*. Did that mean that Angelo had been beyond help? She didn't ask, didn't dare, didn't think she could cope with the answer.

'By the time they freed her, Keira had lost a lot of blood,' Luca continued in a low voice like rough sandpaper. 'Thankfully she was unconscious throughout so was aware of—nothing…'

The *nothing* broke into uneven fragments, and as her heavy lungs tried their best to breathe for her Shannon wondered if Angelo had been aware of nothing.

Angelo. An ache hit low in her stomach. Never to see his lazy grin again or the teasing gleam in his beautiful eyes— 'Oh,' she choked and her legs went hollow, forcing her to sit down again and cover her face with her hands.

'There were problems,' Luca pushed on relentlessly, obviously deciding to get the whole wretched thing said now he had begun. 'Some of which the doctors could fix, some they—could not…'

It was during this next thick pause Luca allowed to develop—presumably to give her time to absorb what he'd said—Shannon suddenly remembered something she should not have forgotten: there was still yet another being involved in this awful tragedy.

A sudden rush of nausea forced her to swallow thickly. Sliding her hand away from her face, she looked up at Luca, her eyes dark and haunted. 'Oh, God, Luca,' she whispered frailly. 'What about the baby?'

Her sister was seven and a half months pregnant—the longest period Keira had managed to carry a baby, one of her many, many attempts to bear Angelo a child. His eyelashes flickered, lowering over dark brown irises to hide his own feelings about what he was about to say. 'They had to do a Caesarean section,' he informed her briefly. 'Keira was haemorrhaging badly and it became a matter of urgency that they deliver the baby as quickly as they could—'

The abruptly spoken words came to a stop again. It seemed that he could only give information in short bursts before he had to pause to gather himself. It was all so dark and utterly wretched, shock piling upon shock upon horror and grief and blood-curdling dread.

'And…?' It took a tight clutching at her courage to prompt him to continue.

'A girl,' he announced. 'She is quite small and needs the aid of an incubator to breathe, but otherwise the doctors assure us that she is fully formed and perfectly healthy. It—it is her mama that gives grave cause for concern. Keira now lies in a coma and I'm afraid the final outcome does not look good.'

In the cold, dark silence that followed, Shannon knew she was slipping into deep shock. Angelo was dead, her sister was dying, their baby daughter needed help to breathe. It couldn't get any worse.

It could, she discovered. 'I'm sorry,' he said gruffly.

But he wasn't sorry, not for her at any rate. It was too late for him to murmur polite words of sympathy when he'd looked at her the way he'd done a few minutes ago. He resented bitterly the fact that he had lost his beloved brother while she, the undeserving one, could still cling to a small thread of hope.

'Excuse me,' she said thickly, 'but I'm going to be sick,' and, dragging herself up from the sofa, she made a dash for the bathroom.

He didn't follow and Shannon did not expect him to—though he had to hear her retching because she hadn't had time to close the door. But she could feel his presence like a scar on her heaving body because this was a scene they had played before, though under very different circumstances.

And remembering that ugly moment made her feel suddenly very bitter that it had to be him of all people to bring her bad news and then witness this.

Trembling too badly to stand unaided, she sank down on the toilet seat lid and tried to think. She had to plan, she had to deal with Luca on a calm and sane footing, because if she was sure about anything in this sudden dizzying nightmare she had been tossed into, then it was that he would have pre-empted her immediate needs and have had travel arrangements put into place before he had even knocked on her door.

It was the way of the man—of the Salvatore family as a whole. Incisive efficiency under pressure was their trade mark. They were rich, they were powerful, they dealt with their enemies in the same way that they dealt with tragedy, by closing ranks and, with shields in place, dealing with the situation as one dynamic force.

All for one, one for all, she mused bleakly. Then she thought about Keira lying in a hospital bed somewhere, and even as the family grieved for Angelo she knew that her sister would still be surrounded by their tight ring of protection. The image should have comforted her but instead she found herself having to make another lurching dive for the washbasin.

Why? Because she was not included. She was the outcast sent into exile for her so-called sins. And the prospect of having to break her way through the Salvatore guard to be with her own sister caused the same nauseating distress that had kept her out of Florence for the last two years.

'Oh, Keira…' she groaned on a sob of anguish. Then she thought of poor Angelo and knew that one constrained sob was not going to be enough, so she switched on the taps and wept with the rush of water drowning out the sound.

Luca wasn't in the sitting room when eventually she went back to face him. The all too familiar scent of him lingered, though, catching at her nostrils and relaying messages to certain senses she did not want disturbed. Strange how she had not picked up on that scent earlier.

Even stranger that she'd dared to tell herself that she was over him.

Well, not any longer, she was forced to accept as she turned to go and find him and spied his overcoat lying across the back of one of the chairs in the old familiar way that brought weak tears springing back to her eyes.

Something had happened to her back there in the bathroom. A door inside her had opened and allowed too many suppressed memories to come flooding out. Memories of love and passion and a promise of perfect happiness turning to dust at her feet. And other memories of a sister she had loved more than anyone. Yet when she'd left Luca she had also turned her back on Keira.

Guilt thudded at her conscience, but it fought with resentment and a deep, deep sense of betrayal that still hurt two years on. There were many ways to break someone's heart for them, she mused bleakly. Luca and Keira both had broken her heart in different ways.

She found him standing in her kitchen by one of the modern white units, his six-foot-two-inch frame dwarfing the room as it did most things—including her more diminutive size. He was in the process of pouring boiling water into her smart glass and steel coffee pot but on hearing her step he turned his dark head. For a brief moment she saw him as she had last seen him two years ago, angry, naked, the natural colour washed out of his skin by disgust and contempt and an appalling knowledge of what he had just done.

Then the image faded and now she saw a tired man living with the strain of grief locked up inside him and a knowledge that life had to go on just as duty must still be done.

He offered her a brief smile before turning away again. 'I thought we both needed this,' he explained levelly, drawing her attention to the freshly made pot of coffee he had prepared. 'I have also made you some toast to help to settle your stomach.'

Following the indication of his dark head she saw a plate sitting on the breakfast counter bearing two slices of lightly toasted wholemeal bread. Her stomach lurched again—not at the thought of receiving anything in its tender state, but because the whole scenario was resurrecting yet more memories of the old times. Times when this wealthy, very sophisticated and utterly spoiled man had surprised her with domestic moments like this.

He owned homes in many prestigious places, owned aeroplanes and helicopters and a beautiful yacht that could take one's breath away. He ran a huge multinational finance company that employed thousands of people right across the globe but he didn't like servants intruding on his privacy, suffered their services as a necessity in his busy life so long as they did their work when he wasn't there. He could cook, he could clean and he made the best cup of coffee she had ever tasted.

But here in her kitchen—acting as if he actually cared about her well-being?

Fresh bitterness welled at his damned hypocrisy. 'I'd rather be going,' she replied with as much composure as she could muster. 'That is presuming you've made arrangements for me to travel to Florence?'

'Of course,' he confirmed. 'But we do not have to leave for another hour. My plane needs to refuel and perform the usual checks then wait for a vacant slot before it can take off again.'

'You mean you've flown here from Florence—today?' Shannon was stunned and it showed in the stifled gasp she released.

'Someone had to break the news to you.' The way he shrugged a broad shoulder was meant to convey indifference to the task but they both knew it was a lie. His brother had just died in tragic circumstances. His sister-in-law lay gravely ill. His mother and his two sisters must need him desperately, yet here he was standing in her small kitchen making coffee and toast for her?

'Wouldn't a message to my answering service have been simpler?'

'Would it?' he said and only had to glance at her for Shannon to know what he was getting at. He had come in person because he knew her. He'd expected her to fall apart just exactly as she had done.

Turning with the coffee pot, he went to place it on the counter next to the plate of toast, then glanced at his watch with its thick gold strap that nestled into a bed of dark hair on a wrist built to lift heavy weights if required to do so. Everything about him was built that way. The formation of his muscular structure showed the power in him yet in some unfathomable way he still managed to appear contradictorily lean and sleek.

His suit was dark, his shirt sky-blue, his tie a slender strip of navy blue silk. Wide shoulders tapered down a long lithe back to narrow hip-bones, the power in his legs and arms lay hidden beneath the expensive cut of his clothes. He could pick her up with one hand—she knew this because he had done it once when she'd challenged him. Then they'd tumbled onto the bed in a fit of laughter because one recently bathed, slippery wet and wriggling naked female was not easy to balance by her seat.

There wasn't a woman alive who didn't have heart flutters when Luca was near them. She had done more than flutter; she'd positively vibrated. He'd personified Man in her estimation and no man since him had come close to equalling him.

'Come and eat your toast.'

The dark tones in his voice made her flesh quiver. Glancing at the plate of toast, she felt a sudden desire to tell him where to go with his demonstration of concern. She didn't need him standing about her kitchen pretending that there was nothing between them but a very loose sister-brother-in-law relationship. They'd *sank* into each other's bodies for goodness' sake! He was passionately Italian and she was passionately Irish. Both stubborn, hot tempered and as temperamental as hell. Standing here watching him stroll about her kitchen was enough to ignite her temper. But common sense was telling her to just shut up and put up if she didn't want full-scale war to break out, because she knew Luca. When his mind was made up about something nothing could budge it. She had learned that the hard way.

Bitterness welled, once more she crushed it down and wondered yet again where she'd got the stupid idea from that she was over him when here she was flailing in the middle of a stomach-curdling crisis and all she seemed able to do was think about him.

Or maybe that was it, she then consoled herself as she used a trembling hand to pull out one of the two high stools that sat in front of her white laminate breakfast bar and hitched herself up onto it. Maybe obsessing about Luca was her mind's way of distracting her from what was really threatening to tear her apart.

'How are your mother and your sisters coping?' she asked as she pulled the plate of toast towards her.

'They're not,' he replied with a blunt economy that turned her stomach inside out. Then he relented slightly, sighed and added, 'They are keeping themselves occupied at the hospital, taking turns to sit with Keira and the baby. It—helps them to be there.'

'Yes.' Shannon acknowledged her acceptance of that.

Luca used that moment to pull out the other stool and sit down beside her. His thigh accidentally brushed against hers as he reached over to pour coffee into her mug. Shannon's mind went blank—although blank was nowhere near the right word to describe the sudden burning sensation that sprang to life low in her abdomen. Nor did the word suit the sudden fire-burst of images that went chasing through her head. Images of what that thigh felt like naked when brushing against her naked thigh, images of her hand stroking along its muscle-packed length and of his hand making the same sensual journey along the silken length of hers.

The old vibrations started up, running riot round her system and warming the sensitive place at her core. In an effort to pretend it just wasn't happening, she reached for a slice of toast and lifted it to her mouth. She bit but didn't taste, tried chewing though she knew she would struggle to swallow. Her mouth was too dry and she needed that coffee.

She needed him to move away so she didn't have to feel like this. She needed to remember why he was here! Oh, God, she thought wretchedly. She was ashamed of herself—she could smell him, feel him, she could even taste him! What was it with her that she couldn't keep her stupid, rotten *appalling* thoughts under control?

Her throat closed as she tried to swallow—hot, bright tears burned in her eyes. She despised herself; she despised him for coming here and doing this to her—for showing her up for the weak-willed, shallow person she had to be to be letting him get to her at a time like this when—

'Milk?' he asked.

Shannon looked at the two mugs of steaming black coffee and recalled how little it had always taken for them to want to fall upon each other. A look, a word, an accidental touch like the light brushing of thighs and they could lose themselves quite appallingly in the pleasures of the flesh. Making love with Luca had been passionate and daring and uninhibited. He had shown her pleasure she'd never known existed, lowered her so deep into her own senses that sometimes she'd struggled to float back out again.

Only twice had he actually hurt her: the first time they'd made love and the last time they'd made love. The first time Luca hadn't understood what kind of woman he'd been dealing with and she hadn't bothered to tell him that he would be her first lover so she'd accepted all the blame. When she'd cried a little afterwards he'd wrapped her in his arms and shown her a different kind of loving with the power of comfort and a need to put right what he saw as his own failure. He had done so, of course, many times and in many, many ways.

'No,' she managed to offer in answer to his question—while her mind rocketed off to recall the second time he had hurt her.

He had been blinded by fury, lost inside a frighteningly jealous rage. He had called her everything from slut to harlot and she had been so appalled that he could see her that way that she'd riled him on with biting sarcasm until he had snapped.

And it had not been the compulsive roar of sex that followed that hurt her, but the contempt with which he'd cast her aside afterwards that had ground her emotions to dust. Since then—nothing. No word, no contact—not even an acknowledgement to say that he had received back his ring.

Therefore—yes, she reiterated very grimly, she was over Luca Salvatore. The simple act of remembering those dark times was enough to kill anything she'd ever felt for him. Even if the truth came up and hit him in the face right now as they sat here pretending to be civilised and he got down on his knees to beg her forgiveness, she would not forgive.

So let her senses respond to his closeness, she invited. Let her foolish pulse quicken and her weak flesh vibrate and her shameful head try recalling the good times if it felt it had to do. But the bad times would always overshadow those good times.

'I'm going to pack a bag.' Getting up with an abruptness that startled him, she walked away without sparing his over-still, over-watchful frame a single fleeting glance.

CHAPTER TWO

LEFT alone in the kitchen, Luca stared into his mug of coffee and wondered grimly if she had actually seen him at all through that glaze of shock that covered her eyes.

Did he really care? he then questioned in outright rejection of what was rumbling around inside him. He already knew the inner Shannon too well to want to make contact again.

Been there, done that, he thought with a cold lack of any humour, then hunched forward and folded his hands around his coffee mug wishing to hell he hadn't come here. In the way he'd always believed that these things worked, life should have drawn a story on her beautiful face by now. She should look distinctly jaded but instead she was more stunningly beautiful than ever.

Lies, all lies, he contended tightly. Those too-blue eyes had turned lying into a fine art. The same with her lush, soft, kissable mouth and the way she held her chin so high whenever she allowed herself to look at him.

Challenge and contempt. He'd seen both in her face before he'd felled her with the news. What did she think gave her the right to look at him like that when she had been the one who had taken another lover into his bed?

His bed. *'Dio.'*

Letting go of his cup, he sprang to his feet on an explosion of anger and disgust, versus a strange, unwanted, stomach-clutching fight with regret.

She had been his woman. In every way he had ever looked at it he had been her man—her love, her for ever after. It had been in her eyes, in her smile, in the way she'd taken him inside her, so why—*why* had she thrown it all away?

A harsh sigh sent him to stand by the kitchen window. The rain was still lashing down outside, the night so stormy it promised to be a rough flight out of England.

Irritation shot down his backbone. Why had he come here?

He wished he knew. He wished he knew what it was that was driving him. Had he really believed that he was man enough to bury the past in this time of tragedy and deal with this situation with understanding and compassion? Or had his motives been driven by something much more basic than that—like a need to assuage this thick bloody grief churning around inside him by witnessing some sign of remorse or regret for what she had thrown away?

Well, so much for the compassion scenario because one look at her standing there at her door, one glance at the way she cowered back against the wall, and his stupid head took him back to the last time he'd seen her cower like that. So he'd pulled the lousy trick with the doors and deserved the contempt she'd thrown back at him for doing it.

And as for signs of remorse?

'*Dio,*' he grated.

He was a fool for coming here in person. He was a fool for expecting to see remorse from a woman who had shown none when she'd been caught cheating on him. He should have stayed where he belonged in Florence with his mother and sisters. He should have left a message on her cell-phone as she'd suggested— There's been a car accident, your sister is dying and my brother is dead.

'Hell,' he cursed. '*Hell!*' as his own brutal words ground his body into a clutch of agony.

Angelo—dead.

His heart began to pound like the rain on the window.

He caught sight of his own iron hard reflection washed by tears he knew he could not shed.

He turned his back on it, grabbing at his neck with tense fingers as the violence within him built like a great balloon making him want to hit something—anything to offset this black pain!

Keira and the baby—he reminded himself forcefully. Think only about them because with them there was still life and where there was life there had to be hope.

On that stern lecture he tugged his cell-phone out of his jacket pocket and stabbed in a set of numbers. Discovering the storm was ruining his signal did not improve his mood. Pocketing the phone, he went back to the sitting room to use Shannon's land-line, hoping that they wouldn't get grounded here until the storm blew over. The sooner they got to Florence, the sooner he could walk away from her.

He was amazed at how badly he needed to do that.

He heard Shannon moving about in the hall while he was still on the telephone. He kept his back to the door as he listened to what his mother was saying and kept his own voice dipped to low-toned Italian as he asked questions, received answers, and felt Shannon's stillness in the door-way like an electric charge to his spine.

The call ended, he turned. She had managed to snatch a quick shower and a change of clothes, he noticed. Gone was the sexy skirt she had been wearing, replaced by faded denims and a sweater that almost blended with her creamy skin. Her hair was up, caught in a neat knot that dowsed most of the flames. But what the prim style took away it then gave back by enhancing the delicate shape of her small oval face, her incredible blue eyes and soft little mouth, which could look Madonna-like but were really weapons of sin.

'No change,' was all he said in answer to the question he could see hovering on her lips.

No change, Shannon repeated to herself. Was that good

or bad? No change said that Keira was still hanging in there. But no change also meant that she was still in a coma, which was no reassurance at all. She wanted to know more— needed to know more and even opened her mouth to demand Luca tell her more. Then changed her mind when she was forced to accept that knowing would probably make her fall apart again and she had to keep herself together if she wanted to get through the long hours of travelling that lay ahead.

So she made her voice sound composed when she said, 'I need to use the phone if you've finished with it. I have to let some people know that I won't be around for a while.'

A nod of his dark head and Luca took a step sideways. Dark clothes, dark eyes, dark everything, he seemed to cast a heavy shadow across her light and airy room. Picking up the receiver, she felt the heat from his grasp still lingering. For some stupid reason, feeling the intimacy that heat evoked made her throat ache all the more as she tapped in the number of her co-partner at the busy graphic design company she and Joshua Soames had built together.

As she murmured huskily, 'Hi, Josh, it's me...' Luca turned and walked out of the room. His shadow remained, though, casting a pall over everything. Taking a deep breath in preparation for a shower of sympathy and concern she just didn't want to have to deal with right now, she began to explain.

Luca reappeared while she was making her second call to confirm that her neighbour still had the spare key to her flat so she could keep an eye on it for her.

'Thanks, Alex, I owe you one,' she murmured gratefully. 'Dinner when I get back? Sure, my shout. It will be something to look forward to.'

The dull throb of silence returned once she'd replaced the receiver. Luca was shrugging into his overcoat and his profile could have been cast in iron. 'Anyone else?' he asked and, at her reply, he flashed her a hard smile. 'Only the two men in your life? You are a consistent little thing, Shannon, I will say that.'

Her response was to walk away without giving him the satisfaction of answer. His reasons to be bitter—imagined or otherwise—were his prerogative, but his right to take cheap shots at her now, when other things were so much more important, filled her with fresh contempt. She wasn't going to explain that Alex was a woman and that Josh was the man who'd saved her life when *Luca* had done his best to ruin it!

He was standing by the front door when she came out of her bedroom wearing a long black woollen coat and a hat pulled down over her ears, both of which had become essential accessories during the winter the UK was enduring this year.

'Is this it?' he asked without making eye contact. In one hand he held her suitcase, in the other the padded black bag that contained her laptop computer.

Settling the strap to her handbag on her shoulder, 'Yes,' she replied. 'Do you have a car outside or do we need to use mine?'

'I have a hire car.'

Turning away, he opened the door and stepped out onto the landing, then went to call the lift while Shannon locked up her flat. They rode the lift like perfect strangers, and left the building to walk into driving rain. Luckily his hire car waited only a few yards away. Using a remote control to unlock it, he swung open the passenger door to allow Shannon to get in and out of the rain before he strode round to the boot to stash her things, finally arriving behind the wheel wet through.

Neither had thought to catch up one of the umbrellas she kept by the front door. Neither seemed to give a damn. As the car engine fired Shannon turned her face to the side window. With only a swipe from a hand across his wet face, Luca ignored the raindrops running down the back of his neck and set them moving with the grim desire to get this over with as quickly as it was humanly possible.

He was angry with himself for making that comment about her personal life. It had placed him in the position of sounding hard and nasty, and could have given the impression that he cared when he didn't. She could have as many Alexes as she liked lining up to take their turn in her bed. Joshua Soames was a different matter. Luca knew all about her close friend and business partner because Keira never ceased to talk about how their graphic design venture had taken off like a rocket from the moment the two of them had begun to trade. The two partners had been friends throughout university, both excelling in computer design. Luca had listened to Keira spouting proud things about her sister even that far back. Only his mood had been more indulgent then—his mind remembering a rather cute, if self-conscious, freckle-faced teenager with a head of gorgeous hair in a pale blue taffeta bridesmaid's dress that managed to wear her rather than the other way around. She'd simply amused him then. He'd *liked* her because despite all her teenage awkwardness she'd had a tongue like a whip, which had entertained him all the way through Keira and Angelo's long wedding breakfast.

Needless to say it was the image he'd used to conjure up of Shannon whenever Keira had mentioned her younger sister. So when, four years later, she'd arrived on her first visit to Florence and he'd found himself confronted by the grown-up version, he had been completely blown away.

Beautiful, he thought, and tightened his grip on the steering wheel. Astoundingly, fascinatingly beautiful. The freckles had gone; her body had filled out to take on a shape that was truly spectacular. And instead of teenage awkwardness he'd been faced with a supremely self-confident graduate with a hunger for life and lethal gift for flirtation. She'd plied him with coquettish looks and her plans to start up her own design company with Joshua Soames and take the world by storm. Older, wiser, and as cynical as hell about people with ideals so grand, he'd listened patiently, answered all her eager questions about financial management, and found it was *he* who was taken by storm.

The first time they'd kissed it had been meant as a brotherly salutation to finish off the evening they'd just spent together listening to Puccini. She had been eager to go to the opera and he had been happy to take her. They'd shared a candlelit dinner at his favourite restaurant afterwards and, even though he had known by then that he was getting in too deep, he had held onto the arrogant belief that he still had control of the situation—until that kiss.

Grimly driving them out of the city now in weather so foul a duck would find shelter, he felt his lips heat at the memory. He had not intended it to be a meaningful kiss, just one of those light exchanges you shared with someone you'd spent a pleasant evening with. But Shannon had fallen into that kiss with the same all-out enthusiasm she threw at life. It had shaken him, sent his libido soaring to a place it had never known was there.

Bringing the car to a halt at a junction, he checked the road either way and used the opportunity to cast a brief glance at her. She was sitting there with her head turned away and that silly little hat pulled down over her ears. Something hot shot from his heart to his loins, then stayed burning there. Only Shannon had ever made that connection, only she had ever been able to turn him into a mass of raging hormones without needing to try.

Ten years his junior, yet divided by almost a millennium's difference in life experience, she'd caught him, trussed him up and packaged him in a box marked 'taken'—by the woman with the amazing hair, the stunning face, a fantastic body and an insatiable set of desires that had him balancing on the edge of fear that she might decide to find satisfaction elsewhere.

Well, he'd got his wish, if that was what he had been looking for. And he should have been relieved he'd found out before he'd placed the wedding ring on her finger. Yet oddly he hadn't been—not once the first flush of anger had worn off, that was. All he'd felt then was regret because at least a wedding ring would have given him a reason to go after her—haul her back by her lovely hair and make her pay for daring to betray him.

Instead he'd enjoyed two years of long, hard, festering about what should have been. And in that time bitterness had turned his view of women so sour he hadn't been able to touch one since.

A great legacy for her to chew on, if she ever found out she'd rendered him impotent, he grimaced as they drove through rain like sheets of ice.

If he throws me one more nasty look I think I might turn round and hit him, Shannon decided as she sat watching his profile via the side-window reflection. Up to now she had watched him slice her one look of utter blinding derision, several of disgust and two of seething sexual denunciation. The roads were bad enough without him distracting himself from his driving by thinking lewd and hateful thoughts.

A slave to his ever-raging libido, she thought. Sex was all that Luca knew. Not *Love* but *Sex*—give me, I need, I want, I have to have. Physical, insatiable, inventive and so good at it that it was no wonder his reputation went before him. Variety—he used to say while grinning unrepentantly when she used to face him with grapevine chatter—is most definitely the spice of life. She should have realised then that she was nothing but a brand new and exciting variety he simply had to try out.

Love? Not this man. He had no idea of the concept if it

didn't attach itself to some physical act. The word? Oh, he'd known how to use the necessary words to gain the required responses. I love you. *Ti amo mio per sempre l'innamorato.* Whispered words in sensual Italian that could seduce a woman to mush.

Then suddenly she was a slut and a harlot, a woman beneath his dignity to know. One mistake—not even *her* mistake—and she had been put out in the cold so fast, she was still dealing with the shock of it two years later.

Over him? she asked. No, she wasn't over him. She was still too angry, bitter and hungry to draw blood to be anywhere near getting *over* what Luca had done to her.

'We will never take off in this weather,' he gritted.

Tears pricked her eyes at the sudden realisation that she had allowed herself to concentrate on Luca instead of on Keira yet again. Oh, may God forgive me, she thought and had to rummage in her bag for a tissue.

'You OK?' Luca had heard her telling little snuffle.

'Fine,' she said, hating him—hating him with every fiber she was made of.

'Not far to the airport,' he said more levelly.

He knew she was crying. But then, he knew her so well. Inside, outside, every which way a man could know a woman he had lived and slept with for half a year before he'd chucked her out. Gritting his teeth together, Luca withdrew inside himself, dark eyes fierce as they pierced the driving rain in his quest to get to the airport and out of close contact with the hate of his life. He had never been more relieved as he was when he saw the lights of the private airport where his plane was waiting for them. He needed some space—air to breathe that wasn't tainted with the scent of this woman.

The hire-car parking bay was under cover. Getting out, he directed Shannon to the departure lounge, then headed off in the other direction to officially hand back the car keys.

By the time he went looking for her, she had removed her hat and coat and was standing in front of the departure lounge viewing window watching the rain pelting down from the sky.

Five feet eight was fairly tall for a woman, but next to him Shannon felt small, frail, delicate. Tonight as he paused to study her slender legs encased in denim and the pale sweater she was wearing he could detect a new fragility in the slender lines of her figure. It was a frailty caused by vulnerability and fear, and realising it made him feel the worst kind of lout for letting his feelings towards her get the better of him.

Smothering the urge to heave out a self-aimed angry sigh, he decided to make it easy on both of them and give her a wide berth. Walking over to the bar, he ordered a stiff drink then remained leaning there staring down at it without drinking, unaware that Shannon had watched his reflection in the window, every grim step of the way.

He hates being here with me as much as I hate him being here, she was thinking heavily, and wished she understood why knowing that caused such a terrible ache deep down inside. She didn't love him—didn't even want to be near him any more, so she was glad when he remained by the bar instead of coming near her—wasn't she?

Forcing her eyes to focus further out into the night, she concentrated on watching the rain hitting the airport lights with almost enough power to smash the glass, while the wind buffeted madly at everything. And inside she prayed fervently that the weather would clear so they could be on their way to what really mattered.

Keira, her beloved Keira, the new baby—and poor, poor Angelo.

Maybe the fates decided to take pity on them because half an hour later Luca appeared at her shoulder. 'They think there is a hole coming in the storm,' he informed her. 'If we can board and be ready, then we might be given the chance to get away from here.'

Getting away sounded so good to her that Shannon instantly turned and went to collect her belongings from the nearby chair where she had placed them. Shrugging into her coat, she pulled on her hat while Luca pulled on his coat. Five minutes later and they were walking side by side yet a million miles apart in every other way.

Magically, halfway to the Salvatore jet the rain suddenly stopped, the wind died away and glancing up Shannon saw the stars appear through a hole in the scurrying clouds. The break in the weather helped to lift some of her fears about Keira. She was going to be all right, Shannon promised herself firmly—*willing* it to be so.

'Choose a seat and belt yourself in,' Luca instructed as soon as they entered the plane. 'I am going to check with my pilot.'

Even as he finished speaking he was disappearing through a door at the other end of the cabin and a flight attendant appeared to take her outdoor things. The man must have known that this was no pleasure trip because his expression remained sober, and once he had quietly suggested the best place for her to sit in the plush cream leather interior he disappeared, leaving her to make herself comfortable in peace.

Two minutes later the plane left the ground and shot towards the star-scattered hole in the clouds. An hour after that and Luca hadn't put in an appearance. Deciding he was deliberately keeping out of her way the same as he had done in the airport departure lounge, Shannon finally felt able to relax the guard she'd been keeping on herself, and almost immediately felt her eyelids begin to droop.

Maybe it was for the best if she slept through some of the journey, she consoled herself after trying to fight the urge for a little while. It might feel as if she was abandoning some kind of vigil she had been maintaining for her sister, but common sense told her that stuck up here she couldn't be more helpless if she tried to be.

So she let herself go, dreamed of her Keira's familiar light laughter and of sweet-smelling babies. She held her vigil there in her dreams, where everyone was whole and healthy and no dark forces came to disturb the beauty of it.

Luca sat watching her for a while, feeling oddly disturbed by how peaceful she was. She used to sleep like this, he recalled. Lying so quiet and still beside him that he'd sometimes had to fight the urge to lean over her and check that she was still breathing. A foolish notion when he had been holding her in his arms and could feel her living warmth pulsing softly against him.

Dio, stop thinking about it, he told himself and pushed his head back into the seat cushion, then closed his eyes and tried to relax. But ugly scenes began playing on the backs of his eyelids, forcing him to open them again.

Angelo—Angelo… He shifted restlessly. Men didn't weep. He wanted to weep. He wanted his brother back so he could let him know one last time how much he meant to him.

Tears began to burn like acid. He got up, hurried down the length of the cabin, then turned to pace restlessly back again. This had been the worst day of his life and it still was not over. He felt as if he had spent the day travelling the world carrying bad news like the grim reaper. He'd broken the news to his mother, to his sisters Renata and Sophia, then taken their disapproval with him to fly to London to break the news to Shannon. Now here he was flying home again with his passenger, who clearly found escape in sleep a better option than staying awake to talk to him.

Did he want to talk to Shannon about anything? he asked himself suddenly.

No, he did not.

Did he want her to wake up?

No, to that question too.

He paced away again, then turned and grimly made his way back to her side. She still hadn't moved a single eyelash. Her face was relaxed but very pale. Her lips were together, soft and flushed with their usual rose-like bloom, but if she was breathing through her nose then he could see no evidence of it, no hint that her breasts were moving up and down.

Don't be a fool, man! he told himself harshly. You know how she sleeps—you *know*! Yet still he found himself leaning over her to place light fingertips against her pale cheek.

Shannon came out of her haven of sleep to find Luca standing over her. He was so close she could feel his breath on her face. Their eyes clashed, two years shot away with the force of a gun crack and she was looking into his face as it had once looked minutes after his loving, one that had shattered her for ever. She saw anger, the contempt and dismay. She saw eyes turned black with the same emotion that had been driving him and felt the full wretched impact of hurt surge up once again.

Tears flooded into her eyes. 'I hate you,' she choked and struck out at him on impulse with a trembling clenched fist.

'Hate?' he echoed and caught the fist before it could land, closing it inside an iron grip. 'You do not understand the meaning of the word,' he bit back harshly. 'This, *cara*, is hate—'

With a tug he yanked her up against him, aiming her mouth up to his so that they collided, and he smothered her shrill cry of protest with the demanding thrust of his tongue. He kissed her in anger, he kissed her in punishment, but it was the heat of his passion that set her struggling wildly to break free. An arm snaked around her waist and she found herself standing with the front of her body clamped to his.

Her fist was released so that he could claim the back of her head and maintain the pressure of the kiss.

He ravished her mouth; he uttered thick curses deep in his throat. Her hair came loose to tumble around his fingers. He kissed her and kissed her until she stopped fighting and started trembling. Two years of abstinence and the reasons for it didn't matter any more because they were back where they'd left off, at war with each other and using sex as their weapon. She scraped her nails down his shirt front, she scored them into his hair, their lips moved in a hungry, sensuous feasting—then as suddenly as it had begun it finished.

Luca thrust her away so violently that she landed in a huddle back in her seat. Dizzy and disorientated, shocked beyond trying to think, Shannon watched him spin on his heel and stride down the cabin. When he reached the far end he picked up what looked like a bottle of whisky, poured some liquid into a glass, then tossed it to the back of his throat.

Staring at the rigid set of his shoulders, she wanted to say something—spit insults at him for daring to grab and kiss her just to prove a stupid point. But her lips felt hot and bruised and she was shaking so badly inside that she didn't think she could make the words coherent. Instead she lowered her face into her hands, let her hair fall around her like a curtain and prayed that he had been too busy punishing her to notice that she had been kissing him back.

The silence after that was like a razor blade slicing through every second they had left to travel. They landed under clear, dark Italian skies but it was cold enough for Shannon to be glad of her warm coat.

Luca had left his car in the airport car park. Shannon climbed into the passenger seat leaving Luca to stow her things. They drove towards Florence in total silence; their only exchange of words since the kiss in the cabin had been his terse information that he'd rung the hospital and there was still no change.

Familiar landmarks began to flash by her window. They were nearing Florence and the closer they got to the city, the more anxious Shannon became. Eventually the car slowed and turned in through an entrance in a high stuccoed wall. Shannon saw a building which, despite the gardens neatly surrounding it, still had the look that all hospitals had, even if this one was obviously a very exclusive place to be ill.

As Luca brought the car to a halt her skin began to prickle. Taking a deep breath in an effort to brace herself, she unlocked her seat belt and got out. Her legs began to shake as she walked towards the hospital entrance. Luca came to walk alongside her but made no attempt to touch.

She didn't want him to touch her, she told herself. But the moment she stepped into the hushed hospital foyer she was having second thoughts about that. Luca indicated towards the lifts. As they stepped into one Shannon began to feel strange—alien to herself almost.

Maybe he sensed it because as the lift doors closed them both inside, he questioned, 'OK?'

She nodded, swallowing on the build-up of tension that had begun to collect in her throat. Her body was tense, her flesh creeping with feelings no one, unless they were about to face a similar situation, could begin to understand. And she was pale; she knew she was pale because her face felt so cold and washed out.

'Don't be alarmed by the amount of equipment you will find surrounding her,' Luca seemed compelled to warn. 'It is standard practice in cases like these to monitor just about everything they can…'

He was trying to prepare her. It was all she could do to give a jerky nod of her head in response. The lift stopped.

Her heart began to pump so oddly that it made it difficult to draw breath.

The doors slid open on a foyer similar to the one they'd walked through downstairs—and Shannon's courage seemed to drop like a stone to her feet, stopping her from moving another inch.

She closed her eyes, tried to swallow again, felt her breasts lifting and falling on small tight gasps for air as a stark sense of dread closed her in. Then the lift pinged, giving notice that it was about to close its doors again. Her eyes flickered upwards at the same time that Luca shot out an arm—not towards her but to hold back those impatient doors.

His eyes were fixed on her, narrowed slightly and shadowed by concern. His face was pale, lips slightly parted on tense white teeth as if he was struggling to control an urge to make a grab for her.

'I'm all right,' she breathed in whispered assurance. 'Just give me a second to—'

'Take your time,' he said gruffly. 'There is no rush.'

No? Shannon fretfully contradicted that assertion. She might already be too late!

Too late… She groaned in silent agony. Too late belonged to the years she had avoided coming anywhere near Florence. Too late belonged to the way she had cut Keira right out of her life for months and even after they'd made up—in a fashion—she'd kept her strictly at an arm's length by being cool, being remote, piling on the guilt and the—

The lift gave another ping and kept on pinging, trying to close its doors against Luca's blocking arm. On a mammoth dragging-together of her courage Shannon made herself move. The first person she saw was Luca's mother. She looked dreadful, her beautifully defined face withered by anxiety and grief.

The ever-ready tears rushed into Shannon's eyes again,

her voice wobbling on the words that had to be said. 'I'm so sorry about Angelo, Mrs Salvatore,' she murmured in unsteady Italian as she moved on instinct, reaching out with her arms to draw the poor woman in an embrace.

It took a few seconds to realise that the embrace was not welcome. Stiff and unbending, Mrs Salvatore was accepting of her touch out of politeness—but that was all. As Shannon drew away, shaken by the cold reminder of how Luca's family felt about her, she saw the other faces bearing witness to her rejection.

Then Luca stepped up behind her, bringing his hands up to curve her shoulders in what Shannon could only describe as a declaration of some kind. He didn't say a single word, but all eyes lifted to his face, then dropped away uncomfortably.

'To your left,' he quietly instructed her.

Dry-mouthed, inwardly struck to her core, Shannon forced herself to start walking again. With Luca's hand still curving her slender nape and with a new kind of silence thickening the air, they entered a corridor that put the rest of his family out of view—thankfully, because she didn't need any cold witnesses when she faced what was to come.

And it came quickly—too quickly. Through the very first door they encountered, in fact. Luca paused, so did she, watching as he pushed the door open then gently urged her to move again. Her body felt heavy, that sense of dark dread placing a drag on her limbs as she made herself step through the opening into a well-lit room with white walls and staffed by a white-uniformed nurse who stood by a white-sheeted bed.

And then there was the white-faced creature lying in the bed.

CHAPTER THREE

IT WAS the point when her control split wide open. Shannon had thought she was prepared, she'd truly believed she was ready to deal with whatever she had to face in this room. But she found she couldn't cope with the sight of her sister lying there so pale and still as if life's essence itself was slowly seeping out of her.

The choked sob that attempted to escape had to be rammed back into her mouth by a shaking fist at the same moment that she took a staggering step backwards, pressing herself against the full muscle-packed length of Luca, who acted like a wall to halt her cowardly retreat. Eyes blurred, throat thick, mouth trembling, she fought to get a hold on herself.

It was awful. It took a fierce effort to force herself forward on legs that didn't feel supportive. Arriving at the side of the bed, she reached for one of her sister's limp hands. It felt warm and that was comforting. Warmth meant life.

'Keira?' she called out unsteadily. 'Keira—it's Shannon. Can she hear me?' she demanded of the nurse. Then, before the woman could answer, her attention honed right back on the white face lying against white pillows. 'Oh, Keira,' she burst out painfully. 'Wake up and talk to me!'

'Here…' a deep voice prompted. A pair of hands carefully eased the overcoat from her shoulders, then a chair arrived at the back of her knees, giving her no choice but to sit.

The diversion stopped her from falling apart as, she realised, she had been about to do. 'H-how deeply unconscious is she?' she asked huskily.

43

'Some of it is drug induced,' Luca offered with what she supposed was meant to be a comfort. The nurse seemed to have slipped away, making her exit without Shannon noticing.

'Has she woken up at all since the accident?'

'No,' Luca answered gruffly.

'Does that mean she doesn't even know she's had her baby?'

'No,' he said again.

Shannon felt her insides begin to burn as a whole new set of emotions went raging through her blood. How many failed pregnancies had poor Keira endured through the years before she'd managed to carry this baby to almost full term? Five or six, Shannon was sure, since she'd married Angelo.

Would a girl child be enough for her? With her own life hanging in the balance here, would her sister now give up on her obsession to give Angelo a male heir?

Angelo—what was she thinking? There was no more Angelo. 'Oh, Keira,' she whispered painfully. How was she going to cope without her beloved Angelo?

Then began long hours of torment. Nothing around her felt real. She sat by the bed and talked to Keira. When she was gently removed from the room by medical staff who needed to check Keira, she sat outside in the corridor and lost herself in grief for Angelo. Occasionally Luca would appear, or his mother or one of the sisters. It didn't occur to her that she was never left entirely on her own or that the family attitude towards her had taken a complete about turn. Perhaps, if she had noticed, she would have started to realise that their sharing of her vigil was a bad sign. But she didn't notice and she rarely spoke, unless it was to Keira—then she talked and talked and talked without remembering a single word.

At one point someone gently asked her if she would like to see the baby. She thought she should do, for Keira's sake, but that was all. So she agreed and was utterly blown away by the tiny scrap of human life lying in her clear plastic cocoon fighting her own little battle.

Keira's daughter—Angelo and Keira's.

She burst into a flood of tears and wept for everyone, her emotions like a driverless vehicle wildly out of control. When she went back to sit with Keira her voice was as calm as a slow-running stream as she talked and talked and talked.

'You've had enough—'

The light touch on her shoulder brought Shannon's limp head lifting from the crisp white sheet that she had not been aware of resting against. Sleep-starved eyes blinked uncomprehendingly up into a determined gaze that was brown flecked with gold.

'You can do no more here tonight, Shannon,' Luca said quietly. 'It is time for us to leave and get some rest now.'

'I…' can be here, she was about to insist, but Luca silenced her with a shake of his head.

'Keira is stable,' he stated firmly. 'The people here know where to contact us if they need to. It is time for us to leave.'

The voice of authority, she recognised. Luca was not going to take no for an answer and if she was honest she knew he was right. She was so utterly used up she was barely functioning on any sensible level.

But it felt like desertion when she made herself get up from the chair and she lifted up one of Keira's hands and pressed a soft kiss to it before leaning over to leave another kiss on her cheek.

'Love you,' she whispered, then she was turning to walk away with wretched tears blurring her progress to the door with Luca following close behind.

'Where are you going?'

She blinked, her sleep-starved brain taking whole seconds to realise they were now outside her sister's room, the door having been pulled shut so silently she hadn't even heard it. 'The baby,' she murmured, waving a decidedly uncoordinated hand in the direction of the nursery. 'I want to…'

'The baby is fine,' he assured. 'I have been with her for the last hour while you sat with Keira.'

An hour? Shannon blinked again. Luca had been with the baby for a whole hour? The picture that produced in her head just didn't correspond somehow with the man she thought she knew.

'I watched the nurse attend to her, then they let me hold her for a while…'

Something passed over his face, a wave of unchecked emotion that emphasised the ring of pain that was circling at his mouth. Guilt made a sudden clutching grab at her aching heart. This man had just lost his beloved brother but, while she had been selfishly absorbed in her sister's plight, Luca had been too busy supporting others to find the time to deal with his own loss. She had been existing in a fog since they'd arrived here, but he'd split his time between comforting his grief-stricken mother or one of his two sisters as well as attending to her.

Now here he stood, doing what he did best: being the strong Salvatore male. But when she looked into his eyes she saw the desolation beneath his glossy black lashes. She also witnessed another painful image of him slipping away to go to the nursery to hold a tiny baby girl who was the only link to his brother.

Her heart ached again, everything ached, for Luca as well as herself.

'Oh, Luca,' she murmured as impulse made her take a step closer to him with soft words of sympathy trembling up from her throat.

He saw it coming. His face closed up. 'Here,' he clipped. 'Put this on…'

He held out her coat. Shannon stared at it, aware that

she'd just had a door slammed shut in her face again. And why not? she asked herself bleakly as she swallowed the words of comfort and felt the tremor that came with them shiver its way to her feet. Her sister was alive but his brother was dead. Accepting comfort from his ex-lover-turned-enemy would be a blow to his dignity he could do without.

So she let him feed her coat sleeves up her arms without uttering another syllable. As the heavy garment settled on her tired shoulders she pushed her hands into its deep pockets to hug the warm wool around her, then walked towards the bank of lifts. The chairs in the foyer were empty now; the rest of the Salvatore family had been sent home to their beds long ago.

The silence between them held as they drove away into the cool dark night. A glance at the clock illuminated on the car dashboard told it was one o'clock in the morning. It felt as if a whole week had gone by since she'd got out of bed yesterday at six in the morning and rushed out to catch the commuter flight to Paris. Such a lot had happened since then. Too much—too much, she thought dully as she rested her head against the soft leather headrest, then closed her hot, tired, gritty eyes.

Luca watched as she slipped into an exhausted slumber and grimaced to himself. He knew the impression he had given her back there in the hospital, but she could not be more wrong about his motives if she'd tried. However, receiving comfort from a warm and sympathetic Shannon right now would have shattered the control he was hanging onto by a thread.

And it was not over yet—though he was aware that Shannon didn't know that. There was more to come—a battle—he predicted, because she was not going to like it when she discovered where she was staying. Let his defences drop before the fight was won and he would turn himself into a

target for someone of Shannon's fiercely stubborn independent nature.

Dio, he thought tiredly as he drove them through the silent streets of Florence. He was not that sure that he wasn't
already that target. A mere glance at her sitting beside him
with her long legs stretched out in front of her, the white
oval of her face so exquisite in repose, he experienced that
telling needle-sharp sting of Man on the prowl.

She got to him. She always had done. Love or hate her,
he *always* wanted her and it was knowing that that made
him such a target. Give her reason to spark and he was going
to catch a light. He was so sure of it that he would try
anything to keep her asleep until he had her safely ensconced in a bed—and he'd put himself on the other side
of the bedroom door.

A sitting duck. Angelo's words, he remembered starkly.
Angelo had said that the two of them were both targets for
a pair of Irish witches to enchant at will.

Angelo… A collapse took place inside his chest. It was
a sensation he had grown familiar with during this long,
miserable day. He missed his brother—already. He wanted
Angelo back. Tears stung hot and dry against the backs of
his eyes and he felt his skin stretch across his cheek-bones
with tension.

His foot hit the accelerator, using a surge of unnecessary
bodily power to release the pressure in his chest. Familiar
landmarks flashed by the side window. He saw a set of
traffic lights ahead glowing red; he aimed for them—felt the
burning rush swell inside him, challenging that bastard
called death. It was compelling, seductive.

Shannon stirred. He glanced at her, saw beauty personified in his stark eyes and, clenching his jaw tight and gritting
his teeth, he forced himself to slow down. One car crash in
the family was enough. The moment of madness eased,

leaving Shannon still asleep beside him with no idea how close he'd come to putting her safety at risk.

The sensation remained, though, burning like acid in his gut, anger at the waste of his brother's life overlaying the numbing sense of grief. It was going to need assuaging and he had a grim suspicion he knew by what source.

It was feeling the car swing sharply down a steep incline that stirred Shannon awake. Opening red-rimmed eyes, she sat up to peer out at the lines of cars parked in the basement car park and, as Luca slotted the car into its reserved parking slot, he waited for recognition to spark.

It didn't happen. Probably too tired to notice anything much, she yawned then opened her door and stepped out. He did the same, eyeing her carefully as she waited in weary silence for him to recover her luggage then walked beside him to the lift.

They stepped into it together. While he used a plastic security card to activate the lift she went to lean against one of the metal cased walls, thrust her hands into her coat pockets, then proceeded to stare at her booted feet.

'You have access, then,' she remarked, smothering yet another yawn.

'Yes, I have access,' was all he said.

'Good of them.'

'Hmm?'

'Angelo and Keira. It's good of them to trust you with security access to their apartment.'

He didn't answer, keeping his expression blank while he wondered if she was even aware that she'd used his brother's name as if Angelo were still alive.

That anger stirred again; he crushed it down. The lift began to rise. He wanted to hit something and wished he didn't feel like this.

'But then, that's nothing new,' she added with a sudden

tinge of bitterness in her voice. 'Security access to each others' homes has always been the norm for the Salvatores.'

'You think that's a bad thing?'

'I think it's bloody stupid,' she replied. 'I know Italian families like to be close, but having the right to walk in and out of each others' homes when they feel like it is taking family unity to the extreme.'

'Because you were once caught out by this—extreme perhaps?'

The taunt hit home. She flinched, then lifted her chin to send him a clear cold stare. He countered it with a thin smile. Mutual antipathy began to sing. The lift stopped. She was so busy defying him to take that comment further that when the lift doors slid open she still did not notice where she was.

So he said nothing and merely mocked her with a gesture of his hand to step out of the lift. Head up, eyes like ice, she walked forward, stooping to collect up her bags from where they sat at his feet before saying tightly. 'Goodnight, Luca. I'm sure you know your own way out again.'

Then she walked—or did she flounce? Luca mused curiously. Whichever, she did it sensationally in her ankle-length coat and flaming red hair; it was almost a shame that reality was about to spoil it.

She was several strides in before she began to take in the décor of rich cream walls and inlaid wood floors on which stood the kind of heavy antique pieces that she would never have connected with Keira's more homely tastes.

Luca watched her freeze, watched her take stock, watched her pull in a sharp breath before she spun to stare at him as he slid the plastic security card back into his leather wallet while the lift doors closed behind his blocking frame.

'No,' she breathed in stricken protest. 'I'm not staying here with you, Luca. No way.'

It took fewer strides to bring her back to him. Eyes bright

with defiance, she snaked a hand over his shoulder to gave the lift-call button a firm press.

'It won't come without my authorisation,' he reminded her gently.

'Then authorise it.'

She was standing so close that he could feel her breath on his face. She smelled of Chanel and the hospital, and the tumbled untidiness of her hair flamed like a warning around her face. She was trying her best to defy him but underneath the defiance he knew alarm bells were ringing because she did not understand his motives for bringing her here of all places, back to the scene of the crime, so to speak.

He could reassure her that he had nothing sinister on his mind and that she had to stay somewhere and even he wasn't so brutal that he take her to a dead man's house then leave her there alone—but it would not be the truth. Something had happened to him during the mad drive here, and he now wanted her so badly that it burned in his gut like a pounding fever. He wanted to pick her up and throw her over his shoulder, find the nearest bed and drop her down on it, then follow with some good, hard sex. No preliminaries, just a quick, hot slaking of all this *stuff* he was struggling to deal with: his brother, her sister—Shannon back here and within his reach. She had made the last two years of his life a misery—the least she could do in reparation was help him assuage his grief!

Shannon knew what he was thinking—it was vibrating all around them like some dark, compelling force. The desire, the old burning attraction, that needle-sharp prick of sexual awareness that made his eyes glow gold and made her need to run the tip of her tongue around the sudden dry curve of her lips.

'No,' she breathed in husky denial.

'Why not?' He watched that telling little gesture and smiled. 'For old time's sake.'

For old time's sake? Her own affronted gasp almost choked her. She couldn't believe he was behaving like this! Didn't it matter to him that there was a life-threatening situation taking place not far away, or that one person had died and another two were fighting a battle with death?

'You ought to be ashamed of yourself,' she told him, then turned on her heel and walked away across the large square entrance hall with all its familiar trappings of wealth, like the exquisite antique chest set against one wall with the magnificent bronze statue of Apollo standing on its top. She strode beneath the wide archway through which she gained access to the rest of the apartment. And she walked with purpose, knowing exactly where she was making for.

The kitchen, which led to the utility room, which in turn led to the rear exit door. A locked rear exit door, she soon discovered. Her heart sank—but not her resolve, she determined as she dropped her bags to the floor then turned, eyes wearing such a hard glint now that they should have turned him to stone where he stood propping up the other door, watching her lazily.

'I'll get out,' she warned, 'if I have to break windows.'

'We are four floors up,' he reminded her.

'Broken windows upset people,' she explained, undeterred. 'They tend to call in the police when glass comes showering down on top of them.'

His hard mouth gave a mocking twist. 'Well, that might have been fun,' he drawled. 'If the glass wasn't shatterproof.'

Her shoulders sagged; this was getting stupid. 'Look,' she snapped. 'It's late. I'm tired—you're tired. We've both had a rotten day! Can we just stop this now?' She tried a bit of pleading. 'Let me out of here, Luca—please!'

'I wish it was that simple,' he grimaced.

'It is!' she insisted.

'No, it isn't,' he returned with a snap that altered his

taunting mood to the grimly serious. 'So let's get a couple of things straight. You are staying here in my apartment, because it is situated so close to the hospital—'

'I'd rather stay at Angelo and Keira's place.'

He stiffened suddenly, dark eyes flaring up with a blistering rage. 'Angelo is dead!' he barked at her. 'So will you stop dotting his name into every damn sentence, for goodness' sake?'

Shannon blinked in surprise, her face turning as white as a sheet. Had she been doing that? She hadn't been aware of it. When she thought about her sister she automatically put Angelo with her. Angelo and Keira—it had always been that way. 'I'm s-sorry,' she stammered, not knowing what else to say.

Luca frowned. 'Forget I said that,' he dismissed, then sucked in a deep breath. 'The point is,' he went on, 'that Angelo and Keira have moved since you were last here. It is now more than an hour's drive out of the city to their new home. My mother is not fit to be on her own right now so she has gone to stay with Sophia, which leaves you with a choice, Shannon,' he offered finally. 'You either stay here with me, stay with Renata, or you go and stay with my mother at Sophia's house.'

Which was absolutely no choice at all, she acknowledged heavily. His mother hated her. So did his sisters. Staying with them would be just a different kind of hell. And anyway, his family had a right to do their grieving together and without an unwanted interloper in their midst.

'There are such things as hotels, you know,' she pointed out stubbornly.

'Are you really so selfish that you would go to a hotel knowing that such a choice would not only offend my mother, but would hurt Keira beyond all that is fair if and when she discovers it?' He sent her a look that stung. 'She will blame the family, she will blame me for not being man enough to put my own feelings about you to one side for her sake.'

'But you aren't putting your feelings aside!' she cried.

'I will if you will.'

'Liar,' she breathed. But as for the rest he was, oh, so frustratingly right that, on acceptance, her ability to remain standing upright any longer disintegrated and she sank wearily against the locked door behind her and dropped her face into her hands.

It was a surrender. He knew it and well and she knew it. But Shannon could not resist dropping one final comment into the throbbing silence that fell. 'I hate you,' she whispered from the all-enveloping shield of her tumbling hair.

'No, you don't,' Luca denied. 'You still fancy the hell out of me and that, *cara*, is what you hate.'

'That's a lie!' The hands dropped so she could spit the disclaimer at him.

'Is it?' His eyes were cold now, hardened by his arrogant belief in what he was claiming. 'Cast your mind back to the kiss on the flight over here,' he suggested. 'If I had not stopped it you would have gone up in a plume of smoke.'

'My God,' she gasped. 'You conceited devil!'

'Maybe.' He gave an indifferent shrug. 'But I know what I know.'

'You kissed me, if you remember!'

'And you fell into it as you always did,' he declared with contempt.

'And you didn't—?'

His grimace conceded that point to her. 'It is going to be really interesting for us to see if we can both survive the next few days without falling on each other again, don't you think?'

'I think you're disgusting!'

A black brow arched, he ran his eyes down the slender body he could see between the gaping sides of her coat.

'Are your breasts tight, Shannon?' he questioned softly. 'Is that place between your legs getting all hot and anxious because we are talking about it?'

She launched herself away from the door with a need to slap his taunting face!

'Sex in the utility room, now that's a new turn-on,' he drawled as she flew towards him. 'But then you never did have any inhibitions as to where or with whom you did it so long as you did.'

Each word was aimed to draw blood from its victim, each mocking glint in his dark eyes was meant to drive her over the edge. She stopped a foot away, trying to push down the rage tumbling around inside her because a part of her was aware that he was provoking her deliberately. His eyes were goading her; his whole lazy, taunting stance was just begging her to take that swipe at him.

'I don't understand why you're doing this,' she breathed unsteadily.

He laughed; it wasn't a pleasant sound. 'Maybe I'm curious as to how much you've learned since you moved on to pastures new.'

'Stop it,' she whispered.

But he wasn't going to stop anything. 'Did you tempt him as you used to tempt me, Shannon?' he questioned curiously. 'Did you tease him into showing you yet another way to reach that mind-blowing final thrill?'

Her arm came up between the glare of their eyes, fixed and warring, and she let fly with her hand. He caught it before it landed its blow, hard fingers closing around her slender wrist to keep the hand suspended a small half-inch from his face.

'We both know that the thrill was all you ever really wanted from me,' he continued remorselessly, 'but did you think you'd exhausted all *my* possibilities? Wrong, darling.' He dared to kiss the tips of her clawing fingers. 'We never so much as scratched the surface. You have no idea what delights you have missed out upon.'

'Shut up!' she choked. He was twisting the truth around to suit his own version of what he believed and she felt so hurt that she actually began to shake from head to toe in response.

Those unremitting eyes held her captive, and his hand gave a tug to bring her hard up against his solid frame. 'I still cannot look at your mouth without remembering how it feels to have it fixed on some intimate part of my anatomy,' he murmured, his deep voice pulsing inside her head. 'I remember each brush of your lips, each sensuous flick of your sexy tongue. There,' he said huskily. 'Does it make you feel better to know that I am still as obsessed with you as you are with me, Shannon, hmm?'

'I am not obsessed with you—I despise you!' she hissed. 'Or am I supposed to have forgotten the way you slaked yourself in me *after* you alleged my so-called other lover had been there before you, or the way that you slid out of my body still heaving from the whole wild experience only to turn on me like an animal? You spat names at me that I wouldn't call any woman!'

His face went white, and her heart was pounding, not with desire but with a rage two long years in the festering that was suddenly blazing hotly inside.

'I apologised,' he bit back.

Did he really? Well, it can't have been such a sincere apology because she couldn't even bring it to mind! 'What you did to me went beyond apologies,' she told him. 'And do you know what made it worse? You didn't care about me enough to listen to what I had to say before you dealt out your punishment. I was judged and found guilty without even the right to a fair trial! Well, I'll tell you something…' Her breasts were heaving, the words shooting from her on the crest of her rage. 'I will let you right off the hook if you like—because I accept the blame. I did it. I took another man to *your* bed, Luca, and I can't tell you how very much I enjoyed the experience!'

'That's enough!' he barked.

He was right and it was. On a sickening wave of dismay Shannon tugged her wrist free from his grasp and reeled dizzily away. She'd spoken lies—all lies. Why had she done that? she asked herself painfully. Why did she always have to tell him what he wanted to hear?

Behind her the silence was throbbing like the heavy beat of a drum. Inside she was quietly tearing apart at the seams. In her heart she was weeping at all the bitterness, and in her head she was feeling so ugly she never wanted to look at herself again.

'Do I win my pass out of here now?' she asked with a dullness that saw off her anger.

For an answer he spun on his heel and strode away.

Shannon wilted on a combination of shocked horror at what they had thrown at each other and a sinking sense of relief because she had finally driven him to let her out of here. Pulling herself together, she went to gather up her bags, then took in a deep breath before following him.

The moment she stepped back into the kitchen she knew she had not won anything. Luca was playing the domesticated man again and filling the kettle. His overcoat had gone, and his jacket and tie. As she stood there her eyes couldn't resist following the ripple of muscle across broad, tense shoulders.

'Take your coat off, dump the luggage,' he said without turning.

'Luca—for goodness' sake…' she pleaded yet again. 'Just let me out of here so I can find a hotel room somewhere.'

'Tea or coffee?' was all she got by return.

'Oh,' she groaned, covering her now-throbbing eyes with a trembling hand. 'Can't you understand?' she cried in a last-ditch attempt to make him see reason. 'I just can't stay in this apartment with you!'

It was no use. The rigid stretch of cotton barely flexed in response as he stood there waiting for the kettle to boil. 'You're nothing but an unfeeling monster,' she told him as her weary body gave up on the whole stupid fight.

'Tea or coffee,' he repeated.

'Oh, choose which you like,' she sighed, and on an act of surrender sank into one of the chairs at the kitchen table, dropped her bags to the floor, then placed her elbows on the table so she could bury her face in her hands.

Another silence rained down around them after that, broken only by the soothing hiss of the kettle as it came to the boil. Shannon kept her face hidden and Luca—well, she was aware that he was standing there, leaning against the worktop and looking at her, but—what the heck? Let him get his fill of her defeat if that was how he got his kicks these days. She didn't care any more, didn't care about anything but getting a warm drink inside then finding a bed she could sleep in.

Observing the weary way she was sitting there with her face buried in her hands, Luca bit his teeth together and angrily asked himself what the hell he'd thought he was doing orchestrating that little scene. Since when did a reasonably sophisticated man of thirty-four taunt an ex-lover with the kind of remarks he had just poured out?

One that needed an escape for all the burning grief that was trampling his insides, he acknowledged heavily.

And Shannon was not just an ex-lover. She was the woman he'd loved. The woman he'd believed he could spend the rest of his life with. Walking into his own home and seeing what he had seen was going to burn in his head for ever.

'I never did manage to discover who the other man was.'

'What—?' Her face came out of her hands, red-rimmed

eyes staring at him as if he had just spoken to her in Greek.
'It makes you a sad kind of man that you even bothered to
try,' she threw back in derision. 'Forget the tea,' she added,
dragging herself to her feet again. 'I'll just take the bedroom.'

With that she hauled up her luggage and walked out of
the kitchen.

Luca let her go, angry with himself for saying something
else he had not meant to say. He stood there listening to her
footsteps taking her down the hallway, listened to a door
being opened, and a grim smile touched the corners of his
mouth because he'd recognised the door as belonging to
what she believed was one of the guest bedrooms. She'd
picked it out deliberately knowing that their old bedroom
was at the other end of the hall.

Standing there tense, hands braced on the worktop, he
waited for her to realise the mistake she'd made. Sure
enough a few seconds later the door closed and her footsteps
continued to the room next door. He hadn't slept in their
old bedroom since the day she'd taken another man to it.
He would have walked out of the apartment and never come
back if it hadn't been too big a step for his pride.

A few seconds later and the next door she had chosen
shut with a telling slam. Only then did he let the air leave
his body.

He must be mad—crazy to continue to let her get to him
like this. What had gone should be forgotten. He wanted to
forget, so why was he standing here feeling as bad as he'd
felt two years ago?

He knew the answer but hell would freeze over before he
would admit it.

The kettle boiled. He watched it happen. Watched it
switch off and still remained standing there until the steam
had died away again. Then, on a growl of frustration that

sounded alien even to him, he turned and followed Shannon's lead by slamming into his own bedroom.

From now on he was going to keep his distance, he vowed grimly. Tomorrow she moved to a hotel. And if they met up again while she was here in Florence then it would be by mistake because he didn't want it to happen.

With that decision made, he stripped off his clothes then strode into the adjoining bathroom, switched on the shower and stepped beneath it. The jet was powerful, the water hot, and as it sluiced down over him he couldn't help but notice what was happening in his lower regions. It made him want to push his fist through the tiled wall in front of him because if Shannon was the only woman who could excite this kind of response in him, then she was right and he was the saddest kind of person indeed.

Shannon opened her suitcase and dragged out a pair of pyjamas, then just stood holding the pale blue strips of flimsy silk in fingers that shook. She despised him, she really did—so why were there tears in her eyes? Why was she feeling so unbelievably hurt because he'd dared to remark on something that should no longer matter to either of them?

If she'd been guilty as charged she might have had reason to feel this wretched. Innocence should bring with it a smug sense of self-righteousness. Only it didn't. Instead it made her want to go and find him, tell the truth and just get it all over with so she could feel comfortable again.

What truth, though? The full truth, warts and all, and other people's secrets? She had tried offering him that truth two years ago only to be scalded by angry disbelief. As far as Luca was concerned she had been caught red-handed trying to tidy away the evidence of another man's recent presence in their bedroom. The rumpled bed had spoken volumes. The packet of condoms had said even more. The fact that she'd dared to try and pass the blame onto someone else had been her final crime in his eyes.

If love had to be tried by such painful methods, then their love was certainly judged that day and found to be utterly wanting in both strength and substance.

And the quicker she got herself out of his orbit, the better it was going to be for both of them, because it was as clear as the nose on her face that he wasn't handling this situation any better than she was.

'Oh, Keira,' she sighed. Just wake up and get well so that I can leave here as quickly as the first flight to London can take me.

Then she thought of Angelo, who had not been given the chance to get well.

Dead.

Her eyes burned. It just wasn't fair. She loved him—everyone loved Angelo. He was that kind of wonderful man.

But no one loved him more than Luca did, she thought painfully. And suddenly she realised she had her reason as to why his behaviour had been so insane.

Remorse raked through her for not realising it earlier. Sympathy followed, along with an aching urge to go and comfort him.

Then she shook on a weary, weary sigh, knowing that the last thing Luca wanted from her was sympathy.

Sex—yes. He'd take the sex as a form of panacea. He'd made that fact only too clear!

On that thought she laid the pyjamas on the bed, removed her clothes, then walked into the adjoining bathroom to step into the shower. The first thing she heard was the sound of water running in the next-door bathroom. It conjured up an image of the naked man in all his god-like proportions, his broad, tanned shoulders, the long golden torso, and the kind of legs built to grip a woman—hard. Her body heated, her breasts grew tight.

Turning on the shower, she forced herself to grimly ignore what was happening on the other side of the wall.

It was bliss to crawl between the cool sheets and put her head down on the pillow, bliss to pull the duvet up to her ears and shut out the rest of the world. Tomorrow I leave here and book into a hotel, was the last thought she remembered having before she dropped like a stone into sleep.

CHAPTER FOUR

CRAMP. Shannon knew what it was even as it brought her screaming out of a deep dark pit of exhaustion. She writhed on the bed, kicking back the covers as her hand shot down to cover the ugly knot that had appeared in her left calf. She groaned and began rubbing at the distressed muscle with the flat of her hand.

It made no difference and if anything only seemed to make her writhe all the more. An agitated need to do something about it before the pain tore her apart sent her agony-bright eyes shooting around the darkened bedroom in search of help from something—anything!

But then her cramping muscle twisted a little tighter and she tumbled off the side of the bed to land in a heap on hard, polished wood squirming and whimpering like a wounded animal.

She had never suffered from cramp in her life before, so she had no idea what to do to ease it. She tried shaking the offending leg, then rubbing it again when the shaking did nothing but make her teeth sing. In sheer desperation she tried to stand up on the dizzy idea that if she could manage to reach the bathroom she could apply something warm to the muscle in the hope heat would help release the angry spasm. But she never made it because the moment she placed any weight on the leg the pain became so unbearable that she landed back on the floor amidst a shrill and shaken cry.

The bedroom door suddenly flew open, and light from the hallway poured into the room. 'What the hell—?' a harsh voice demanded.

Luca stood there. She stared helplessly up at his lean, dark bulk silhouetted against the light. 'Cramp,' she groaned.

It was all she could manage.

To give him credit he didn't need to be told twice. In a couple of strides he was kneeling beside her and gripping the offending leg with ruthless fingers, then began manipulating the cramped muscle in a way that set her teeth singing again.

'I should have known something like this would happen,' he gritted over her whimpered cries of protest. 'When was the last time you bothered to drink anything? You must be dehydrated, you fool!'

Fool or not, she was beginning to see stars now, tears were streaming down her face. 'It hurts,' she cried over and over and kept hitting the floor with a fist while he kept up his grim manipulation of her leg.

Miraculously, though, his form of torture began to ease the other. Sheer relief from the pain brought her out in a shivering cold sweat. 'Aah!' she gasped out shakily. 'That has to be the worst pain I've ever felt in my life.'

But Luca wasn't listening. His dark face locked with anger, he had twisted to pull the light quilt from the bed and was grimly bundling her shivering body into it. Without a word he gathered her into his arms and stood up to carry her out of the bedroom then down the hall and into the kitchen where he finally dumped her on a chair at the table.

Not quite knowing what had hit her, Shannon sat huddling into the quilt while she stared at him in a state of near shock as he crossed the floor and opened the fridge door. A second later he was placing a clean glass tumbler and a bottle of water down on the table.

'Drink,' he commanded.

In mute obedience Shannon unscrewed the bottle top and—ignoring the glass—drank straight from the bottle. Ice-cold, the water was like nectar to her parched mouth and burning throat. After drinking down half the bottle she slumped back in the chair and closed her eyes while she tried to grapple with what had just happened. Her leg felt as if someone had kicked it; the pain had left her shaken and weak. Her head ached with one of those dull throbs that came with too much stress and she felt so tired she could fall asleep where she was sitting.

A sound beside her forced her eyes to open. Luca was leaning against the table beside her chair staring down at his own bare feet. He looked tired and pale, the long day's strain etched into the hard contours of his face.

'Sorry I woke you,' she mumbled.

'I was not asleep,' he replied, and the way he said it told her that he had been lying there thinking about his brother, loving him, hurting for him, wishing the last twenty-four hours had never been.

Her heart turned over, an aching sympathy curling around it. She wanted to reach out and touch him gently, offer words that might help to ease his grief. But there were no such words and she didn't dare mention Angelo's name because whenever she did Luca went ballistic. It was such a helpless, hollow feeling to know that she was not the person he wanted to confide his feelings in.

She would have been, once upon a time. He used to tell her everything. They would lie in bed with limbs tangled and talk and talk and—

'Drink.'

Her eyelashes fluttered against her cheek-bones, then lifted to find him looking at her. His eyes were dark—dark as ebony, sleepy and sultry, his lashes curved and spiky and just begging her to—

She looked away quickly before the senses she could feel beginning to stir took a dangerous grip. Picking up the bottle, she drank some more, hoping the cold water would cool what was beginning to heat. She didn't want to want Luca. She didn't want to remember things about him that she'd learned years before. He was her past. She'd moved on since then.

And just because he was leaning here wearing only a short, hastily tied robe did not mean she had to conjure up memories of the body beneath the robe. So what if this particular man was built to push the female sex drive into meltdown? Sex was sex. These days she looked for deeper things in a relationship like friendship, caring and respect. One day she might even find a man she felt she could trust enough to give him these things. She hadn't stopped looking because of one bad experience. It was just that she hadn't found him yet.

Lifting the bottle to her lips, she drank again. The only illumination in the room came from the down-lighters that were integral to the wall units. The light barely reached the centrally placed table but what did manage to reach cast a warm, seductive glow. And it was quiet, so quiet she thought she could hear the unsteady beat of Luca's heart.

Or was it her heart that was beating unsteadily?

Of course it was her heart. He was too close and she wished that he weren't. Lifting the bottle again, she kept her eyes carefully averted from him and tried to pretend that they were complete strangers.

But averting her eyes didn't do anything but give her imagination a chance to list every detail about him. The length of his legs, for instance, the power in his golden thighs. The robe he was wearing could cover what it liked without making much difference to her for she knew every inch of him, the shape of each separate vertebra in his long, supple spine. She knew the wonderful feel of his satin skin and the contrasting crisp coils of hair that covered his chest. She knew how firm his stomach was, how taut the muscles were in his lean behind. She could draw a picture of every sleek detail from his long brown toes to even longer fingers.

Oh, stop it! she railed herself as a sensation she knew only too well made her squirm. Move away from me! she wanted to yell at him, but instead took another gulp at her drink because saying anything of the kind would be tantamount to confessing what she was thinking and she would rather cut out her tongue than let him know what was inside her head.

A sigh shook her. The kind of sigh that was supposed to ease tension, not help to intensify it—yet that was exactly what this particular sigh did. It intensified everything she was thinking and feeling until the atmosphere began to sing. She wanted to run but remained glued to her seat. She wished those legs weren't right in her field of vision, yet couldn't make herself look the other way.

'What time is it?' she asked with a touch of desperation.

'Three-thirty,' he supplied and even his voice worked its own kind of magic on what was happening to her. It was low and deep and dark and gorgeously accented. It tugged at her heartstrings, which in turn tugged at more susceptible things.

She ached on a silent groan. Will I ever get over him? The first love syndrome, she thought helplessly. They say that you never really recover from your first true love.

'How is the muscle?'

Like a wooden puppet, she put a hand down to rub the offending calf. It still felt tight but it was no longer knotting.

'OK,' she replied and drank some more water. It came as a shock to realise that somewhere in the last few minutes he had exchanged her empty bottle for a full one. 'How many of these do you want me to drink before you'll let me go back to bed?'

It was said in an effort to lighten the tension, and he

dutifully laughed. But the low sound only set her flesh tingling. 'Keep going until I tell you to stop,' he replied.

Then the silence came back. Her pulse began to race, the previously even rhythm of her breathing shattering so badly that she shifted restlessly on the chair in an effort to contain it all. The action made one of the thin straps of her flimsy top slide off her shoulder. Finding herself in real danger of exposing a tightly thrusting nipple, she reached up to tug the offending strap back into place again—only to clash with long brown fingers as they went to do the same thing.

Both of them went absolutely still with fingers resting against fingers, while her flesh began to heat. She glanced up. It was instinctive. What she saw sent her heart-rate into overdrive.

He was looking at her body. His dark eyes were hidden beneath those spiky black lashes as they grazed over a smooth white shoulder, then dipped lower to the rounded slopes of her breasts.

He wanted to touch her.

'No,' she breathed in shaky rejection and made a clumsy grab at the slipping duvet.

Her denial brought his lashes up. Black heat from his eyes shot towards her and held her trapped in a dark, dark mesh. The duvet remained where it was, lying in a soft, squashy heap on her lap and the sting of desire leapt through her blood, tripping sensual switches as it went.

He knew—he knew. Everything about him was turning dark on the knowledge. Dark eyes, dark heart, a searing dark ardour that coiled itself around the both of them. Nothing about him was light any more, or gentle or soft. He wanted her but didn't want to want her. She returned the resentful feeling.

His fingers began to trail across her shoulder. Moving with a tantalising slowness until they reached the long column of her neck, then slid sideways, combing her tangled hair away from her nape. Shannon stopped breathing. Luca did the opposite. Pulling a deep, hard breath of air into his lungs, he moved, dipping his dark head to fasten white teeth on the creamy flesh he had just exposed.

Sensation shot through her like a thousand pinpricks; she gasped and quivered, then stroked her cheek against his face. Animal, they were animals, she the purring preening she-cat responding to her demanding mate. His hands slid beneath her arms and lifted her onto her feet. His mouth moved from nape to her mouth and she stood on one foot, favouring her cramped leg as she sank herself into the all-consuming heat of his kiss.

What had been threatening to spark between them from the moment they'd first faced each other across the threshold of her London flat now flared up with spectacular energy. They kissed as they used to kiss, long and deep and holding back nothing. Her arms went around his neck; the duvet lay around her feet. He moved his hands down her slender sides, moulding her fine-boned feminine shape, then gripping her waist to draw her between his legs. He was still leaning against the table but the robe had slid apart at his waist. She felt the heat of him, the powerful thrust of his sex against her stomach, and knew that she was not going to be the one to stop this.

Would he stop it? She moaned against his mouth in horror of it happening. He took the groan to mean something else.

'No way,' he muttered, and explained his meaning by shifting his hands again. Her pyjama bottoms slithered downwards to come to rest at her knees. She accepted the force of his thrust between her thighs and held him there while the kiss went on and on and her pyjama top was eased away from her breasts. He touched, she went wild for him. Her fingers clutched at his hair and her thighs tightened their possessive grip. On a dark growl he picked her up and began walking without allowing the kiss to break until he let go of her and she landed in the middle of a rumpled bed.

For a horrible moment she thought he was going to turn and walk away. It would be just punishment in his eyes, she knew that. But, far from walking away, Luca stripped off his robe and came to join her, ridding her of the flimsy scraps of blue silk before sliding his powerful frame over the top of hers and returning his mouth to hers.

They kissed right through the whole tempestuous journey. Not once did either of them attempt to break free. They touched with hands and the sensual shift of their bodies; when they needed more he penetrated her with a single silken thrust. She cried out against his mouth; he answered the cry with a grunt that raked the back of his throat. Her fingers had a tight grip on his hair again, her legs were wrapped around him, like two tight clamps. He moved to a primitive rhythm, his chest rasping against her breasts.

Animal? Yes, it was animal. A hungry coupling of two wild creatures that did not want to think about the past or the present or even the future. They just wanted—*needed* this.

This came with a power to make her lose contact with reality. Gasps, groans and shudders arrived in unison. Mingled sweat and body-heat and, finally, body fluids that left them wasted and eventually shocked.

He got up the moment he was physically able. Snatching up his robe, he slammed out of the room. Shannon watched him go with her heart in her eyes, then curled into a ball and sobbed her heart out.

He hated her—despised himself for touching her at all.

When daylight came, she opened her eyes to a pale sun seeping through the window and with her body aching like mad and her heart locked into a dull throb. She continued to lie there for a while, reluctant to move when moving meant having to face Luca.

Then she remembered Keira, and was grimly pushing Luca to one side and hurrying into the bathroom.

Choosing the first things out of her case that came to hand, she pulled on her jeans and added a clean blue top, then repacked the case. She wasn't staying here another night.

As she opened the bedroom door the seductive aroma of fresh coffee teased her senses, the thought that Luca was up and about made those same senses squirm. She didn't want to see him. If she could get away from here without having to face him she would do.

She never wanted to have to set eyes on him again.

But there he stood, looking very sombre and civilised in beautifully cut black silk trousers and a crisp white shirt. He was standing by a kitchen unit playing the domestic again. Her stomach dipped; she followed it by placing her bags down by the kitchen door.

'Sit down,' he invited. 'This won't be a minute.' He indicated the large pot of coffee brewing beside him.

But he didn't turn to look at her as he said it, which spoke volumes to her. Too ashamed of himself? If so, he wasn't the only one to feel that way.

'Did you ring the hospital?' she asked him stiffly.

He nodded. 'There is still no change,' he supplied.

'Then I would rather be going.'

'After we have eaten,' he came back uncompromisingly. 'I don't think either of us got around to eating much yesterday.'

We ate each other, Shannon thought bitterly. 'I don't—'

'We played this scene in your kitchen, Shannon,' he cut in. 'I see no use in doing it again.'

In other words, shut up. Pressing her lips together, she moved to the table and sat herself down. If he sticks toast under my nose I shall probably throw it back at him, she decided mutinously. Then felt a wave of panic wash over her when he turned suddenly as if she'd said the words out loud.

Not that she was afraid of him—only his expression. She preferred to keep looking at his back. In fact she would prefer it a lot more if she did not have to look at him at all! So she kept her eyes lowered as he crossed to the table, and placed the coffee pot before her.

Then he went still because he'd noticed her bag standing by the door and a new tension began to suck the oxygen out of the air. He was going to say something about last night, she was sure of it. If he did she was out of here even if that meant jumping down the lift shaft.

'About last night...'

She shot to her feet like a bullet.

'I want to apologise for—'

She moved on trembling legs towards the door.

'Shannon...'

'No!' She swung on him furiously. 'Don't you dare start telling me how much you regret it! Don't you dare, do you hear me, Luca? Don't you *dare*!'

'I hear you,' he said very quietly.

She looked at him then, really looked at him and saw exactly what she'd expected to see—his handsome dark features locked into a cold stone wall of self-contempt and regret. A sob caught in her throat. She wanted to hide her shame. She wanted the ground to open up and swallow her whole!

'Keira has to be all that matters here,' she pushed out unsteadily. 'You—m-me—*we* don't matter. I won't let you force me into running away this time!'

'I don't want you to run,' he sighed out irritably.

The question— Then what do you want from me?—sang in a silence that hung.

She didn't ask it. Instead she lifted trembling fingers to her mouth, tried to swallow, then lowered them again.

'I have to move to a hotel—today,' she told him.

There was a movement of tight male muscle, a flash of black fury hitting his eyes. 'And I have to claim my brother's body today!' he lashed at her harshly. 'What do you think is more important right now?'

She took a jerky step backwards, shaken to her roots by what he'd said. 'I'm so sorry,' she whispered painfully 'I didn't know!'

'I know that,' he snapped, still frowning blackly as he swung away again. 'We are both having to deal with an intolerable situation,' he said tightly. 'Needs cross, emotions get out of control. It has to be expected that our priorities will clash.'

Wise words, she acknowledged, if she was able to ignore the fact that she had been so wrapped up in her own grievances and distress she'd allowed herself to forget all of his.

And what were her grievances? she asked herself. So, they'd done the unforgivable last night but both had been guilty of falling into that particular dark pit, greedily assuaging one set of emotions, then overwhelming them with a different set.

Because Luca had pulled away from her afterwards did not mean she could shift all the blame onto him. In fact, while she was being brutally honest here—if he hadn't pulled away, then she probably would have.

The new silence gnawed at the tension in the atmosphere. She wished she could say something to make them both feel better but she couldn't think what. He was standing there wearing a rod of iron strapped across his broad shoulders, and his fingers were gripping the worktop with enough power to put dents in to the solid black marble.

'Sit down again,' he gritted.

Sit down, she repeated to herself, and looked down at the way her bags were standing at her feet like a childish defiance. Without saying a word she picked them up, turned and left the kitchen. Walking down the hall, she went back into the bedroom, put the bags down by the bed then walked back the way she had come. Fingers fluttered momentarily, coinciding with the deep, shaky breath she took before she pushed open the kitchen door and stepped back in.

Luca was still standing where she had left him, long brown fingers still gripping the worktop like a vice. She wanted to go to him, put her arms around him and *show* him just how badly she felt for forgetting what really mattered. But instead she crossed to the table and sat down.

And the silence pulsed in her eardrums, it throbbed in her stomach and pulled at the flesh covering her face. *Move*! She wanted to shout at him. *Say* something—*anything*! I've said I'm sorry. I've made the climb down. I don't know what else to do!

Maybe he tapped into her thought patterns—he'd always been able to do that. He turned, walked towards the table. The predicted rack of toast was set down in front of her.

'I will organise a hotel suite for you,' he announced curtly, then left her alone to swallow the unpalatable fact that her climb down had been a complete waste of time.

An hour later and she was at her sister's bedside, delivered there by Luca who, once he'd checked on Keira, left again, his lean face scored by the grim task that lay ahead of him, one that would to strip his self-control to the bone.

Tears for them all flooded her eyes as she sat gently stroking Keira's soft brown hair. She and her sister were so unalike in so many ways, she thought fondly. The colour of their hair, for instance, and the differences in character. Where she was bright and independent and naturally self-confident, Keira had always been shy and unsure of herself. Meeting and falling in love with Angelo had put stars in her eyes and an anxious pallor on her soft cheeks. She could never quite believe that a dashingly handsome man like Angelo could fall in love with a timid little mouse like her.

So she'd worked hard all her marriage to make herself feel worthy of her man. It had infuriated Shannon to watch it sometimes. 'You spoil him too much. He'll start treating you like a doormat if you don't watch out.'

But Angelo had remained faithfully besotted to his Irish mouse. It was the mouse who'd taken Shannon by surprise by turning into a sly little fox. 'Idiot,' she whispered and was suddenly fighting a battle with fresh tears again.

What followed was a long and hard nerve-flaying day in which Shannon divided her time between Keira and the nursery.

By two o'clock she was beginning to feel drained of emotional energy and was actually glad to be given some respite from her bedside vigil when a team of medical staff appeared and she was ushered away.

She needed some air that did not smell of the hospital. So she bought a sandwich in the downstairs cafeteria and took it with her to eat outside. The sun was bright and the air was cool, fresh—clean. Walking through the neatly laid gardens, she found a bench in the sunshine and sat down, unwrapped her sandwich and tried to empty all thoughts from her head so that she could attempt to eat at least.

Luca tracked her down ten minutes later. Her hair was up scrunched into a twist of narrow black ribbon, and the curve of her slender neck looked disturbingly vulnerable to him. The thought made him grimace because he wasn't thinking of vulnerable as in fragile, he was thinking vulnerable as in ripe for tasting. His tongue even moistened at the prospect, and he wished that he didn't have to look at her through the eyes of a recent lover.

But he did. Giving in to his baser instincts might have been a stupid mistake but he was now stuck with the results of it. Last night he had gone a little insane. He had lost control of himself. Two years ago she'd left him, taking his manhood with her when she went. Last night she gave it back to him. He should be pleased. He should be feeling the triumph of retribution and be able to walk away free and whole and ready to get on with the rest of his life, but all he felt was...

Need, greed—it had many names but they all came wrapped up in the same package. He wanted more and no amount of self-aimed contempt was going to change that.

Maybe he should go out and find himself a woman. There were certainly a lot out there more than willing to share his bed. Maybe now that Shannon had released him from his sexual prison he could even do both himself and these other woman some of his old macho justice.

But he didn't want them; he wanted this one. This red-haired, white-skinned, blue eyed betrayer who made his body sing.

A wry smile played with the tired corners of his mouth as he started walking again. The slight tensing in Shannon's shoulders as she'd sensed his approach gave that smile a different edge. Love each other or hate each other, they could still tune into the others presence like wild cats sniffing territorial scent.

Stepping around the bench, he paused for a moment to study the strain in her face. Her hair might burn like fire in the sunlight but her cheeks were pale, her eyes too dark and there was a telling hint of hurt about the way she was holding her mouth.

On a heavy sigh, he remembered why it was that he had come to find her. Slipping free the single button holding his jacket together, he sat down next to her with a long sigh.

'I'm sorry there was no one here with you,' he murmured quietly. 'It has been a—tough morning for everyone, I'm afraid.'

She turned to look at him, expression guarded as she looked into his face. He was beginning to look haggard, he knew, and did not bother to hide it. 'I thought it was tough enough five years ago when we had to do this for my father but...' He stopped, mouth tightening on words he didn't want to say but knew in the end that he had no choice. 'My mother collapsed and has had to be sedated. Renata is finding it difficult to cope. Sophia offered to come here to sit with you but she is needed by Mama.'

'I understand,' she returned.

'Do you?' Luca wished that he did. It felt as if the whole family had been involved in that car crash—himself and Shannon included. 'It's a mess,' he muttered and leaned forward to rest his forearms on his knees, his throat working on the now-permanent lump stuck in it. 'I've got people dropping like flies all around me. Formalities to deal with. A company that refuses to stop running just because I want it to. The phones keep on ringing. We are sinking beneath a wave of sympathy that, to be honest, I could do without right now.' His voice was growing husky—he could hear it.

Would she scream abuse at him if he also admitted that he wanted to pick her up and carry her off to the nearest bed to lose himself in her for an hour or two?

'The thing is, Shannon, I need to ask a big favour...'

She tensed. He grimaced as his mind made a connection with what he'd been thinking and what he'd just said. But, of course, Shannon didn't know about that.

'I need to be sure you are OK, you see,' he went on. 'Thinking of you alone in some faceless hotel room when you are not here does not make me feel OK.' He turned his head to look at her. The sunlight was trying its best to put some colour onto her drawn cheeks but it wasn't succeeding, and her mouth looked so vulnerable he wanted to—

'So I would like to take back my offer to find you somewhere else to stay. I want you to go on living at my place. I will move out if you prefer,' he offered, watching her carefully for some kind of reaction, but he wasn't getting one. 'But I would rather stay there too. That way I will know you will not be on your own if the—'

'Don't say it,' she said.

'No,' he agreed, looking down at his long fingered hands hanging limp between his spread knees.

While Shannon looked at the top of his dark head, watching the sun gloss it with a silken sheen. If the worst happens during the night, was what he had been going to say. Having shared her time between Keira and the baby, she was more than aware that the 'worst' wasn't very far away. As she watched the baby grow stronger with every passing hour she watched the baby's mama slowly fade.

'About last night,' he inserted suddenly.

Shannon sucked in a sharp breath. His hands moved, flexing tensely before pleating together, and she saw a nerve at the edge of his jaw give a jerk.

'I went a little crazy,' he admitted. 'I am ashamed of myself for taking my—feelings out on you.'

'We both went a little crazy.' She shifted tensely.

'It won't happen again,' he promised.

'No,' she agreed.

'So will you stay at my apartment?'

She looked down at her lap where the remains of her half-eaten sandwich lay slotted in its triangular casing and watched it blur out of focus on the onset of tears. 'Keira isn't ever going to wake up, is she?' she whispered.

Luca didn't answer for a moment, then he shook his dark head. 'I don't think so,' he responded huskily.

'I'll stay,' she agreed on a thick swallow.

Luca sat back against the bench suddenly and the air hissed out from between his teeth in a tense, taut act of relief. A moment later something dropped on her lap next to the sandwich carton.

It was a plastic security card. 'Access,' he explained. 'You might need it if I cannot get here to collect you.'

She nodded.

'If I cannot make it then my driver Fredo will come for you. You remember Fredo?'

'Yes.' Another nod while she stared down at the card. Fredo was a wiry little man with amazing patience—he needed it for the hours he tended to hang around waiting for Luca to appear.

'Good,' he said. 'Then I don't have to worry about you getting into the back of some stranger's car.'

It was a joke. She hadn't expected it. It surprised her enough to force a small laugh out of her. Luca laughed too, one of those deep, soft, husky sounds of his that caressed the senses. But it all felt so strange and wrong to be laughing in the circumstances that soon they both fell silent and still.

'You don't have to worry about me at all,' she thrust into that stillness.

'Worry is not the word that shoots into my head,' he countered. 'Someone should be here with you supporting you through this. Here.' Something else landed on her lap. She stared in surprise at the sight of her own mobile telephone. 'It was in my overcoat pocket. I found it this morning,' Luca explained. 'Here is my private number. Log it in the phone's memory. Don't hesitate to call me if you need me, Shannon.' It was a serious threat more than polite reassurance.

Then he stood up so suddenly that he made her blink. Big and lean and dark and tense, he blocked out her sunlight. She felt cold—bereft. He was going to leave and she wanted to fling herself at him and beg him to stay!

But he had duties to return to and she had a bedside vigil to keep.

'I have to go.' He stated the obvious and tension zipped through the air like electric static. 'Use the phone, do you hear me?'

Shannon pressed her lips hard together and nodded. He

turned and strode away without glancing back and she remained sitting there with the sun trying to put back the warmth he had taken with him.

It didn't.

Luca had never felt so inadequate or useless in his entire life as he did when he walked away from her like that. But he had things to deal with, lousy, throat-locking, soul-stripping *things* that could not be put off.

But his mind was locked into Shannon—or was it his heart? He didn't know. What he did know was that Shannon might have betrayed him two years ago but he was betraying her now by not being there when she needed him.

And it had to be him. That was the other part of his inner conflict that was flaying him alive. He did not want someone else to be there with her. He didn't even want to think about her leaning on someone else.

'*Dio*, leave me in peace!' he rasped when the land-line on the desk began to ring.

It was a reporter wanting him to make a statement. This was not the first insensitive lout he'd had to deal with today and probably would not be the last. As he was replacing the receiver Renata put her head round the door to look him a question. She'd added ten years in twenty-four hours. They all had.

'No,' he said. 'It was the press, not the hospital.'

Renata remained hovering in the doorway and he knew she wanted him to hold her. Walking across the room, he took her in his arms and let her weep into his shoulder and wished it could be OK for him to break down and weep.

'How is Mama?' he asked when the flood subsided.

'She's awake now, and looking a little stronger,' Renata told him, then added carefully. 'Luca, about Shannon—'

'Don't go there, Renata,' he warned thinly and was glad of the excuse to move away from her when the phone rang again. His sister hovered for a few seconds longer, silenced by his censure and waiting to find out who was calling before slipping away once she knew the call was business.

He did not want to discuss the rights and wrongs of Shannon staying with him at his apartment. He did not want to discuss Shannon with anyone—period.

His personal assistant was asking him a question that required his full concentration. Luca gave it to him and dealt with the problem as if it were perfectly normal to make corporate decisions while the world lay in rubble at his feet.

It was while he was in the middle of a curt, clipped sentence that his private cell-phone began to beep.

Shannon. He was certain of it. He dropped the other phone as if it were a hot brick.

His fingers shook as he made the connection. All she could manage to say to him was, 'Please—will you come?'

CHAPTER FIVE

Luca came to a stop in the doorway, a thick breath labouring in his chest. He was too late. She had called him too late. Now he was having to stand here and witness just how alone she must have felt.

The doctors had advised him to take her away now, but how did you prize those slender white fingers from her beautiful, beautiful sister's fingers for the last time?

Tears hit his eyes and remained there, burning like acid, though he did not let them fall. It was going to happen soon, he knew that. Soon he was going to give way to all of this hard, aching grief and cry himself empty, he promised himself.

But for now he wanted to hit something again, put his fist through a window or a wall. The pain it would cause had to be more bearable than what he was suffering right now, he thought grimly as he made himself walk forward on legs that felt hollow and slowly went down on his haunches next to Shannon's chair. She didn't even notice, but as he gathered up her free hand her eyelashes flickered and she looked at him.

'It's over,' she whispered.

'*Sì,*' he murmured unevenly. 'I know.'

Her eyes drifted back to her sister's quietly serene face and she forgot he was there again for a while, then the sound of a muffled sob came from somewhere behind them, and glancing round Luca saw that the rest of his family had arrived.

He'd taken off without them with Fredo driving like a madman leaving the others to find their own way here, now they poured forward, crowding the bed to begin this next wave of unbearable grief. As they pressed around the bed he saw Shannon become aware, blinking blank and dazed eyes at the sudden commotion, and he knew by instinct that she was not going to cope with the Italian way of letting feelings pour out like this.

With his jaw set like a closed vice, he reached across for her other hand and with gentle fingers began carefully easing it away from Keira's hand.

Shannon gasped and looked him a pained protest. But he shook his head. 'It's time to let go, *cara*,' he told her gently.

For a moment he thought she was going to refuse. She looked back at her sister with glistening tears drawing a film across her eyes and it ripped him apart inside because he knew those tears displayed the beginning of acceptance.

A few seconds after that she allowed him to complete the separation, allowed him to ease his arm around her waist and help her to her feet. The others flooded towards her now, crowding her by reaching out to embrace her and murmuring their tearful phrases of condolence; his mother looking dreadful, his weeping sisters and their sober-faced husbands all taking their turn.

Shannon accepted their embraces from within a cocoon of dazed bewilderment and clung tightly to one of Luca's hands.

Keira was gone.

Angelo and Keira. Was it all right for her to use their names together like that now? She looked up at Luca standing big and dark like a guard beside her; his handsome face was locked up again, mouth grim, eyes hot. It wasn't the face to which you asked such a question, she thought, and allowed him to guide her towards the door, leaving her sister surrounded by people who'd always loved her unstintingly.

There was consolation in that somehow.

'The baby,' she said as they reached the quietness of the corridor.

'Not now,' Luca said and kept her moving—away towards the lifts, then down and across the ground floor foyer out into the late afternoon sunlight. It was cold and she shivered. She saw Fredo was there looking solemn as he held open the rear door to a big silver car. Luca guided her inside, then followed. Almost as soon as the door closed behind him he was reaching for her and drawing her into his arms.

They stayed like that for the time it took Fredo to deliver them to the apartment, Shannon leaning limply against him, lost somewhere inside the mists of shock while he gave her what he instinctively knew she needed—his silent strength.

He continued to hold her close as they walked across the main foyer of the apartment block; he kept her wrapped in his arms as they rode the lift. When they reached the apartment she suddenly broke free and headed straight for her bedroom. Luca needed to use a few moments to put a clamp on what was threatening to break loose from inside him, then he followed with the intention of making sure she was all right before he left her alone to her grief.

But it did not work out like that. One glance at her lying curled on her side in the middle of the bed and he was kicking off his shoes, dragging off his jacket and tie, then joining her.

It was really quite pathetic the way she accepted his arms as they drew her in, and near impossible not to shed tears with her when she began to weep quietly.

When she eventually went silent he reached beneath and tugged out the duvet, then covered them both.

'I don't—' she went to protest.

'You are so cold you're shivering,' he cut in huskily. 'Stay here with me like this for a little while,' he encouraged. 'Once you warm up a bit I will go and leave you in peace.'

'I don't want you to go.' It was so soft and weak he almost missed it. But he didn't miss the way her fingers drifted across his shirt front and settled in a tremulous curl around his nape. Her breath feathered along his jawline, her breasts felt soft against his ribs and a slender leg slid across his thighs as she pressed herself closer as if it was the only place she wanted to be. He closed his eyes and wished it did not feel so good to be needed by her like this.

That need continued through the ensuing dark days when Shannon was aware of very little if Luca was not there to make her.

'Eat,' he'd say and she would eat. 'Sleep,' and she would curl up in her bed like a child and close her eyes obediently.

In the mornings they would share breakfast, then Luca would drive her to the hospital to be with the baby while he went off to attend to—other things. In the afternoon he would arrive back at the hospital to spend a little time in the nursery before taking Shannon back to his apartment to ply her with more food and make her talk about work, her life in London, Keira and Angelo—about anything so long as she was made to use her brain.

She moved around as if surrounded by a fog, though she didn't mind. It might be cold but it was oddly comforting— she liked it. The Salvatore family were being kind to her. They had managed to put their resentments aside in these days of a shared grief. Mrs Salvatore invited her to come and stay with her, but Shannon declined. 'I want to stay with Luca,' she explained, too lost in her fog to see that the invitation had been issued to get her *away* from Luca. But it would not have mattered if she had been aware of it because Luca himself happened to overhear the invitation, and turned it down.

The only time the fog cleared was when she was with the

baby. In fact her world began to revolve around the tiny and sweet, tragically orphaned daughter of Angelo and Keira.

Having had personal experience, Shannon knew exactly how it felt to be orphaned at birth. She and Keira had been brought up by a spinster aunt who'd come to Dublin and carried the two girls off to live with her in England. Shannon knew all of this because Keira had told her. Only three years older than herself, yet Keira had remembered it all so vividly. Maybe it was Aunt Merrill's no-nonsense efficiency at that time that had turned the frightened and bewildered Keira, who was missing her mother, into such a timid mouse, whereas Shannon had never known anything else but Aunt Merrill's no-nonsense, 'I don't have time to deal with this' attitude, so she'd learned to be independent very young.

Aunt Merrill shocked everyone by marrying and moving to live with her new husband in South America only weeks after Keira's wedding and while Shannon was in her first term at university. It had not occurred to either sister that the woman they'd sort of relied upon had been chafing at the bit waiting for the moment when her responsibility towards them would finish so that she could get on with her own life. Neither of them had resented their aunt for doing that, but with Keira living in Florence and busy building her marriage, Shannon had been left alone to fend for herself while she'd finished her education. What emerged from those years of self-sufficiency was a bright and super-confident young woman brimming with a zest for life.

Her aunt knew what had happened to Keira and Angelo because Shannon had rung her up to break the news. Merrill offered her sympathy but said she would not be able to attend the funerals because she had too many commitments. When Aunt Merrill had fulfilled her commitments to her sister's children she'd well and truly cut them out of her life.

Looking down at the small baby she held cradled in her arms, 'It will never be like that between you and me,' she vowed softly. 'You, my precious, will have my lifelong love.'

Luca appeared, striding into the nursery like a dynamic force wearing one of the sombre dark suits she'd grown used to seeing him in over the last week. He looked tired, drained to the dregs of his energy by too much heartache and too many painful, emotion-stripping formalities to deal with. But his face softened into a smile when he saw Shannon cradling the small pink bundle in her arms.

'She's been unplugged,' he exclaimed in soft surprise as he came down on his haunches to brush a gentle finger along the baby's pink cheek.

'Half an hour ago.' Shannon smiled too. 'They just came in and took out the leads and tubes and handed her to me.'

'May I take her?' he requested, and without hesitation he received the tiny person into the crook of his arm.

Straightening up, Luca strolled away to the window, his dark head bowed as he gazed down at his brother's child. She was exquisite. A tiny pink rosebud Angelo would have fallen instantly in love with.

Well, I've done it for him, he thought adoringly. Angelo's daughter was never going to feel the loss of her father's love, he vowed, and lowered his head to seal the vow with the light brush of his lips to her petal-soft cheek.

'I must formally register her birth soon,' he remarked as one thought led him onwards. He'd become quite the expert on the official procedures required for registering birth and death, he mused. 'This little angel needs a name.'

'She already has one,' Shannon said, then flushed when he lifted his eyes to send her a sardonically questioning glance.

'Well, this is interesting,' he drawled, and he glanced back at the baby. 'It seems you have a name no one else knows about, *mia dolce piccola*. Perhaps your Aunt Shannon would like to share it with us?'

Aunt Shannon suddenly looked distinctly defensive. 'I call her Rose,' she murmured. 'It—it's Keira's middle name.'

'I know it is,' Luca said quietly. 'I was merely wondering if there was a second or two when you considered giving all of us an opportunity to offer up our own suggestions…?'

He could see by the frown pulling at her brow that there had not been a second when she had considered such a thing. 'I haven't gone over your head and made it official. It's just *my* name for her,' she then said uncomfortably. 'If you have any objections then just—'

'I like it,' he cut in, making that point clear, though his eyes narrowed slightly as a sudden suspicion began to play with his head.

If Shannon had decided on the baby's name without consulting with anyone else, could it be that she was harbouring ideas of possession that did not include anyone else?

He studied her tired face with its blue eyes set in saddened darkness and the downward turn that had taken virtual permanent control of her beautiful mouth. Her skin looked so delicate it reminded him of finely stretched silk—touch it and it would tear apart.

His gaze drifted lower, moving over the black jeans that made her legs look more slender than ever and the navy-blue top that hid nothing he couldn't picture for himself. She barely ate and it was showing. She barely slept—though he was aware that she did not know he listened to her as she paced his apartment in the dead of night. She was beautiful but bruised, beautiful but lost in her own world of grief that shut out everyone else.

But he had plans for this baby. He had plans for her aunt. Aware though that this was not the time to voice those plans, he continued amiably, 'If I could make a small addition—for my mother's sake, you understand. We could name her Rosita, use Rose as our name for her and add Angelina, in Angelo's memory—what do you think?'

Shannon thought it sounded so beautifully appropriate that it brought the ready tears to her eyes. 'Yes, I would like that,' she whispered and was too lost in thoughts of Angelo and Keira to notice how the baby girl had just become fully Italian.

'Here…' Luca said, and gave her back the baby, watched the tears drift away to be replaced with a loving smile and was quietly satisfied with the smooth way he had handled this. 'Say your farewell, then we must be going…'

They had the ordeal of a double funeral to get through tomorrow and Shannon needed something to wear. She knew this because they had discussed it over breakfast this morning and she had reluctantly agreed to let him take her shopping. But by the scowling expression she sent him he knew she had changed her mind.

'No way,' he firmly vetoed the look. 'You need the break from here and a change of scenery—*I* need the same. You never know,' he added lightly as she stood up and without comment went to lay the baby down in her cot. 'We might even catch ourselves enjoying it.'

Oddly enough they did enjoy themselves. Luca took her back to the apartment for a quick shower before they headed into the city. Shannon changed into the only dress she had brought with her to Florence—a deep sapphire-blue long-sleeved knit thing that clung to her slender figure and highlighted the colour of her eyes. She applied some make-up for the first time in a week, brushed out her hair and decided on impulse to leave it loose. Slipping her feet into a pair of slender-heeled shoes, she then went to look for Luca—and found him in the sitting room stretched out on one of the brown sofas reading a magazine while waiting for her, just as he used to do.

The familiarity of the pose brought her to a standstill in the doorway. It jolted her right out of her comfortable fog. He looked so achingly beautiful, so long and dark and sleek and so much her kind of man that her heart turned over. When he caught sight of her standing by the door, the sight of his easy smile took away her ability to breathe.

When he tossed the magazine aside to rise lithely to his feet she knew she had got herself into deep trouble here because everything about him was drawing her to him, like that old magnetic pull they used to share. He'd changed his suit for casual dark grey trousers and a soft black leather jacket worn over a wine-red shirt. In sharp suits he was expensive and dynamic; in casual clothes he became—dangerous.

And now he had gone still—other than for slumber-dark eyes, which were roaming over her as if he too were only just seeing her for the first time this week.

'Quite an exquisite transformation,' he murmured softly, and began walking towards her.

Shannon watched him come through guarded eyes because she knew what he was thinking. He was thinking—mine—sex—I want. She recognised the sensually possessive gleam. Her stomach muscles gave an agitated tingle, the tips of her breasts stirring in their old electric response to him.

'Beautiful,' he murmured, then bent to touch her mouth with his and maintained the light contact until he felt her lips quiver before he lifted his head again. 'Ready to go?' he enquired with subtle innocence.

Her uncertain nod came with an equally uncertain frown because she knew that kiss had been a deliberate gesture—like a warning foretaste of what was to come.

Did she want what was to come? She didn't know yet—

she didn't even know if she wanted to leave here at all feeling as unsettled and confused as she did.

'Then let's do it,' he said, as if he were answering the questions she was asking of herself.

They drove into the centre of Florence, winding through the back streets until they reach the pedestrian zone where Luca parked the car. It was warmer than it had been since she'd arrived in Italy and the sun was bright so she left her coat in the car and they set out walking.

Luca settled a hand at her waist as if it had every right to be there. The top of her head reached to just above his shoulder; every time he spoke to her he turned to look her deep in her eyes. She could feel herself becoming mesmerised yet couldn't seem to do anything about it. Even though she knew he was deliberately building the intimacy between them, she was just too susceptible to slap him down.

That was the trouble with tragedy and grief, she excused her own weak behaviour—it sapped your strength to fight.

They turned heads as they walked together. It had always been this way for them because they made such a striking contrast—he the tall, dark man of Florence and she the white-skinned slender creature with hair that flamed.

A man stopped to utter something candidly naughty about them to Luca in Italian and when Shannon made the translation she couldn't resist an impulsive laugh. Luca grinned, white-toothed and wicked. The stranger looked momentarily shocked at Shannon's laughing response, then he was grinning as he went on his way leaving them to do the same.

They reached the great *Duomo* cathedral with its gleaming white ribs set against terracotta tiles. As they walked beneath its mighty shadow Shannon did what she knew she had been aching to do and slipped her arm around Luca's lean waist.

Luca didn't want it to stop. He did not want to take her into one of the élite shops on *Via dei Tornabuoni* and snuff out her lingering smile by shrouding her in black mourning clothes. So he diverted them into the elegant café *Giacosa* and ordered cappuccino and pastries, which they shared while he carefully set her talking about her life in London and her graphic design business until she was talking away with all her old zest and enthusiasm, shooting him questions, picking at his brains—and other parts of him, just as she used to do.

It was mad, he knew it. Allowing himself to become bewitched again was a fool's way to go. But he had plans for Shannon and if those plans were a poor excuse for letting her inch her way back into his system then he was ready to fool himself that he was in control.

Shopping in Florence was a serious occupation. No one knew how to shop better than the Italians. They were born with an innate sense of class and unquestionable style. Luca was no different, so it was he that decided on a suit because of the sleek, timeless classicism of its beautiful fabric and wonderful cut. After buying the suit they window-shopped on *Via dei Tornabuoni*, stopping to buy bag and shoes, before moving on to *Via dei Pecori* to select the rest of the things she required. The moment an assistant settled the first black veil on Shannon's head Luca saw the change come over her face and knew she'd remembered why they were doing this, so he distracted her with an extravagant showering of expensive lingerie, which made her blush, then smile.

They took her purchases back to the car, then Luca suggested that they walk down to the river to watch the sun go down. Shannon agreed, aware that he was peeling back the years to a different time when everything was wonderful and they used to do this kind of thing often. Luca was as irresistible as he had been back then. Smiling, talking naturally with him while holding hands as they strolled along the *Lungarni* and onto the *Ponte Santa Trinita* to watch the sunset on the Arno, was like dipping her hand into very hot water—and discovering that she liked it.

'Oh, just look, Luca…' she prompted softly as the river turned into a silk ribbon of fire and warmed the famous face of the *Ponte Vecchio*—the next bridge in the line. 'How do you ever get used to looking at this?'

They were standing shoulder to shoulder against the bridge looking down the river, but he turned at her words to run his gaze over her face tinted golden by the sun and her hair shot with flames. 'I don't,' he said.

Inner flutters took flight in her stomach because she knew he was referring to her, not the view. She glanced at him. 'Now that was corny,' she chided, 'and very un-Italian of you.'

'It is the truth—why pretend?' He shrugged lazily.

She was suddenly racked by a cold shiver as the cool water rising from the river touched her skin. 'I'm cold,' she said and pushed away from the bridge to begin walking back the way they had come, aware that she'd left Luca still leaning there absorbing the change in mood.

He soon caught up with her, though, his leather jacket arriving across her shoulders along with his arm to hold it there. 'Thank you,' she murmured a trifle stiffly.

'Prego,' he drawled with a lightness that told her he was going to ignore the mood change and his arm remained where it was across her shoulders, casual yet intimate and possessive.

'Where shall we eat?' he asked after a moment.

'It's too early for dinner.' For an Italian, anyway.

'You prefer to go back to the apartment now?'

No, she didn't. Going back meant making a decision about what came after they got there and she knew she wasn't ready to do that yet. But she was also remembering his liking for the super-smart restaurants frequented by the

Florentine élite. Etiquette was everything in those places, along with a seriously adhered-to code of dress.

'Somewhere small and casual, then,' she said carefully.

He smiled. 'The prompt was not necessary, *cara*.' It was his turn to chide. 'I was thinking of that little place we used to go to off *Via Delle Belle Donne*—you loved the *panzanella* there, if I recall…'

Its warm, cosy atmosphere was just what Shannon needed. She relaxed again. The food was delicious and the man she shared it with was—perfect.

He sat across a small table with the candlelight flickering on his golden face and fed her small titbits of food with the tips of his long fingers, plied her with a crisp, dry white wine. And he talked, mesmerising her with deep-timbred tones soaked in intimacy and he did it in Italian to force her to concentrate only on him. When she spoke he dipped his eyes to watch her mouth move, kissed it with those eyes to make her lips tremble, then flicked his gaze back to her eyes to make her aware that he knew what was happening to her.

It was the foreplay in a long seduction, she knew, because she'd been caught up in its spell so many times before. He was making love to her with his eyes, with his voice, with every intimate weapon he had in his super-sensual armoury.

'Why?' she asked him suddenly.

'Because I want you,' he answered, not even attempting to misunderstand the question.

Faults and all? she was about to challenge when his fingertips came up to rest against her mouth. 'Don't question me—ask yourself what you want.'

She wanted him, she admitted. She had always wanted him. She wanted tonight to go on for ever and the past to disappear altogether and for the sadness of tomorrow to never come.

So when he kissed her as they left the restaurant she let him, his hands gently crushing her shoulders beneath his leather jacket, the light brush of the bodies a teasing taster for what was to come.

On the way back to the car Luca suddenly left her side with a murmured excuse and disappeared into one of the little shops that sold everything. He came out a few minutes later carrying a box, which he handed to Shannon with a lopsided grin. It was a box of chocolate-coated truffles, more confirmation of what they were going to be doing soon because they always used to indulge in chocolate-coated truffles, feeding them to each other while reclining on the bed, still wearing the bloom on their naked flesh from a long, slow loving.

He was pulling out all of the stops here to recreate their old magic. And she was so busy blushing that she almost missed his other hand slipping something small into his pocket, and even then she just assumed it was some folded paper Euros and dismissed the incident to the back of her head in favour of—other things.

They continued walking towards *Duomo* with anticipation beating a tender pulse of its own. They got into his car as that pulse grew quicker. They drove without speaking, which speeded it all the more. They climbed out of the car and arrived at the basement lift. He reached out to press the call button at the same time that his other hand drew her close.

'You're trembling,' he said.

She tried a laugh that didn't quite work, then his mouth was capturing hers and they were kissing so deeply she was unaware that the lift had arrived until he broke away to manoeuvre them inside its cool metal casing. Then he was propping her up against the wall with his body while he activated security. They rode the lift with his hands cupping her hips, and his lips pressing small kisses all over her face.

She did not push him away. She did not say no to this, so why was she beginning to feel anxious the closer they came to that point at which she was going to move beyond the point of saying no?

The lift doors opened; their bodies separated as they stepped out.

Everything was the same—*everything*. The cream walls, the inlaid floor—Apollo standing to one side of the arch. Electric lights burned, softly activated by a time switch so no one ever arrived here in the dark.

She moved on legs that felt like sponge now, her heart beating oddly in her breast.

Did she want this?

Luca was behind her—close behind her. The lift doors closed and he was turning her round to face him again, capturing her eyes and keeping the past safely merged with the present with the luxurious dark promise burning in his. His jacket was taken from her shoulders and tossed aside on a nearby chair. His hands replaced it, closing over slender shoulders, then stroking down her arms before moving to the tingling base of her spine where he pressed her into arching contact with his body and recaptured her mouth with a deep, deep kiss that sent the question marks flying away.

They moved on to her bedroom, the door closing them into their carefully constructed world where no outside forces were allowed to intrude. She put the box of truffles aside on a chest of drawers, then wound her slender arms around his neck, her head tilting sideways as her mouth searched for his again, lips parted, warm and pulsing with invitation. The breath shuddered from him as he accepted the invitation and he shuddered again when she rolled her tongue around the inner tissues of his mouth. They were joined—already—even without the rest of what was to come. It had always been like this for them.

They kissed like that for ages, immersing themselves in a deep, dark, sensual mist. He stroked her arms, he stroked her body, he slid his hands beneath her hair and slowly slid down the zip to her dress. She sighed at the pleasurable caress of his fingers against the silk-smooth flesh on her back, stretching and arching in perfect accord with his demands as he urged her arms down so he could peel the dress away. The tight cuffs on the sleeves snagged on her hands and he gave a sharp tug to get them free. Then he was collecting up her wrists and kissing them as if to soothe away that small piece of violence—because violence had not been allowed to come into this room with them. It belonged to the past when they'd fallen on each other in a rage of untrammelled lust.

No, she thought, don't remember that, as another moment of indecision feathered her skin.

The dress slithered to the floor, and Luca followed its progress with the dark glow of his eyes while his hands moved on to unclip her bra. Pretty cups of blue lace trailed away from two pale globes with protruding crests of tight rose-pink. He licked one of them and she released a gasp of pleasure, closing her eyes on that unwanted moment of question in favour of this. Her shoulders went back, her head tilting with them so as to lift her breasts up towards his mouth.

Luca laughed; it was a soft and low sound of recognition. She had always been a delightfully receptive lover. He moved his tongue to the other breast and elicited the same response. In the right mood he could make her come just by standing here doing this and nothing else.

But not tonight, he told himself as he sent his hands stroking across skin like satin, gently moulding her slender body then bringing the arching of her hips into contact with the waiting thickness between his. She felt the thrust of his penis and moved against it, instinctive and unreserved when it came to pleasuring the senses.

'Undress me,' he said.

She opened her eyes, blue slow to focus, but smiling a

siren's sensual smile when they did. She reached out to free buttons, smoothing back fabric to reveal the power built into his chest and scraping fingernails through the dark springy hair that covered finely leathered dark golden skin. The shirt fell away and she leant forward to trail wet, warm kisses from one bulging pectoral to the other while her fingers went to unzip his trousers so they could slide inside to explore.

It was a touch like no other. Luca closed his eyes as a wave of desire rolled over him. His breath scored his throat and she whispered something incoherent. When he opened his eyes he saw her tongue running a moist circle around her lips and he knew why it was doing it.

She could hide nothing—never could. Heat roared up from the pit of his very essence and on a growl he picked her up and took her to the bed, bent to throw back the quilt, then laid her on the cool white sheet. She watched him strip off his clothes, still hiding nothing of what she wanted as she followed his movements with her sensual eyes and matched them by stripping away stockings and blue panties, long legs slithering against white linen giving him tantalising glimpses of womanly folds hidden within a burnished copper cloud.

His mouth wanted to swoop and take possession. But not yet, he thought and gave his hand the pleasure of sliding between those restless thighs as he came down beside her, leaving his mouth free to take what it needed from her hungry, hunting mouth.

They kissed, they touched, they rolled together; when he plunged fingers inside her she groaned in shuddering delight. He knew everything about her, where to touch, what to do to launch her into space.

'Need you,' she kept on saying over and over. 'Need you—need you,' until he was dizzy with hearing it, with triumph, with a need of his own that piled on the heat.

Her hands weren't still. He might know Shannon inside and out but she was as well acquainted with him. She knew where to stroke to get his senses roaring, she knew how to torment him and earn herself a flame-hot response, until his blood sang and his breathing became ragged. By the time he let her guide him into her he was already lost to everything but her and this raging pleasure.

She arched her hips in hungry welcome; he made his deep, plunging thrusts without holding anything back. She clung where she could and he rode her like a man chasing after something he should never have lost. The heat of her electrified his senses, her tightness enclosed the length of his shaft. Their mouths were fused, their hearts thundering, their flesh bathed in sweat, limbs gripping or clinging, all parts of them trembling in a hot and gasping journey towards the mercurial finish.

She toppled first, taking him with her, the rippling response of her orgasm fiercely exciting his own. He groaned and kept on groaning with each shuddering stab of his body that released his juices into the path of pulsating muscles that greedily gathered them in.

Eventually it slowed, the tight, speeding rush of the senses steadied, tension eased and he became aware that Shannon was taking his full weight. He slid away from her, then lay on his back with his eyes closed, waiting for the silver-white flood of deep satiation to become a slow ebb.

After a while he found the energy to look at her. She hadn't moved at all. Levering himself up onto a forearm, he looked down to find that her eyes were still closed and she looked quite pale. Had he hurt her? Anxiety shot tension back into his shoulders because he could have done; there had been moments there when he had been lost in a blackness that had roared in his head.

'OK?' he asked huskily and touched his lips to her soft

lips, then gently fingered some damp strands of hair from her cheek.

Her lazy, 'Mmm,' swam through him in a river of relief.

'Then open your eyes and look at me,' he commanded. 'I don't like it when you lie so still.'

Her eyelids fluttered upwards, dusky lashes spiky with mascara—and she smiled. 'You're so wonderful, do you know that?' she told him softly.

In true macho style he agreed with a lazy grin, then touched another kiss to her lips. He had just enjoyed the most amazing experience in his entire life and managed to take his woman along with him. So he felt wonderful.

'Truffles,' she announced suddenly, and was going from satiated stillness into live-wire movement within the single blink of an eye.

Allowing her to wriggle from beneath him, Luca lay on his side and watched through slumber-dark mocking eyes as she climbed off the bed and strode across the room to collect the box of chocolate-coated truffles from where she had placed them on the chest of drawers by the door.

The moment that Shannon picked up the box, something began to nag at her from the back of her mind. She turned round slowly, frowning down at the chocolate-coated truffles while trying to capture whatever that niggling something was.

It was then that it hit like a blinding flashback bursting forth to replay itself. She saw Luca coming out of the shop wearing that smile on his face as he handed her the truffle box. But it was what his other hand was doing that she was focusing on now. She'd thought he'd been sliding some folded Euros into his pocket. She could see it so clearly now that she couldn't believe she had made such a stupid mistake!

He hadn't gone into that shop to buy truffles! Those had

been a mere afterthought to the more serious purchase he'd made.

A packet of condoms. He had bought condoms in preparation for the carefully nurtured love-fest!

'I cannot look at you without wanting to be inside you,' he murmured in a low, dark rasp.

Her chin jerked as she lifted her face to look at him. He was lying in typical, relaxed Luca fashion, on his side with his dark head propped up on a hand and a long, powerful leg casually bent. The naked pose hid nothing. Not the breadth of his chest or the length of his long torso covered with dark hair. Nor did it cover that other cluster of hair that surrounded his sex.

A proud and very potent sex.

She began to shake, with rage or with terror—she wasn't sure which and it was probably a combination of both.

'You bastard,' she spat at him. 'I hate you!'

CHAPTER SIX

'*COSA?*' Luca's languid dark eyes showed surprise and bewilderment.

'I h-hate you,' Shannon repeated. 'You *knew* you'd done it without the first time and you didn't bother to tell me!'

He sat up, a frown pulling his black brows together across the bridge of his nose. 'What are you talking about?'

'Condoms,' she enlightened. 'Y-you bought some tonight from the shop you got these truffles from. I saw you put them in your trouser pocket.'

'*Sì,*' he confirmed, not seeing the problem. 'We tempted fate the last time,' he admitted. 'I was not going to take the same chances this time—why are you looking at me like that?'

Because it was getting worse by the second. With a start of screaming alarm, Shannon dropped the box of truffles to make a dive for his trousers where they lay discarded on the floor. Trembling fingers dipped into a pocket and came out with a cellophane wrapped packet.

She didn't even need to speak. Luca saw the packet and caught on at last. '*Idiota,*' he breathed, then had the absolute utter gall to offer her a lazily sheepish grin. 'We never did like those things, did we *cara*? Too much messing around when we were under the influence of much more compelling forces.'

She threw the packet at him. It impacted with a god-like bronze shoulder then dropped with ironic accuracy onto his lap. 'I will never forgive you,' she snapped at him furiously. 'How could you take such risks with me, Luca? How could you!' she cried.

He stared at her for a moment longer, then his own mood altered. 'We both took the risks, *cara*,' he pointed out grimly. 'We fell upon each other without doing much thinking at all, if you recall. It was not a one-way slaking.'

'I wasn't trying to say it was!'

'Then what are you so mad about?' he snapped, rolling off the bed to land on his feet on the other side of it.

She could barely get any words out across the lump of incredulous fury strangling her throat. 'I'm standing here in real danger of already being pregnant and you wonder why I'm mad?' she choked.

'Pregnant? What is this?' he demanded. 'You take the pill,' he stated with supreme confidence, 'and this kind of joke is not funny!'

'You can bet it's not funny,' Shannon breathed hotly. 'Because I am *not* on the pill—why the heck do you think I'm so upset?'

A thick silence clogged up the air for a second. Then, *'Madre di Dio,'* he muttered, 'we have been talking about different risks.'

'What different risks?' she shot at him, bewildered.

'Why are you not on the pill?' he shot back.

'Why did you buy condoms if you believed I was?'

He didn't answer. Instead he grabbed the back of his neck and swung his back to her, leaving Shannon to use up the next few suffocating seconds drawing her own conclusions, which she did with a shuddering gasp of dismay. 'Is what you're *not* saying here,' she framed very slowly, 'that you've been indulging in unsafe sex with other women and *still* didn't think to protect me for my health?'

'I don't believe this conversation.' He turned on her angrily. 'I do not indulge in unsafe sex and I am perfectly healthy!'

'Oh, you're so very positive about that!' she snapped.

'Sì!' he declared.

'If that's so and you obviously thought I was taking the pill, then why did you bother to buy the—?'

The answer arrived before she'd even finished asking the question. The sudden taut cast that arrived on his face was like a physical slap of confirmation. The condoms had been bought to protect *him*. He thought *he* was at risk from *her*.

Shannon stopped trembling. It was amazing, she realised, how calming the ice-cold wash of truth could be. She was the bad guy here, the one that took different men to her bed.

And he was the man who had hurt her once too often.

'Get out of my room,' she said, then turned and walked into the bathroom, thrusting the door shut behind her with a foot as she went.

The door didn't even make it into its housing before it was thrust open again by an angry hand. 'I did not mean what you thought I meant,' a still-naked Luca uttered stiffly.

'Yes, you did.' Snatching a bathrobe from the hook behind the door, she wrapped herself in it.

'I denied your charge,' he defined angrily, 'which did not mean I was then throwing the blame onto you!'

No, Shannon thought bitterly, his silence did that for him.

'But we have been apart for two years and no one—man or woman—in their right minds takes unnecessary risks these days!'

'You did—twice!' she flashed.

'And so, *mia cara*, did you,' he returned.

There was no answer to that so she didn't offer one; instead she picked up a towel and tossed it at him. 'Cover yourself,' she said with contempt and went to push past him, but he stayed her with a hand on her arm.

'Stay right where you are,' he commanded darkly. 'We have a problem here and we need to talk about it.'

'I think we've done enough of that.' She tried to tug free.

But he was not going to let her. 'Two years ago you took

the legs from under me,' he threw at her harshly. 'Now here
you are doing the same thing to me again!'

'Where do you think my legs are?' she cried. 'You've
just issued me with the worst insult a man can pay the
woman he's just sank his body into!'

He winced. 'I apologise.'

'It's not enough,' she tugged.

His fingers tightened. 'Then what do you want me to
say?'

'Nothing!' She was feeling so chilled it was as if she had
ice running in her veins. 'I just want you to leave this room.'

'But I can't do that. You could be carrying my child—'

'Oh—don't *say* that!' She rounded on him, hair flying,
face white, tears beginning to blacken her eyes. 'I don't
want to have your baby!'

He paled. 'You may not be left with the luxury of
choice!'

If anything put the lid on the whole wretched mess, then
that declaration did. A strangled sob escaped. Luca answered it with a teeth-grinding curse, then let go of her arm
and moved away from her, wrapping the towel around the
lean, bronzed, tightly moulded buttocks as he went.

Spying the box of truffles lying on the floor, he stooped
to pick it up and put it back on the chest of drawers with a
thump that said a lot about the feelings rumbling inside him.
His hand went back to his neck, grimly grabbing onto the
rod of tension that was threatening to snap muscle there.

One part of him was searching for words that would put
right the ugliness of what had just happened, but another
part—the angry part—was telling him to let it drop because
the truth was the truth, even when it was a bitter-tasting
truth.

He *had* been thinking of himself with the risk thing. She
did have a sexual history he could not afford to ignore. How
many different 'boyfriends' names had Keira dotted into

conversations in her stubborn, stubborn determination to keep Shannon's name alive in his head? Had Keira really believed that it made him feel great to know that Shannon was getting on with her life while his own stagnated?

Keira… He'd allowed himself to forget about Keira and his brother Angelo in this madness. He released a sigh, closing his eyes on a picture of his beautiful but slightly obsessive sister-in-law who used to remind him of a fragile spark of electricity travelling along an endless loop of wire supported by the strong, patient, loving Angelo. That spark had been snuffed out now along with its support, leaving behind a shattered family, an orphaned baby girl and Shannon, who had been knocked about enough by this tragedy without him knocking her about some more.

Dio, he thought. It was not supposed to be like this. Hurting Shannon had not been part of his plan. His sole objective when they'd set out this afternoon had been to remind her how good it used to be between them, not how ugly it could be. He'd wanted her receptive to what they could have again if they both wanted it badly enough—before he'd meant to hit her with his big proposition.

On the bed, after the loving, while sharing a chocolate-coated truffle. His planning had been meticulous. He even had a bottle of champagne and two glasses chilling in the fridge ready to help them celebrate after she'd said yes to his carefully rehearsed speech.

Now all he had was a block of ice standing somewhere behind him hating his guts, which left him wondering heavily what the hell was he supposed to do now to rescue the situation?

Then—*Dio*, he thought again. Where was his head? Nothing had changed here except the mood in which the next part took place and the main thrust of his argument!

Lowering his hand from his neck, he turned to face her. She was still standing in the bathroom doorway looking about as receptive to reason as a cat would be to the mouse it held in its teeth.

Was he a mouse? The hell that he was, he thought grimly and braced himself in readiness for what he was going to say next. 'Marry me,' he announced, reducing his well rehearsed and reasoned speech to the basic bottom line of it. 'Then all of this stops being a problem.'

A cold stone block of silence followed. Shannon continued to stare at him through those sapphire eyes and he received a very, very erotic sensation across his neck that made him think of cats and mice and—teeth.

Then she moved, and the erotic sensation slithered down his body to pool around his sex. 'Well, it must have hurt you to say that,' she drawled deridingly.

'No,' he denied.

Shannon felt her mouth flick out a cold little smile in response. Did he think she hadn't noticed the way he'd had to brace himself before making that outrageous suggestion?

And outrageous it was after what they'd just exchanged. He still hated and resented her beneath all of that throbbing desire she could see pounding at his magnificent chest. She was sure of it now—how could she not be?

'I am not having your baby.' She stated it firmly, grabbing the crux of this proposal and crushing the life out of it before it became a terrifying monster in her head. 'And even if I was unfortunate enough to be pregnant, I only have to think about Keira to gauge my chances of carrying a baby full term.'

'Don't say that.' He frowned. 'You are not your sister. You—'

'So for us to consider marriage on the slimmest chance of my being pregnant is really stupid,' she interrupted him. 'But, even if I *am* pregnant and *did* manage to carry the baby full term, I would *not* marry a man who thinks that not only am I promiscuous but I'm irresponsible with it!'

'I don't think you are promiscuous!' he denied. 'And we are not getting back into that.'

As far as Shannon was concerned they'd never left it! 'Can't trust me to stay faithful, then!'

He thrust out his chin. 'I can trust,' he insisted.

Her own chin went up, blue eyes defying the lying swine to prove that statement. 'Who was I planning to be with the night you came to my London flat?' she challenged.

His frown dragged the two black bars of his eyebrows together. 'How should I know?'

'You heard me make two telephone calls—both of which were to men—and drew some pretty quick assumptions that both of them were my lovers! That makes me pretty sluttish and untrustworthy wife material, don't you think? Add those two lovers to my irresponsible behaviour regarding sex and either one of them could be the father of this fictitious child!'

He dismissed that line of argument with an impatient flick of one long-fingered hand. 'One of those calls was to a woman.'

Surprise widened her eyes. 'Who told you that?'

'Joshua Soames,' he replied. 'He called here the other day to talk to you while you were at the hospital. I asked the question, he set the record straight.'

He'd actually pumped her business partner for information about Alex? 'And you call that trusting me?'

The frown darkened. 'Stop this,' he grated. 'Do you think I am an idiot? If you are not on the pill then you are not in a relationship. And don't start going on about slutting,' he dismissed with another flick of that hand when she opened her mouth to answer him. 'This is too serious an issue to be bouncing insults off each other. If you are pregnant it will be because I made you so, in which case I want to be there for you. If you have to go through what Keira went through, then I want to be there to support you as Angelo supported Keira. So I am offering you a serious commitment here.' He began walking towards her, closing a gap Shannon did not want closed. 'I am offering marriage—now—before the timing of conception can become an issue. I am offering it without any prejudice from the past getting in the way. And I would appreciate an honest and unprejudiced answer from you instead of razor sarcasm.'

Shannon stood through it all, watching his face and his expressive hands in fascination while listening to the slick dynamics of his clever brain as he put together his offer outlining all the positives for marriage and ignoring the negatives such as—no love, no respect, no emotional commitment, no mention of his family's horrified response.

She felt like a business he was trying to take over. He was being very cool and practical and even a little arrogant, though the arrogance was rather an attractive feature of his sales pitch. His ulterior motive? For the moment she couldn't think of one, she was too engrossed in the seductive power this man possessed when he turned himself into a trouble-shooter. She'd always liked it, been an absolute sucker for it once upon a time. Get him in professional mode discussing the rudiments of corporate management and she would be stripping him naked as he talked.

She'd seen him work this kind of magic on a room full of hard headed women while giving a talk at a business-women's convention. By the time he'd stepped off the po-dium to rapturous applause there had not been a woman in the place who had not been fantasising about him. She had been the lucky one to get him alone, though, and tap into the fantasy.

She could feel the same charismatic pull now trying to draw her towards him like a magnet. The voice was seduc-tive, the beautiful accent was seductive, the expressive way he used his hands made you visualise them moving over your skin. The serious mouth that pretended he did not know it was happening was seductive; the serious eyes that waited politely for her to offer her response were seducing her into uttering the response he wanted to hear.

He was lethal, she acknowledged. But she'd also come up with the answer to his ulterior motive.

Sex.

He might be able to keep the mask of his face under control but he was not having the same luck with the rest of his body. He'd said at much before as he lay on the bed watching her as she went to get the box of truffles. 'I cannot look at you without wanting to be inside you,' he'd confessed. What they could do for each other was still jumping all over his senses with a desire to do it all again and again.

He was hooked, on the slut who always did have the instinctive sensual expertise to turn him inside out. So— why not marry her? was his very male answer to a nagging problem. If her betrayal with another man had not got in the way two years ago, he would have committed himself to her body and soul then and without a single regret for his lost single status. He was still prepared to do that because, despite all that had happened, the sex was still mindlessly good. And the irresistible little sweetener to his outrageous proposal was that he could have it all without all the old emotional stuff getting in the way.

She called it thinking on his feet, seeing a chance to have his cake and eat it at the same time. Somewhere in the last hour she had been elevated to his idea of the perfect woman. A woman, in other words, who would be absolutely great to have as a permanent fixture in his bed but would not expect or get anything else from him once they were out of that bed.

The bastard, she thought. He hadn't bothered to mention his darling family or the fact that they had all just lived through the worst seven days of all of their lives and still had the worst day to come. This was a window of opportunity and he was not going to let the chance pass by.

She felt cold—iced over by his calculation, the speed with which he could assess and decide. He had done it to her before—two years ago in this very apartment when he'd walked in on a frankly suspicious scene, assessed and come to a decision with the blinding speed of light. That was the moment that she'd become a slut in his eyes and nothing she said afterwards could change that belief.

She shivered, she felt so cold. Inside—outside—and found herself fighting a battle with her tongue that wanted her to blurt out the truth. What would he do if she brought it all out into the open again? she wondered. Would he respond as he had done the last time by accusing her of daring to soil her sister with her own sins?

And what had Keira done? she then recalled painfully. Her sister had begged her to say nothing. Begged her to understand why she could never confess the truth to Luca, not even for Shannon's sake. 'He will tell Angelo. How could he not? If it was the other way round I would have to tell you or I could not live with myself!'

Those words were emblazoned on her heart for ever now. Because despite everything Keira had said she *had* told Luca, she had tried to save herself at the expense of Keira's marriage to Angelo.

But Luca had refused to believe.

Keira had been everyone's vision of the perfect woman, therefore Shannon had to be the sinner.

His opinion was not about to change because he'd discovered he could not keep his hands off her. He was still going to go on resenting her presence in his life and never trusting her alone with any man and probably using the sex as a darn great way of exacting punishment for betraying him.

So, did she say—Believe me about Keira and I might consider your proposition, or did she say—?

'My answer is no,' she announced, then turned and walked back into the bathroom, having the sense to shoot home the bolt this time before she sank down onto the toilet seat to bury her face in her trembling hands and silently cried her eyes out.

Because she knew that despite the long, hard lecture she had been a tongue tip away from tarnishing her poor sister's image in his eyes for ever by insisting he listen to the truth. She even had proof to back her story up, though not here, but back in London.

Luca stood with the sound of that bolt sliding home ringing in his ears and was damned hellish angry for opening himself up to that cold little no.

Who did she think she was, turning down his frankly very generous offer? She was lucky to be getting one. Did she think he wanted to attach himself to a natural-born siren with eyes constantly on the lookout for the next man?

But she was carrying his child. In his mind it was already a statement of fact—it had to be or his arguments crumbled to dust at his feet. If the witch believed he was going to allow her to walk away carrying that child with her, then she was in for a very big shock.

Turning on his heel, he walked out of her room and down the hall into his own room. Once safely shut away in there he went to take a shower—while planning his next line of attack.

There was a moment once his anger had cooled and he began to think like a rational man again that he questioned what the hell it was he was trying to do to himself by getting involved with her again.

Trust? He could never trust her out of his sight! Shannon had been right when she had faced him with that.

Did he really want a future of forever wondering who she was with when she wasn't with him?

No, he damn well did not.

Of course he could not trust her. Just as he could not dare to trust his own judgement where she was concerned, because if anyone had suggested to him that she was playing around behind his back two years ago he would have laughed in their faces—before knocking them flat.

The old dark feelings returned with a vengeance. Pushing his head beneath the shower spray, he rinsed off shampoo and saw images of that afternoon when he had come home unexpectedly to find Shannon standing in the doorway to the bedroom trying to block him from seeing the truth.

And what a truth. 'What are you doing back?' She could not have appeared more horrified to see him.

'I could ask you the same question. You were supposed to be in London until tomorrow.'

'I came back early.' She tried pulling the bedroom door shut behind her.

'So did I,' he answered absently. 'I needed some papers from my safe…' Instinct made him step around her and push the door open again.

'Damn,' he muttered as soap got in his eye. Switching off the shower, he reached for a towel and tried not to let his mind take him into that room as he wiped the stinging soap away.

The room was a mess. The bedding pulled back and lying half on the floor. He picked up the scent of male cologne. Not his cologne, not his red silk boxer shorts that he pulled quite calmly from the tangle of white sheeting. He never wore silk underwear; he never wore red. He preferred cotton, black, white, grey—any damn colour but red.

'Who do these belong to?' He saw himself swing round in time to catch her sliding something into a bedside drawer.

'I came back to f-find it like this. I don't know wh-what—'

His hand reached out to open the drawer Shannon had pushed shut. He saw her stiffen then start to tremble, then lower her eyes when he drew out the packet of condoms.

Condoms, bloody condoms, he thought viciously. The blight of his bloody life!

One was missing—not that it mattered that one was missing; the fact that they were there at all was enough to turn his blood to bile. They did not use condoms. And that scent—that damned strong male scent had clung to his nostrils while he'd stood there trying to deal with what it was he was being forced to face.

'I can explain...' She'd sounded deep-voiced and husky, like someone suffering from an intolerable amount of anxiety and stress.

Without saying a word he put the packet back in the drawer and closed it, then turned to look at her. 'Before you jump to your rotten conclusions—it wasn't me, Luca, it wasn't me!'

'Who, then?' he challenged.

Her face was white, her eyes black pools of utter torment; tears trailed down her cheeks and worked at her throat. 'Keira,' she whispered.

Keira. Of all the lying excuses she could have come up with, she had to choose to place the blame on the one person who would never betray her man—never. Her willingness to do that to her own sister broke his calm. What followed had been another nightmare that had lived inside him ever since.

A telephone began ringing somewhere, bringing him out of the blackness of that second nightmare to discover that he was standing in the bathroom staring at the ceramic tiles covering the floor where water was dripping from his body to form a pool around his brown feet. He lifted his head and caught sight of his face in the mirror. It was not him. It was like looking at a stranger. A man with no colour and no warmth.

Only Shannon could do this to him.

And he had offered her marriage again?

Pulling on a bathrobe, he made himself walk on legs that felt oddly stiff, as if he had just run a marathon. Maybe he had done—run a marathon through agony, lies and deceit.

He had left his jacket on the chair by the lift. His mobile phone was in one of its pockets and he strode through the apartment to collect it. The call was from Marco, his assistant. He frowned at the lateness of the hour and felt a hard snap of irritation because if Marco was still in the office then he was probably being snowed under trying to keep up in his absence.

He was bringing the call to an end when Shannon appeared in the archway. She was wearing the skimpy blue pyjamas beneath a thin blue cotton wrap, which hung open down her front. Her face was scrubbed and shiny, her hair piled up on top of her head leaving her slender neck exposed. Her eyes were like two dark bruises set on a background of porcelain white and her mouth looked tiny, pinched and—pink.

Hunger roared to life inside him followed by a self-contempt that wrapped itself like a steel band around his chest. He turned his back on her to listen in grim silence to whatever it was Marco was asking him. The poor devil sounded harassed and bone weary. Luca knew both feelings. Shannon still hovered in the archway; he wondered what she wanted.

'Just leave it for tonight, Marco,' he commanded quietly. 'The business is not going to go down the tubes if you go home and get some sleep.'

He ended the call and dropped the phone onto his jacket,

then had to flex his shoulders before he could bring himself to turn and face Shannon again.

She blinked at the toughness hardening his features. 'I'm sorry to intrude,' she apologised stiffly. 'But we left my shopping in the car and I need to hang up my suit…'

He sighed at the stupid oversight and the pendulum swing of his emotions took yet another violent swerve. What kind of selfish bastard was he to be adding to her stress at a time like this?

Misreading the reason for his sigh, she walked towards him with her hand outstretched. 'If you let me have your car keys I'll go and collect the bags myself.'

Let her loose in a basement car park at this time of the night dressed like this? 'Not while I still breathe,' he hissed, making her frown because she didn't understand.

And he was not going to enlighten her.

'I'll go,' was all he said, and turned to get his wallet and car keys from where he'd placed them on the table by the lift.

She was waiting at her bedroom door when he came back with her shopping bags.

'Thank you.' She took them from him.

'Prego,' he replied.

She took a step back, and closed the door in his face.

A sudden blistering urge to push the damn door open again and have this out almost had him doing just that. Then common sense arrived and along with it a burst of frustration, which had him aiming a clenched fist that didn't quite land on the oak panelling.

Then he went back to his own room to fester in silence.

While Shannon threw herself down on the bed to cry her eyes out again.

She hated him but she loved him and that was her toughest problem—she loved, loved—*loved* the brute!

* * *

The next day was a day Shannon hoped she would never have to endure again. From the moment she donned the black outfit the full weight of what she was about to face took her deep, deep inside herself.

She met Luca in the foyer. A fleeting glance at him standing there in his sombre black suit, white shirt and black tie, his lean face drawn into a pale grey mask of steely composure, and she knew he was feeling the same way she did. He studied her briefly, taking in her own waxen composure before he enquired expressionlessly if she was ready to leave.

Fredo drove them in a black limousine that made no attempt to disguise what it was. Even the day had decided to wear a grey cloud cast as if it knew that this was not a day to fill with warm sunlight.

They didn't talk; both had their faces half turned to the car's side windows, preferring to remain sunk into their own bleak thoughts.

They barely touched unless Luca was taking her arm to politely help her in or out of the car.

They arrived at his mother's house to find that the whole vast and scattered Salvatore family had congregated. Everyone was subdued, grave, but kind and sympathetic towards Shannon, which was nice of them given their knowledge of her past relationship with Luca—not that anyone but the closest family members knew what had happened, only that they'd parted under bitter circumstances. But still, Shannon appreciated their willingness to put all of that aside for today at least—though some could not help throwing curious glances at herself and Luca, who was never more than a step away from her side, though they did not acknowledge each other's presence.

From the moment they stepped out of the house everything took on a bleak, dreamlike quality that led them frame by agonising frame through the ensuing hours. Mrs

Salvatore was bereft. Each time she broke down the whole sombre gathering felt its rippling effect. And it was heart-rending to watch her cling to her surviving son as if she was afraid to let go in case he was lost to her too.

Renata and Sophia clung to their husbands, Tazio and Carlo. One sister was older than her surviving brother, the other slotting in between Luca and Angelo. Both were stunningly beautiful, as were all the Salvatores, and their two men had been picked to complement their outstanding looks and great name.

Shannon clung to no one, though she knew that Luca somehow always managed to keep himself within arm's reach of her just in case she broke down, but she didn't; she just kept her head lowered and did her grieving silently beneath her black lace veil.

She almost cracked at her first sighting of the two flower-decked coffins. And again later when she stepped into the church and was shocked by how many more people there were packed into it. Friends and colleagues, she presumed, most of whom were strangers to her but not to Angelo and Keira. In her heart all these people represented life surrounding the tragic couple as they made their journey to their final resting place.

She didn't shed tears throughout the service. She didn't do anything other than go where she was instructed to go, sit, stand, kneel, wait—follow. The waxen mask of her composure took its worst beating during the graveside ceremony. Mrs Salvatore almost collapsed and Luca had to support her in both his arms. Sophia wept, Renata wept, the whole flower-bedecked site seemed to rock beneath the rolling weight of everyone's grief.

Afterwards they made the journey to the Salvatore family villa set high above Florence on the outskirts of Fiesole. It was a beautiful place steeped in the fabulous trappings of wealth collected over centuries and surrounded by the most exquisite gardens big enough to lose yourself in. It was a place used by all factions of the Salvatore family for throwing extravagant parties. Today it became a place shrouded in sorrow, where the whole congregation gathered to pay their respects to the family.

Mrs Salvatore was led away to her private apartments so she could have a few minutes to compose herself. Luca, his two sisters and their husbands took up the role of hosts as the many formal reception rooms began to fill with black-clad sombre people and sober-dressed serving staff that mingled amongst them carrying white-linen-covered silver trays holding a choice of refreshment.

And Shannon had never felt so lost and alone in her entire life as she did as she wandered aimlessly from room to room, smiling politely at those who offered her their sympathy and murmuring all the right phrases in response, but she felt strange inside, oddly out of place as if she did not belong here and she knew why she felt that way.

She had just buried her sister, yet she felt as if her right to grieve had been hijacked by this great, heaving wave of Salvatore grief. It was silly, selfish and unfair of her to think this way, but telling herself that did not remove the feeling. Everyone spoke in Italian and she wanted to speak English. She wanted to remember her sister in their own language and scream at the top of her voice— Let me have my sister back!

Someone caught her arm as she was stepping out of one room into another and she was hustled into a quiet alcove set into the side of the grand staircase. Luca loomed over her like a dark shadow.

'The British stiff upper lip is still in use, I see,' he drawled sardonically.

CHAPTER SEVEN

IF HE only knew what was going on inside her head, Shannon thought. 'I didn't see you showing signs of letting your composure crack,' she countered distantly.

'It is cracked inside—bleeding, in fact.' Luca surprised her with the gruff admission. 'Here, drink some of this,' he said and put a glass in her hand.

'What is it?' she asked suspiciously.

'Brandy. It might help warm you up. You look in danger of turning into an ice sculpture.'

She drank some of the brandy and was annoyed with herself afterwards because it went straight to her eyes.

'Don't,' Luca husked.

'You started it,' she blamed, stretching her eyes wide to stop the tears, and lifted a set of fingers to press them against her trembling mouth.

His sigh arrived with the gentle touch of a long finger as it brushed a stray lock of hair from her cheek. It was contact enough to make her want to throw her arms around his neck and sob her heart out.

Someone appeared on the periphery of their vision. It was Renata; she took one look at the intimacy of their little one-to-one and tensed. Luca's older sister was one the nicest people anyone would wish to meet, but she struggled to look at Shannon without showing her disapproval.

'Mama has come down and is asking for you, Luca,' she informed her brother stiffly.

'I'll be there in a minute,' he said without taking his eyes from Shannon.

'Mama said—'

'A minute, Renata,' he interrupted incisively.

There was a pause that set the fine hairs on Shannon's body tingling and kept her eyes firmly fixed on the black silk knot of Luca's tie, then Renata spun away leaving an uncomfortable silence behind her.

'That wasn't very nice,' she chided.

'I don't feel like being nice,' he clipped in reply. 'For the whole of this terrible day you have looked like a lonely piece of fragile porcelain someone put down and forgot to pick up again. I want to pick you up and never put you down.'

It was Shannon's turn to murmur an uneven, 'Don't.' He had no right to be saying things like that to her—especially not after the way he'd used her last night.

'We need to talk. Last night was a mess,' he said abruptly, hooking right into her thoughts again. 'It should not have ended the way that it did.'

'I don't want to discuss it.' She made a move to follow in Renata's footsteps.

Luca blocked her exit from the alcove with a broad shoulder that effectively held her captive. 'We have to talk about it,' he insisted. 'There are things I should have said last night that got lost in the war. But they are about to come up and hit us both in the face so I need you to listen.'

'Listen to what—more insults?'

'No,' he denied on a rasp of impatience. 'The marriage thing,' he explained. 'You said no to marrying me for our child's sake but—'

'There is no child!' she inserted sharply.

'Luca…' It was the softer voice of Sophia that interrupted this time, sounding very cautious. 'I am sorry to disturb you but Signor Lorenzo has arrived. He wants to…'

A string of near-silent curses left Luca's lips while Shannon closed her eyes and prayed to God that Sophia hadn't heard what she'd said. 'I'm coming,' he bit out in grinding impatience.

Sophia wasn't up to pushing her point as her older sister had done, because she walked away without saying another word, leaving Shannon trapped in the alcove by a man who was literally pulsing with frustration and a burn in his eyes that made her think of—

Stop it, she thought painfully. Don't *do* this to me here! She dragged in a tense breath. 'Go to your mother, or Mr— whoever,' she said tautly.

But Luca was not going anywhere. 'Just listen,' he instructed, 'because I do not have time for this but I know it must be said!' He took a deep breath, impatience fighting with something Shannon couldn't quite put a name to but it set her trembling as he caught her eyes again and began feeding words to her in a quick, sharp rasp. 'I want you to think about Rose. I want you to put your own feelings aside, and my feelings, for that matter, and think about her and what is best for her.'

'Rose will come home with me. I mean to—'

'No!' he shot at her forcefully. His hands came up to grip her shoulders, the sudden angry shift of his body almost knocking the glass of brandy out of her hand. 'I knew you were planning something like this,' he bit out like a curse, 'but it cannot be like that.'

'Why not?'

'Because—'

'Luca…' There was no dismissing the owner of this particular voice. It belonged to Mrs Salvatore herself. Shannon almost sagged with relief when he let go of her shoulders on a sigh of surrender and turned to his mother.

'Father Michael has to leave now but he says you wanted a word with him before he— Oh, Shannon,' Mrs Salvatore cut off to acknowledge. 'I did not see you standing there.'

Which was a blatant untruth because if this wasn't part

of a conspiracy to stop whatever it was the family believed they were doing in this alcove, then Shannon would eat her hat.

Then she smashed that bit of untimely sarcasm when she saw the devastation written in the older woman's face. Luca's mother had every right to want her remaining son all to herself just now, she thought guiltily, and managed to squeeze past Luca to offer his mother a smile.

'Luca brought me a drink,' she explained.

'So thoughtful of you, Luca,' Mrs Salvatore nodded in approval. 'It seems to have done the trick, Shannon, and put some of the colour back into your cheeks. You needed it, poor dear,' she added on a husky quaver. 'Today has been such an ordeal for all of us.'

'Yes, such an ordeal,' Shannon endorsed as the full power of it came clattering back down upon her head. To her surprise, Mrs Salvatore reached out to put her arms around her and brushed a kiss on both of her cheeks. 'I will miss Keira so much,' she confided thickly—and she said it in English.

It was almost Shannon's undoing. She had to swallow the tears and was able only to nod and return the two kisses because she knew she couldn't speak. Luca's mother seemed to understand that because she patted her gently before releasing her, then turned her attention to her son.

'I don't understand why you need to speak with Father Michael but I don't think you should keep him waiting.'

'No,' her son agreed.

Shannon took this as her cue to make good her escape, 'Excuse me,' she murmured, and was about to melt quietly away when Luca stopped her with the touch of long fingers to her arm. 'OK?' he asked huskily.

She kept her eyes lowered, swallowed and nodded, but he didn't appear impressed. She could feel his irritation, his frustrated desire to finish what he had begun. But he couldn't and he knew that he couldn't. 'Think about what I said,' he clipped out eventually.

Not if I can stop myself, Shannon thought bleakly, but nodded because his mother was listening. Then she slipped her arm free of his fingers and walked away, aware of his eyes following her—aware that his mother's eyes were doing the same.

She looked so damn fragile he knew she was going to have to break soon, Luca was thinking grimly.

'I hope you know what you're doing,' his mother said.

He looked down into the pale, anxious face of this woman he loved without question and wished he could love Shannon that way again. 'I know exactly what I'm doing,' he assured her soberly.

'Still…' his mother heaved in a breath of air '…it is best not to make hasty decisions while you are feeling so vulnerable.'

The comment amused him enough to have him tilt a mocking eyebrow. 'I wish I knew what you were talking about,'

'You and Shannon,' he was informed. 'It only takes a pair of eyes to know that you two are sleeping together.'

'*Madre!*' he admonished.

'Why else would you insist that she stay at your apartment?' She shrugged off the censure. 'Why else would Shannon refuse my invitation to stay with me? The sparks fly between you like electricity and it took three—*three*—people to prize you out of this alcove.'

'Maybe that was because we did not want to be *prized* out,' Luca suggested dryly.

His mother was not impressed. 'It is a known fact that life clings to life in times of tragedy,' she persisted stubbornly. 'I can understand it—even sympathise with it. I cannot imagine another situation in which the two of you could be thrown together again so powerfully. But you now have Father Michael waiting to talk to you and Angelo's lawyer awaiting his turn. I am concerned about what it is you are planning to do.'

There was a lot he could say in reply to this, but Luca's attention was already fixed elsewhere. Throughout his mother's very sensible lecture his eyes had followed the glowing crown of Shannon's head as she moved amongst the darker heads clustered at the other end of the hall. He'd watched her pause, listen, accept embraces of sympathy, watched her pretend to sip at the glass of brandy she still held in her hand. She seemed fine, composed, coping admirably—yet a niggling sensation was clawing at his instincts.

'Luca, please listen to me,' his mother urged anxiously. 'I don't want to see the two of you hurt each other again!'

His eyelashes gave a reluctant flicker as he made himself look away from Shannon and into his mother's worried face. Lifting his hands to cover his mother's fingers where they rested against his chest, he drew them to his lips to kiss them gently, then firmly lowered them to her sides. 'I love you,' he told her gently. 'It breaks my heart that you let yourself worry about me. But we are going to have to finish this later, *mi amore…*'

Because something more urgent was tugging at him. And to lift his gaze back to the spot where he had last seen Shannon only to discover he couldn't see that distinctive flame head of hers anywhere turned that tug into a roar that had him striding away, passing by the tall, slender figure of Father Michael and the more rotund Emilio Lorenzo without even seeing them.

Where did she go—?

Shannon had opened the door and slipped quietly inside the Salvatore library with its beautiful pale wood-panelled walls and light blue furnishings, and ornately corniced bookcases filled with rows of priceless books. It was quiet in here, and so free of other people that her shoulders dipped in relief. Luca had hustled her into thinking when she did not want to think. Now she had an ache building behind her eyes that was promising to develop into a blinding headache if she didn't snatch a few minutes to herself.

At first she walked across to the window to stare out at the gardens laid out with classical Italian formality and awash with the yellow and purple heads of the season's first spring flowers. There was a moment when she was tempted to open one of the French doors and step out onto the terrace to breathe in some fresh air. But the greyness of the day warned her it was cold out there, and instead she turned to face the room again and was drawn towards the huge white marble fireplace where a burning log fire sent out flickering fingers of inviting warmth.

She was about to sit down in one of the winged chairs flanking the fire when she saw the row of silver framed pictures standing on the mantel top. Her heart gave a pained little flutter as she put down her glass on a small table, then went to study each picture in turn.

They were all there in their wedding finery and standing beneath the same stone archway to the same church they had visited today. Renata with Tazio, Sophia with Carlo—even Mrs Salvatore stood with her handsome husband whom Shannon had never been fortunate enough to meet, but she still knew that if he'd walked by her in the street she would have known who he was because Luca looked so much like him.

And then there was the picture of Angelo and Keira. Reaching up with fingers that weren't quite steady, she gently floated them over the faces of these two happy people she would never see smile like this again. It came then, breaking free on an anguished sob followed by another and another that sent her sinking to her knees where she knelt, hugging herself as she rocked to and fro, pouring out everything she had been so staunchly holding in.

The door flew open and a cluster of people came to a stunned halt in its opening. She didn't know, had no idea that Luca had been causing quite a scene out there because he couldn't locate her. She didn't know that he'd found her until he was dropping to his knees in front of her and was uttering something thick and uneven as he gathered her up against him.

'I can't bear it, I can't bear it,' she could hear herself sobbing as he lowered his dark head over hers, and she could feel the tremors shaking him.

Someone else uttered a broken sob and a different hand arrived at the base of her spine. It was Luca's mother's hand. Despite her concerns Mrs Salvatore was no match for the depth of Shannon's broken-hearted grief. Tears thickened her voice as she offered words of comfort. Over by the door several others struggled to keep their tears in check.

But it was Luca who held her, Luca's composure she could feel tearing apart at its seams.

'*Idiota,*' he muttered as she buried her face in his throat and washed him with the deep, gulping agony of her tears. 'I take my eyes off you for two short seconds and you disappear to do this! Why are you so stubborn?' he demanded unevenly. 'Why do you insist on believing you can carry all of this grief without help from me? Don't I know better? Don't you always fall apart eventually? When we are married I am going to shackle you to my side, then I will not need to—'

'I am not marrying you,' Shannon sobbed into his throat as a chorus of shocked gasps ran around the room. She didn't hear them.

Luca ignored them, his fingers dislodging the clip holding up her hair so the thick, flaming mass uncoiled over his fingers as he pressed her closer. 'Yes you are,' he gritted. 'It is your fate—*my* fate.'

'What are you are saying?' It was Renata who spoke so scandalously.

'Nothing you would not have heard by the end of today,' he supplied while Shannon sobbed all the harder, and he wondered how long he had left before he joined her in all of this agony.

'Then you are a fool!'

'*Sì*,' he acknowledged. 'Tazio, have Fredo bring the car to the door, if you please,' he requested. 'I am taking Shannon home.'

He climbed abruptly to his feet with Shannon still clamped to the front of him. 'Can you stand or do I carry you?' he asked her.

'I am not going to marry you.' Shannon found strength from Renata's dismay to lift her tear-washed face and burn the words up at him. 'Look at those pictures, Luca—*look*!' she insisted with a wave towards the mantel top. 'They're all happy to be marrying each other. Are we happy? Are *they* happy that you're even thinking of marriage to me?'

Luca did not look at the row of pictures on the mantel top or the real versions of those people who were clustered around the door. He looked at Shannon; he looked *into* Shannon. 'Angelo and Keira will be happy for us,' he stated. 'Their daughter will be happy for us when we adopt her into our new family. And you're—'

Shannon's heart leapt to her throat, 'Don't you dare say it!' she choked out. 'I'm not—'

'Already pregnant with our own precious child?'

The next mass gasp was followed by a comprehensive silence. Mrs Salvatore's hand still lay against Shannon's back, but it was removed jerkily.

'How could you?' Shannon whispered.

'It was surprisingly easy,' Luca mocked her with a look.

'Are you now going to make Renata's wishes come true and make a fool of me again?'

Well, are you? Shannon was forced to ask herself. She looked into the wry, slightly rueful face of this man she had loved for so long she couldn't remember when she began loving him, and thought— No, I won't do it again.

Her tears cleared away, her shaky composure slipped quietly back into place. Moistening her trembling lips, she turned in the circle of his arms and faced this family she had once felt such a welcome part of but now—

'Luca and I are getting married,' she announced in a voice that refused not to shake. 'I'm sorry if you don't like it but its wh-what we both w-want.'

'So we plan to do it next week in a quiet ceremony in respect of our recent loss,' Luca took over. 'You are welcome to attend but it is not a duty I expect you to take up if you cannot bring yourselves to wish us well in this.'

No one spoke—no one. There wasn't a single good luck, God damn you or even a dismissive go to hell, you pair of fools. It was a suffocating, suffocating blanket of perfect silence until—

'Well, bravo,' a smooth male voice commended, and Father Michael detached himself from the small group.

He began walking towards them, a tall, slender man with silver hair and a look of a Salvatore etched in his lean face. He paused to touch slender white sympathetic fingers to Mrs Salvatore's shocked cheek, then continued on until he came to a stop in front of them.

'I now understand your desire to arrange this hasty wedding service, Luca.' He smiled as he reached out to shake his hand. 'This should have happened two years ago, of course, but next week is good. I for one am very happy for you both.'

There were so many hidden messages in what he'd said that it caused a wave of discomfort to shift through their audience. Shannon couldn't cope. She had taken enough. Fresh tears were throbbing in her throat and she knew she was in danger of falling apart again.

She certainly didn't need the priest to swing the attention to her. But that was exactly what he did. 'Welcome to the Salvatore family, Shannon,' he sanctioned, bringing his hands to rest on her shoulders. 'Having come to know your sister well over the years, I know how hard she prayed for this to happen.' He bent to place kisses on both of her cheeks. 'She can be at peace now, *cara*,' he murmured for her ears only. 'For her sake try to be at peace with it yourself.'

It was then that she knew that Father Michael knew everything. Keira must have confessed all to the priest. Her shoulders shook as the tears threatened to burst forth again and she broke free of Luca's arms to sink into one of the winged chairs with different hurts, different emotions, all clamouring to take a bite out of her.

Father Michael moved back across the room, gathering Luca's mother beneath his arm as he went and herding the rest of his subdued flock before him through the door. 'Take the poor child home, Luca. I will stay and deal with the other business you have pending here,' were the final complacent words spoken in the Salvatore library for long seconds after the door closed.

'I can't believe you did that.' Shannon broke into the silence.

'I am having great difficulty believing that you backed me up,' was Luca's drawling reply. 'Here…' The glass of brandy was retrieved from the reading table and slotted between her fingers. 'Drink,' he commanded.

Drink, she repeated and spent a few seconds toying with the idea of tossing the drink in his face. Then Luca asked grimly, 'What did Father Michael say to you that almost had you shattering again?'

And she took a sip at the brandy because she suddenly needed it. 'Nothing,' she mumbled. 'What was the *other* business he mentioned as he left?'

'Last will and testaments,' he supplied. 'Emilio Lorenzo is Angelo's lawyer. He is here to read Angelo and Keira's joint will. But there is one specific section, which deals with the unlikely event of their dying at the same time. It is that part which concerns you and me.'

'What do you mean?' She looked up at him with the question. He was standing with an arm resting against the mantel top, his expression grim as he stared into the leaping log flames.

'If you will accept a loose translation from memory, it says that in the event of both parties dying together their joint estates will be placed into trust for any surviving children they might have. The trust to be administered by you and me.' He shifted his gaze to her face to watch as she absorbed this surprising news. 'We are also given joint guardianship of any children they may have,' he added. 'So, you see, even if you want to adopt Rose for yourself, you cannot without my agreement, just as I cannot adopt her without yours.'

And there was the crux of this marriage business, Shannon realised. Forget everything else. Luca had known about the will all along. He must have felt the noose close around his neck the moment he'd read it because, being who he was, not only was he not going to allow his brother's child to be brought up by anyone but himself, but he was not going to let Shannon have power of say over what had to amount to a large chunk of Salvatore stock without him having power of say over her. Good grief, she could almost see the cogs spinning inside his head at the prospect. If he didn't marry her then she was at liberty to marry someone else—a man, moreover, whom she might allow to dabble his fingers in Salvatore business.

She laughed; it was all suddenly so clear. 'You've had our marriage planned from the moment Keira died, haven't you?' she murmured.

'Yes.' He didn't even bother to lie.

'And the carefully constructed trip down memory lane yesterday, culminating in the big seduction scene, was the precursor to a marriage proposal.'

'I did intend to explain about the will first,' he declared in his own defence.

While sharing chocolate-coated truffles in their bed of passion. 'Shame all of that other stuff about condoms got in your way,' she said.

'We fight like wild cats, *cara*, we always have done,' he reminded her softly. 'Neither of us is inclined to give way.'

Resting her head against the corner of the chair, she looked at him standing there with the firelight playing dynamic tricks with his smoothly handsome face—and wondered why she wasn't angry with him.

Because she'd given up, she realised. He had claimed that neither of them gave way in a fight, but she knew she had given way by backing this marriage thing.

Why? Because she loved the ruthless devil. Because she was being handed an opportunity here that would never come her way again. Father Michael had been right when he'd said it was time for her to be at peace with herself. If being at peace meant letting herself to love Luca, without the old resentments tagging onto it, then she could do that now. The fact that Luca could not allow himself the same peace was not his fault, but the fault of circumstances even she could accept had been pretty damning at the time. But he had loved her once, and if that look in his eyes wasn't telling her he was fighting hard not to love her again then she didn't know him at all.

He was hers. Everything he did and said demonstrated that he was hers. Even this last bit of manipulation had been an act of possession meant to cloak his true feelings or he would not have gone for the all-out seduction last night, but chosen the cool-headed business proposition he'd been forced to put into action only when the seduction had failed.

'When you smile like that the hairs on the back of my neck start to tingle,' he murmured darkly. 'It reminds me of very sharp teeth.'

Ignoring that, 'Your family isn't going to like this,' she warned him. 'Once they've recovered from their shock they're going to come down on you with every objection they can find.'

'Do I appear to give a damn?' He arched an eyebrow.

Her heart gave a flutter because—no, he didn't. 'I won't take a load of flak about the past,' she declared. 'If you bring it up, I'll walk, taking Rose with me and let you fight me for her through the courts.'

'What past?' he countered, filling her with a heady kind of heat because the man standing here wasn't thinking about anything but the length of her slender, silk-covered legs and how tightly they could grip him when he needed them to.

She uncrossed those legs and crossed them again slowly, sensually, and watched the flickering firelight catch hold of the gold flecks in his eyes.

'You provoking little witch.' He knew what she was doing.

'*Sì,*' she drawled unconscionably.

He moved like lightning. The glass she was cradling between her fingers disappeared. She was aided to her feet by two hands that circled her slender waist. His kiss devoured—*devoured*. Hunger, thirst, punishment, desire—you name it, he put it all into that one hot kiss.

'Let's go home,' he growled as he set her mouth free.

Reality arrived to give her an uncomfortable kick. Going 'home' as Luca called it meant going out there and facing the disapproval of his family.

'I'm—sorry,' she murmured, moving a step away from him.

'What for?' he asked.

'For falling apart when I was determined not to, and for causing that awful scene to happen at all.'

'The outcome of it was always going to happen,' he answered, then reached for her chin, lifted it so she had to look into his eyes. 'If you are carrying my child, we marry,' he stated flatly. 'If you are not carrying my child but you want to be a mother to Rose, then we marry. Either way— we marry.' He shrugged to declare that he'd covered it all.

'I am not carrying your child,' she stated adamantly.

Luca frowned. 'Why are you set against it?'

'I told you.' She tried to release her chin but he refused to let her, his long fingers simply moving to encompass one of her cheeks. 'I don't want to go through what Keira went through so many times.'

'Why do you fear that you will have the same problems?'

Her breasts shuddered on a small sigh. 'My mother died in childbirth,' she told him. 'How can I *not* expect it to be the same for me?'

'Because Keira did not die giving birth to Rose, she died because of a terrible freak accident.'

'And all of those dreadful disappointments she suffered year after year?' She shook her head, and still did not manage to dislodge his fingers and thumb. 'I know it must sound very cowardly, but I just can't put myself through that.'

'Did your mother have many miscarriages?'

'No,' she admitted. 'But she—'

'Then you are mixing two separate tragedies together here and frightening yourself with the results, so stop it,' he said quietly. 'Nothing is going to happen to you. If you are pregnant, then we will find you the best medical attention. If you are not and you really do continue to fear it, then Rose will be our only child—our special gift from Angelo and Keira.'

'Will that be enough for you?' Oh, she knew she sounded pathetically wistful, but his answer was so important to her.

'*Idiota,*' he chided, and pulled her towards him as he lowered his head and kissed her again but differently.

This kiss seemed to seal something, though what exactly, Shannon wasn't sure.

And the gauntlet of disapproval wasn't nearly as bad as she expected it to be, mainly because almost everyone but the immediate family had left while they'd been hiding in the library and as for the rest—well, Shannon had to assume that they knew what was in Angelo and Keira's will by now because there was an air of acceptance about their manner, which was marginally better than disapproval.

Luca's mother put it into words. 'This has been the worst week any of us could be forced to go through. It places everything that went before it in the shade. As Father Michael pointed out to us, our thoughts must be with Angelo and Keira's baby and I cannot think of two people who will love the child more than both of you will. Please, Shannon—can we make this day a fresh beginning for all of us instead of such an unhappy end?'

It was an olive branch she had never expected. It could have brought the tears flooding back if she hadn't glimpsed the cynical expression on Renata's face.

'Why is it that Father Michael has so much influence with your family?' she asked Luca as Fredo drove them away.

'Did you not know?' He turned a surprised frown on her. 'He is my uncle—my father's brother. Everyone in my family listens to him—even me, when I have to.'

They married a week later. Father Michael performed the ceremony. Luca pulled out all the stops and insisted she wear the frothiest wedding gown she could find. The fact that his motives were driven by the silly fuss she'd made about silver-framed pictures did not pass Shannon by.

The family was there to offer support. She was really surprised to discover that Renata's husband Tazio had offered to escort her down the aisle and that Sophia wanted to stand witness for her while Carlo did the honours for Luca.

Spreading it around, she mused hollowly as she stood beneath the stone archway with Luca at her side. Camera bulbs flashed. They were caught for posterity, though she felt no sense of belonging—yet.

It would come, though, she told herself determinedly. It had to do for Rose's sake if not for her own—and she had not placed all her future in Luca's hands without being prepared to fight tooth and nail to belong eventually.

She told Angelo and Keira that—quietly inside her head as she laid her bridal flowers on their grave.

They flew to London after the wedding. Shannon had a life to pack up and ship to Florence, including a job she had no intention of stopping because she had become a wife and was about to become a mother. She'd talked it over with Luca and they'd agreed that she could work from his apartment and commute to London when commitments made it necessary. So they'd also agreed to employ a nurse to help care for Rose, and even found the ideal candidate in one of the nurses at the hospital who'd been helping care for the baby since her birth. She'd grown so attached to Rose that she jumped at the chance of coming home with her when she was eventually allowed to leave the hospital. But that moment was a still few weeks away because Rose had to remain in her safe hospital environment until she had reached her proper birth date, which meant that Shannon had a few weeks' grace to get used to her new working regime and get organised for a baby before Rose and the nurse joined them.

Her business partner Joshua thought she was mad giving up everything to become a martyr to the Salvatores—as he saw it. But then, Joshua was a typical high-octane twenty-four-year-old with ambition shooting like steam from his ears. He could think of nothing worse than tying himself down to anything but his desire for success. It was when Luca pointed out to him that, with Shannon's fluent grasp of Italian and his own influential contacts, having her based in Florence could only be good for business. After that Joshua was almost packing up for her, he was that eager for her to get back to Florence. But, on a personal level, he was the closest friend she had in her life and he was concerned that she was going to be hurt badly again if she didn't take care.

She knew he was right, yet she was happy in an odd, quiet kind of way. She was letting herself love Luca and he couldn't be more supportive of her plans if he tried, though she didn't think love came into his reasons for pulling out all the stops in his effort to make this marriage work. And no one could make her question the passion they shared on a nightly basis in the luxurious surroundings of his London apartment or those other sensual interludes conducted while packing up her flat, where he was supposed to be helping but spent most of his time trying to get her out of her clothes.

No matter how she tried to she could not rid herself of the feeling that the bubble was going to burst at any second. But even thinking like that did not prepare her for the speed with which the bubble did burst.

It began five short days into their marriage. Luca received a call from his PA that resulted in him having to fly back to Florence immediately. Shannon hadn't finished packing up her flat so it meant he had to go back without her. He didn't like it—she didn't like it. Their marriage was too new and much too fragile for them to be risking a separation so soon. Before he left they made love as if they were never going to be together again and by the time he kissed her goodbye she was so close to changing her mind and going with him she was actually shocked as to how desperate she felt.

The next few days seemed to stretch out before her like an empty desert. She filled her time in by visiting her clients and soothing their concerns about her change in location. When she wasn't with clients she was packing and listening to Alex, her neighbour, wax enviously about the new life she was about to embark on with one of the sexiest men alive.

The sexiest man alive rang her each evening—and during the day if he could find the time. She missed him. She missed Rose and couldn't wait to get back to them.

Her things were shipped off to Florence by special courier. She was actually on the brink of booking her own flight there when the supermodel she'd met with in Paris called up to say that she would be in London in two days and wanted another meeting. It was too good an opportunity to pass up so she decided to stay a few days longer. Luca went on a cursing spree, then when he had calmed down he informed her that her things had arrived and she had better be following them soon or he would come and get her.

She liked the angry, possessive way he said that. It was all very nice, very float half an inch above ground. Nice place to be. She hugged the feeling to her as she went about her business the following day. Then it suddenly struck her that she hadn't done anything about proper contraception, so she made an appointment with her doctor with the happy idea that she could surprise Luca when she got back to Florence with the news that he wouldn't have to keep using the dreaded condoms he hated so much. The doctor was filling in a prescription slip when she thought to question him about whether it was safe to start taking pills when there was a small chance she might be pregnant.

'Well, let's find out,' he said.

CHAPTER EIGHT

Luca rang that evening while Shannon was standing in the bedroom staring at the pale reflection in the dressing mirror that was hardly recognisable as her own face. Her phone was within fingertip reach and she answered with a wispy, 'Hi.'

'Hi yourself,' he echoed lazily. 'What are you doing?'

Falling apart, she thought. 'Nothing,' she answered. 'I've just got in. W-what about you?'

'I am still at the office. I have a few—things I need to do before I can leave. But doing nothing sounds inviting,' he then murmured, sounding husky and dark and gorgeously intimate. 'Maybe we could do this nothing together. Would an interlude of telephone sex appeal to you?'

Shannon watched long, mascara-tipped lashes folding down over sapphire blue eyes then lifting up again. 'Not right now,' she refused. 'I'm—' falling apart '—about to take a shower,' she improvised hazily.

'Well, if that image does not encourage telephone sex then I am in a worse state than I thought.' He laughed. 'Are you undressed already? If so you are going to have to wait while I play catch-up.'

'N-no.' She watched her eyes blink again. 'I've just got in.'

'You've already told me that.' There was a moment of silence, a hint of tension suddenly whipping down the line, then— 'Are you all right, *cara*?' he asked.

'Fine,' she said.

'You don't sound fine.'

And he no longer sounded husky, she realised, and made

140

herself turn her back to the mirror so she could try to concentrate. 'Sorry,' she said. 'I've had a—rough day.'

'Doing what?'

Did she tell him—cold like this via a telephone? 'I…' A hand went up to cover her forehead, confusion and shock making it impossible to think. 'I w-went shopping, bought too much then—' she couldn't tell him, not like this '—then couldn't remember where I parked m-my car.'

'You sold your car last week,' he reminded her softly and there was no gentleness in that soft tone. He was becoming cross and suspicious of this whole crazy conversation.

Pull yourself together! she told herself tautly, and heaved some air into her lungs and managed to make it sound like a laugh as it left her again. 'I know. Isn't that stupid? I shopped till I dropped then went looking for a car I don't even have any more!' Swinging away from her own lies, she walked on shaking legs over to the bed. 'See what you've done to me?' she said as she sat down. 'I'm losing my mind and it has to be your fault because I was absolutely fine before you came back into my life.'

'So, I make you lose your mind, that's OK. I can live with that,' he accepted quietly. 'Now tell what's really wrong?'

He wasn't taking the bait. She felt the tears start to press at the back of her eyes. 'I have a headache,' she quavered honestly.

'Ah, the classic headache,' his mocking sigh whispered into her ear. 'No wonder you don't want telephone sex with me.'

The diversion had worked—he was sounding husky again. She liked husky, it squeezed tightly at her heart but she still liked it. 'I'm missing you,' she added for good measure. 'And I'm missing Rose. Have you seen her today?'

'We spent the afternoon together, and we missed you too,' Luca returned still frowning because that instinct he possessed where Shannon was concerned was telling him she still had not told him what was really upsetting her. 'She has changed so much in a week that you won't know her, I promise you. She has her mama's eyes and—' He stopped when he caught the sound of movement. 'Would you prefer it if I called back later when you've had your shower and you feel—?'

'No!' she protested. 'I l-like listening to your voice.'

'While doing what?' he asked. 'I can hear you moving around.'

'I'm making myself comfortable on the bed,' she told him as she crawled up the bed and curled up on his pillow.

'Wouldn't you rather I go so you can—?'

'No!' she responded. 'Tell me more about Rose,' she encouraged.

So he did in low-toned, husky Italian, while Shannon listened with the phone tucked between the pillow and her ear and for extra comfort tugged another pillow towards her so she could hug it as if it were him.

While Luca reclined in his chair behind his desk in his office and wondered what was really troubling her, because something certainly was.

Was it grief? Had he caught her at a bad moment when she had been thinking of her sister? Hell, why not? he thought. Hadn't he been sitting here thinking about Angelo and the gut-wrenching task that lay ahead of him this evening when he eventually found the courage to enter his brother's office to begin clearing it out?

His gut gave him a thick thump just by his thinking about it. 'You've gone quiet,' he said huskily when he realised that her muffled little responses had faded away. 'Are you asleep?'

'Almost,' her whispered response trailed into his ear and down through his body like a lover's caress.

He sat forward, reaching out to pick up the bunch of keys

that had been sitting on his desk staring at him for the last few hours. 'I will let you go, then,' he murmured, deciding it was time that he got the deed done with.

'OK,' she said, but she didn't sound happy about it, which made him smile.

'I will call again in the morning.'

'Early,' she told him and his smile became a rueful grin. 'I…miss you…' she added.

And the grin faded when his heart turned over and squeezed painfully because *miss you* wasn't enough. He wanted to hear *I love you Luca*, in that same soft, serious tone she used to use to say those words to him.

'I miss you too.' The keys bit into his palm as he clenched his fingers around them because he knew he couldn't say it either, though he wanted to.

The call ended. He sat staring at his cell-phone while a bleak feeling of dissatisfaction gnawed its way into his senses, tempting him to call her back and just say the damn words and get it over with. But how did he do it? How did a man admit he was still in love with the same woman who had betrayed him two years ago?

He didn't, was the easy answer—and he stood up abruptly, then turned the phone off altogether just to make a point. Angry, fed up and frustrated with himself, he shifted his attention to the bunch of keys in his other hand and on a few tight, self-aimed curses stepped around his desk and headed for the door that linked his brother's office to his.

He didn't call.

After spending a sleepless night tossing and turning, counting off the minutes and the hours until she would hear his voice again, Shannon didn't know if she was hurt or angry that he had not bothered with the promised early morning call.

So she tried calling him, only to discover that his phone was switched off. Had he let the battery run down? she wondered, and refused to listen to the little voice in her head reminding her that he had several spare batteries to cover such an eventuality, because the idea of a flat battery was a more acceptable reason for him not calling her than him just forgetting to do it.

By twelve o'clock she was fretting because he still hadn't called, and when she tried his number she received the same automated message telling her the telephone she was trying to connect to was not available, which also forced her to acknowledge that her flat-battery theory was stupid so— where was he? What was he doing that was so important it would make him switch off his phone?

A leap of panic had her ringing the hospital in Florence in case Rose had taken ill. Nerves rattling, heart racing, she listened to a nurse reassuring her that the baby was fine but, no, Signor Salvatore had not been in to visit the baby as yet that day.

At two o'clock she attended her meeting with the super-model, determined to hang onto her professional persona even though she wanted to jump up and down and shout or fall apart as she usually did in times of crisis.

An hour later she was standing in a street somewhere in Mayfair, with a new contract secured and due to meet Joshua at their offices to bring him up to scratch about the contract before they headed off to their local wine bar to celebrate.

But she didn't do anything. She just stood in that cold Mayfair street and called Luca's number again. When there was still no response, she began calling every number in Florence she had logged in her phone in an effort to track him down. He wasn't answering at the apartment. She'd tried his office, his mother, even both of his sisters to no avail. No one seemed to know where he was or why he was not contactable. Everyone was as bewildered as she.

And she needed—*needed* to talk to him!

She hit the panic button. She didn't know why she had to hit it at that precise moment standing in a busy street, but before she knew it she'd made the decision and was in a taxi and heading directly for Heathrow.

She managed to get a seat on a flight into Pisa leaving within the hour and only then had the sense to check if she had her passport with her and was relieved to find it still stashed in her bag from the last time she'd used it.

'What do you mean, you're on the way to Florence?' Joshua shouted at her down the phone. 'We have a surprise farewell party waiting here for you!'

'I'm s-sorry,' she apologised. 'Tell everyone I'm sorry. But I have to go, Josh, it's important.'

'You mean *he's* important.'

Oh, yes, she thought. I just didn't realise how much until I couldn't reach him. 'I can't get in touch with him and I'm—scared.'

It reminded her of the last time he'd done this to her. The same thick clutch of anxiety was dragging her aching heart around her insides as if looking for somewhere to hide from what his silence had to mean.

'This is different, Shannon.' Joshua toned down his anger when he heard the anxious quiver in her voice. 'You managed to sort out your old differences and you're *married* to him.'

But they hadn't sorted anything out. They'd merely agreed to put it all on a shelf marked 'pending'.

'When did you last speak?'

'Last night.'

'Last night?' Joshua choked. 'For goodness' sake, Shannon, how often is a busy man like Luca Salvatore supposed to contact his wife to keep her happy? You're going over the top here, sweetheart,' he told her bluntly. 'Take a deep breath and calm down, then remind me not to get myself stuck in the marriage trap if this is the kind of hassle I will have to look forward to.'

She laughed. Josh was right. She took that deep breath. Her silly, stupid nerves began to calm down. 'Thanks,' she said.

'Don't mention it,' Joshua drawled. 'Now, are you going to revert to your original plan to fly out to Florence tomorrow and come back here for a booze-up with your brethren?'

'No,' she said and felt her anxieties erupt again. 'I still have something to tell him that can't wait.'

'Don't tell me, let me guess,' Joshua sighed. 'You've got to fly a million miles just to say *I love you, Luca*!'

'One day you're going to meet your own Waterloo, Joshua, and I want a front seat when it happens,' she snapped at his sarcasm.

'Am I right?' he challenged.

'No,' she said and glanced at her watch. Her flight was about to be called. 'I'm going to tell him that I'm pregnant with his child.'

She cut the connection before Joshua could blurt out his response to that announcement, then just stood staring at the waves of people flowing through the airport, stunned by what she was feeling now she'd let herself say the words out loud.

Fear mainly, mixed with a stammering sense of excitement that was threatening to make her legs give out. She made for her departure gate before it happened, took her seat on the plane in a mindless daze.

It was dark when she landed in Pisa. From there she had to catch the train into Florence, then hire a taxi to take her the rest of the way.

And in all of that time and travel, Luca still had not tried to contact her cell-phone. Joshua might think she was being silly expecting him to, but she didn't. In fact silly didn't even touch what she was feeling. Angry, hurt, indignant—

offended better described what was fizzing inside her as she rode the lift up to Luca's apartment.

The first thing she saw when she stepped out of the lift was her packing cases stacked up against a wall. The daunting task of having to unpack them all again brought her to a halt for a few seconds while she allowed herself a silent groan.

Then she moved off through the arch looking for Luca without holding out much hope of finding him here, since she'd rung and rung here only to have the answering service take over each time.

So it came as a shock to throw open the sitting room door and find what she did. The room looked as if a bomb had been dropped on it; papers and documents were strewn everywhere. But it was the sight of Luca stretched out on one of the sofas that held her frozen. He was wearing the trousers to one of his dark suits and a wine red shirt tugged open at his throat. His shoes were missing, his jacket, his tie, and even as the smell of hard alcohol assailed her nostrils she saw a squat glass half filled with something golden he had slotted between a set of long fingers and the half-empty bottle of whisky standing on the low table an arms reach away from him.

Every picture tells a story, Shannon thought grimly. And this one told her that he was asleep—lost in a drunken stupor, she suspected indignantly—the glass moving up and down with the rhythm of his deep breathing where it rested on his chest!

While she had been worrying herself out of her head about him, rushing to catch planes *and* letting down all her work colleagues—Luca been right here enjoying his own private boozing party!

Her eyes took on a murderous glitter. Taking a sharp step forward, she lifted a hand and sent the door into its housing with a very satisfying crash.

Luca jolted like a man shot, opened his eyes and through a bleary haze of alcohol saw her standing there. For a full ten seconds he couldn't move a single muscle, wondering if he had conjured her up from the deepest, darkest nightmare he had ever had in his life.

'So this is why no one can get hold of you!' Her voice lashed itself against his fragile senses.

'Madre de Dio,' he groaned and rolled into a sitting position. 'What are you doing here?' he demanded bemusedly. 'Have I lost a whole day?'

'Try switching on your phone, then you would know,' she snapped. 'And I think it's more important that you explain what the heck you think you're doing here?'

'Don't shout,' he groaned, making a grab for his aching head.

'Don't shout?' she repeated, her voice lifting a full octave. 'I've just flown halfway across Europe worrying why I can't get in touch with you and I find you happily ensconced in here rolling drunk! Why shouldn't I shout?'

'I was not expecting you—all right?' he uttered thickly as her decibels played havoc with his head.

'That makes it OK?' She wasn't impressed. 'I married a closet drunk, is that it? And what are all these papers doing scattered about the—'

She stopped suddenly. Luca felt his blood turn from pure malt whisky to ice. Lowering his hand from his eyes, he was just in time to see her start to bend to pick up a piece of paper. 'No,' he rasped. 'Don't—' and leapt to his feet.

But he was too late. Shannon already had the notepaper in her trembling fingers. Her heart began to pump unevenly. She tried to take a breath and found that she couldn't. She knew this notepaper. Her mouth ran dry, her eyes beginning to sting as she looked around her and saw more of the same scattered about.

Then she noticed the others that were not quite the same but she still recognised them.

'What have you done?' She began darting round the room picking up the papers as a heaving ball of agony built in her chest. 'Why have you got these?'

These being Keira's letters to her—Keira's *private* letters! And not just Keira's letters to her that she'd had safely stored away in a packing case, but her letters to Keira were here too!

'You've been through my private papers.' She didn't want to believe it. 'You must have gone through Keira's as well!' She lifted her head to look at him and went pale when she saw the expression on his face.

He didn't even look guilty, but hard and angry. 'How could you?' she whispered.

'But they made such a revealing read,' he said bitterly. 'All that begging you did before your tone turned to ice.'

Then he took a gulp at his whisky when she flinched.

'Y-you sh-shouldn't have read them.' She was shaking so badly she could barely get the words out. 'They w-were not yours to read.'

'Do you mean the one where she begs you not to tell me about what she'd done because I would have to tell Angelo?' he threw back. 'Or the one where she promises you *faithfully* that she will never do such a wicked thing again!'

Oh, dear God. Shannon swallowed across a throat that was paper-dry suddenly. 'Sh-she was afraid of losing him.'

'My besotted brother? He would have forgiven her if she'd taken her lover to his *own* damn bed!'

This time when she flinched he swung his back to her. Shannon could see the angry muscles flexing across his shoulders as he took another pull on his drink. Her head was buzzing, and she was trembling so badly that she only just made it to the nearest chair before her legs gave out.

'Sitting ducks,' Luca muttered.

Still lost in a shocked daze, 'I b-beg your pardon?' she said.

'Angelo and me,' he enlightened. 'A pair of sitting ducks for a pair of lethal witches.' He uttered a hard laugh. Everything about his was hard from the iron-cast profile to the tightly clenched angry stance.

'Now hold on a minute.' She pushed out a protest. 'Don't use that derisive tone on me because I don't recall you forgiving me for my so-called sins, Luca.'

'You should have told me the truth.'

'I *tried* telling you the truth but you refused to believe me!'

'Not then—*now*!' He swung on her harshly. '*This* time around!'

'Why would I want to tarnish the memory of a beautiful person whose only fault was she needed to be loved too much by too many people?'

It was his turn to go white. 'You mean the man she took to our bed was not the *only* one?'

'Yes, he was the only one!' She jumped up furiously. 'She adored Angelo—you know that she did! But their marriage was in trouble,' she tagged on reluctantly, and began pacing the floor while staring at the letters still clutched in her fingers because she couldn't stay still and look at Luca while she talked about this. 'Angelo was fed up with performing according to calendars and menstrual cycles so he s-stopped coming home every night. Keira decided he didn't love her any more so when some guy came along and showed her she was still lovable, she fell for his silver-tongued charm like a brick.'

'How do you know all of this?' If Luca had been pale before, he was a grey colour now. 'None of what you have just said is in those letters.'

'It was happening while I was here living with you.' She turned, to find his face had blurred now, and knew she was about to give way to tears. 'Didn't you notice that those six months must have been the only months my sister wasn't pregnant at some stage?' she questioned unevenly. 'Or that Angelo was working incredibly long hours every day?'

'We were in the middle of some big company changes,' he dismissed impatiently.

'You still managed to come home to me every night.'

'Are you suggesting that Angelo was going to someone else?' he barked out furiously.

'I wouldn't have a clue!' she cried. 'The important point here is that Keira believed that he was!'

'And you knew she was feeling like this and did not bother to bring her concerns to me?'

Which brought them right back full circle, Shannon noted heavily—but she still lifted her chin, eyes tear-bright as she challenged him. 'If Angelo had been having an affair and you knew about it, would you have told me?'

He stared at her for a moment, then turned away, his answer lying in the thick silence that clattered down around the two of them. Sibling loyalty was the pits when it encroached on your own life, Shannon thought painfully.

'I'll be honest,' she dropped into that silence. 'I was selfish. I was madly, madly in love and so happy I didn't want to think about anyone else but you and me. So I told Keira not to be silly and more or less left her with no one to turn to for—' Her voice broke; she struggled to recover it. '*Why* did you have to bring all of this up again?' she choked out. 'She didn't even do anything! Can you believe that? I'd gone to London to pack up my life there, then missed you so much that I came back early—hey,' she mocked then, '*déjà vu*!' and swallowed hard on the next lumps of tears to grab at her aching throat. 'You were supposed to be in…' She couldn't remember.

'Milan,' he provided.

She nodded, pressed her trembling lips together in an ef-

fort to control them then grimly forced herself to go on. 'I
came back to your apartment to find this strange man in our
bed and a scantily dressed Keira standing beside it tugging
at the sheets and sobbing at him to get up and get dressed
because she couldn't do it.' The scene could still set her
senses reeling with horror and shock. 'Th-then they saw me
standing there and Keira ran and locked herself in the bathroom leaving me to tell the guy to get the hell out. By the
time you arrived, I'd got the whole story out of her and sent
her home with the promise that I wouldn't tell a soul so
long as she never did such a stupid thing again!'

'You don't need to go on,' he put in thickly.

'No,' she agreed and began to shiver so badly she had to
hug herself. 'But you tell me what I was supposed to do
next, Luca?' she demanded. 'Because I still don't have an
answer to that!'

'You still should have told me.'

Shannon almost stamped a foot in frustration. 'I did!' she
cried. 'You refused to believe me!'

'*Once!*' He swung around to scorn that. He looked pale
and hard and tough and cold. She shivered again. 'You mentioned her name *once* before it was quickly withdrawn
again!'

'Because you almost took my head off!'

'I think I'm going to do it now,' he gritted and actually
took a step towards her before he pulled himself up with an
angry hiss that rattled with fury. 'This is going nowhere,'
he uttered.

He was right and it wasn't. She felt sick and hurt and
angry and bitter, and he looked like the cold, dark stranger
who'd walked into her flat several weeks ago. Where had
all the new tender warmth gone? Why did it always have
to be other people's problems that tore them to shreds like
this? Maybe because they never should have come together
in the first place, she answered her own bleak question.

Maybe it was fate's way of saying—Get out of each other's lives, for goodness' sake. You don't belong together.

When you went straight to the bottom line what did they have worthy of keeping them together? 'Great sex,' she muttered, that was all.

'Cosa?'

'You and me and going nowhere,' she enlightened dully. 'We have great sex and nothing else really.'

It was his turn to flinch. 'There is more to this relationship than what takes place between the sheets,' he insisted.

Was there? Shannon stared down at the letters trembling in her hands and thought about that statement. 'You married me because you thought you had no other option,' she told him. 'You did it for Rose's sake, *and* because of the great sex! But most of all, Luca, I think you married me because you needed to be sure you kept some control over who controlled me and my say over Angelo's heavy stock share in the Salvatore empire.'

'That is utter rubbish,' he discarded.

'Is it? Then why did you feel you had to go through my private letters?' she challenged. 'You had to be looking for something important to do such a wicked thing! Did you hope to find something to use against me in court if this stupid marriage didn't work? Proof about my ill-gotten lifestyle, maybe, that would say I was an unfit mother for Rose and totally unfit to be a co-guardian of her inheritance!'

'Madre de dio,' he breathed. 'I do not believe this. You could not be more wrong!' he charged.

But Shannon wasn't listening. She had suddenly spied another letter lying half hidden beneath a chair and made a dive for it. It was one of her letters to Keira. Tears flooded into her eyes.

'How could you?' she choked, kneeling on the floor and attempting to sift the letters into some kind of order on her lap while her fingers shook and her eyes burned. 'How could you go to her house and hunt through Keira's private papers like a—'

'I didn't,' he sighed.

She looked up. 'Didn't what?'

'Did not go to Angelo and Keira's house.' He put it in plainer words. 'I have not been there since…'

He couldn't bring himself to say it; instead he uttered a thick curse and sank back onto the sofa, dropped the glass onto the low table, then bent over to scrape long fingers through his hair.

'Then how did you get your hands on her letters?' she demanded.

Luca covered his face with his hands and wished the alcohol had done its job and completely numbed his brain. He didn't want to think; he didn't want to look at what he'd been doing last night, or what the future was going to mean now he'd discovered what he had.

'I was clearing Angelo's desk out in his office,' he told her. 'The letters were hidden at the back of a drawer…'

'Oh, dear God,' Shannon breathed, and he knew she'd already leapt ahead of him to the next part as this bleak, miserable mess began to unfold.

'I don't know how long Angelo had known about them or if Keira knew that he had them at all,' he pushed on, spelling it out for her anyway. 'But the fact is that my brother knew the truth about what happened two years ago, yet he could not bring himself to come and tell me.'

And there was the reason for the angrily scattered letters and his whisky binge, he admitted heavily. Not only had he discovered the truth about two years ago, but he had also realised that the brother he loved had kept from him the one thing Angelo of all people had known was important to him.

Shannon was innocent.

'I have spent the last two years believing I had the right to hate you with every damn day that went by,' he ground out huskily. 'Huh, what a joke. It was me that let you down, and my own brother could not tell me that!'

'He was protecting Keira.'

For some reason that remark shot sparks down his backbone. 'And that makes it OK?'

'No,' she admitted. 'But Angelo and Keira are no longer here to defend themselves, so I can't see the use in raking over it all again.'

'I refused to believe you—make me defend that!'

She sighed and got up. 'Can you defend it?'

'*You* should have told me—showed me those letters. You owed it to me.'

'Ah, so it's my fault. Good defence,' she commended.

'I did not mean that.'

'Then what did you mean?'

'I don't know, damn it!' he snapped and picked up his drink.

'Any more of that stuff and you'll fall over the next time you stand up,' she said tartly and started walking towards the door.

The glass was slammed back down on the table. It was amazing how quickly a man the size of Luca could move when he was provoked enough, Shannon noted as he swung to his feet and rounded the sofa and was standing over her before she'd even blinked. His hands grabbed her shoulders, the next thing she knew she was being pinned against the nearest wall.

'Very macho,' she murmured, but she was trembling again.

'I won't let you leave me,' he bit out thinly.

'I didn't say I was going to.' She frowned.

'You can hate me for the rest of our lives but you will do it right here, where I can see you doing it.'

His eyes were so black she felt as if she were falling into them, his hands possessive, his mouth tensely parted but gorgeous with it, and his breath so loaded with whisky fumes that they began to go to her head. 'OK,' she agreed hazily.

Frustration raked across his features. 'Take me seriously,' he snapped.

'I've only just got here!' she shot back at him. 'Why the heck are you expecting me to leave again?'

'You were going to the door.' Now he was trembling.

'To put these letters away with my other things!' she cried.

'You should be stuffing them down my disbelieving throat!'

She went one better, caught her bottom lip in her teeth and aimed the flat of her other hand at the side of his face. She didn't know where it came from but for some stupid reason the tears were back in her eyes. 'That's for going through my private possessions,' she heaved out shakily as her finger marks drew lines on his cheek. 'And if I h-had the strength left I w-would hit you again for upsetting me when I was already upset before I got here!'

'Why were you upset?'

'I'm—pregnant,' she whispered and watched as all that domineering macho anger turned into a block of stone. He didn't even swallow. In fact he didn't do anything.

'S-say something,' she stammered, then did something herself. Her vision went funny, all woozy and washy. She closed her eyes and knew she was going to faint.

'Shannon…?' was the last hoarse word she heard uttered before everything went black.

Luca cursed and caught her to him as she began to slide down the wall. Then he kept on cursing as he gathered her into his arms and turned to carry her to one of the sofas. She looked like death and he wanted to hit something— himself preferably.

Pregnant—

For a couple of seconds he seriously thought he was going to join her in her get-out swoon. Then concern for her took over—a concern that should have *always* been hers!

Dio, he hated himself. He was the worst kind of man a woman would want in her life—one that did not believe her and did not trust her and made her pregnant when it was what she feared the most!

'Shannon…' He called her name but she made no response to it.

Twisting his body, he dipped his fingers in the whisky glass, then turned back to moisten her bloodless lips with it. She was so limp and lifeless his skin began to prickle. Getting up, he went to get his cell-phone from his jacket pocket. The moment he switched it on half a dozen messages popped up on the screen. He'd intended to use the phone to call for a doctor but for some crazy reason he found himself opening text messages.

'I need to talk to you. Shannon.'

'Where are you? Shannon.'

'I'm coming to Florence. Shannon.'

'I'm frightened. Please call me. Shannon.'

'Why won't you speak to me? Shannon.'

He couldn't even swallow.

'I need to hear your voice, Luca!'

'Luca—'

His attention reeled back to the owner of those pitiful messages, lying there on the sofa with a slender white hand now covering her mouth.

'I think I'm going to be sick,' she whispered frailly.

CHAPTER NINE

LUCA leapt at Shannon, tossing the cell-phone aside to gather her back into his arms.

'I don't believe you sometimes,' he gritted as he made for the door with her head resting on his shoulder and his husky voice rumbling against her cheek. 'I suppose you flew all of this way without taking on refreshment again? When will you learn to be sensible? Last time it was cramp, this time you faint and now you feel sick. If you had waited until tomorrow my plane would have delivered you here in comfort. Why do you always have to mess up my plans? I am smashed out of my head and I cannot think straight. What man wants his woman to catch him like this?'

'Wife,' Shannon mumbled.

He pulled to a stop in the hallway, mind locked on the single word as if it were alien to him. Then his chest heaved.

'*Sì,*' he confirmed and started moving again, shouldering his way through the bedroom door, then making straight for the bathroom where she was noisily, humiliatingly sick into the toilet while he squatted behind her holding back her hair and spitting out curses that sang in her head.

By the time it was over it was all she could do to sink weakly against him. Her head was swimming; his curses still echoed in her head. She was trembling and shivering on the aftermath of her nausea, her skin felt clammy and the last thing she needed right then was for him to move her again. He picked her up, flushed the toilet, then slammed down the seat so he could sit down on it with her still wrapped in his arms. Muscles began flexing all over him as he stretched out a hand towards the washbasin and just managed to reach a tap and turn it on. Two seconds later a damp cloth arrived on her face. It was so refreshing she just closed her eyes and gave in to his grimly silent ministrations with the back of her head resting in the hollow of his shoulder and her legs dangling limply along the length of his.

Eventually he went still. Her world began to steady. She could feel the pound of his heart against the back of her head. The whole urgent shift from sofa to bathroom could not have taken more than two minutes yet she felt as if she'd just climbed Mount Everest and had a suspicion that he felt the same.

She released a small sigh.

'Feeling a little better?'

'Mmm.' She became aware that her hair was plastered across the front of his shirt. She lifted a weak hand with the intention of gathering the long, straight strands together— but Luca caught the hand and held onto it. The next thing she knew he was lifting it to his lips.

'Forgive me,' he murmured.

'What for?' she sighed.

'Not listening to you and believing in you when I should have done.'

'It looked bad. I knew that.'

'But I should have given you a fair hearing,' he insisted. 'I should not have—'

'You promised me that we wouldn't do this, Luca,' she snapped out suddenly, wriggling her fingers free and finding the strength to stand on her own two feet. 'No raking up the past, we said.'

'I did not know what I know now when we agreed to that.'

'But I did,' she said, using angry fingers to hunt out a tube of toothpaste and a toothbrush. 'What has changed for me other than you now know the truth?'

'Everything has changed for me.' He stood up, restless now, angry and tense.

'And you can't live with that?'

'Not right now—no,' he replied and walked out of the bathroom.

Shannon stood with the toothbrush loaded with toothpaste and listened tensely for him to leave the bedroom. If he does I'm finished with him, she told herself fiercely. If he walks away from this, I am out of here and booking into a hotel!

The toothbrush went into her mouth. She glared at her own washed out reflection in the bathroom mirror while she scrubbed at her teeth. Her hair was a mess, full of strand-tangling static, and if she'd started out today looking good enough to make the supermodel scowl again then she certainly did not look like that now!

It was easier to look away—better to look away because the bedroom door still hadn't slammed to mark his exit and the sheer tension in waiting for it to happen was making her tremble again. She turned on the cold tap, angrily cleaned her toothbrush, then bent to rinse out her mouth. The moment she lowered her head a fresh wave of dizziness set the floor rocking beneath her feet, forcing her to cling to the washbasin or fall in a jelly-legged heap. 'Oh,' she sobbed out in angry frustration. This just wasn't fair!

A strong arm hooked around her waist to take her weight again. The toothbrush was snatched away. He didn't even curse this time, but simmered in magnificent silence as he bent to hook the other arm around her knees then carried her out of the bathroom with his profile set in iron again.

'You're doing a lot of hefting and carrying for a drunk,' she remarked acidly.

'Discovering that my wife is pregnant has a way of sobering me up.' He deposited her on the edge of the bed.

'Oh.' She'd forgotten she'd told him that. 'Do you mind?' she asked warily.

'Do *I* mind?' He released a hard laugh and got down on

his haunches and began undoing the buttons on her jacket. 'You find out you are pregnant. You get so scared that you cannot even bring yourself to tell me when I call you last night.' The jacket came off. 'So we have this strange conversation where I think as if I am helping you through a lonely period of grieving for your sister—'

'I grieve all the time.'

'I am aware of that—so do I!' he snapped, pulling her jumper off over her head and making her hair crackle with static. 'But last night you were scared, and I *felt* your fear.' The flat of his palms tamed her hair. 'You should have told me what was worrying you and I would have flown straight back to London to be there for you.'

He started on the zips to her boots next. 'I know,' she said.

'Then why didn't you tell me?'

'Because it isn't something you tell someone over the telephone,' she answered defensively. 'I wanted to tell you properly—face to face.'

'But I ruined that for you too.' The boots came off. He stared at her feet. 'You're wearing my socks,' he sighed.

Shannon wriggled her toes. 'Another illusion shattered.' She smiled. 'I don't sleep around. I don't tell you all my secrets. I wear men's socks underneath my boots.'

There was an earthy, frustrated animal growl as he reared up to his full height. 'How can you joke about this?' he demanded.

'What do you want me to do?' she flared up at him. 'Fall into a fit of screaming hysterics instead? OK.' She jumped up to face him furiously. 'I'm pregnant when I don't want to be pregnant and it's all your fault!'

Her dreadful accusation hung in the silence. 'I'm sorry,' she burst out in anxious remorse. 'I didn't mean—'

He spun on his heels and walked away—out of the bedroom altogether this time, and he didn't even slam the door.

She wished he had. She wished he'd yelled back at her then flattened her on the bed! What she'd said wasn't even true because she did want this baby! She was just so terribly scared of what lay ahead of her.

'Oh, damn—*damn*!' she bit out angrily and turned back to the bathroom with the decision to lose herself in the shower in the vague hope it would ease away some of the awful stress. By the time she'd walked into the bathroom she had changed her mind in favour of a long soak in a warm scented bath.

Or maybe the bath was a delaying tactic before she had to go out there and face Luca again because she knew she had some serious apologising to do for that final remark and she had never been very good at apologising to him.

An image of that cold-eyed look he'd sent her before he'd walked out jumped up to hit her conscience again. Her lower stomach quivered.

'Don't you start,' she muttered. 'You're too tiny to have an opinion.'

Then she realised who it was she was talking to and a different kind of quiver ran through her. 'Oh, God,' she sighed. I am in such an emotional mess.

Piling her hair up on top of her head, she stripped away the rest of her clothes then stepped into the bath. As the warm, silky water closed around her she tried very hard to relax and put everything else out of her head.

It worked—in a fashion. A whole, long, uninterrupted hour later, bathed, dressed in her blue pyjamas with the matching wrap and smelling of sweet-scented bath oils, she let herself out of the bedroom and padded on bare feet to the kitchen in search of something to eat. She still felt a bit shaky but the nausea had receded, leaving her stomach growling for food.

The kitchen was in darkness. No sign of Luca, but for now she was glad about that. Flicking on the light switch, she went to put the kettle to boil, then turned to open the refrigerator door to see what there was to eat.

Nothing she fancied eating, she realised as she gazed at the unappetising fridgy type things that got left in there because nobody wanted them. There was a wedge of cheese—was she allowed cheese in her condition? There were eggs—was she allowed eggs? She didn't even know if she was allowed to drink the milk—was it pasteurised or unpasteurised that was bad for pregnant women?

Sighing, she gave up and walked out of the kitchen, crossed the hall and walked into the sitting room. It had been cleaned up since she'd been carried from it, she noticed. No sign of the whisky bottle, but the letters lay neatly stacked on the table. The traitors, she thought, then made herself turn to where her senses were telling her Luca stood, staring out of the window at the dark night.

He'd changed his clothes for a pair of dark grey trousers and casual black sweater that finished at his waist. His hands were lost in his trouser pockets and there was something about the way he was standing there that made him look lonely and bleak and about as remote as he could do.

'I'm—sorry,' she burst out anxiously. 'I really didn't mean to heap all the blame onto you. It's just that I'm—'

'Frightened,' he put in for her.

But he didn't turn to look at her as he said it, and there wasn't a single muscle on him anywhere that so much as flexed. Another clutch of remorse played havoc with her conscience and she knew she was going to have to do a bit more than utter an apology if she was ever going to feel comfortable with herself again.

They needed physical contact and lots of it.

Luca watched her come towards him via her reflection in the darkened glass. Her hair was piled up on top of her head and she was wearing the blue pyjamas. Her face had a scrubbed clean look to it but it also wore the strain of the last twenty-four hours.

If she touched him he'd had it. If she uttered one small damned unfair feminine sob then he promised himself he was going to turn and toss her onto the nearest sofa and slake all of this bloody *guilt* burning inside him with a hard hot session of lust.

She had no right to look so beautiful. She had no right to look so delicate and frail. She was pregnant with his child. An odd sensation skittered down his torso and gathered in his crotch. He wanted to turn and wrap her in his arms and promise her that he would make sure everything was fine for her. He wanted to pick her up and carry her back to bed and *show* her how much he meant it, but—

Was it safe for them to make love in her delicate condition?

Was it safe for Shannon to have his baby at all?

That odd sensation in his crotch dissipated then regrouped to turn itself back into pangs of guilt. She was innocent of all charges two years ago. She had married him knowing he'd still believed she'd cheated on him. Why had she done that? What made this beautiful woman tick inside if she was prepared to throw her life away on a no good cynic like him, not once, but twice!

She disappeared out of his field of vision, his throat closed because he knew what was coming next. She was going to touch him. She was going to try to make amends when it should be him making those amends.

Her hands arrived first, sliding around his waist. He watched them via the window reflection begin travelling up the wall of his stomach until they came to rest against his chest. He *felt* them arrive and had to close his eyes as her cheek came to rest against his back.

'I'm hungry,' she mumbled sulkily, 'and there's nothing to eat in the fridge.'

'If you had come back tomorrow as planned we would have a full stock of fresh provisions,' he responded coolly.

A new silence fell. He felt her stiffen a little, opened his eyes to watch the crescents of her nails curl to dig into his flesh. 'A bigger man would take pity and let me off the hook now,' she told him.

A bigger man would not have to retract his fingers into fists in his pockets so they couldn't follow the hardening rise of his sex, he thought dryly.

And a bigger man would turn and take her in his arms, then tell her how much he loved her—without bringing in the sex. But his chance to say those words to her had come and gone the night before during a long telephone conversation when words like I love you would have meant something because he had not known then what he now knew.

So what did he do? Keep his earlier promise to himself and throw her down on the nearest sofa, or did he go for the big one, say the damn words to get it over with, then see what the hell he got back?

Shannon could feel his heart pounding; she could feel the way he was holding every muscle taut like a barrier against her. And he didn't say a single word.

It was rejection of the worst kind. A rejection she just hadn't anticipated so it had the capacity to hurt all the more. Now she didn't know what to do, didn't know how to pull away from him and keep her dignity at the same time.

Then she thought, Oh, just do it! and slid her hands away, then took a step back.

Luca realised he'd left too long a gap without responding the moment she stepped back from him. By the time he'd had the sense to turn to look at her she was already walking back to the door.

'Come back here,' he growled impatiently. 'I was about to suggest I order food in from the restaurant down the street.'

'I'll make a sandwich,' she said and kept on going.

'Don't be so stubborn, damn it,' he exploded. 'Just tell me what you would like and I will order it!'

Shannon paused in the doorway to glance back at him, and discovered that he'd decided to turn and face her at last. The lamplight was catching the damp gloss of his hair now and his skin had recovered some of its warm golden glow. He was so handsome, she thought achingly. So much her kind of man that even when he played the arrogant bastard she still loved him more than he deserved.

'I'll have pizza, then,' she said. 'Thank you.' It was a very prim little thank you that gave her time to watch his top lip give a twitch of distaste before she turned away. The Luca Salvatores of this world never ate pizza. To them it was an insult to Italian cuisine.

She wandered back into the kitchen with a twitch to her mouth that was pure wicked amusement. The kettle was just coming to the boil as she entered. She went to reach up for the coffee beans, then suddenly stopped again.

Was she allowed coffee?

Was she allowed tea?'

Pregnant.

That frisson ran through her again. It happened each time she let herself so much as *think* that word. It was scary but exciting but scary—

The kitchen door swung open and Luca strode in. He kept right on going through to the utility room where he kept his racks of wine.

'Red or white?' he called.

Was she allowed wine?

She didn't reply.

He came to lean in the doorway with his dark eyes hooded and a sardonic tilt to his mouth. He was waiting for an answer. She refused to look at him.

'I'll just have water, I think,' she said and reached for the loaf of crusty Italian bread sitting on the counter and began hacking at it with a bread knife.

The silence came back. They were becoming really good at dragging out the tension without uttering a single word, she noted as he continued to stand there trying to outguess where she was coming from and probably deciding that she was being awkward when she wasn't being awkward, she told herself mulishly.

Then he moved, levering himself upright, and she frowned furiously at the loaf of bread because she knew she wasn't only being awkward, she was almost fizzing with offended pride at his rejection before.

So if he had any sense he would keep his distance because if he dares to touch me now I'm likely to go for him with this knife!

He knew it too, the swine, because he hit so fast that he had the knife from her hand and put safely out of reach before she could even blink.

'OK.' He spun her round. 'Let's have this out.'

'Have what out?' She glared at his chest. The sweater he was wearing was made of the softest cashmere and she already knew how smooth and warm it felt to touch so she didn't need to fold her hands across her body to stop herself from finding out. 'I don't want to have anything out.'

'Well, I do,' he said. 'And I want to start by apologising for being a stiff-necked boor back there.'

Her shrug of indifference to his apology forced him to pull in a deep breath.

'I also apologise for misjudging you two years ago. I am sorry I read your letters and I'm sorry that I led you to believe I was marrying you for Rose's sake and to keep control of Salvatore stock.'

Her chin came up. 'Are you saying you didn't marry me for those reasons?'

He took in another of those breaths. 'I am saying I'm

sorry if I gave you that impression,' he persisted. 'And stop trying to turn this into another fight!'

'I'm not,' she denied while her blue eyes locked for battle.

He opened his mouth to answer, then closed it again when he took the mammoth decision not to take her on. 'Let's stick to the issues,' he gritted. 'What is important now is that we have two babies and your health to consider, which means we've got to stop fighting all the time and start to organise our lives to accommodate everyone's needs. So tomorrow we see a doctor and attempt to put all your fears at rest about your pregnancy. Then we are going to need somewhere else to live that is out of the city. Somewhere both you and Rose will breathe healthier air that will also be big enough to give us all our own bit of space. It is also important that we move quickly because Rose might be released from hospital next week and we are going to have to pull out all the stops to organise ourselves before that happens. We are going to need a full complement of staff—'

He was doing it again and playing the trouble-shooter, planning everything as if they were embarking on a new business project.

'You don't like servants littering up your house.' She tossed in a spanner.

'Do I have a choice?' he countered. 'You are pregnant and about to become a full-time mother, which has to take priority over my likes or dislikes.'

'Very good of you,' she commended.

'I wasn't trying to be a good boy, Shannon,' he sighed impatiently. 'I am trying to be practical. I would like to think *you* were going to be sensible and accept that you can't maintain a full-time career as well as everything else, but I don't hold out much hope of convincing you of that.'

'Too right,' she agreed. 'Is there anything else you've

decided about our future while you had this private meeting with yourself?'

She was still gunning for a war. Luca's eyes narrowed. He was just trying to decide whether to let her have war when the bell by the lift gave a short ring, announcing that their food had arrived.

Problem solved, he thought with relief as he swung away and strode out of the kitchen, wishing he knew where they were going from here because one thing was certain—they had resolved nothing and, if anything, become more entrenched in hostilities than they had been before.

He sanctioned the lift to come up, then stood sizzling in his own angry frustration while he waited for it to arrive. A waiter stood there holding a flat pizza box. Luca exchanged it for some money, then sent the lift doors sliding shut again. The owner of the restaurant must think he'd lost his head ordering pizza. If he'd been asked the question he would have given an affirmative by reply. He lost his head a long time ago to a red-haired witch with blue eyes and a nature that was more stubborn than his own!

He turned and strode back to the kitchen. Shannon had laid the table. He placed the pizza box down in the middle, then opened the lid. The moment she looked at it he could see she didn't want it. She just stood there by the table staring at it as if it were the worst offering he could have presented.

'What now?' he asked and his voice sounded husky, though he didn't know why it did.

'It's got cheese on it.'

'Pizza usually has cheese on it.'

'I forgot,' she murmured, then pressed her lips together and to his surprise they started to shake. 'I don't think I can have cheese. I don't think I can have eggs or milk or coffee or—anything in case it's bad for the baby!'

He was momentarily stunned. It had never occurred to

him that babies and certain foods did not go together. Was she right? Hell, what did he know? This was as new to him as it was to her.

She looked up at him then and his heart tilted. It was amazing how such a tough woman could turn into weak, vulnerable baby in a blink of an eye. 'No, don't cry,' he said and now his voice was sounding thick. 'Surely the odd slice of pizza cannot be dangerous?'

'I don't know. That's the point. I only asked for it to annoy you,' she admitted. 'But I did intend to eat it.'

'*Idiota,*' he sighed. 'Look, do you want me to order something else? I can have it here in—'

'No, I don't want anything else.' Then she really knocked him sideways when she ran sobbing from the kitchen, leaving him standing there feeling punch-drunk by the swing of emotions that had been taking place here tonight.

Shannon slammed into the bedroom and threw herself face down on the bed. She wished she knew what was wrong with her. She had never felt so messed up in her entire life! She wanted one thing, then she wanted the exact opposite. She wanted to keep hitting out at him and she wanted desperately to cling! It wasn't fair—none of it was fair.

The bed depressed as he came to lie down beside her. 'Stop it,' he said. 'Or you will make yourself sick again.'

'I'm frightened!' She punched the pillow by her head because she hated—*hated* feeling like this.

'I know.' He released a sigh and gathered her in.

'I'm so fed up with everything always going wrong for us, Luca! I thought we had it all sorted, now it's all gone haywire again and—'

'Now listen to me, you crazy little hellion,' he cut in fiercely, coming to loom over her so he could give her shoulders a gentle shake. 'Nothing is going to go wrong.

You are not your sister and you have got to stop thinking that you might be, do you hear?'

She looked at him through big, dark, make-me-believe-it, pleading eyes and— To hell with it, Luca thought, and gave in to what he had been aching to do all evening. He lowered his head, then crushed her trembling mouth. It took about two seconds after that for the sobs to start slowing. Another second later and she was kissing him back.

And if this wasn't worth fighting to hell and back for then life wasn't worth living at all, he thought as they both gave in to what they knew they should not be giving into until they'd consulted with a doctor. They made love with fire and passion. When it came time to join they did it with such gentle care and tenderness that it was a whole new mind-blowing experience on its own.

Afterwards they fell asleep in each other's arms while the pizza dried up in its box in the kitchen, and they awoke the next morning pretending they didn't feel guilty and worried that they'd tempted fate to spring yet another lousy deal on them with a doctor's report that sex was out for the next eight months, because both of them knew they'd struggle to stay the course.

CHAPTER TEN

FORTUNATELY the doctor said no such thing. He was very understanding of Shannon's fears and reassured her that her sister's problems had been a personal physical weakness and nothing genetically linked. She was fit and healthy. There was absolutely no reason why she shouldn't have a perfectly normal pregnancy and he told them to go away and get on with their marriage. 'Enjoy.' He grinned and wished them well as they left.

They were dazed—both of them. They'd become so used to bad luck dogging them that good news was difficult to accept.

The moment they were alone Luca pulled her into his arms and kissed her. 'I am off the hook,' he announced with feeling, and she laughed because she understood exactly what he meant because she felt the same way herself.

Rose was beautiful. Shannon couldn't believe the changes in the baby girl since she'd last seen her. She was all pink and cute with her mother's blue eyes and her father's silk dark hair. She cried as she held her. It was silly to cry because in reality she was so filled with love for this tiny, tiny sweet creature that she should have been laughing.

The nurse who was going to come with Rose when they left the hospital was called Maria. She was young and dark and so incredibly shy that she blushed every time Luca sent her a smile. He played on the shyness, being an utterly incorrigible Latin male. Then he would look at Shannon holding Rose and his expression would alter to a dark, dark, heavy-lashed density that would liquidise her insides. A teasing Latin male and a desiring Latin male were two different people: one was harmless, the other—wasn't.

When it was time for them to leave to go and visit a house Luca wanted to show her, it was Maria's arms that were waiting to take the baby.

Tension fizzed in the atmosphere as they drove out of Florence. It belonged to that old breathtaking excitement they'd used to share in those first few heady days and weeks before they'd become lovers, when their awareness of each other had been so needle-sharp it had been electric. This time it came from a new sharp sense of belonging. They were joined by the seed Luca had planted inside her and she was nurturing.

She was going to have Luca's child.

Her hand crept out to cover his where it moulded a squat racing gear stick. He didn't say a word but his fingers spread a little to gather hers in and the fizz had something physical to feed off as they drove on into the Tuscan countryside, passing through Fiesole on their way.

'This house isn't going to be another Salvatore Villa, is it?' Shannon quizzed dubiously.

'Wait and see.' Luca grinned, and it was one of those lazily teasing, natural white toothed grins that wrenched at her vulnerable heart.

Everything about her felt vulnerable today. She felt soft and serene and unbelievably female. It was the oddest sensation yet warm and nice. Until her meeting with the doctor she had been a worrying tumble of excitement and fear. She was still scared but now she felt joyful with it.

'You look so beautiful today,' Luca murmured huskily.

Could he see how she was feeling? She had to assume so because, even when they'd thought they'd hated each other, he had still been able to pick up on her every thought and emotion as if they belonged to him.

And maybe they did.

They pulled off a lane onto a clay driveway that took them through pastureland that gave way to the most perfect shallow valley with woodland and meadows and even a narrow stream.

Her first sighting of the house set her gasping. 'How did you find this?' she asked breathlessly.

'It belongs to me.' He sent her a wry smile. 'I was left it by my maternal grandfather.'

'Your mother used to live here?'

'Don't sound so shocked,' he mocked. 'She did not become a Salvatore until she married one,' he reminded her dryly. 'She was a Monteriggioni; they were wine growers,' he extended. 'They owned huge tracks of land around here and produced some of the best wine in Tuscany. When the wine industry had to modernise to keep up with New World wines, my grandfather decided he was too old for such radical change so he sold on the vineyards but kept the house and a large piece of surrounding land. As children we all loved to come and stay here because we were allowed a kind of freedom we could never be allowed in the centre of Florence.'

Shannon could understand why. This beautiful place was a haven to children.

Then there was the house.

Luca stopped the car, then sat back to give her a few minutes to absorb the two-storey frontage with rough stone walls, a clay roof and long, narrow windows with green shutters.

'How old is it?' she asked curiously.

'Fifteenth century, at a guess,' he said. 'The guessing part is because we could not trace it back further than the fifteenth century—which does not mean it was not here.'

Getting out of the car, he came round to open her door and help her to alight. Their hands linked again. He began drawing her towards a pair of solid-looking front doors.

Shannon was shocked to step through them then find herself standing in what she could only describe as country rustic. No grand display of priceless art collections. No exquisite renaissance furniture that made you want to stand and admire rather than use.

'It's amazing,' she murmured as they walked slowly from room to room of pure old-fashioned magic. The rough plastered walls were plain painted, the floors beneath her feet cool stone leading to wood then back to stone again. Every room was fully furnished and looked as if it hadn't been altered in centuries. 'I can't believe you never told me about this place.'

'It never came up in conversation.'

'Well, it should have done,' she chided. 'It's so wonderful.'

'*Grazie,*' he said. 'My grandparents left it to me because from being quite small I had apparently always claimed that this would be where I would live when I had a family.'

He was being gently mocking but she could hear the affection in his voice. 'And did you make that claim?' she asked.

'*Sì,*' he admitted. 'So now you know you have married a countryman at heart instead of an arrogant Florentine.'

Shannon turned to study him curiously. He was standing beside her dressed in one of his sharp business suits and looking about as glossy as a man of means could look. He should appear totally out of place here but oddly he didn't; she only had to superimpose a casually dressed Luca over the sharp-suited one to know he would look very at home.

'Then you're both,' she declared and wandered away to check out the next room, aware that his gaze was following her and aware that he'd read some kind of challenge in that remark.

Sexual challenge. It was all around them. Last night they had come together in a fever of passion they knew they should have resisted. Today all need to resist anything had been removed, so the passion shimmered like the sun coming in through the slats covering some of the windows.

They moved on through room after room arguing lightly over which wing would be a family wing and which would be reserved as work space. 'We could move in here today and not have to do a single thing to it,' she said eventually. 'Who has been keeping it this clean?'

'We used to have a housekeeper called Fantasia,' Luca said. 'She was here for so long I cannot recall a time when she wasn't.'

Shannon spun from the view she had been admiring through one of the windows. 'But she isn't here now?'

'Sadly no. She passed away a couple of years ago.' He walked off to straighten a painting that was hanging crooked on a wall.

'You were fond of her,' she probed.

'I adored her,' he sighed, standing back to check his handiwork. 'She ruled my life with a rod of iron and the best *osso buco* you could ever taste.'

'Impossible to replace, then.'

'*Sì,*' he agreed. 'So we won't even try. Instead we will have a very young, very modern team of staff to go with our very young and very modern family.' He swung round to face her suddenly. 'Do you want to take a look upstairs now?'

Oh, my, Shannon thought as desire coiled through the air like a magic love potion. She let him take her hand again to lead her up one of several staircases she'd noticed as they'd walked the ground floor.

They checked out bedroom after bedroom, found the nursery wing with just about everything a child could desire. It was like an enchanted place that had become lost in time. Everything was old and well used like the rest of the house, the only obviously updated features being the exquisite bathrooms—one attached to every room.

'Where are the staff?' she thought to ask as they stood in one of the larger bedrooms containing a huge four-poster bed that reached up to the high beamed ceiling.

'I gave them the day off so we could look around—uninterrupted.'

And Shannon swerved away from the heavy-lashed expression to pretend a deep interest in the handmade rug covering the richly polished floorboards beneath her shoes.

'Well...' she tried to take in some air by lifting her chin and turning full circle '...you will certainly have your own space here just as you wanted.'

'If that was a subtle hint for me to choose my own bedroom, then forget it. I sleep where you sleep.'

Her heart tripped a couple of beats.

'So take your pick,' he invited.

Her cheeks began to heat. Other parts of her began to join in. 'Some other time,' she said nervously and started backing away because he was most definitely stalking.

'But you look tired.'

'I do not,' she denied as the backs of her legs hit the edge of the bed and she knew she'd been carefully herded.

'You need to take regular rests. The good doctor said so.'

'Not for what you have in mind,' she derided. 'Don't you dare!' she protested when his hand lifted to tug at his tie.

But he did dare. Another stride and he was standing right in front of her. The tie came off, his jacket landed on the polished wood floor. She had a choice now, Shannon knew that. She could fight or she could surrender. His dark eyes flamed as he began undoing the buttons on his shirt. A deeply bronzed chest appeared with its covering of deliciously inviting dark hair.

Her eyelashes flickered in time with her accelerated heartbeat. The heat and the scent of him were going to her head.

'You planned to do this in this room, didn't you?' she murmured accusingly.

'Of course. It is the best room. Are you going to undress yourself or do you want me to do it?'

Still hovering between fight and surrender, she drew out the moment for a few long seconds. Then she relaxed her shoulders. 'This is your seduction, *caro*,' she murmured provocatively.

So he removed his clothes with a tantalising slowness. He teased her senses with hands that knew exactly where to touch. They made love into the afternoon and fell asleep together, as they did every night afterwards in that same bedroom with its big four poster bed and windows that overlooked the rolling Tuscan hills.

Rose came home. It was quite a shock to Shannon's system to find herself fully responsible for this precious little being who was so dependent on her for everything. But with Maria's help she managed. She learned to be a mother. It took weeks to feel really confident but she got there in the end.

She worked most mornings in her office. The afternoons were dedicated to Rose. Luca was busy—very busy. With Angelo gone he was having to do the work of two but breakfast time belonged strictly to Rose. And no matter how busy he was he still came home every night to share a meal with Shannon and, of course, the four-poster bed.

On the surface everything seemed absolutely perfect. Shannon was carrying her baby with an ease that surprised everyone. She was happy with her new life and it showed in the way she quite simply glowed. Luca's mother was so delighted to learn that they were moving into her old home that she was rarely away. She clung to Rose and, Shannon suspected, assuaged her grief for her lost son by pouring love into his baby daughter. Sophia became Shannon's mentor in everything to do with baby concerns. Renata still continued to hold herself aloof but as the months rolled on even she unbent and began to like her again.

Everything was pretty much perfect. Like the calm after a terrible storm, everyone seemed willing to work together to help make this new life they were building run as smoothly as it could. Shannon was happy. She felt healthy and alive and so enervated that nothing could bring her down. She even flew to London a couple of times during the early months to consult with clients. Though she did so in the pampered luxury of Luca's private jet with Rose and Maria along because she refused to be separated from her baby, and Fredo was there to drive her everywhere she needed to go.

She worked, she played, she made love with Luca. The only tiny, tiny cloud on her sunny horizon was that Luca had not once said he loved her. The look in his eyes told her he did but the words were never spoken, so she didn't say them either and just hoped that he could see in her eyes what she could see in his. One day we will feel safe enough to say it, she assured herself. I can be patient. Everything else is as perfect as it can be. She could feel her baby living inside her and had never felt so complete as a woman. She loved her house, her life, her family and it showed. She radiated contentment and happiness.

She forgot to be scared.

August arrived with a simmering heatwave. Florence heaved under its enormous weight. The streets throbbed with day-tripping tourists and those residents of Florence who could do moved out into the country or took their annual vacations simply to escape.

Even Luca decided to work from his office at the house rather than brave the hot, heaving flood in the city. Shannon was almost eight months pregnant and so incredibly beautiful it made his heart ache every time he looked at her. Rose had blossomed, developing an enchanting little personality of her own. She had recently discovered how to crawl and was causing minor mayhem wherever she was set loose.

She was doing so now, he observed with a grin as he lounged in the terrace doorway looking out towards the garden. He'd just changed out of casual shorts and a loose tee shirt into a suit because he had a meeting to attend in Florence, which meant braving the gridlock that clogged up the city in heat that seared. He did not want to go. He wanted to stay right here and watch the baby girl fight for her freedom while Shannon, looking amazing in a fitted white shift that moulded the heavily pregnant shape, held firm to the straps of Rose's little white dungarees.

They were supposed to be sitting quietly beneath the shade of a sun umbrella but Rose had different ideas. She'd spotted one of the resident cats and was determined to chase it.

'No, Rose, no,' Shannon said firmly. 'The sun is too hot, you must—'

The baby broke loose. Luca was still trying to work out how Shannon had allowed it to happen when he saw her lunge forward in an effort to catch Rose again. Then the lunge suddenly changed into something else entirely. He saw her freeze like a statue for a second, then her cry hit his eardrums as her face contorted and she slumped to the grass in a ball of pain.

His heart punched a hole in his throat as he launched himself into movement. He ran across the terrace and onto the grass to fall to his knees beside her and placed a hand on the rounded curve of her spine.

'What happened—what?' he demanded sharply.

'Pain,' she gasped and even as she said it the next agonised spasm shot through her, forcing the breath from her throat on a sharp, keening cry.

The sound pierced the heat-laden sunlit air like the bay

of a wounded animal. Dropping down even lower he curved his arms right around her as her fingers pawed desperately at the ground. *'Cara,'* he kept saying, *'cara,'* because he did not know what to do and she was so paralysed by the pain.

He must have called for help though he did not recall doing it. People came running from all directions. Someone scooped up the escaping Rose, another yelled for Maria. The nurse came at a run and joined him on her knees beside Shannon, who was heaving in air then not breathing at all as her whole body locked inside a soul-raking, thick, extended moan.

'What's happening—what's happening?' she gasped out a few seconds later. 'This can't be right, can it?'

'Your baby has decided to arrive early and is in a great hurry,' Maria said. 'We need to get you to the hospital very quickly, *signora.*' Then she looked at Luca with urgent dark eyes and added, 'Very quickly, *signor,*' and Luca felt his blood run cold.

Then the next paroxysm caught hold of Shannon and he was plunging himself into incisive efficiency, making decisions and snapping out orders as he climbed to his feet with Shannon in his arms.

'Luca,' she sobbed. 'I'm frightened.'

'Shh,' he soothed through teeth locked by tension. 'Everything is going to be fine.'

He began striding towards the house with Shannon's fingers clutching at his neck and Maria running along beside him while countless other people scattered like flies. Fredo was waiting in the outer courtyard with the rear door to the Mercedes open and his face drawn with concern.

'The local hospital, *signor,*' Maria advised gravely.

'Get going!' he rasped even as he got in the rear seat of the car with Shannon.

Fredo leapt up then raced around the bonnet. The car took

off down the drive like a bullet kicking up red clay dust as it went. Shannon's fingernails were scoring crescents into the side of Luca's neck and those God-awful breath-locking groans were filling the car.

The contraction eased, leaving Shannon weak and trembling. Her fingernails eased their grip on his neck. Then she rolled her head against his arm and opened her eyes to look at him. It was like looking into hell.

'It's the same,' she whispered and he knew she was talking about Keira.

'It is not the same,' he bit out sternly. 'It is happening a few weeks early, that is all. Have you not got enough to do here without scaring yourself too?'

Her eyes clung to the ferocity of his expression, drawing strength from it as the next pain hit. This time there was no let-up. Fredo drove like a maniac. They hit gridlock on the outskirts of Fiesole. Fredo sat on the horn until cars and coaches began reluctantly edging out of their way. A traffic policeman on a motorbike suddenly appeared beside them. Fredo spoke to him, and the guy only had to glance into the rear of the car and a second later he was cutting them a corridor through the traffic with Fredo riding on his back wheel.

They arrived at the hospital entrance to a waiting team of medics. The moment Luca climbed out of the car with his burden they were swooping down on them. They wanted to place her on a trolley but Shannon wouldn't let go of him. Luca had to be tough with himself and lower her down there with her fingernails still clutching his neck with enough force to draw blood.

What followed became a mind-locking blur of swinging doors and medics throwing questions at him that he tried to answer without biting off their heads. Shannon had a tight grip on one of his hands now and was not going to let go, forcing the medical team to work round him.

Eventually someone found him a chair and suggested that he sit down. He did so without relinquishing his grasp on Shannon's hand and leant closer so he could curve an arm across the crown of her head as if he was trying to protect her from all of this.

'It is going to be OK,' he whispered fiercely. 'Very healthy babies are born at thirty-five weeks.'

She nodded. 'We have Rose as living proof.'

He nodded too and held her frightened gaze while trying hard not to recall all of Keira's tragedies before Rose. From then on everything happened so quickly it threw everyone into a panic as the baby arrived with a speed that took everyone by surprise.

'You have a son,' the attending doctor announced, then there was a scurry of activity, 'Do not be alarmed that you cannot hear him cry. My team are working on that; give them a few seconds.'

But those few seconds felt like a lifetime. Luca held Shannon's gaze and counted those seconds with each throbbing drumbeat of his heart. Shannon was so still he knew she was doing the same thing while all around them everyone else got on with their tasks as if it were nothing unusual for them to deliver five-week premature babies for parents with a family history of tragic premature births.

Then it came—that first weak little cry that wound its way around everyone. Shannon released a single strangled sob of relief and Luca had to close his eyes while he fought a hard battle with control.

Then another cry came—and another. 'You have a fighter,' someone remarked. 'This little man is going to be fine…'

Luca paced the corridor outside Shannon's room and tried to come to terms with the miracle he had just witnessed. Why did women willingly put themselves through it? Why did men cling to the belief that they had the right to make it happen at all?

A nurse came out of Shannon's room. 'You can go back in now.' She smiled.

He shot through the door like a bullet to find Shannon reclining against a bank of pillows and looking calm and serene and so achingly beautiful that he did not hesitate. Making directly for the bed, he sat down on it and looked deeply into her soft blue eyes.

'I love you,' he said, then fastened his mouth on hers in the gentlest kiss meant to seal that declaration. 'I wanted you to know that before we exchanged another word,' he explained as soon as he broke contact. 'I should have said it months ago but I did not think it would mean anything after—'

Shannon's fingers came up to cover his lips, and she smiled a tender smile. 'Just say it again,' she instructed softly.

He heaved in a tense breath and caught her fingers, passion glowing from dark, dark eyes. 'I love you—*ti amo*,' he repeated huskily. 'Always—*sempre e per sempre*.' He kissed her fingertips and watched her eyes begin to mist with happy tears. 'You are my life—*lei è la mia vita*. My soul—*la mia anima*.'

Shannon couldn't stop the small chuckle. 'You don't have to repeat everything twice.'

'Yes, I do,' he stated fiercely. 'I owe these words to you. I owe you for every single day I have let pass by without telling you how much you mean to me.'

'I never said them to you,' she pointed out candidly.

'You had no need to say anything. You married me knowing what I believed, that was enough.'

'And you married me believing what you thought you knew,' she countered. 'Does this mean I have to say the words back to you for you to know I feel the same way about you?'

'*Sì*,' A hint of his old arrogance appeared. 'What man lays his heart bare without expecting his love to do the same for him?'

'Idiota.' She laughed softly and twisted her fingers free so she could wind her arms around his neck. 'I love you,' she whispered. 'I always have and I always will—even though you are a fraud,' she informed him teasingly. 'You decided that today was a good day to tell me because I gave you a beautiful son and you're so full up with love and pride you don't know what to do with it.'

'Ah, well…' He sent her a lazy grin. 'There is that too, I suppose.' Then immediately he was serious. 'We are never doing this again,' he announced huskily. 'That a woman in the twenty-first century should have to go through so much to give birth is barbaric.'

'Primitive acts of untrammelled lust bring forth primitive results,' Shannon countered. Then she frowned. 'Why are you staring at me like that? I wasn't that awful, was I?'

'You were amazing.' He took her face between his hands and kissed her again—with fierce passion this time. 'You were strong and courageous and I was a useless waste of time and space. I—'

'You held my hand and kissed me all the way through,' Shannon reminded him gently. 'You kept me strong, Luca.'

'We are still never doing this again,' he maintained. 'I married you to love and cherish, not to force you to be strong!'

'Where is my son?' she fretted suddenly. 'When they took him away they said they would only be gone a few minutes. That was—'

'Be at peace. He is in safe hands.' He soothed her with the gentle caress of his fingers to her cheek. 'My mother has him.' He grinned then.

'Your mother is here?' Shannon widened her eyes in surprise.

'Sophia and Renata too.' He nodded. 'The last I saw of them they were trying to decide if he looked Irish or Florentine.'

'Oh, goodness me!' Shannon gasped in horror. 'He hasn't grown red hair since I last saw him, has he?'

'No, it is still as dark as mine.' Luca laughed. Then suddenly wasn't laughing. 'He is beautiful. *You* are beautiful. I adore red hair. I adore you. And when I get you home again I will enjoy showing you how much I adore you.'

'You're talking sex already,' Shannom sighed out chidingly.

'I am talking *love*,' Luca corrected and set about showing her the difference.